"AFTER HIM!"

At the bawled orders, monks ran to get weapons, saddle horses, turn loose the monastery hounds.

That command alarmed Argyros, but it was the last one he heard. He thundered through the open gates. His horse's muscles surged against his thighs; the wind of his headlong gallop tore tears from his eyes. St. Gall's fields of wheat, rye and barley blurred by on either side. Someone in one of the watchtowers sounded a horn.

To escape the all-seeing eye up there, he made for the woods, where he hoped Wighard was still waiting. Silent as a shadow, Wighard stepped into the roadway. "Fine ruction you stirred up back there," the Anglelander observed. "D'you have the spell, man?"

"The answer, yes."

"Then we'd best not wait around, eh?"

"Harry Turtledove is a very talented science fiction writer."
—Orson Scott Card

ISAAC ASIMOV PRESENTS

AGENT OF BYZANTIUM

HARRY TURTLEDOVE

WORLDWIDE.

TORONTO • NEW YORK • LONDON • PARIS
AMSTERDAM • STOCKHOLM • HAMBURG
ATHENS • MILAN • TOKYO • SYDNEY

For John and Steve,
who went through it with me

AGENT OF BYZANTIUM

A Worldwide Library Book/November 1988

ISBN 0-373-30301-7

First published by Congdon & Weed, Inc.

Sections of this book have appeared in different form in the July 1985,
November 1985 and January 1986 issues of *Amazing Science Fiction Stories*,
and in the August 1986, March 1987 and April 1987 issues of *Isaac Asimov's
Science Fiction Magazine*.

The Ifs of History

by Isaac Asimov

There have been so many occasions when the fate of humanity seems to have hung on the outcome of a single event that might have fallen this way or that with equal probability. What if Lincoln had said, "I don't feel like going to the theater tonight, Mother. I have a headache." Or what if Gavrilo Princip's gun had misfired when he aimed it at Franz Ferdinand of Austria?

My own favorite "if of history" involves a scientific discovery. Leo Szilard was a Hungarian scientist who had been driven out of Europe by Hitler's anti-Semitic policies. He knew that uranium fission, recently discovered, might make a nuclear bomb possible and he wanted to be sure Hitler didn't get it first. He labored to get scientists in the field to practice voluntary secrecy and keep their discoveries to themselves.

Then, he and a pair of fellow exiles, Eugene Wigner and Edward Teller, labored to get still another exile, Albert Einstein, to write a letter to President Franklin Roosevelt, urging him to set in motion a secret project to build a nuclear bomb before Hitler did. Szilard knew that only Einstein possessed enough weight to be persuasive.

The letter was sent in 1941, Roosevelt listened and, late in the year, he finally signed a directive that set up what came to be known as the Manhattan Project.

Now he signed it on a Saturday, and our society being what it is, people are often reluctant to do anything on a weekend. I could imagine Roosevelt tossing his pen onto his desk on the particular Saturday, and saying, with a touch of irritation, "The hell with it. Let's take it easy. I'll sign it first thing Monday." It would have been such a natural thing to do.

Except that he *did* sign it, and it was on Saturday, December 6, 1941. If he had waited till Monday, he might never have signed it for Sunday, December 7, 1941 was Pearl Harbor day and, after that, by the time things cooled down, the whole business about the Manhattan Project might have been one with the snows of yesteryear.

What would have happened? Would Germany have gotten the bomb first? Would World II have ended without the bomb and would the Soviet Union have gotten it first during the Cold War? Would no one ever have developed the bomb? You could write three different stories about three different consequences from this one little if of history—if Roosevelt had yawned and said, "I'll do it Monday."

It's not easy to write such an if-of-history story. One little change might give birth to another and still another, until a later period becomes radically, almost unimaginably, different from what we now consider reality. Or else such a change may produce a difference which, through some kind of social inertia manages to converge until a later period is reached which is almost identical with what we call reality except for a few amusing—or ironical—changes.

Science fiction writers occasionally dare the difficulty. There are two examples I have remembered with love over the decades. One is L. Sprague de Camp's "The Wheels of If," which appeared in the October 1940, *Unknown* and which dealt with a world in which the Moslems had won the battle of Tours, and the Celtic Church had won out over the Roman Church in the British Isles. The other is Ward Moore's "Bring the Jubilee" which appeared in the November, 1952, *Magazine of Fantasy and Science Fiction* and presented a world in which the Confederacy had won the Battle of Gettysburg and had established its independence. The latter was particularly touching because characters in it would fantasize the consequences if the Union had won the battle and America had remained intact. What a Utopian world they imagined would have resulted.

Well, now we have another attempt at an elaborate if-of-history. What if Justinian's attempt at reestablishing the Roman Empire had *not* overstrained it? What if the Byzantine Empire had been able to hold off the Zoroastrians of Persia and if Islam had never arisen to destroy the latter and permanently cripple the former. Might Byzantium have then carried Graeco-Roman culture, intact and in full, into the future?

Read Harry Turtledove's imagined result.

PREFACE

I'm a science-fiction writer and a historian. The combination is not as uncommon as it sounds—to name just a few, Barbara Hambly, Katherine Kurtz, Judith Tarr, Susan Shwartz, and John F. Carr all use what they studied in college to give depth and authenticity to the worlds they create. In my case the connection between the two is even tighter. Were I not a science-fiction reader, I probably never would have ended up studying Byzantine history. I was in high school when I read L. Sprague de Camp's classic *Lest Darkness Fall*, in which he dropped a modern archaeologist into sixth-century Italy. I started trying to find out how much he was making up and how much was real, and I got hooked. The rest, in more ways than one, is history.

This book, then, draws heavily on my academic background. It's set in the early fourteenth century of an alternate world where Muhammad, instead of founding Islam, converted to Christianity on a trading mission up into Syria. As a result, the great Arab explosion of the seventh and eight centuries, which in our world spread Islam from the Atlantic to the frontiers of China, never happened. The Roman Empire (which in its medieval, eastern guise we usually call the Byzantine Empire) never lost Syria, Palestine, Egypt, and north Africa to the invaders, never had to fight for its life in Asia Minor or defend Constantinople in a siege that, if lost, would have sent the Empire crashing into ruin.

Freed from such desperate pressure in the east, the Empire took a more active hand in western Europe than it could in our universe. Over the centuries, it took Spain back from the Visigoths, Italy from the Lombards, most of the southern coast of France from the Franks. To the western states that kept their freedom, Constantinople was to be envied as much as it was feared.

In the east, the history of Rome's ancient rival Persia also differed greatly from its fate in our world. Without the Arab invasions to lay it low, it remained the other great power in the world west of China, the one nation that could treat with the Empire as an equal. Sometimes the two states clashed openly; more often they quietly maneuvered to gain an advantage here, to stir up trouble in each other's lands there. Each continued to dream of and work for the final victory neither had ever seen.

Such is the world of Basil Argyros, soldier and agent of the Empire. It is perhaps a more conservative world than our own, at least in the sense of having changed less drastically from classical times. But no world, as Argyros learns (not always to his comfort), stands still forever.

A final note on chronology: the Byzantines did not often use the Incarnation as the starting point for their era. The *etos kosmou* (year of the world) ran from September 1 to August 31 and was reckoned from the Creation, which Byzantine scholars dated to September 1, 5509 B.C. Thus *etos kosmou* 6814, the year in which this story begins, runs from September 1, 1305, to August 31, 1306.

1 ETOS KOSMOU 6814

The steppe country north of the Danube made Basil Argyros think of the sea. Broad, green, and rolling, it ran eastward seemingly forever, all the way to the land of Serinda, from which, almost eight hundred years before, the great Roman Emperor Justinian had stolen the secret of silk.

The steppe was like the sea in another way. It offered an ideal highway for invaders. Over the centuries, wave after wave of nomads had dashed against the frontiers of the Roman Empire: Huns and Avars, Bulgars and Magyars, Pechenegs and Cumans, and now the Jurchen. Sometimes the frontier defense would not hold, and the barbarians would wash over it, even threatening to storm into Constantinople, the imperial capital.

With a deliberate effort of will, Argyros drew back from the extended nautical metaphor into which he had fallen. What with the motion of his horse beneath him, it was threatening to make the scout commander seasick.

He turned to his companion, a blond youngster from Thessalonike named Demetrios after the city's patron saint. "Nothing so far. Let's ride on a littler farther."

Demetrios made a face. "Only if you say so, sir. I don't think the devils are anywhere around. Couldn't we just head back to camp? I could use a skin of wine." Demetrios fit three of the military author Maurice's criteria for a scout: he was handsome, healthy, and alert. He was not, however, markedly sober.

Argyros, for his part, did not quite pass the first part of Maurice's test. For one thing, his eyebrows grew in a single black bar across his forehead. For another, his eyes were strangely mournful, the eyes of a sorrowing saint in an icon or of a man who has seen too much too soon. Yet he was only in his late twenties, hardly older than Demetrios.

He said, "We'll go on another half mile. Then, if we still haven't found anything, we'll call it a day and turn around."

"Yes, sir," Demetrios said resignedly.

They rode on, the tall grass brushing at their ankles and sometimes rising to tickle their horses' bellies. Argyros felt naked in his long goat's-hair tunic. He wished he had not had to leave his mail shirt behind; the Jurchen were ferociously good archers. But the jingle of the links might have given him away, and in any case the weight of the iron would have slowed his mount.

He and Demetrios splashed across a small stream. There were hoofprints in the mud on the far bank: not the tracks of the iron-shod horses the Romans rode, but those made by the shoeless hooves of steppe ponies.

"Looks like about half a dozen stopped here," Demetrios said. His head swiveled as though he expected all the Jurchen in creation to burst out from behind a bush and ride straight for him.

"Probably their own scouting party," Argyros judged. "The main body of them can't be far behind."

"Let's go back," Demetrios said nervously. He took his bow out of its case, reached over his shoulder for an arrow to set to the string.

"Now I won't argue with you," Argyros said. "We've found what we came for." The two Roman scouts wheeled their mounts and trotted back the way they had come.

The army's hypostrategos—lieutenant-general—was a small, hawk-faced man named Andreas Hermoniakos. He grunted as he listened to Argyros's report. He looked sour, but then he always did; his stomach pained him. "Fair enough," he said when the scout commander was through. "A good trouncing should teach these chicken-thieves to keep to their own side of the river. Dismissed."

Argyros saluted and left the lieutenant-general's tent. A few minutes later, a series of trumpet calls rang out, summoning the army to alert. As smoothly as if it were a drill, men donned mail shirts and plumed helmets; saw to bows and lances, swords and daggers; and took their places for their general's address and for prayer before going into battle.

As was true of so many soldiers, and especially officers, in the Roman army, John Tekmanios was Armenian by blood, though he spoke the Latin-flavored Greek of the army without eastern accent. From long experience, he knew the proper tone to take when speaking to his troops:

"Well, lads," he said, "we've beaten these buggers before, on our side of the Danube. Now all that's left is finishing the job over here, to give the barbarians a lesson they'll remember awhile. And we can do it, too, sure as there's hair on my chin." That drew a laugh and a cheer. His magnificent curly whiskers reached halfway down the front of his gilded coat of mail.

He went on, "The Emperor's counting on us to drive these damned nomads away from the frontier. Once we've done it, I know we'll get the reward we deserve for it; Nikephoros, God bless him, is no niggard. He came up from the ranks, you know; he remembers what the soldier's life is like."

Having made that point, Tekmanios used it to lead to another: "Once the battle's won, like I said, you'll get what's coming to you. Don't stop to strip the Jurchen corpses or plunder their camp. You might get yourselves and your mates killed and miss out on spending your bonus money."

Again, he got the tension-relieving laugh he was looking for. He finished, "Don't forget—fight hard and obey your officers. Now join me in prayer that God will watch over us today."

A black-robed priest, his hair drawn back in a bun, joined the general on the portable rostrum. He crossed himself, a gesture Tekmanios and the whole army followed. *"Kyrie eleison,"* the priest cried, and the soldiers echoed him: "Lord, have mercy!"

They chanted the prayer over and over. It led naturally to the hymn of the Trisagion—the Thrice-holy—sung each

morning on arising and each evening after dinner: "Holy
God, holy mighty one, holy undying one, have mercy on
us!"

After the Trisagion usually came the Latin cry of *"Nob-
iscum Deus!"*—God with us. Tekmanios's priest, though,
had imagination. Instead of ending the prayer service so
abruptly, he led the army in a hymn composed by that great
author of religious poetry, St. Mouamet.

"There is no God but the Lord, and Christ is His son,"
Argyros sang with the rest. St. Mouamet was a favorite of
his, and after Paul probably the most zealous convert the
church had ever known. Born a pagan in an Arabian desert
town, he came to Christianity while trading in Syria and
never went home again. He dedicated his life to Christ,
producing hymn after impassioned hymn, and rose rapidly
in the church hierarchy. He ended his days as archbishop of
New Carthage in distant Ispania. Canonized not long after
his death, he was, not surprisingly, venerated as the patron
saint of changes.

Once the service was done, the army formed up, each of
the three divisions behind the large, bright banner of its
commanding merarch. The moirarchs or regimental commanders had smaller flags, while the banners of the tagmata—companies—were mere streamers. The tagmata were
of varying size, from two hundred to four hundred men, to
keep the enemy from getting an accurate estimate of the
army's size by simply counting banners. A small reserve
force stayed behind to protect the camp and the baggage
train.

The horses kicked up clods of earth and a thick cloud of
dust. Argyros was glad to be a scout, well away from the
choking stuff. The men in the second battle line would
hardly be able to breathe after an hour on the move.

The scouts rode ahead, looking for the dust plume that
would betray the Jurchen army, just as their own was being
revealed to the enemy. Argyros chewed a handful of boiled
barley meal and ate a strip of tough smoked beef. He
swigged water from his canteen. From the way Demetrios
grinned and smacked his lips when he drank in turn, Ar-

gyros suspected that his flask, contrary to orders, held wine. He scowled. Combat was too important a business to undertake drunk.

To give credit where due, the wine did not affect Demetrios's alertness. He was the first to spot the gray-brown smudge against the sky in the northeast. "There!" he shouted, pointing. When several of his comrades were sure they saw it too, a scout raced back to give the word to Tekmanios.

The rest of the party advanced for a closer look at the Jurchen. All the nomad tribes were masters at spreading out their troops to seem more numerous than they really were. Given over to disorder, they did not fight by divisions and regiments as did civilized folk like the Romans or Persians, but mustered by tribes and clans, forming their battle lines only at the last minute. They also loved to set ambushes, which made careful scouting even more important.

The terrain sloped very gently upward. Squinting ahead to lengthen his sight as much as he could, Argyros spied a group of plainsmen at the top of a low rise: undoubtedly the Roman scouts' opposite numbers. "Let's take them out," he said. "The high ground there will let us see their forces instead of them being able to watch us."

Nocking arrows, the scouts kicked their horses into a trot. The Jurchen saw them coming and rode out to defend their position, leaving behind a few men to keep observing the Roman army.

The nomads rode smaller horses than their foes. Most of them wore armor of boiled leather instead of the heavier chain mail the Romans favored. Curved swords swung at their sides, but they had more confidence in their horn-reinforced bows.

A Jurchen rose in his stirrups (which were short, plainsman-style) and shot at the Roman scouts. The arrow fell short, vanishing into the tall steppe grass. "Hold up!" Argyros called to his men. "Their bows outrange ours, so we can't possibly hit them from this far away."

"I'm stronger than any damned scrawny Jurchen!" Demetrios shouted back as he let fly. All he accomplished was to waste an arrow.

A horse screamed as a shaft pierced its flank. The beast ran wild, carrying the scout who rode it out of the fight. A moment later a Jurchen clutched at his throat and pitched from the saddle. The Romans raised a cheer at the lucky shot.

An arrow flashed past Argyros's ear with a malignant, wasp-like buzz. He heard someone grunt in pain close by. From the inspired cursing that followed, he did not think the wound serious. Along with the rest of the scouts, he shot as fast as he could. Forty arrows made a heavy quiver, but they were spent so fast in combat.

The Jurchen also filled the air with hissing death. Men and horses fell on both sides. The Romans bored in, knowing their mounts and armor would give them the edge in a hand-to-hand fight. Argyros expected the plainsmen to break and run like a lump of quicksilver smashed with the fist. Instead they drew their sabers, standing fast to protect the little group that still stood on the rise.

One of those nomads—an older man, his hair almost white—was holding a long tube to his face; its other end pointed toward the main Roman force. Argyros would have crossed himself had he not held his sword in his right hand. It looked as though some Jurchen wizard had invented a spell for projecting the evil eye.

Then he had no attention to spare for the wizard, if that was what he was. A nomad in a sheepskin coat and fox-fur hat was slashing at his face. He turned the stroke awkwardly, cut down the Jurchen. The plainsman leaned away. He grinned at his narrow escape, teeth white in a swarthy face made darker still by grease and dirt.

They traded blows for a minute or so, neither able to hurt the other. Then out of the corner of his eye Argyros saw a tall lance bearing seven oxtails coming over the rise: the standard of the Jurchen army. "Break off!" he shouted to the rest of the scouts. "Break off, before they're all on top of us!"

Unlike the Franco-Saxons of northern Gallia and Germany, the Romans did not make war for the sake of glory. They felt no shame in pulling back in the face of superior force. Their opponents, who had been hard-pressed, were glad enough to let them go.

Argyros looked around to make sure all his surviving men had disengaged. "Demetrios, you fool, come back!" he screamed. The scout from Thessalonike had succeeded in breaking through the picket line of Jurchen and, perhaps buoyed by the grape into thinking himself invincible, was charging single-handed at the little group of nomads that included the man with the tube.

His folly got what folly usually gets. He never came within fifty yards of the Jurchen; their arrows killed him and his mount in quick succession.

There was nothing Argyros could do to avenge him, not with the whole nomad army coming up. He led the scouts off to another small rise, though not one with as good a view of the upcoming battlefield as the one the Jurchen held. He sent one of his men to report the situation to Tekmanios and another to bring back more arrows. He hoped the fellow would return before the plainsmen took too great an interest in his little band.

Whenever he got the chance, he kept an eye on the Jurchen scouting party, which was now a good mile away. Riders went back and forth in a steady stream. Squint though he would, he could not quite make out the nomad with the tube. He frowned. He had never seen anything like that before, which automatically made it an object of suspicion.

The scouts cheered. Argyros's head whipped around. The Roman army was coming into sight. Seen from the side, as the scouts did, Tekmanios's plan was plain. He had a couple of tagmata on the right wing riding slightly ahead of the rest, concealing a strong force behind them that would dart out to outflank the Jurchen once the two armies were engaged. From the nomads' angle of view, the outflankers should have been invisible.

But they were not. Maneuvering without the neat evolutions of the Roman cavalry, but with great rapidity, the Jurchen shifted horsemen to the left side of their line. "They've spotted the screen!" Argyros exclaimed in dismay. "Gregory, off to Tekmanios, fast as your horse will take you!"

The scout galloped away, but battle was joined before he reached the general. The Roman outflankers never got a chance to deploy; they came under such heavy attack that both they and a detachment of troops from the second line had all they could do to keep the Jurchen from flanking them.

Nothing if not resourceful, Tekmanios tried to extend the left end of his line to overlap the nomads' right. The Jurchen khan, though, might have been reading his mind. The attempt was countered before it had fairly begun. It was not that the nomads outnumbered the Roman forces; they did not. But they seemed to be spotting every move as fast as Tekmanios made it.

The scout returned with the arrows. "I'm just as glad to be here," he said, tossing bundles of shafts from his saddlebags. "They're too fornicating smart for us today."

A horn call sounded over the din of battle: the order to retreat. Withdrawal was always risky; it turned with such ease to panic and rout. Against the nomads it was doubly dangerous. Unlike the Romans and Persians, the plainsmen, more mobile than their foes, liked to press pursuit to the limit in the hope of breaking the opposing army.

Even if he had been beaten, though, Tekmanios knew his business. In a retreat it mattered less for the Jurchen to be able to anticipate his movements; they were obvious anyway. His goal was simply to keep his forces in some kind of order as they fell back to camp. And they, recognizing holding together as their best hope, obeyed his orders more strictly than they would have in victory.

With the Jurchen between them and their countrymen, the Roman scouts swung wide of the running fight. Away from landmarks familiar to him, Argyros steered by the sun. He was surprised to notice how low in the west it had sunk.

At last he spotted a line of willows growing along a river-bank. They were also visible from camp. "Upstream," he said, pointing.

The scouts were the first troops to reach the camp: not surprising, for they did not have to fight their way back. The men of the tagmata guarding the baggage train crowded around them, firing anxious questions. They cried out in alarm when Argyros and his comrades gave them the bad news. Then, as they were trained to do, they hitched their oxen to the wagons and moved the wains into place behind the camp ditch to serve as a barricade against arrows.

That work, in which the scouts lent a hand, was not finished when the Roman army, still harassed by the Jurchen, drew near. Several oxen were shot and had to be killed with axes before their rampaging upset the wagons to which they were yoked.

Tagma by tagma, the Roman cavalry entered the campsite by way of the four gaps in the ditch. The companies that held off the nomads while their comrades reached safety scattered caltrops behind them to discourage pursuit to the gates. Then they too went inside, just as the sun finally set.

That night and the next three days were among the most unpleasant times Argyros had ever spent. The moans of the wounded and the howls and shouts of the Jurchen made sleep impossible, and little showers of randomly aimed arrows kept falling into the camp until dawn.

As soon as it was light, the nomads tried to rush the Roman position. Concentrated archery drove them back. They drew out of range and settled down to besiege the encampment.

Andreas Hermoniakos helped lift the Romans' spirits. He went from one tagma to the next, saying, "Good luck to them. We're camped by the water, and we have a week's worth of food in the wagons. What will the Jurchen be eating before long?"

The question was rhetorical, but someone shouted, "Lice." The filthiness of the nomads was proverbial.

The lieutenant-general chuckled grimly. "Their bugs won't feed even the Jurchen more than a couple of days.

Eventually they'll have to go back to their flocks." So it proved, though the plainsmen persisted a day longer than Hermoniakos had guessed.

After scouting parties confirmed that the nomads really had withdrawn, Tekmanios convened an officers' council in his tent to discuss the Romans' next move. "It galls me to think of going back to the Danube with my tail between my legs, but the Jurchen—may Constantinople's patron St. Andreas cover their khan with carbuncles—might have been standing with their ears to my mouth as I gave my orders. One more battle like that and we won't have an army left *to* take back to the Danube."

"They shouldn't have been able to read our plan that well," Constantine Doukas grumbled. He had commanded the right meros, the one whose screening force and flankers the nomads had discovered. "They would have had to be right on top of us to see anything amiss. The devil must have been telling the khan what we were up to."

Hermoniakos looked down his long, straight nose at the grousing merarch. "Some people blame the devil to keep from owning up to their shortcomings."

Doukas reddened with anger. Argyros normally would have sided with the lieutenant-general. Now, though, he stuck up his hand and waited to be recognized; he was very junior in this gathering. Eventually Tekmanios's attention wandered down to the far end of the table. "What is it, Basil?"

"The devil is more often spoken of than seen, but this once I think his excellency Lord Doukas may be right," Argyros said. That earned a hard look from Hermoniakos, who had been well-disposed toward him until now. Sighing, he plunged ahead with the story of the tube he had seen in the hands of the white-haired Jurchen. "I thought at the time it had to do with the evil eye," he finished.

"That's nonsense," one of the regimental commanders said. "After our prayers before the battle and the blessing of the priest, how could any foul heathen charm harm us? God would not permit it."

"God ordains what He wills, not what we will," Tekmanios reproved. "We are all of us sinners; perhaps our
prayers and purifications were not enough to atone for our
wickedness." He crossed himself, his officers imitating the
gesture.

"Still, this is a potent spell," Doukas said. The commanders around him nodded. Trained in Aristotelean reasoning, he reached a logical conclusion: "If we do not find
out what it is and how it works, the barbarians will use it
against the Roman Empire again."

"And once we do," Tekmanios said, "we can bring it to
the priest for exorcism. Once he knows the nature of the
magic, he will be better able to counteract it."

The general and all the officers looked expectantly toward Argyros. He realized what they wanted of him and
wished he had had the sense to keep his mouth shut. If Tekmanios had it in mind for him to kill himself, why not just
hand him a knife?

"COWARDLY WRETCH!" Andreas Hermoniakos exploded
when Argyros came to him the next morning. "If you dis-
obey your general's orders, it will be the worse for you."

"No, sir," the scout commander said, speaking steadily
in spite of the heads that turned to listen. "It will be the
worse for me to follow them. To do so would be no less than
suicide, which is a mortal sin. Better to suffer my lord Tekmanios's anger awhile in this world than the pangs of hell
for eternity in the next."

"You think so, eh? We'll see about that." Argyros had
never realized what a nasty sneer the lieutenant-general had.
"If you won't do your duty, by the saints, you don't deserve your rank. We'll find another leader for that troop of
yours and let you find out how you like serving him as his
lowest-ranking private soldier."

Argyros saluted with wooden precision. Hermoniakos
glared at him for close to a minute, his hands curling into
fists. "Get out of my sight," he said at last. "It's only because I remember you were once a good soldier that I don't
put stripes on your worthless back."

Argyros saluted again, walked away. Soldiers stepped aside as he went past. Some stared at him; others looked away. One spat in his footprint.

The line of horses was only a couple of minutes away from the lieutenant-general's tent, but somehow, in the mysterious ways news has of traveling through armies, word of Argyros's fall got there before him. The horseboys gaped at him as they might have at the corpse of a man blasted by lightning. Ignoring that, he mounted his horse without a word and rode to the tent of Justin of Tarsos, until a few minutes ago his aide and now, presumably, his commander.

Justin turned red when he saw Argyros coming, and redder still to receive his salute. "What are your orders for me, sir?" Argyros asked tonelessly.

"Well, sir, uh, Basil, uh, soldier, why don't you take Tribonian's place in the eastern three-man patrol? His wound still pains him too much for him to sit a horse."

"Yes, sir," Argyros said, his voice still dead. He wheeled his horse and rode out to the eastern gate of the camp, where the other two scouts would be waiting for him.

Having made up the patrol roster, he knew who they would be: Bardanes Philippikos and Alexander the Arab. Justin had been kind to him; both were steady, competent men, though Alexander did have a ferocious temper when he thought himself wronged.

It was plain Argyros's presence made them nervous. Bardanes's hand twitched in the beginning of a salute before he jerked it down to his side. And Alexander asked, "Where to, sir?"

"You don't call me 'sir'; I call you 'sir.' And you tell me where to go."

"I've wanted to do that for weeks," Bardanes said. But he spoke without malice, using the feeble joke to try to get rid of the tension he felt. To meet him halfway, Argyros managed the first smile since his demotion.

Still, it was the quietest patrol on which he had ever gone, at least at first. Bardanes and Alexander were too wary of him to direct many words his way, and his being there kept them from talking between themselves about what they most wanted to: his fall.

Bardanes, the more forward of the two, finally grasped the nettle. The camp had long vanished behind them; there was no evidence of the Jurchen. The three horsemen could not have been more alone. And so Argyros was not surprised when Bardanes asked, "Begging your pardon, but what was it you fell out with the lieutenant-general over?"

"I made a mistake at the officers' meeting," Argyros replied. He tried to leave it at that, but Bardanes and Alexander were waiting expectantly, so he went on, "I showed Hermoniakos to be in the wrong for taking Constantine Doukas to task. After that, I suppose all I would have had to do was blink at the wrong time and Hermoniakos would have come down on me."

"That is the way of things when you mix in the quarrel of men above your station," Alexander said with Arab fatalism. "Whether the bear beats the lion or the lion the bear, the rabbit always loses."

"Lions and bears," Bardanes snorted. "A damn shame, if you ask me."

"No one did," Argyros said.

"I know," Bardanes said cheerfully. "Another damn shame they didn't break some other officers I could name instead of you. There's more than one I owe plenty to, and I'd enjoy getting some of my own back. You, though—well, shit, you're a hard-nosed bastard, aye, but I can't deny you're fair."

"Thank you for that much, anyhow."

"Don't mention it. It's as much as we can hope for from an officer, and more than we usually get. You'll find out."

They gradually drew near another tree-lined creek, a good spot for a band of Jurchen to be lying in ambush. Bardanes and Alexander both unconsciously looked in Argyros's direction; old habits died hard.

"Let's split up," he said, accepting that in their eyes he still held rank. It warmed him for what he was about to do, but only a little. "You two head down to the south end of the stand. Remember to stay out of arrow range. I'll go north. We'll all ford the stream and meet on the other side.''

The other two scouts nodded and took their horses downstream. Neither looked back at Argyros; their attention was on the trees and whatever might be lurking among them. As he had told them he would, he rode north. He splashed over to the eastern side of the stream. But he did not turn back to meet the other Romans. Instead he kept heading northeast at a fast trot.

He could imagine the consternation Alexander and Bardanes would feel when they came to the rendezvous point and found he was not there. The first thing they would do, no doubt, would be to race back to the western bank of the creek to see if he had been waylaid.

When they discovered he had not, they would follow his tracks. They would have to. He wondered what they would do when they saw the direction he was taking. He did not think they would follow him. He was riding straight toward the Jurchen.

Even if they did, it would not matter. By then he would have a lead of half an hour and several miles: plenty of time and distance to confuse his trail. In the end, his erstwhile companions would have only one choice—to go back to John Tekmanios and report he had deserted.

Which was only fair, because that was exactly what he intended to do.

THE BIGGEST WORRY, of course, was that the first Jurchen he met would shoot him on sight. But when he came riding up openly, one hand on the reins and the other high in the air, the nomad horseman was bemused enough to decide that taking him into camp would be more interesting than using him for target practice. He was not, however, bemused enough to keep from relieving Argyros of his bow, sword, and dagger. The Roman had expected that and did not resist.

The tents of the plainsmen sprawled in disorderly fashion over three times the ground the Roman camp occupied, although Argyros thought the Jurchen fewer in number. The black tents themselves were familiar: large, round, and made of felt. The Romans had borrowed the design from the plainsmen centuries ago.

Men walked here and there, clumping about in their heavy boots. The nomads spent so much time on horseback that they were awkward on the ground, almost like so many birds. They stopped to eye Argyros as the scout brought him in. He was getting tired of people staring at him.

The khan's tent was bigger than the rest. The oxtail standard was stuck in the ground in front of it. Argyros's captor shouted something in the musical Jurchen tongue, of which the Roman knew nothing except a couple of foul phrases. The tent flap drew back, and two men came out.

One was plainly the khan; he carried the same aura of authority Tekmanios bore. He was a small, stocky man in his mid-forties, narrow-eyed and broad-faced like most of the nomads, but with a nose with surprising arch to it. A scar seamed his right cheek. His beard was sparse; he let the few hairs on his upper lip grow long and straggle down over his mouth, which was thin and straight as a sword cut.

He listened to the Jurchen who had first encountered Argyros, then turned to the Roman. "I am Tossuc. You will tell me the truth." His Greek was harsh but understandable.

Argyros dipped his head. "I will tell you the truth, O mighty khan."

Tossuc made an impatient gesture over the front of his tunic. The garment was of maroon velvet, but of the same cut as the furs and leathers the rest of the Jurchen wore: open from top to bottom, fastened with three ties on the right and one on the left. The khan said, "I need to hear no Roman flattery. Speak to me as to any man, but if you lie I will kill you."

"Then he will not speak to you as to any other man," chuckled the Jurchen who had accompanied the khan out of his tent. His Greek was better than Tossuc's. He was white-haired and, rare among the nomads, plump. His face somehow lacked the hardness that marked most of his people. The Roman thought he was the man who had had the tube that caused his present predicament, but had not come close enough during the fighting to be sure.

Seeing Argyros's gaze shift to him, the plainsman chuckled again and said, "Do not place hope in me, Roman. Only you can save yourself here; I cannot do it for you. I am but the shaman of the clan, not the khan."

"You also talk too much, Orda," Tossuc broke in, which seemed to amuse Orda mightily. The khan gave his attention back to Argyros. "Why should I not tie you between horses and rip you apart for a spy?"

Ice walked up Argyros's back. Tossuc was not joking; the Roman thought him incapable of joking as his shaman had. The ex-commander of scouts said, "I am no spy. Would a spy be fool enough to ride straight to your camp and offer himself up to you?"

"Who knows what a Roman spy would be fool enough to do? If you are no spy, why are you here? Quick, now; waste no time making up falsehoods."

"I have no falsehoods to make up," Argyros replied. "I am—I was—an officer of scouts; some of your men will have seen me and can tell you it is so. I told the Roman lieutenant-general he was wrong in a council and showed him it was true. As reward, he took away my rank. What was I to do?"

"Kill him," Tossuc said at once.

"No, because the other Romans would kill me too. But how can I serve the Empire after that? If I join you, I can gain revenge for the slight many times, not just once."

The khan rubbed his chin, considering. Orda touched his sleeve, spoke in the nomad tongue. He nodded, short and sharp. The shaman said, "Will you swear by your Christian God that you speak the truth?"

"Yes," Argyros said. He crossed himself. "In the name of the Father, the Son, and the Holy Spirit, by the Virgin and all the saints, I swear I have left the Romans after my quarrel with Andreas Hermoniakos, the lieutenant-general."

Orda heard him out, then said to Tossuc, "His truth is not certain, khan, but it is likely. Most of these Christians are too afraid of this hell of theirs to swear such an oath wantonly."

"Fools," Tossuc grunted. "Me, I fear nothing, in this world or the next." It was not meant as a boast; had it been, Argyros would have paid no attention to it. Spoken as a simple statement of fact, though, it commanded belief—and the Roman knew only too well he was not without fear himself, for the khan inspired it in him.

"Maybe it is as you say," Tossuc said at last. "If it is, you will not mind telling all you know of the Roman army." He bowed with a mocking irony more sophisticated than anything Argyros had thought to find in a nomad, waved for the Roman to precede him into his tent.

"Do not step on the threshold," Orda warned. "If you do, you will be put to death for the sin. Also, as long as you are among us, do not piss inside a tent, or touch a fire with a knife, or break a bone with another bone, or pour milk or any other food out on the ground. All these things offend the spirits, and only your blood will wash away the offense."

"I understand," Argyros said. He had heard of some of the Jurchen customs, just as the plainsmen knew something of Christianity. A couple, though, were new to him. He wondered nervously if Orda had left anything out.

The Roman had never been in the tent of a nomad chief; its richness surprised him. He recognized some of the displayed wealth as booty from the raid across the Danube: church vessels of gold and silver, hangings of cloth-of-gold and rich purple, bags of pepper and cinnamon and scarlet dye.

But some of the riches the Jurchen had produced for themselves. The thick wool carpets, embroidered with stylized animals or geometric shapes, would have sold for many nomismata in the markets at Constantinople. So would Tossuc's gold-inlaid helmet and his gem-encrusted sword, scabbard, and bowcase. And the cushions, stuffed with wool and straw, were covered in silk.

Except for a looted chair, there was no wooden furniture. The life of the Jurchen was too mobile for them to burden themselves with large, bulky possessions.

Tossuc and Orda sat cross-legged with a limberness that Argyros, years younger than either, could not match. The khan began firing questions at him: how big was the Roman army? How many horses did it have? How many men were in the first meros? In the second? The third? What supplies did the baggage wagons carry?

On and on the interrogation went. After each of Argyros's replies, Tossuc would glance toward Orda. The Roman could not read the shaman's flat, impassive face. He knew he was not lying; he hoped Orda did too.

Apparently he did, for at last Tossuc fell silent. The khan reached over his shoulder for a jar of wine, another bit of plunder from the Empire. He drank, belched, and passed the jar to Orda. The shaman took a pull, then belched even louder than Tossuc had. He offered Argyros the wine. The Roman drank in turn, saw both nomads watching him. The belch he managed was paltry next to theirs, but enough to satisfy them. They smiled and slapped his back. Tentatively, at least, he was accepted.

After riding with the Jurchen for a couple of weeks, Argyros found himself coming to admire the nomads he had fought. It was no wonder, he thought, that they raided the Roman frontier districts whenever they saw the chance. Living as they did on the yield of their herds alone, never stopping to plant a crop or settle down, they provided themselves with food and shelter but no more. Luxuries had to come from their sedentary neighbors, whether through trade or by force.

The Roman came to see why the plainsmen judged wasting food a capital crime. The Jurchen ate anything they came across: horsemeat, wolves, wildcats, rats all went into the stewpot. Along with other imperial troopers, he had called them louse-eaters, but he did not think of it as anything but a vile name until he saw it happen. It sickened him but also made him understand the harsh life that made the nomads the soldiers they were.

For, man for man, they were the finest warriors Argyros had ever met. He had known that for years; now he saw why it was so. They took to the bow at the age of two or three and began riding at the same time. And herding and hunting and struggling to get enough to eat merely to stay alive hardened them in a way no civilized man could match.

He was glad he was a good enough archer and horseman not to disgrace himself among them, though he knew he was not equal to their best. And his skill at wrestling and with the dagger won him genuine respect from the Jurchen, who had less occasion than the Romans to need the tricks of fighting at close quarters. After he had thrown a couple of plainsmen who challenged him to find out what he was made of, the rest treated him pretty much as one of themselves. Even so, he never lost the feeling of being a dog among wolves.

That alienation was only strengthened by the fact that he could speak with only the few nomads who knew Greek. The Jurchen speech was nothing like the tongues he had already learned: along with his native language, he could also speak a couple of Latin dialects and a smattering of Persian. He tried to pick it up, but the going was slow.

To make matters worse, Tossuc had little time for him. Planning each day's journey and keeping peace among his people—who quickly turned quarrelsome when they drank—kept the khan as busy as any Roman provincial governor. And so Argyros found himself seeking out the company of Orda the shaman more and more often. Not only did he speak better Greek than any of the other plainsmen; his mind also ranged further than theirs from the flocks and the chase.

Constantinople, the great capital from which Roman Emperors had ruled for almost a thousand years, was endlessly fascinating to the shaman. "Is it really true," he would ask, "that the city is almost a day's ride across, with walls that reach the clouds and buildings with golden ceilings? I've heard tribesmen who visited the city as envoys to the imperial court speak of these and many other wonders."

"No city could be that big," Argyros replied, sounding more certain than he was. He was from Serrhes, a town in the province of Strymon in the Balkans, and had never seen Constantinople. He went on, "And why would anyone build walls so high the defenders could not see their foes down on the ground?"

"Ah, now that makes sense." Orda nodded in satisfaction. "You have on your shoulders a head. Now what of the golden ceilings?"

"It could be so," Argyros admitted. Who knew what riches could accumulate in a town unsacked for a millennium?

"Well, I will not tell Tossuc," Orda laughed. "It would only inflame his greed. Here, have some kumiss and tell me more of the city." All through the Empire, even here on the plains beyond its border, Constantinople was *the* city.

Argyros took the skin of fermented mare's milk from the shaman. Drinking it, he could understand why Tossuc so relished wine. But it did make a man's middle glow pleasantly. The nomads loved to drink, perhaps because they had so few other amusements. Even the Roman, whose habits were more moderate, found himself waking up with a headache as often as not.

One evening he drank enough to poke a finger at Orda and declare, "You are a good man in your way, but eternal hellfire will be your fate unless you accept God and the true faith."

To his surprise, the shaman laughed until he had to hold his belly. "Forgive me," he said when he could speak again. "You are not the first to come to us from the Romans; sooner or later, everyone speaks as you just did. I believe in God."

"You worship idols!" Argyros exclaimed. He pointed toward the felt images of a man on either side of the doorway into Orda's tent and to the felt udders hanging below them. "You offer these lifeless, useless things the first meat and milk from every meal you take."

"Of course I do," Orda said. "The men protect the men of the clan; the udders are the guardians of our cattle."

"Only the one God—Father, Son, and Holy Spirit, united in the Trinity—gives true protection."

"I believe in one God," the shaman said imperturbably.

"How can you say that?" Argyros cried. "I have seen you invoke spirits and take omens in all manner of ways."

"There are spirits in everything," Orda declared. When Argyros shook his head, the shaman chuckled. "Wait until morning, and I will show you."

"Why wait? Show me now, if you can."

"Patience, patience. The spirit I am thinking of is a spirit of fire, and sleeps through the night. The sun will wake it."

"We will see," Argyros said. He went back to his own tent and spent much of the night in prayer. If God had cast demons from men into the Gadarene swine, surely He would have no trouble banishing a heathen shaman's fire-spirit.

After breakfasting on goat's milk, cheese, and sun-dried meat, the Roman tracked down Orda. "Ah, yes," Orda said. He pulled up some dried grass and set it in the middle of a patch of barren ground. The nomads were always careful of fire, which could spread over the plains with devastating speed. More than Orda's talk of the night before, that caution made Argyros thoughtful. The shaman thought he could do what he had claimed.

Nevertheless, Argyros kept up his bold front. "I see no spirits. Perhaps they are still sleeping," he said, echoing Elijah's gibe to the false priests of Baal.

Orda did not rise to the bait. "The spirit dwells in here," he said. From one of his many pockets he drew out a disk of clear crystal—no, it was not quite a disk, being much thinner at the edges than in the center. It was about half as wide as the callused palm of the shaman's hand.

The Roman expected an invocation, but all Orda did was to stoop and hold the piece of crystal a few digits in front of the dry grass, in a line between it and the sun. "If it is supposed to be a fire spirit, aren't you going to touch the crystal to the tinder?" Argyros asked.

"I don't need to," the shaman answered. Blinking, the Roman came around for a better look; this was like no sorcery he had ever heard of. When his shadow fell on the

crystal, Orda said sharply, "Stand aside! I told you last
night, the spirit needs the sun to live."

Argyros moved over a pace. He saw a brilliant point of
light at the base of the yellow, withered blade of grass. "Is
that what you call your spirit? It seems a trifling thing
to—"

He never finished the sentence. A thin thread of smoke
was rising from the grass, which had begun to char where
the point of light rested. A moment later, the clump burst
into flames. The Roman sprang away in alarm. "By the
Virgin and her Son!" he gasped. Triumph on his face, Orda
methodically stamped out the little fire.

Argyros felt about to burst with questions. Before he
could ask any of them, a shouted order drew him away from
the shaman. A nomad used many gestures and a few words
of Greek to set him repairing bird nets made of rawhide
strips. By the time the plainsman was finished telling him
what to do, Orda had gone off to talk with someone else.

As he worked, the Roman tried to puzzle out why his
prayers had failed. The only answer he could find was that
he was too great a sinner for God to listen to him. That gave
him very cold comfort indeed.

IT WAS EVENING before he finally got another chance to talk
with the shaman. Even after most of a day, he was shaken
by what he had seen, and gulped down great swigs of kumiss
before he nerved himself to ask Orda, "How did you find
that that spirit lived in the crystal?"

"I was grinding it into a pendant for one of Tossuc's
wives," Orda answered. Argyros had not met any Jurchen
women; the khan's raiding party had left them behind with
a few men and most of their herds, for the sake of moving
faster. The shaman went on, "I saw the little spot of light
the fire spirit makes. Then I did not know its habits. I put
the bright spot on my finger and burned it. The spirit was
merciful, though; it did not consume me altogether."

"And you still claim to believe in one God?" Argyros
shook his head in disbelief.

"There are spirits in all things," Orda said, adding pointedly, "as you have seen. But the one God is above them. He gives good and evil to the world. That is enough; he does not need prayers or ceremonies. What do words matter? He sees into a man's heart."

The Roman's eyes widened. That was a subtler argument than he had expected from a nomad. He took another long pull at the skin of kumiss—the more one had, the better the stuff tasted—and decided to change the subject. "I know why you use that fig—figure of speech," he said accusingly, punctuating his words with a hiccup.

"And why is that?" The shaman was smiling again, in faint contempt. He had matched Argyros drink for drink and was no more than pleasantly drunk, while the Roman was acting more and more fuddled.

"Because you are like Argos Panoptes in the legend." After a moment, Argyros realized he was going to have to explain who Argos Panoptes was; Orda, after all, had not enjoyed the benefits of a classical education.

"Argos had eyes all over his body, so he could see every which way at the same time. You must have learned some of the magic that made him as he was." He told how he had led the Roman forces who had tried to attack Orda and the Jurchen scouting party on their little rise during the battle. "Wherever you pointed that tube, you seemed to know just what the Romans were going to do. It must have been a spell for reading the officers' minds."

The shaman grinned, in high good humor now. "Your first guess was better. I do have these eyes of Argos you were talking about." His sibilant accent made the name end with a menacing hiss.

Argyros started to cross himself, but checked the gesture before it was well begun. Even without Orda's remarks, the church vessels Tossuc had stolen showed how little use the Jurchen had for Christianity. And no wonder—the Empire used religious submission as a tool for gaining political control. Now that he was living with the nomads, the Roman did not want to antagonize them. But he felt a chill of fear all the same. He had always thought of Argos as a character from pagan legend, and from ancient pagan legend at that. To conceive of him as real, and as still existing thirteen centuries after the Incarnation, rocked the foundations of Argyros's world.

Shivering, the Roman said, "Let me have the kumiss again, Orda." But when the Jurchen shaman passed him the skin, he almost dropped it.

"Aiee! Careful! Don't spill it," the shaman exclaimed as Argyros fumbled. "Here, give it back to me. I won't waste it, I promise."

"Sorry." The Roman still seemed to be having trouble getting control of the leather sack. Finally, shaking his head in embarrassment, he handed it to Orda. The shaman tilted it up and emptied it, noisily smacking his lips.

"Tastes odd," he remarked, a slight frown appearing on his face.

"I didn't notice anything," Argyros said.

"What do you know about kumiss?" Orda snorted.

They talked on for a little while. The shaman started to yawn, checked himself, then did throw his mouth open till his jaw creaked. Even in the flickering lamplight, his pupils shrank almost to pinholes. He yawned again. As his eyelids fluttered, he glared at Argyros in drowsy suspicion. "Did you—?" His chin fell forward onto his chest. He let out a soft snore as he slumped to the carpet.

The Roman sat motionless for several minutes, until he was certain Orda would not rouse. He rather liked the shaman and hoped he had not given him enough poppy juice to stop his breathing. No—Orda's chest continued to rise and fall, though slowly.

When Argyros saw the nomad was deeply drugged, he got to his feet. He moved with much more sureness than he had shown a few minutes before. He knew he had to hurry. As shaman, Orda gave the Jurchen—and their horses—such doctoring as they had. A plainsman might come to his tent at any hour of the night.

Several wicker chests against the far wall of the tent held the shaman's possessions. Argyros began pawing through them. He appropriated a dagger, which he tucked under his tunic, and a bowcase and a couple of extra bowstrings. As soon as he was done with a chest, he stuffed Orda's belongings back into it; that way a visitor might, with the Virgin's aid, merely reckon the shaman too drunk asleep to be wakened.

Half of Orda's gear was for sorcery of one kind or another. Argyros wanted to take much of it with him to examine when he had the chance, but he was too pressed for time and too leery of magic he did not understand.

There! That was the tube he had seen Orda wielding against the Romans. He had thought it made of metal, but it turned out to be black-painted leather over a framework of sticks. Sure enough, there were two Argos-eyes, one at either end, glassily reflecting the light of the lamps back at him. Shuddering, he stuck the tube next to the knife, draped his tunic to hide the bulge as best he could, and sauntered out of the shaman's tent.

His heart was pounding as he approached the long line of tethered horses. "Who goes?" a sentry called, holding up a torch to see.

Argyros walked toward him, a grin on his face. He held up the bowcase. "Buka on the southern patrol forgot this. Kaidu rode in to sleep and told me to fetch it." He spoke in a mixture of Greek and the few words of the plains speech that he had.

After several repetitions and a good deal of pantomime, the sentry understood. Argyros was ready to go for his knife if the Jurchen disbelieved him. But the nomads had used him for such menial tasks before, and Buka was not renowned for brains. The watchman laughed nastily. "That stupid son of a goat would forget his head if it weren't stuck on tight. All right, get moving."

The Roman did not catch all of that, but he knew he had gained permission. He rode south, as he had said he would. As soon as he was away from the light of the campfires and out of earshot, though, he swung round in a wide circle, riding as fast as he dared through the darkness. Away from the camp stench, the plain smelled sweet and green and growing. Somewhere in the distance, a nightjar gave its sorrowful call.

The waning crescent moon rose after a while, spilling pale light over the steppe. That made it easier for Argyros to travel, but also left him more vulnerable to pursuit. So much depended, he thought as he urged on his rough-coated little mount, on when the Jurchen discovered Orda in his drugged sleep. Every yard of lead he gained would make him harder to catch.

He used every trick he knew to make his trail hard to follow. He splashed along in the shallows of streams, doubled back on his own main track. Once he was lucky enough to come across a stretch of ground where the herds of the Jurchen had passed. He rode through it for a couple of miles: let the nomads enjoy picking out his horse's hoof-prints from thousands of others.

Dawn was painting the eastern sky with pink and gold when Argyros began looking for a place of refuge. His horse still seemed fresh enough—the nomads bred tougher beasts than the Romans—but he did not want to break down the only mount he had. Moreover, he was so exhausted himself that he knew he could not stay in the saddle much longer.

He felt like shouting when he saw a line of trees off to his left. That meant a stream—fresh water; with a little luck, fish or crayfish; maybe even fruits and nuts. And, if worse came to worst, he would be able to fight from cover.

He let his horse drink, then tethered it close to the water, where, he hoped, no chance observer would spy it. After setting aside the dagger and tube he had stolen, he lay down close by the animal, intending to get up in a few minutes to forage. His belly was growling like an angry bear.

The sun in his eyes woke him. He looked about in confusion; the light was coming from the wrong direction. Then he realized he had slept half the day away. He breathed a prayer of thanks that the nomads had not come upon him unawares.

There were freshwater mussels attached to several stones near the edge of the stream. He smashed them open with a flat rock and gobbled down the sweet orange flesh. That helped his hunger a little. He tried to scoop a fish out of the water with his hands, but he did not have the knack. Some of the trees bore plums—hard, green plums. He sighed. He would have to hunt soon. Now, though, he was more interested in the tube.

He thought for a moment that he had broken it; surely it had been longer than this when he took it from Orda's tent. Then he saw it was not one tube, but two, the end of the smaller cleverly fitted into the larger. He extended it out to its full length again.

He looked at the eyes of Argos again. In daylight, with time to examine them, they did not so much resemble real eyes. They looked more like the crystal in which Orda had trapped the fire spirit. Argyros had been about to break the tube open to see what was inside, but that thought stopped him. Who knew what sort of demon he might release?

Maybe he could see what the demon was like. Slowly, ready to throw the tube down in an instant, he held the larger end to his face, at the same time murmuring, "Mother of God, have mercy on me!"

The horned, leering face he had feared did not leer out at him. What he saw was even stranger; he had, after all, known about demons since he was a child. But what was he to make of a tiny circle of light, far smaller than the diameter of the tube could have accounted for, appearing in the middle of a field of blackness?

And in the circle—! He snatched the tube away, rubbed at his eyes in disbelief. Repeating his earlier prayer, he cautiously brought the tube up once more. Sure enough, there were the trees on the far bank, but minute, as if seen from an immense distance instead of a couple of hundred feet. And they were—by the Virgin, they were—upside down, their crowns where their roots should be and the stream above them where the sky belonged.

He lowered the tube, sat tugging at his beard in perplexity. For the life of him, he could not see how looking at the world as if it were minuscule and head over heels would help the Jurchen beat the Romans. On the other hand, maybe he did not yet fully understand Orda's magic.

Well, what could he do that he had not done? At first he could not think of anything. Then it occurred to him that he had looked through the big end of the tube both times. What would happen if he tried the small one?

He held it to one eye and closed the other so as not to confuse himself any more than he already was. This time the circle of light in the midst of the blackness was larger. But where before the image in that circle had been perfectly sharp—albeit tiny and topsy-turvy—now it was a confusing, fuzzy jumble of colors and indistinct shapes. Argyros thought of St. Paul seeing through a glass, darkly, although *blurrily* would have been a better word here.

He took the tube away from his face, rubbed his eyes. Orda had known how to make the accursed thing work; was he too stupid even to follow in a barbarian's footprints? Maybe so, but he was not ready to admit it.

He pointed the tube at the very top of a tall oak across the stream, paid careful attention to what he saw through it. Sure enough, the bottom of the vague image was sky-blue, the top green. No matter which end one looked through, then, the tube inverted its picture of the world.

How to make that picture clearer? Perhaps, Argyros thought, Orda had a spell for his own eyeballs. In that case he was beaten, so there was no point worrying about it. He asked the same question he had before: what could he try that was new?

He remembered that the tube was really two tubes. The Jurchen shaman had obviously done that on purpose; it would have been easier to build as one. With a growl of decision, Argyros pushed the apparatus as far closed as it would go.

He looked through it again. The image was even worse than it had been before, which Argyros had not thought possible. He refused to let himself grow disheartened. He had changed things, after all. Maybe he had been too forceful with his push. He drew the smaller tube out halfway.

"By the Virgin!" he breathed. The picture was still blurred, but it had cleared enough for him to see branches and leaves on the trees on the far side of the creek—and they looked close enough to reach out and touch. He pushed the tube in a bit, and the image grew less distinct. He drew it out again, to the point where he had had it before, and then a trifle beyond.

Even when the distant leaves were knife-edge sharp, the image was less than perfect. It was still slightly distorted, and everything was edged with blue on one side and red on the other. But Argyros could count individual feathers on a linnet so far away his unaided eye could barely make it out against the leafy background.

He set the tube down, awed. Aristophanes and Seneca had written of using a round glass jar full of water as a magnifying device, but only for things close by it. No ancient sage had ever envisioned so enlarging objects at a distance.

Remembering the classic authors, though, made him think of something else. That water-filled jar would have been thin at the edges and thick in the center, just as were Orda's crystals. And if that was so, then doing peculiar things to light was a property of such transparent objects and could take place without having a fire spirit trapped at all.

Argyros breathed a long sigh of relief. He had been horrified when his prayers did not stop Orda from making fire with the crystal. But if he had been praying for the overthrow of a natural law, even one he did not understand, his failure became perfectly understandable. God worked miracles only at the entreaty of a saint, which the Roman knew he was not. He had been in the field so long that even the Jurchen women, skin-clad, greasy-haired, and stinking of rancid butter, would have looked good to him.

He closed the tube and stowed it in a saddlebag. Now all that remained was to take it back to the Roman army. Roman artisans would surely be able to duplicate what the nomad shaman had stumbled across.

"CHRIST, THE VIRGIN, and all the saints, but I'm an idiot!" Argyros burst out two days later.

His horse's ear twitched at the unexpected noise. He paid no attention, but went on, loudly as before, "If the eyes of Argos will help Tekmanios see his foes at a distance, they'll do the same for me. And with only the one of me and heaven knows how many plainsmen looking for my trail, I need to see more than Tekmanios ever will."

He took the tube out of the saddlebag, where it had rested undisturbed since he put it away there by the stream. After a bit, he stopped berating himself for stupidity. The eyes of Argos were something new; how was he to grasp all at once everything they were good for? Old familiar things were much more comfortable to be around. At the moment, though, this new device was more useful than any old one would have been.

He tied his horse to a bush at the base of a low rise, ascended it on foot. At the very top, he went down to his belly to crawl through the grass. Even without an Argos-eye, a man silhouetted against the sky was visible a long way.

But now, he was no longer startled when the world turned upside down as he put the tube to his eye. He scanned in a full circle, pausing wherever he spied motion. Without the tube, he would have fled from a small cloud of dust he spotted to the south. With it, he was able to see it was only cattle, not horsemen, kicking up the dust. He could continue on his present course, riding around the nomads to reach the Roman army before Tekmanios took it back to the settled lands south of the Danube.

Tossuc and Orda would guess what he was aiming at, of course. But the steppe was so wide that he did not think the Jurchen could catch him by posting pickets in his path. They would have to stumble across his trail, and that, *theou thelontos*—God willing—would not happen. It certainly would not, if his prayers had anything to do with it.

Once another four days had gone by, he was confident God had granted his petition. He was farther south than any line the nomads would have set to waylay him. Better still, he had just come upon tracks he recognized as Roman—the horses that had made them were shod.

"Won't do to get careless now," he said aloud; he noticed he was talking to himself a good deal, to counteract the silent emptiness of the plains. He quoted Solon's famous warning to King Kroisos of Lydia: "Count no man happy before he is dead." And so, to be safe, he used the eyes of Argos again, looking back the way he had come.

The magnifying effect of the tube seemed to send the Jurchen horsemen leaping toward him. Even seen head over heels, the grim intensity with which they rode was terrifying. They had not yet spied him; they were leaning over their horse's necks to study the ground and stay on his trail. But if they had gained so much ground on him, they would catch sight of him soon—and the last phase of the hunt would begin.

He dug his heels into the horse's flanks, but the most he could extract from it was a tired, slow trot. Only a beast from the plains could have done as much as this one had; a Roman horse would long since have foundered. Even the nomad animals had their limit, though, and his had reached it.

He looked back again. This time he could see his pursuers without the tube. And they could see him. Their horses, fresh because they had not ridden the same beast days on end, came galloping forward. It would not be long before they were in arrow range. He might pick off one or two of them, but there were far more than that in their band.

All hope died when he saw another party of horsemen ahead. If the Jurchen were in front of him as well as behind, not even the miracle he did not deserve would let him escape. Those other riders had also spotted him and were rushing his way as quickly as the plainsmen behind: racing to see who would kill him first, he thought as he set an arrow in his stolen bow and got ready to make what fight he could.

Because they were approaching instead of pursuing, the riders from ahead drew near first. He drew his bow to shoot at the closest one, but the winking of the sun off chain mail made it hard to reckon the range.

Chain mail . . . For a second, his mind did not grasp the meaning of that. Then he lowered the bow and shouted as loudly as he could, "To me, Romans, to me! A rescue!"

The oncoming horsemen drew up in surprise, then pounded past Argyros toward the Jurchen. He wheeled his weary horse to help them. The two parties exchanged arrows at long range. The nomads, as always, were better archers than the Romans, but they were also outnumbered. They could not press the attack home; a pair of charges were beaten back.

Argyros whooped exultantly as the Jurchen sullenly rode away, shooting Parthian shots over their shoulders in their withdrawal. Then his mount gave a strangled scream and toppled, an arrow through its throat. He had no chance to jump away. The beast fell on him, pinning him with its weight. His head thumped against the ground. The world turned red, then black.

HIS HEAD ACHED abominably when he came back to his senses; the rest of him was one great bruise. Most of all, though, he felt relief that he was no longer crushed beneath the dead flesh and bone of his horse. He tried his limbs, one after the other. They all answered to his will. Gritting his teeth, he sat up.

Half a dozen Roman scouts were standing around him in a tight circle. He craned his neck back to look up at them—that hurt too. Among the soldiers scowling down were Bardanes, Alexander, and Justin of Tarsos.

"So you find you do not love the barbarians after all," Alexander said when Argyros's eyes met his. He smiled. It was a singularly unpleasant smile, the expression a falcon might wear when about to swoop on a field mouse.

"I am afraid, Basil, you cannot undesert," Justin said. He sounded sorrowful; for a soldier, he was not a cruel man. But there was no yielding in him either. He went on, "Going over to the enemy has only one penalty."

Bardanes, who was standing by Argyros's right side, did not say anything. He kicked the returned Roman in the ribs.

One of the men behind him—he did not see who—kicked him in the back.

Alexander laughed. "You get what you deserve now, for running out on us." His foot lashed out too.

Argyros realized they were going to kick him to death, right there. He rolled into a ball, his arms drawn up to protect his face and head. "Take me to Hermoniakos!" he shouted—actually, the words came out more like a shriek.

"Why should we bother the lieutenant-general, when we can deal with you ourselves?" Alexander said. Argyros yelped as a boot slammed into his thigh.

"Wait," Justin said.

"What for?" Bardanes spoke for the first time, though his foot had been more than eloquent. Neither he nor Alexander could forget that Argyros had ridden away from their patrol, putting them at risk of being thought accessories to his desertion.

"Because I am your commander, and I order it!" Justin snapped. That was not enough; he could read the mutiny building on the faces. He added, "If Argyros wants to see the lieutenant-general so badly, we should let him. Hermoniakos has more ways to make death interesting than boots, and the temper to use them."

The scouts considered that. Finally Alexander chuckled. "Aye, that's so. The hypostrategos is a regular little hornet when he's angry. All right, we'll let him do this bastard in. I wonder what he'll come up with."

Argyros heard it all as though from very far away. None of it seemed to have any meaning; the only reality was his pain. The additional discomfort of being dragged to his feet and then lashed over a horse's back like a corpse hardly registered. Mercifully, he never remembered most of the journey back to the Roman camp.

He did recall waking in horror as he jounced along, and exclaiming, "My saddlebags!"

"Shut up," Alexander growled. "Nothing is yours anymore. We've got 'em along to share out amongst ourselves, if you stole anything from the Jurchen worth the having."

Argyros passed out again; Alexander took his sigh of relief for an anguished grunt.

The next time he roused was when they cut the bonds from his wrists and ankles and he slid to the ground like a sack of barley. Someone threw a pail of water in his face. He groaned and opened his eyes. The world spun more dizzily than it had when he looked through the tube.

"So you asked to come before me, eh?" He picked out Andreas Hermoniakos's voice before his vision would focus on the lieutenant-general.

"Answer his excellency," Justin of Tarsos said. Alexander stepped forward to kick him again, but Hermoniakos halted him with a gesture. Another bucket of water drenched Argyros.

He managed a sloppy salute, wondering whether his right wrist was broken. "I beg to report—success," he said thickly. He had a cut lip, but he did not think any of his teeth were missing—his arm had taken the kick intended for his mouth.

To the amazement of the scouts, the lieutenant-general stooped beside him. "Where is it? What is it?" he demanded. In his urgency, his hand clamped on Argyros's shoulder. Argyros winced. Hermoniakos jerked his hand away. "Your pardon, I pray."

Argyros ignored that; he was still working his way through the two earlier questions. "The tube—in the saddlebag," he got out at last.

"Thank you, Basil."

As Hermoniakos rose, Alexander put into words what his comrades were feeling: "Sir, this is a deserter!"

"So you obviously thought," the lieutenant-general snapped. "Now fetch a physician at once. Yes, soldier, you!" Alexander fled in something close to terror. Hermoniakos turned on the other men. "The desertion was staged, of course—you had to think it real, so you would say as much if the Jurchen captured you. I never imagined you would be more dangerous to Argyros than the nomads."

When the lieutenant-general stooped by the saddlebag, a couple of scouts seized the opportunity to sidle away. The rest looked at each other, at the ground, or into the sky—anywhere but at the man who had been first their commander and then their victim.

Several of them exclaimed as Hermoniakos took out the tube: they had seen Orda with it too, in the scouts' skirmish before the battle against the Jurchen. Justin of Tarsos solved the puzzle fastest. "You sent him out to steal the magic from the plainsmen!"

"Yes," Hermoniakos said coldly. He turned back to Argyros. "How do I make the spell work?"

"I don't think it is a spell, sir. Give it to me." He took the tube with his left hand, set it in the crook of his right elbow—yes, that wrist was broken, no doubt of it. Awkwardly, he drew out the smaller tube what he thought was the proper distance. Bardanes Philippikos made a sign against the evil eye as he raised it to his face.

He made a last small adjustment and offered the tube to Hermoniakos. "Hold it to your eye and point it at that sentry over there, sir."

The lieutenant-general did as Argyros suggested. "Mother of God!" he said softly. Argyros was not really listening to him. The approaching footsteps of the army physician were a much more welcome sound.

"WELL DONE, well done," John Tekmanios said a few days later, when Argyros was up to making a formal report to the general.

"Thank you, your illustriousness," the scout commander said. He sank gratefully into the folding chair to which Tekmanios waved him; he was still a long way from being steady on his feet. He accepted wine, although he was not used to having a general pour for him.

"I wish there had been two of those tubes for you to take," Tekmanios said: "one to keep and one to send back to Constantinople for the craftsmen to use as a model to make more." He paused awhile in thought. Finally he said, "Constantinople it is. I'm pulling back to our side of the river before long. If I got by without your eyes of Argos all these years, I'll last another month."

Argyros nodded. He would have decided the same way.

The general was still in that musing, abstracted mood. "I wonder how that barbarian happened to stumble onto the device when no civilized man ever did."

Argyros shrugged. "He found that one crystal, ground properly, would start a fire. He must have wondered what two would do, and looked through them when they were in line."

"I suppose so," Tekmanios said indifferently. "It's of no consequence now. We have the tube; it's up to us to find out all the different things we can do with it. I don't suppose the first men who got fire from Prometheus—if you believe the myth—knew everything it was good for, either."

"No, sir," Argyros agreed. That sort of speculation fascinated him. Christianity looked ahead to a more perfect time, which had to imply that times past had been less so. The concept was hard to grasp. Things had been the same for as long as he could remember, and in his father's and grandfather's time as well, from their tales.

Tekmanios had been thinking along a different line. "There also remains the problem of what to do with you."

"Sir?" Argyros said in surprise.

"Well, I can't keep you here in the army any longer, that's plain," the general said, raising an eyebrow at having to explain the obvious. "Or don't you think it would be awkward to go back to command men who've beaten you half to death?"

"Put that way, yes, sir." The scouts would be terrified of him. They would also fear his revenge, and might even arrange an accident for him to beat him to the punch. "What then?"

"As I said, you did a fine job ferreting out the Jurchen secret. It just so happens that George Lakhanodrakon is a cousin of my wife's."

"The Master of Offices, sir?" The Master of Offices was one of the most powerful officials in the Roman Empire, one of the few with the right to report directly to the Emperor himself.

"Yes. Among his other duties, he commands the corps of magistrianoi. How would you like to be the one to take your precious tube down to Constantinople, along with a letter urging your admission to their ranks?"

For a moment, all Argyros heard was "Constantinople." That was enough. Along with every other citizen of the Empire, he had heard stories of its wonders and riches for his entire life. Now to see them for himself!

Then the rest of what Tekmanios had said sank in. Magistrianoi were elite imperial agents, investigators, sometimes spies. They served under the personal supervision of the Master of Offices, the only man between them and the Emperor, the vicegerent of God on earth. Argyros had dreamed of such a post for himself, but only dreamed.

"Yes, sir! Thank you, sir!" he said.

"I thought that might please you," Tekmanios said with a smile. "It's your doing more than mine, you know; you've earned the chance. Now it's up to you to make the most of it."

"Yes, sir," Argyros said again, slightly deflated.

The general's smile grew wide. "Take a couple of more days to get your strength back. Then I'll send you and your tube back to the Danube, with a good strong resupply party along to keep you in one piece. You can get a riverboat there and sail down to Tomi on the Euxine Sea, then take a real ship on to the city. That will be faster and safer than going overland."

The grin looked out of place on Argyros's usually somber features, but he could not help wearing it as he bowed his way out of Tekmanios's tent. Once outside, he looked up into the heavens to give thanks to God for his good fortune.

The pale, mottled moon, near first quarter, caught his eye. He wondered what it might look like through the eyes of Argos. Tonight, if he remembered, he would have to find out. Who could say? It might be interesting.

Basil Argyros felt trapped behind the mounds of papyrus on his desk.

Not for the first time, he wondered if becoming a magistrianos had been wise. When he had been an officer of scouts in the Roman army, the post seemed wonderful, dashing, exotic.

Argyros had thought his new job would be similar to the old, only on an Empirewide scale. He had not realized how little time agents spent in the field and how much sifting minutiae. The imperial bureaucracy was thirteen centuries old. There were a lot of minutiae to sift.

He sighed and went back to the report he was drafting, which dealt with the foiling of some Franco-Saxon merchants' efforts to smuggle purple-dyed cloth out of Constantinople. The petty princes and dukes of Germany and northern Gallia—the southern coast, of course, belonged to the Empire—would pay almost anything to deck themselves in the fabric reserved for the Roman Emperor.

But even though Argyros had detected the try at escaping with contraband, he had had nothing to do with actually arresting the barbarians. All he had done was spot a discrepancy in a silk-dyer's accounts, which hardly gave him the action he craved.

He sighed again. At last the report was through. A good thing, too: advancing twilight was making it hard to see to write. He signed the report and dated it: "Done in the year of the world 6816, the sixth indiction, on July 16, the feast-day of St.—"

He paused in annoyance, stuck his head out the door of his office, and asked a passing clerk, "What feast-day is it today?"

"St. Mouamet's."

"Thanks." Argyros scowled at his own stupidity. He should never have forgotten that, not when Mouamet was one of his favorite saints on the calendar.

Argyros's sour mood evaporated as he walked down the stairs of the Praitorion, the imperial office building in which he worked. After all, here he was on the Mese, the main street of Constantinople, the most splendid city in the world. Had he not joined the magistrianoi, likely he never would have set foot in the imperial capital.

A procession of black-robed priests came down the Mese from the west, heading toward the great cathedral of Hagia Sophia. Some priests carried upraised candles, others wooden crosses, while one bore the image of a saint. Argyros piously crossed himself as he heard the hymn they were chanting: "There is no God but the Lord, and Christ is His son."

He smiled. If all else failed, that hymn would have reminded him whose day this was. Though Mouamet was almost seven centuries dead, his religious verse still had the power to move any good Christian.

The magistrianos stood watching until the procession had passed, then went up the Mese in the direction from which it had come. His own home was in the central part of the city, between the church of the Holy Apostles and the aqueduct of Valens.

He quickened his steps. His wife Helen would be waiting for him, and so would their baby son Sergios. His long, usually somber face softened as he thought of the boy. Sergios was getting old enough to know who he was when he came home at night and to greet him with a large, toothless smile. Argyros shook his head in amazement at how swiftly time passed. A couple of months ago, the baby had been only a wailing lump. Now he was starting to be a person.

Helen and Sergios alone should have sufficed to reconcile Argyros to being a magistrianos. Had he not come to

Constantinople, he never would have met her, and their son
would not have been born. That was disturbing even to
think about.

He turned north off the Mese, picking his way through
the maze of smaller lanes. Thanks to sound planning and
strict laws, even those were cobbled and a dozen feet wide,
nothing like the cramped, muddy back alleys of the Balkan
town where Argyros had grown up. Even balconies could
not come closer than ten feet to the opposite wall, and had
to be at least fifteen feet above the ground, to let light and
air through.

As darkness descended, shops and taverns began clos-
ing, spilling out their patrons. The whole world came to do
business in Constantinople. On the streets were Persians in
felt skullcaps, the ancient rivals of the Roman Empire;
beaky Arabs, men of Mouamet's blood, wearing flowing
robes; flat-faced, long-unwashed nomads from the northern steppe; blond, blustering, trousered Germans. Men from
every part of the Roman Empire mingled with the foreign-
ers: stocky, heavily bearded Armenians; swarthy Egyptians, some with shaven heads; broad-faced Sklavenoi from
the lands near the Danube; Carthaginians; Italians; even a
few Ispanians staring about in amazement at the wonders of
the city.

Then there were the Constantinopolitans themselves. To
Argyros, who had lived in the capital for only a couple of
years, the locals seemed much like the black-capped little
sparrows with whom they shared it. They were bustling,
cheeky, always on the lookout for the main chance, ever-
lastingly curious, and quick to lose interest in anything no
longer new. Of a steadier, more sober nature himself, he
found them endlessly fascinating and altogether unreliable.

He also found them exasperating, for they were self-
centered to the point of being blind to others. That was lit-
erally true: he watched scores of people walk past the man
in the gutter as if he did not exist. He might have understood had the fellow been a derelict, but he was not. He was
clean and well-groomed, his brocaded robe of good qual-

ity. He did not look as though he had been overcome by drink.

Muttering under his breath, the magistrianos bent to see what he could do for the man. Perhaps he was an epileptic and would soon come back to his senses. Many people still had a superstitious fear of epilepsy, though Hippokrates had shown more than four centuries before the Incarnation that it was a disease like any other.

Argyros reached down to feel the fellow's forehead. He jerked his hand away as if he had touched a flame. And so, almost, he had; the man burned with fever. Peering closer, the magistrianos saw a red rash on his face and hands.

"Mother of God, help me!" he whispered. He rubbed his right hand over and over again on his robe and would have paid many gold nomismata not to have touched the man's skin.

"You!" he called to a passerby whose clothes and, even more, whose manner proclaimed him to be a native. "Are you from this part of the city?"

The man set his hands on his hips. "What if I am? What's it to you?"

"Quick as you can, fetch the medical officer." Every district had one, to see to the drainage system and watch out for contagious disease. "I think this man has smallpox."

"MAYBE YOU WERE wrong," Helen Agryra said later that night. "Or even if you were right, maybe there will be only the one case."

"I pray you're right," Argyros said. As he had many times before, he wondered how his wife managed to look on the bright side of things. He sometimes thought it was because she had eight or nine fewer years than his own thirty. But he had been no great optimist in his early twenties. He had to admit to himself that her nature simply was sunnier than his.

They contrasted physically as well as emotionally. Argyros was tall and lean, with the angular features and dark, mournful eyes of an icon. The top of Helen's head barely reached his shoulder. While her hair was dark, her fair complexion, high wide cheekbones, and blue eyes spoke of Sklavenic ancestors.

Sergios, Argyros thought, was a lucky little boy: he looked like his mother.

Helen went on, "I don't understand how it could be smallpox, Basil. There hasn't been an outbreak in the city since my father was a boy."

"Which will not keep God from sending another one if He decides our sins warrant it."

She crossed herself. *"Kyrie eleison,"* she exclaimed: "Lord, have mercy!"

"Lord have mercy, indeed," he agreed. In crowded Constantinople, smallpox could spread like wildfire. Except for the plague, it was the most frightful illness the Empire knew. And whole centuries went by without the plague, but every generation, it seemed, saw a smallpox epidemic, sometimes mild, sometimes savage.

Helen had a knack for pulling Argyros away from such gloomy reflections. "Neither of us can change God's will," she said with brisk practicality, "so we may as well have supper."

Supper was bread with olive oil for dipping in a stew of tuna and leeks, and white raisins for dessert. "Delicious," Argyros said, and meant it, though he was still not used to eating fish so often. In his upcountry hometown, the meat in the stew would have been goat or lamb. But fish was much cheaper here by the sea, and though he made more as a junior magistrianos than he had in the army, he had not had to rent a house or support a family in those days...and Helen was talking about hiring a maidservant.

Fish, then.

After she cleared away the dishes, Helen nursed Sergios in a beechwood rocking chair she had bought after he was born. While she was nursing, she would talk only about small, pleasant things. That was one of the few rules she imposed on her husband; she firmly maintained that breaking it made her give less milk. The way Sergios has squalled hungrily the couple of times he tried to nurse after

Argyros, full of his own affairs, ignored the rule made him keep to it thereafter.

Sometimes the restriction irritated him. Now he was just as glad of it. He told Helen about one of his fellow magistrianoi whose wife had twins a couple of weeks younger than Sergios and who did not look as though he slept at all anymore. She gave him the neighborhood gossip, either gleaned from the view from the balcony or traded with other women among the market stalls.

Sergios fell asleep while she rocked him. She carried him to his crib. He would probably stay asleep until somewhere close to sunrise. Argyros sighed in relief as he thought of that. It had been only a few weeks since the baby woke two or three times every night, crying for his mother's breast.

She might have been reading his thoughts. Her eyes answered his. "Shall we go to bed?" she asked, adding mischievously, "But not, I think, to sleep."

"No, not to sleep," Argyros said. His fingers undid the clasps of her blouse, which she had fastened again after feeding Sergios. The urgency with which he took her made her gasp in surprise (for he was usually more restrained), but not in displeasure.

Spent afterward, she slept almost at once, her legs and rump pressed warmly against him. He lay awake himself. His thoughts lit now here, now there, until he realized why he had been so importunate: that helped hold worry away for a while.

He grimaced in the darkness. That was not fair to Helen, or flattering to his own motivations.

It did not help him rest, either.

The magistrianos went to and from the Praitorion fearfully for the next few days, dreading what he might see on the way. He distrusted the way everything remained utterly ordinary, and feared it to be a cruel deception—though it was cruel only to him, for he had seen the stricken man, while the city remained unaware of its danger. But after a while he began to believe Helen had been right or that the fervent prayers the two of them had sent up were being answered.

He held to that belief as long as he could, even after fewer magistrianoi and other functionaries began coming to work each day. Life was chancy at the best of times, and any illness dangerous: doctors could do so little against sickness. Prayer offered more hope than nostrums.

But when one missing man after another was reported down with a fever, Argyros's alarm returned. And the day he found out the first of them had broken out in pustules, he decided the Praitorion could do without him for a while. He was not afraid anyone would accuse him of shirking. Already half the people rich enough to own second homes outside the city were moving out to them "for the sake of fresh air." The rumble of leaving carts full of household goods went on day and night.

Most Constantinopolitans, of course, could not afford to flee. Nevertheless, the streets grew empty. People who did stir abroad looked at each other warily. Smallpox might have been God's curse, but everyone knew only too well it could be caught from a sick man.

The price of grain fluctuated wildly. One day almost all the mills in the city would be open and almost all of them empty. Then, for no reason any man could find, only a handful would operate, with people lined up around the block to buy.

Argyros felt he was taking his life in his hands whenever he went out to buy food. Helen wanted to share the burden with him, but he said no so sternly he got his way. "How would I feed Sergios if something happened to you?" he demanded. "I'm not built for the role, you know."

"How would I feed him if you get sick and can't feed me?" she replied, but she did not press the point. The thought of danger to her baby was enough to make her listen to him.

He did not tell her he would have acted the same way if the smallpox had come the year before, when they were still childless. Any risk he could spare her he would.

Only churches stayed crowded while the smallpox was loose in the city. Priests and layfolk alike petitioned the Lord to return His favor to the people and end the epidemic.

People also rushed to the liturgy for more personal divine reasons: to pray for the health of their loved ones—and for their own.

When Helen wanted to pray at the great church of Hagia Sophia, Argyros could not refuse her, nor did he make any great effort to. A trip to church, he reasoned, was different from a shopping expedition. God might be angry at Constantinople, but surely he would not smite them in His own house.

Carrying Sergios in her arms, Helen went out into the city for the first time in several weeks. She exclaimed at how still the streets were: "It's as if this were some country town, not the city!" Her voice echoed off houses.

"It's quieter here," Argyros said, remembering Serrhes. "True, the towns have only a handful of people next to Constantinople, but they're also much smaller, so they can seem crowded."

They walked east along the Mese toward the great church, whose dome dominated the city skyline. The stalls of the horse market in the forum known as the Amastrianum were empty; no one had any beast out to sell. A quarter-mile farther down the street, a few lonely sheep bleated in their pens in the forum of Theodosios. The farmers who had brought them to market stood around scratching their heads, wondering where their customers had gone.

"Poor souls," Helen said with her ready compassion. "They must not have heard aught's amiss."

"I'm surprised the gate guards didn't warn them," Argyros said, but on second thought he was not surprised at all. The guards at a minor gate, say the gate of Selymbria or that of Rhegion, might well have decamped, leaving the portal standing wide for rustics to saunter straight into the city.

The magistrianos shouted across the square to the farmers. At the dread word *smallpox*, they crossed themselves in alarm and began rounding up their animals. "I wish we were coming home from church instead of on our way there," Argyros said. "A sheep could feed us for days."

"We would have got a good price, too," Helen sighed. "Ah, well. I hope their owners get home safe."

Only in the Augusteion, the square on which Hagia Sophia fronted, were there signs Constantinople was not a ghost town. Even there, the booksellers' cubicles and perfumers' stalls were all closed. But some food shops were operating, to serve the people who came to the great church to pray. Argyros smelled breaded squid frying in olive oil and garlic. His stomach rumbled hungrily. He had to force himself to walk past the smoking charcoal braziers.

People filled the great church's colonnaded atrium. Argyros waved to a clerk he had not seen for several days. Other such meetings were going on all over the atrium. Many folk felt as he did, that going to church was the one safe outing they could make.

Keeping a protective arm around Helen, he led her into the exonarthex, the hallway between the atrium and the church proper. He bent to kiss her and Sergios, saying, "I'll meet you right here after the services."

"All right," she said, and turned away to head for the stairs up to the women's gallery: as in any other church, men and women worshiped separately.

Someone close by let out a loud sneeze.

"Your health," Argyros said politely.

Entering the nave of Hagia Sophia was an experience overwhelming enough to make the magistrianos forget for a while that smallpox was running free in the city. No man could enter the great church and remain unmoved. When Justinian rebuilt it after the Nika riots, he had chosen the two best architects he could find and let them draw on the resource of the whole Empire. The result deserved his boast when the magnificent structure was complete: "O Solomon, I have vanquished you!"

Polished marbles of green, red, yellow, polychrome, drawn from the Bosporos, Greece, Egypt, Isauria; gleaming lamps—gold, silver, brass; a forest of columns with intricately carven acanthus capitals; four semidomes, each full of mosaic-work ornament: all led the eye up to the central dome that was the grandest triumph of Justinian's brilliant builders.

Supported on pendentives, it reached 180 feet above the floor. Forty-two windows pierced its base; the rays of sunlight shining through them left the dome eerily insubstantial, as if it were floating in space above the church rather than a part of it. The ever-shifting light glittered off the gold mosaic tesserae in the dome and off the cross of Christ at the apex.

Had that dome not existed, the great church's sanctuary would have sufficed to seize the eye. The iconostasis in front of the altar was of gold-plated silver, with images upon it of Christ, the Virgin, and the Apostles. The holy table itself was pure gold, encrusted with precious stones. So were the candelabra, the thuribles, and the eucharistic vessels: ewers, chalices, patens, spoons, basins. Red curtains with cloth-of-gold figures of Christ and Sts. Peter and Paul flanked the altar.

As always, the divine liturgy took Argyros out of himself, made him feel no longer a man alone in the world but part of the great Christian community, past, present, and future. The liturgy was ancient, ascribed to St. John Chrysostom, the theologian and scholar who had been patriarch of Constantinople less than a century after Constantine refounded the city.

The service was celebrated with splendor appropriate to its surroundings. The slow dignity of the prayers, the rich silks of the priests' dalmatics and chasubles, the sweet incense emanating from the thuribles, the choruses of perfectly trained men and boys that sang the hymns—all added together to convey to both spirit and senses the glory of God.

Prayers for the dead appeared twice in the service, after the reading of the Gospel and in the prayer for the church before communion. That was customary; it stressed the bond between the living and the dead and the close relationship between this world and the next. In this time of pestilence, though, the prayers were specially poignant.

Argyros shook his head in sorrow when at last the priest sang St. Symeon's song of leavetaking, removed his vestments, and brought the service to an end. Hagia Sophia seemed to bring the world to come so close to this one. Returning to simple mundanity was never easy afterward.

Helen, as she usually did, looked at things from a different perspective. "Thank you for taking me, Basil," she said as they were walking home. "I needed to be reminded how God still watches over us."

She was without the dogged curiosity Argyros brought to his faith, but he often thought her belief the purer. She accepted where he, by nature and training, always looked to question. The longer the smallpox epidemic went on, the more he saw good people dying along with the bad, the more he began to wonder why God was not watching more closely.

His mind still shied from the notion. Undoubtedly God had His reasons. When He wanted Basil to learn them, Basil would.

"THAT WAS DELICIOUS, dear," Argyros said, putting aside his plate of garlicky lamb stew with real regret.

"I'm glad you enjoyed it," Helen said. "Would you like some more?" She offered him her own plate.

"You've hardly touched it," he said in surprise. "You'll have to do better than that. I remember my mother and my older sister back in Serrhes saying they were hungry all the time while they were nursing."

"I have been too, till now," Helen said, a little defensively. "I just haven't felt much like eating, the last couple of days."

"Do you think you're pregnant again?" Argyros asked, remembering how nauseated she had been when she was first carrying Sergios.

But she shook her head. "This is different; more like I'm tired all the time." She laughed. "I don't know why I should be. You've helped a lot around the house, and I've hardly been out since we prayed at the great church a couple of weeks ago."

She stood to pick up the dishes and take them back to the kitchen, where she would set them to soak. She paused to undo the top two clasps of her tunic. "I think the heat lately has helped take away my appetite," she said, fanning herself with her hand.

Argyros's thick eyebrows shot up. Summer in Constantinople was hot and sticky, but the latest bad heat wave had broken three days before. He rose from the table, went around, and kissed her on the forehead.

She smiled. "What was that for?"

"For you, of course," he answered easily, returning her smile. He would not show her the twinge of fear he felt, but it was there. Under his lips, her skin had been warm and dry.

She slept restlessly during the night and was a long time falling back to sleep after she got up to feed Sergios. So was Argyros, but for a different reason.

Helen woke in the morning with a headache. "Would you go out and pick me some willow twigs?" she asked; the bitter sap in them was soothing.

Argyros did as she requested. Along with its splendid buildings, Constantinople boasted several large parks, one not far from the church of the Holy Apostles. Many Constantinopolitans, city dwellers for generations, would not have known a willow tree from a rosebush. The magistrianos, from his childhood in a small Balkan town and also as a veteran of life in the field, had no trouble finding what he sought. He used his dagger to slice off a handful of the youngest, tenderest shoots, then hurried back to his home.

He gasped in dismay: though the day was warmer than the previous couple had been, Helen huddled under every blanket in the house. He could hear her teeth chattering across the room. "So cold, Basil, so cold," she whispered, but when he put his hand to her head he found her burning hot.

"Mother of God, help me, help us," he exclaimed. He knelt beside her, sponged her brow, made her chew on the twigs. Their juice also fought fever, though how much it could do against such a raging heat he did not know.

When he had made her as comfortable as he could, he rushed out again, to the home of the district medical officer. That worthy was a small, delicate-featured man named Arethas Saronites. He looked tired unto death. When the magistrianos stammered out that his wife was sick, Saronites only brushed back a lock of his light brown hair from his eyes and said, "You're Argyros, from the street of the pillowmakers, aren't you?"

At Basil's nod, the medical officer said, "God grant her healing," and made an addition to the long list on his desk. He looked up, surprised to find the magistrianos still there. "Will there be anything more?"

"A doctor, damn you!"

"One will be sent you."

"Now," Argyros said in a voice like iron. Of its own volition, his hand slipped toward his knife.

Neither the tone nor the motion affected Saronites. "My dear sir, one in ten in the city is ill, maybe one in five. We do not have the physicians to treat them all at once."

Deaf to his words, Argyros glanced into the hallway. "You had better desist, or Thomas there will put an arrow through your brisket," Saronites warned.

The archer had his bow drawn and aimed. "You are not the first," Saronites said kindly. "How can I blame you for trying to help your loved one? You will get your physician in your proper turn, I promise you."

Shamed and beaten, Argyros gave a brusque nod and left. When he got home, Helen was sitting in the parlor, nursing Sergios. "Have a care, darling, or he may catch your sickness," the magistrianos said. He refused to say "smallpox"—if he did not name it, he could still hope it was not there.

Except for two spots of hectic color high on her cheeks, Helen was very pale. Her eyes glittered feverishly. But she was not shivering anymore, and she answered him steadily: "I know, Basil, but he can starve too, and my breasts have milk in them. Do you think I could get a wetnurse to come into this house while I'm ill?"

Argyros bit his lips. No woman would risk herself thus, and he knew it. Nor could he condemn them for that, just as Saronites had not grown angry when he tried to take more than his due to Helen. "Cow's milk?" he suggested at last.

Helen frowned. "It gives babies a flux of the bowels," she said. After a moment, though, she muttered, half to herself, "Well, that's a smaller chance to take." Her voice firmed. "Yes, go get some. But how will you feed it to him? They take so little, sucking at rags soaked in milk."

Argyros knew she was right about that. He plucked at his beard. His time as a scouts officer had got him used to improvising, to using things to fit his needs, no matter what they were intended for. And unlike the routineers who staffed most of the Roman bureaucracy, he had to stay mentally alert to do his job. So—

He snapped his fingers. "I have it! I'll use an enema syringe. By squeezing the sheep's bladder, I can make as much milk as Sergios wants flow through the reed into his mouth."

Sick as she was, Helen burst out laughing. "The very thing! What a clever husband I have. Oh—buy a new one."

"Yes, I suppose I should, shouldn't I?" Argyros smiled for the first time that day. As he went out again, he felt a small stir of hope.

Constantinople's dairies were small, because there was not much room for grazing in the city. For the same reason, most of the dairies were at the edge of parks so the cattle could crop the grass there. The magistrianos hurried to the park where he had cut off the willow shoots that morning.

He waited impatiently while the dairyman squeezed out a jug of milk. "You have a sick child?" the man asked.

"No—his mother."

"Christ grant she get well, then, for her sake and the lad's." The dairyman and Argyros crossed themselves. The former went on, "Terrible, the smallpox. Me, I spend most of my time praying it'll stay away from my family."

"So did I," the magistrianos said bleakly.

"Aye, and many besides you. I've more praying to do, though, for my wife Irene's given me three sons and five daughters.'' The dairyman bobbed his head. "I'm Peter Skleros, by the way.''

Argyros gave his own name, then said, "Eight children! And all well?''

"Aye, even little Peter, my youngest. He's only three, and just starting to help get the dung out of the barn. Poor little fellow got a blister last week and had us all with our hearts in our throats, but it was only the cowpox.''

"What's that? I never heard of it,'' Argyros said.

"You'd have to be a dairyman or a farmer to know it. Mostly the cow's catch it—you'd guess that from the name, wouldn't you?'' he chuckled, "—but sometimes them as keep 'em get it too. I had it myself, years ago. But that's not here nor there—we're all well, and if God wants to let us stay so, why, I'll keep on thanking Him and praising His name. And I'll add a prayer or two for your family while I'm about it.''

"I thank you. May God hear yours more than He has mine.''

"You pray for yourself, sir, too,'' Skleros said. "I can see by looking that you've not had the smallpox. It'd go hard if it came on you along with the rest.''

"Yes, it would.'' The magistrianos shook his head; he had not thought about that. He made himself put the worry aside. Short of fleeing his wife and child, he could not lessen the chance he would take the disease. He clapped the lid on the jar of milk, tucked it under his arm, and headed home.

"I hope to see you again,'' the dairyman called after him.

"So do I,'' Argyros said.

But when he got home, he forgot about Sergios and what his son needed, though the baby lay howling in his cradle. Helen must have set him down before she tried to return to her own bed, but she had not made it there. Argyros found her sprawled senseless on the floor. When he touched her, he swore and prayed at the same time: her fever was back, worse than before.

She was a dead weight in his arms as he picked her up; absently, he wondered why unconscious people seemed so much heavier to carry.

She half-roused when he set her on the bed. "Go away," she muttered. "Go away."

"Hush." He did leave her for a moment, to soak a rag in a ewer of water. On the way back, he blew on it to make it cool, then set it on her forehead. She sighed and seemed to lose touch with the world again. He sat beside her, took her limp hand in his.

So passed the day. Argyros stayed by his wife, sponging her face and limbs with moist cloths and holding her still when the fever made her thrash about. She came partly to herself several times and kept urging him to get out. She would not listen to him when he told her no, but repeated her demand over and over.

Finally she revived enough to ask him, "Why won't you go?"

"Because I love you," he said. A smile lingered on her lips when she lapsed back into stupor. He had said that dozens of times while she was unconscious; it warmed him that she'd finally understood.

He left the bedroom only when Sergios cried. He was clumsy cleaning the baby—Helen had done most of that—but he managed. Before he gave Sergios the milk-filled syringe, he smeared the tip of the tube with honey. The old midwife's trick made the baby suck lustily, though he did make a face at the unfamiliar taste of his food.

Near dusk, he cooked some thin barley gruel to feed Helen. As an afterthought, he stirred some honey into that, too: Helen was hardly thinking more clearly than Sergios. She ate about half of what he'd made, less than he thought she needed, but better, he supposed, than nothing.

The thin waning crescent moon was rising in the east when exhaustion clubbed Argyros into sleep. A few minutes later, Sergios's howling woke him. He stumbled out to take care of his son and heard the first cockcrow just as the baby was nodding off.

His eyes were full of grit; he could feel himself walking in slow motion, as if the air had turned thick. Perhaps because he was so tired, the idea of going to Helen's family for someone to help struck him with the force he imagined

Christianity had hit St. Mouamet. He took along the empty jar that had held milk. While one of Helen's younger brothers or sisters came to watch over her and the baby, he would go back to Skleros's dairy and refill it; or he would send them to get the milk if they feared entering a disease-filled home.

Helen's father was a notary named Alexios Moskhos. As always, several dogs started barking when Argyros knocked on his door; on holidays, Moskhos liked to go into the countryside and hunt rabbits. The magistrianos waited for his father-in-law to come cursing and laughing through the pack to let him in.

He heard Moskhos approach, but the door did not open. Instead, Moskhos cautiously called through it, "Who's there? What do you want?"

"It's Basil. I need help—Helen's sick." He explained what he needed.

There was a long silence. Then Argyros listened in disbelief as his father-in-law said, "You'd better go, Basil. I'll pray for you, but no more than that. No one here's been ill, and no one's going to be if I have anything to do with it. I'll not hazard all of mine against one already poxed."

"Let me hear your wife say that," the magistrianos exclaimed.

"It's for her I do this."

"Why, you gutless, worthless—" Indignation choked Argyros. He hammered on the door with his fist. "Let me in!"

"I'll count three," Moskhos said coldly. "Then I set the hounds on you. One—two—"

The magistrianos left, cursing; he could tell his father-in-law would do what he'd said. What made it somehow worse was that Argyros understood. He wondered what he would have done had Helen been well and Moskhos come to him for aid.

He was honest enough to admit he did not know.

Peter Skleros's mouth turned down when Argyros came to buy more milk. "I was hoping your lady might just have, oh, eaten something spoiled that made her ill," he said as he led the magistrianos into his barn. "But that's not so, is it?"

"I'm afraid not. I wish it were."

"And I," the dairyman said. As he had said, his little son, also named Peter, was helping to clean the barn. He took the boy by the arm and brought him up to the magistrianos. "I wish it could have been like this." There were three pockmarks, close together, on little Peter's wrist. They looked like smallpox marks, but no smallpox victim escaped with so few.

"This is your cowpox, eh?"

"Yes." He patted the boy on the bottom. "Run along, son; the gentleman is done with you now." To Argyros: "Here, I'll get your milk." He pulled a stool up beside a cow.

"Your family is still well?"

"Yes, praise the Lord, the Virgin, and all the saints. Good of you to think to ask, sir, with your own troubles on your mind." He handed the magistrianos the jar of milk, waved away payment. "Really, it's not enough to bother over. You take it, and keep your boy strong till your wife is better."

Against the dairyman's insistence, Argyros could only accept as gracefully as possible. He compared Skleros's behavior to that of Helen's father and could only shake his head. Like combat, the epidemic brought out the best and the worst in people.

When he got home, it was as if he had not left. Helen's fever still raged. Sometimes she knew him, but more often she was lost in a world of mostly unpleasant dreams. He tried to keep her cool, but the burning heat of her forehead dried his compresses almost as fast as he put them on.

Sergios drank the cow's milk. His father hoped he was taking enough. As with Helen, he supposed anything was better than nothing.

The next morning, Helen felt a little better. She was lucid more often, and did not seem as hot. By contrast, Sergios was fussy. As Helen had predicted, his insides resented the new food he was getting. He spent a lot of time crying, his

legs drawn up to his belly against gas pains. Argyros thought
he felt warm, but would not have sworn to it.

A knock on the door that afternoon made the magistrianos jump. He got up from beside Helen and hurried to
the entrance hall. "There's sickness here," he called,
expecting whoever it was to beat a hasty retreat.

Instead, to his amazement, rumbling laughter answered
him. "I'd not be here if there weren't," said the man outside; his Greek had a strong Italic Latin flavor. "I'm a
doctor, or so they tell me."

In his relief, Argyros had to try three times before he
could work the latch and throw the door wide. The man
who brushed past him was a vigorous sixty, stocky and
broad-shouldered. His big nose had been well broken
sometime in the distant past; he wore his graying beard high
on his cheeks to cover as many old pockmarks as he could,
but it did not hide them all.

He barked laughter when he saw Argyros looking at him.
"Oh, I was pretty enough once," he said, "but when you
get as old as I am, it doesn't matter worth a damn anymore
anyway. Now tell me who's got it and where they are." He
set hands on hips and waited.

"This way, ah—" The magistrianos paused, flustered
both by the doctor's blunt manner and because he did not
know the man's name.

"I'm Gian Riario, if you're wondering," the doctor said.
"Ioannes Rhiarios, if you'd rather have the Greek like most
people here." As the original language of Rome, Latin was
still co-official with Greek but had less prestige than the
tongue of the richer, more anciently civilized eastern half of
the Empire.

"I speak Latin," Argyros said mildly. "If you'd rather
use it—" Riario shook his head, gestured impatiently. The
magistrianos went on, "Before you go farther, I have to tell
you I fear it's the smallpox."

"You waiting to see if I run?" Riario said and laughed
again. He ran his fingers over his pocked forehead. "I've
had it already, and I'll not catch it again. You can only get

it once, no matter what the old wives say. Either it kills you, or it leaves you alone afterward.''

"Is that really true?''

"It's true, or else I'd've been dead five hundred times this past month. Come on, who's sick here? Wife? Brats? Not your mistress, or you'd be keeping her somewhere else.''

"My wife,'' the magistrianos said, refusing to be drawn; he recognized that Riario's abrasiveness had no malice behind it. "My baby son is well so far, thank God.''

"Aye, it's very bad in babes. Well, take me to your woman, then''—Riario yawned till his jaw creaked—"for I've more stops after this one.'' For the first time, Argyros noticed the dark pouches under the physician's eyes. The man was close to working himself to death.

The magistrianos led Riario back to the bedroom, saying as they went in, "I think Helen is better today than she has been for the last couple of days.'' Indeed, his wife had her wits about her and managed a smile for Argyros and for the doctor when he was introduced.

Riario at the bedside was nothing like Riario with someone who did not need him. He felt Helen's forehead, murmured, "Oh, very good,'' and reached for her wrist to take her pulse. "Very good,'' he repeated, his eyes on her face.

She smiled again, then made an apologetic gesture and scratched at her cheek. The doctor did not seem to notice. "You'll be up and about before long,'' he said. "Now I'm just going to check to see that your baby's doing well too. Does he look like you, or is he homely like his father?''

She giggled.

Riario snorted. "You come with me, sirrah, and leave your lady at peace,'' he said to Argyros. When they were in the hall, out of earshot of the bedroom, he let out the sigh he had been holding back.

The magistrianos seized his arm. "She's better, not so?'' he demanded, remembering barely in time to keep his voice down.

"It often seems that way,'' Riario said, "just before the pocks come. You saw that rash she was picking on her face? That's how it begins.''

Argyros heard him as though from very far away. Young, bright Helen's cheery face pitted and slagged with scars like this old doctor's? It was not that he could not love her afterward. He knew he could; he cherished her for much more than the outward seeming of her body. But he feared she could not love herself disfigured, and her sorrow would take the summer from his year.

Riario might have read his mind, "Don't fret over her looks," he said bluntly. "Fret over whether she lives. The pocks are the crisis of the disease. If they begin to scab over and heal, she's won. Otherwise—"

"Is there nothing you can do?" The magistrianos knew he was pleading and did not care.

"If there were, don't you think I'd've done it for myself?" Riario's laugh was harsh. "I hate smallpox, and even more I hate being helpless against it. If it's God's curse as they say, why, I curse God back for it."

Argyros crossed himself at the blasphemy, but the physician answered with a two-fingered obscene gesture Italians often used. Riario grated, "If you'd watched as many men—aye, and women like your wife, and babes like your babe—as I have die in pain, and all you could do was close their eyes when they'd gone, you'd understand. When God smote Egypt, Pharaoh got off lucky, for He didn't send him smallpox."

He shook his head and seemed to come back to himself. "Show me your son, as long as I'm here." The bitter edge returned for a moment: "Not that I'll be able to do any good if he does have it."

But Riario's interest revived when he saw the jar of milk and the syringe by Sergios's cradle. "What have we here?" he asked. Argyros explained. The doctor rubbed his chin and nodded. "Clever. A trick I'll have to remember."

He picked up the baby, felt Sergios's forehead with his hand and then, as if not sure what it told him, with his lips. "A touch of something there, maybe," he said at last, "but who knows what? These little ones take all sorts of fevers. If it's bad, you'll find out soon enough."

Again, he was gentle with his patient, cuddling Sergios and making him smile before he put him down. To Argyros he said, "I'm sorry I can't offer more hope. No doubt you'd rather have a doctor who tells you sweet-sounding lies."

"No, I prefer an honest man," the magistrianos said, which startled Riario but also seemed to satisfy him.

The physician gave a jerky nod and headed for the street. "Another mission of mercy," he said, rolling his eyes to show how much mercy he expected to bring. "Good fortune to you, Argyros; I'll call again in a few days, or when I have the chance." He nodded again and was gone.

Over the next week, Argyros learned why Riario hated smallpox so much. He watched helplessly as the disease's characteristic rash spread over Helen's face, arms, legs, and even onto her belly and back.

At first the marks were red and raised. They must have itched ferociously, for Helen scratched them till they bled. Her fever was back full force and left her wits wandering. Argyros finally had to use rags to tie her hands to the bedposts to keep her from clawing herself in her delirium.

In the moments when her wits partly cleared, she wept all the time, moaning, "I'll be ugly, Basil, ugly. How will you be able to want me anymore?" Nothing he said could get through to her to convince her she was wrong. That wounded him almost as much as being there hour by hour, day by day, watching the ravages of the disease grow ever worse. Sometimes he wondered if he was going mad. Sometimes he wished he could.

Most agonizing for him was how little he could do even to make her comfortable. He sponged off her sores several times a day. The coolness might have helped her fever a little, but none of the ointments of grease and honey and other less easily named ingredients that he bought did the least thing to help her itching.

Argyros could not make her eat much, and the days of fever wasted her. She grew very thin.

The only times he left the house were his daily trips to buy milk for Sergios. The baby was growing as used to his makeshift feedings with the syringe as he had been to his mother's breast. That saddened Argyros too, although he was relieved his son's fever had grown no worse.

He got to know Peter Skleros and his large family well: they were the only healthy people he was seeing. Once or twice he caught himself resenting them for escaping the smallpox and immediately felt ashamed for his meanness.

He could not help being glad to get out of the house, though, and it was only natural that sometimes he invented small delays to keep from going straight back with his milk. He would help Skleros's children keep the dairy buildings clean, lead the cows to and from their grazing at the park. Once he even did his own milking.

"Here, Sergios," he said with foolish pride when he gave the boy some of that jar. "Your father drew this with his own hands. Doesn't it taste especially good?"

Sergios was not impressed.

Helen got worse. The red patches on her skin turned to blisters, filled at first with a clear liquid and then with pus. When they broke, as they sometimes did in her thrashing, the smell was foul. She would not eat at all after that, and drank only a little water. She had no more control over her bodily functions than Sergios had.

Her breathing grew harsh and labored. Along with the pox, her skin began to look bruised. Though she was still delirious, she moved less and less. All these signs terrified Argyros, who ran to the church of the Holy Apostles for a priest to give her the last rites.

Though that church was second only to Hagia Sophia, it had but few ecclesiastics to serve it. Some were dead; others fled. Only one would go back to his house with him when he told them Helen had smallpox.

He cursed the rest for cowards. The priest, whose name was Ioasaph, set a hand on his arm. "They are no more than men, my son. Do not ask for what is beyond their strength."

"How do you dare come, then?"

Ioasaph shrugged; his thick brown beard bounced on his chest. "God will do with me as He wills. Whether I stay or come, I am in His hands."

The magistrianos wondered what Riario would say to that.

Then all such small thoughts crumbled to ashes within him, for when he and the priest returned to his home they found Helen dead. Ioasaph prayed over her body, then turned to Argyros. "She is at peace at last and out of pain."

"Yes," Argyros said dully. He was surprised he did not feel more. It was like a sword cut: the damage was done, but the pain would come later.

Ioasaph said, "You must understand, this is God's will. She has gained eternal life, against which this world and its suffering are but a moment."

"Yes," Argyros said again, but he could not share the priest's calm confidence. Having been with Helen all the while, he found he could not see why heaven had to be purchased with a week of hell.

After a while, Ioasaph left. Argyros hardly noticed. He sat staring at Helen's body. Even in death she had no repose, but lay contorted.

He did not know how long he stayed by the bed they had shared. Sergios's cries finally roused him. He changed and fed the baby. He had joked with Helen about that, back in another lifetime.

Remembering their laughter reached him as the brute fact of death could not. He set down his son and buried his face in his hands. The tears came then, and for a long time would not go.

At last, moving stiffly as one of Hephaistos's bronze men in the *Iliad*, he made himself go do what he had to. Arethas Saronites's sympathy sounded forced; the medical officer had said the same words too many times these past weeks. So too with his final advice: "Go home and wait for the burial party. It will come soon."

Two shaven-headed convicts bore Helen away to one of the large, newly dug graves outside the city. An overseer with a bow stood by. If the convicts lived through the epidemic, they would go free.

Had it not been for Sergios, the magistrianos would have given way to despair. The baby was far too little to understand his mother was dead; he only knew he needed some-one to take care of him. He did not give Argyros much time to dwell on his own grief.

Argyros thought once more about getting the boy a wet-nurse. Before, he had balked because he did not think one would come into a house of sickness. Now he did not want to expose Sergios to more outsiders than he had to. The baby was all he had left to remember his wife by. He did not count her family. After he sent the message telling them she was dead, he intended never to have anything to do with them again.

When the knock on the door came, he thought it was his father-in-law, come to try to make amends. His hand was on his knife hilt as he went to the front of the house. But instead of Alexios Moskhos, Gian Riario stood waiting.

The doctor's shoulders sagged when he read Argyros's face. "Oh, damnation," he said. "She was young and strong, and if she pulled through the crisis I thought I'd be able to help her. These are the hard ones to lose."

"What do you know about that?" the magistrianos lashed out at him.

"Do you think I was never married?" The question, and the raw hurt behind it, brought Argyros up short. After a moment, Riario went on, "Your baby is still well, I hope?"

"Yes."

"Something, anyway. I wasn't so lucky," the doctor murmured, more to himself than to Argyros. He grew brisk again: "Listen—if you so much as mislike the way he breaks wind, call me. I live on the street of the church of St. Symeon, six doors up from the church. Do you write? Yes? Good—you can leave a note on my door if I'm not there, and I probably won't be. Even if he farts funny, do you understand?"

"I do—and thank you."

Riario snorted, very much his cynical self again. "You'd thank me more if I really had a hope of doing something."

"You try."

"Well, maybe so. As I told you, the smallpox has done everything to me it can. I'm not afraid of it anymore." He laughed harshly. "Futile, aye, but not afraid."

The magistrianos was afraid: he and Sergios were still vulnerable. After Riario left, he went back and fed the baby. Every syringe of milk his son gulped down felt like a triumph—what could show health better than a strong appetite?

Sergios was cranky the next day, but not enough to worry his father, in spite of Riario's words. Argyros went on with the melancholy tasks that sprang from Helen's death. He was packing her belongings in sacks and boxes to take them to St. Symeon's church, where the deacons could distribute them to the needy.

Then the baby started crying again, and Argyros's head came up without his having to think about it. He knew the difference between fussy cries and those that meant something was really wrong. He hurried into Sergios's room, expecting that one of the fibulae he had used to fasten the baby's linen had come undone and was poking his son, or some similar minor catastrophe.

But nothing was obviously wrong. Sergios was not even wet. The crying stopped; Sergios seemed listless. Shrugging, Argyros bent to lift him out of the cradle and cuddle him. He almost dropped him—the baby's skin felt much too warm.

Icy fear shot up Argyros's back. As if to deny the reality of what his fingers told him, he filled the syringe bladder with milk and offered it to his son. Sergios gave a couple of halfhearted sucks, then spit up the little he had eaten. Argyros wrapped him in a blanket and dashed for Riario's house.

By good luck, the doctor was there. His eyes narrowed when he saw the baby. "Fever?" he asked sharply.

Argyros nodded, unable to make himself say yes out loud.

"It could be any of a myriad things," the doctor said. He cocked an eyebrow. "They do fall sick of other illnesses than smallpox, you know."

"Yes, and also from that. How will you know if it is?"

"The rash, of course, if it appears." Argyros was certain four days of waiting would drive him mad. That must have been plain on his face, for Riario went on, "It acts faster in infants than with adults. If no eruptions show up by tomorrow, or the next day at the latest, you've probably escaped."

He disappeared into the back of the house and returned with a small stoppered vial. "Here's poppy juice from Egypt. It will help the little fellow sleep, and that will do some good. I'll be by tomorrow morning to look at him again." He clapped the magistrianos on the back. "Even if it is smallpox, not everyone dies of it."

"No," Argyros agreed. He could not help remembering, though, what Riario had said before about smallpox and infants. He put that thought down by brute force as he carried Sergios home.

He gave his son a dose of the poppy juice and waited until the baby had fallen into a heavy, drugged sleep. He sniffed at what was left of the jar of milk he had bought the day before. His nose wrinkled: it was sour. As soon as he was sure Sergios would not wake, he hurried to Skleros's dairy.

The dairyman's wife greeted him at the door and exclaimed over his grim visage. Maria Sklerina's plump features went pale when, flat-voiced, he told her Sergios was sick.

"Mother of God, not your little son too, after your wife!" she said, crossing herself. "I thank the Lord every day for sparing Peter and me and our eight, and he and I both added you to our prayers. Who can say why God does as He does?"

"Not I," Argyros replied. He scratched absently at the back of his hand, which itched.

Maria said, "Here, give me your jug and let me fill it for you. I know you won't want to spend a moment more than you have to away from him. They're dear, aren't they, even when they're so small you know loving them is such a gamble?" Her eyes grew sad. "We lost two babies ourselves, my husband and I, and mourned them almost as much as if they'd been grown. And we're luckier than most families we know."

"Indeed you are," Argyros said; his own parents had raised only three children out of seven births.

He was glad not to have to make any more conversation as he followed her out to the barn. She rinsed the jar and drew fresh milk from a cow that looked amazingly bored with the whole process. As her husband had before, she refused to take his money. He felt the sting of tears as he thanked her; any small kindness touched him deeply.

Still mostly asleep, Sergios ate a little and did not throw it up. That gave Argyros enough hope to seek his own bed. His rest, though, was fitful, and Riario's knock not long after dawn came as a relief. He sprang up to let the doctor in.

But Riario had no good news to give him. He hissed in dismay when the magistrianos led him into Sergios's room. "The first eruptions already," he grunted, and Argyros saw he was right. Raised red patches were beginning to cover the baby's face, just as they had Helen's. But with Helen, they had taken four days after the onset of the fever to appear. This was only the next day for Sergios.

"Is that bad?" Argyros asked, already afraid he knew the answer.

"Yes," the doctor said baldly: he was not one to mince words. "The faster the disease goes through its course, the worse the prognosis."

"What can I do to help him? There must be something!" The magistrianos kept running the nails of one hand over the back of the other. He was not even aware he was doing it.

Riario sadly shook his head. "Only what you did for your wife. Keep the tot as comfortable as you can. Bathe him in cool water to try to fight the fever. Do your best to see he eats—he needs his strength. Come to me when you need more poppy juice. Pray, if you think it does any good."

The physician's callous attitude toward prayer had shocked Argyros the first time he heard it. Now he only nodded. He still believed prayer could help the sick—but only sometimes.

Then Riario left, and he was alone with his son, alone to fight the inexorable progress of the smallpox. He had thought nothing could be worse than tending Helen had been. Now he saw he was wrong. It was as if some malign spell had accelerated the disease so he could watch Sergios get worse hour by hour. Nothing he did slowed the illness in the slightest.

The only mercy—a small one—was the poppy juice. It spared the baby the torment of itching Helen had gone through. Sergios hardly knew how, as the day waned and dusk fell, the pus-filled vesicles spread over his body. The end came not long after lamplighting time. The baby gave a small sigh and stopped breathing. For several minutes, his father did not realize he was dead.

When he did, he fled the house that had seen his young family begin and end as if it were accursed. To him, it was. For two coppers, he would have put a torch to it, no matter if the blaze set half Constantinople afire. He wandered blindly through the dark lanes and alleys of the city.

He was walking past the church of St. Symeon when he noticed where he was. Later, he saw it was probably not chance that had led his feet thither. He made for Riario's house. Of all the people he knew in the city, the doctor was most likely to grasp his anguish and, in grasping, help temper it.

When a knock sounds in the middle of the night, men commonly come to the door with a lamp in one hand and a cudgel or knife in the other, ready to fend off footpads. Because of his trade, though, Riario was used to such rude summonses. He opened the door at once, still wrapping his blanket around him. "Yes? What is it?" He held up a taper to see who his caller was.

His face fell when he recognized Argyros. "So soon as this, eh?" he said, and did not wait for a reply. "You'd better come in. I have some wine that could use drinking."

Riario filled and lit several lamps in his living room, threw a couple of robes from a chair to the floor, and waved the magistrianos into it. The rest of the room was strewn with clothes, books, and medical oddments. Men who live alone are usually very neat or anything but. The doctor was of the latter group.

"Here." He put an earthenware jug in front of Argyros and got one like it for himself. He did not bother with cups. "Drink," he said.

Argyros drank. Like a sponge, his grief sucked up the wine and left him all but untouched. He put down the jar. "Why?" he cried, a groan that filled the room.

"Ask God when you come before Him in judgment," Riario said. "I intend to. He'd best have a good answer, too, or I'll make Him pay. One day I had a wife I loved, two daughters I couldn't afford to dowry, and a face I didn't mind seeing in a mirror. A couple of weeks later... But you know about that."

"Yes, I know about that." Argyros drank deeply. After a while he went on, "I wish I had caught it too. Why am I here and untouched, when they're gone?" He rubbed at the back of his hands.

"*Never* wish you had smallpox," Riario said, most seriously. "Never. Poison yourself if you want, or jump off a building, but never wish that on yourself. Be thankful you don't know what you're talking about."

His eyes bored into the magistrianos, seeming to glow in the lamplight. Abashed by the force of that stare, Argyros raised the winejar to his lips again. Riario's glance shifted. Even after he had been drinking, he missed very little. His eyebrows shot upward. He whispered, "Be careful what you wish for. You may get it."

"Huh? What are you talking about?"

"Look at your hands, fool!"

Setting down the jug, the magistrianos did. He felt his heart stumble with fear. On his fingers and the backs of his hands were several of the hateful blotches he had come to know so well. A couple were already turning into blisters.

"It's impossible!" he burst out. "I'm not sick!"

Riario stood beside him, felt his forehead, took his pulse with sure, careful fingers. "You're *not* sick," he agreed at last. It sounded like an accusation; the doctor was scowling. "Why aren't you? Those are smallpox sores. Why don't you have more of them?"

"I don't know." Absurdly, Argyros felt guilty.

Riario kept poking and prodding at him, trying to figure out why he was not worse. He could not fathom it himself. He had watched the smallpox lesions disfigure Helen before they killed her, had seen them devour his son, and here he had this harmless handful. If God was giving him his wish, it was a mocking gift.

Then he smacked his forehead with the heel of his hand. "I'm a fool!"

"I'm willing to believe it," Riario said, "but why do you say so?"

"I don't think I have smallpox at all."

"What are those, then?" The doctor jerked his chin at the blisters on Argyros's hands.

"What did the dairyman call it when his little boy had it? Cowpox, that's what it was. I milked cows a couple of times, getting milk for Sergios."

"You're right, and I'm the one who's the fool." Riario shook his head in chagrin. "I've seen cowpox often enough, on milkmaids and such scared spitless they had smallpox instead. It's just that now, with so much of the real sickness everywhere, I naturally thought of it first and didn't even worry about the other."

Still grumbling to himself, the doctor left the room. He came back with two jugs. "That calls for more wine."

"I don't want to drink to celebrate," the magistrianos said.

"Then drink to drink, or drink for oblivion, or drink to stay with me, because I intend to. Just drink." Riario used a scalpel to cut into the pitch sealing the winejar's cork, worked it free, raised the jar to his mouth, and tipped his head back.

Argyros followed suit. At last the sweet wine began to reach him. He stared owlishly toward Riario. "What the devil good are you miserable doctors, if you can't even cure anybody who falls sick?"

Riario did not get angry. Instead, he buried his head in his hands. "How I wish we could. Give us what credit we deserve, though: we set bones, we tend cuts and burns, sometimes we even do some good with the knife."

The magistrianos nodded. "Oh, aye, I've seen all that in the army. But I've also seen campaigns fail before they started because half the men went down with a bloody flux, and no one could do anything about it."

"Yes, I know; those things happen." Riario hesitated, then continued slowly, seeming to reveal a long-cherished dream at which he feared Argyros would jeer: "What I really wish is that we could do something about disease before it started."

Indeed, the magistrianos had all he could do not to burst into derisive laughter. "How would you do that?"

"How do I know?" Riario said irritably. "I keep thinking of King Mithridates of Pontos—you know, the one who gave Rome such a fight in the time of Sulla and Pompey. He made himself so immune to poisons by taking lots of small doses that when he really needed to kill himself he had to get one of his mercenaries to do it for him."

"Wonderful," Argyros said. "Where are you going to get a little dose of a disease? And—"

He stopped, his mouth hanging open. He thought of Paul Skleros, his plump happy wife, and their eight children, all healthy while smallpox raged through Constantinople. He thought of the cowpox marks he had seen on small Paul—and surely the rest of the family would have had that ailment too. He thought of Riario's own words, of how people coming down with cowpox were afraid they had smallpox.

"By the Virgin and all the saints," he whispered.

"What?" Riario still sounded as though he regretted bringing his vision out where the magistrianos could see it.

Then, stammering, his tongue thick with wine, Argyros set his own insight before the doctor. When he was done, he waited for Riario to call him an idiot.

He watched Riario's hands slowly curl into fists. His face took on an expression Argyros did not recognize for a moment. Then he remembered his army days and suddenly riding into a clearing where a wildcat was stalking a squirrel. The cat had borne that same look of hungry concentration.

"To hit back, oh, to hit back," Riario breathed. "Do you realize the weapon you'll have put into physicians' hands if you're right, Argyros?"

"If I'm right," the magistrianos repeated. "How could you find out?"

"I know what I'd like to do," Riario replied at once: "Dab some pus from a smallpox sore into a cut on somebody who's already had cowpox. If the poor sod didn't come down with smallpox after that, he never would."

"I thought you would say that. Do it."

"With whom?" the doctor asked scornfully. "Who'd be madman enough to take a chance like that?"

"I would," Argyros said.

"Don't be a jackass, man. If you're wrong, you take the disease for real, not just in your foolish wishes."

The magistrianos spread his hands. "Why should I care? My life is in ruins anyhow."

"That's the wine talking, and your sorrow."

"In the morning I'll be sober and tell you the same thing. As for my sorrow ... if I live to be old as Methuselah, I'll never lose it. *You* should know that."

Riario flinched, grimaced, reluctantly nodded. All the same, he said, "Go home and go to bed. If you're fool enough to come back in the morning, well, we'll talk about it. If not, I can't blame you; that's for certain."

Argyros did not want to go home; the memories of the past weeks were too bitter for him ever to want to live in that house again. In the end, his legs decided the matter. They might as well have been jelly when he tried to rise. His head spun like Scylla's whirlpool. He slumped back into his chair and passed out.

WHEN HE WOKE his pounding head made him think he had died and gone to hell. He groaned, and then groaned again at hearing his own voice.

Riario was moving about; listening to him also hurt. The doctor said, "There are two cures for a hangover. One is raw cabbage, the other a bit more wine. Cabbage always makes me belch. Here."

Argyros thought his queasy stomach would reject the cup Riario pressed on him, but the wine stayed down. After a while, he began to feel human, in a melancholy way.

Riario's haggard look and red-tracked eyes said he was suffering too. He picked up a chunk of bread, shuddered, put it down again. "I'm getting too old for this kind of thing."

"I'm half your age, and I was too old years ago." The magistrianos sat bolt upright and regretted it. "The small-pox!"

Riario regarded him with bleary curiosity. "You still want to go ahead?"

"I said I would, didn't I? I remember that. It's one of the last things I *do* remember."

"Let me look at you," Riario said and took the magistrianos's hands in his own. Argyros looked with him. Clean brown scabs were already forming over the cowpox blisters. The doctor grunted. "Aye, you're healing from it. Come along, then. If you're after a nameless grave in the cemetery of Pelagios with the other suicides, I'll help put you there."

"If you were so sure that was going to happen, you wouldn't try this," Argyros said.

"I suppose not. But then, I wouldn't try it unless I was certain I'd miss the disease."

Having had the last word, Riario paced the house, waiting for someone to report a new case of smallpox. He began to grumble; by this time yesterday, he had been wanted in three places at once. But noon was still a long way away when a woman began pounding on the door, crying, "My husband! Come quick! The pox has seized my husband!"

Argyros and Riario both screwed up their faces at the bright morning sunshine. Lost in her own concern, the woman never noticed. She unquestioningly accepted Argyros as another doctor.

The magistrianos's stomach almost rebelled when he stood by the sick man's bed. The fellow reminded him too sharply of what he had gone through with Helen and Sergios. Smallpox lesions covered his face and limbs; as yet, they held clear fluid, not pus. "Will he live?" Argyros asked quietly, so the man's wife, who was sobbing in the next room, would not hear.

"He may well," Riario answered. "The fever's not as high as it often is, and his pulse is very strong."

He eyed the magistrianos. Argyros willed himself to nod.

The doctor pulled a scalpel from his bag; Argyros thought it was the same one he had used to open the wine the night before. He made a small cut in the side of the magistrianos's right thumb. Argyros nearly jerked his hand away. Holding still to be deliberately injured, he found, was harder in some ways than going into battle.

Humming tunelessly, Riario pierced a couple of the sick man's blisters with the scalpel. He pressed the liquid from them into the wound he had made on Argyros's hand and wrapped a bandage around it. He gave the scalpel a thoughtful look. "If this had smallpox poison on it, I suppose I ought to wash it before I use it again."

He went out a few minutes later to tell the sick man's wife to do all the things Argyros had done for Helen: bathe him against the fever, keep him quiet—all the palliatives that did no harm, and not much good, either. They did not pretend to cure.

His thumb had begun to throb. It did not matter. If he was right, here was something better than a cure, for anyone who had once had cowpox would never get smallpox at all.

If he was wrong—well, Riario had already spelled out what would happen if he was wrong. One way or the other, he would know soon.

HIS VISITS TO RIARIO became a daily ritual. The doctor would examine him, feel to see if he had a fever, check his pulse. Then Riario would growl, "Still alive, I'd say," give him a cup of wine—a *small* cup of wine—and send him home again.

The routine gave him something around which his life could coalesce once more. So did his work, to which he returned about a week after Sergios died. The corps of magistrianoi was still badly shorthanded, with some members dead and others mourning loved ones or caring for the sick. The number of things to be done, though, remained the same. Exhaustion was an anodyne hardly less potent than wine.

After three weeks, only a pale scar remained from the cut on Argyros's thumb. He began to lose patience with Riario's stock phrase. "Think I'm likely to stay that way?" he asked pointedly.

"Oh, yes, I've thought so for some time," the doctor said. "There is another problem, though: for all we know, you may have been immune to smallpox even before you got the cowpox. You nursed your wife and son without catching it, you know."

Argyros stared at him, appalled. He felt betrayed. "Then what I did was worthless?"

"No, no, no, no. You're part of a proof, but only part. I've done some checking lately. Did you know that it's not just the Skleroi who escaped smallpox, but almost all the dairy families in the city?"

"No, but that would make sense, wouldn't it? They'd be the ones most likely to get cowpox first instead."

"So they would. That's really what decided me you'd guessed right, whether you yourself were immune or not. By now, I've given cowpox to a couple of dozen people and tried to give them smallpox afterward."

"And?" Argyros wanted to reach over and shake the answer out of Riario. "By the Virgin, tell me this instant how they are?"

The doctor grinned his lopsided grin. "Still alive, I'd say."

"Then if, say, the city prefect made everyone in Constantinople come forward to get a dose of cowpox, or if babies got it not long after they were born—"

"—None of those people would come down with small-pox later," Riario finished for the magistrianos. "That's my best guess. I've already started telling other doctors, too. The word will spread."

Awe on his face, Argyros crossed himself and bent his head in prayer.

"Here, what's all this in aid of?" Riario demanded after the magistrianos had spent several silent minutes.

"I was apologizing to the Lord for daring to question His will," Argyros answered humbly. "Now at last I see His purpose in the anguish He sent me and those I love—loved." Purpose or no, that correction brought sorrow with it. Argyros quickly went on, "Had they not been taken ill, I never would have stumbled across the truth that will save so many more from a like fate. Truly I am but an instrument of His will."

"Oh, hogwash," the doctor said. "What of all the others who got sick and died in the epidemic? If God killed all of them just so two would draw your attention, He strikes me as bloody wasteful."

"No," said Argyros. "Consider—were many people not sick, I would have gone to a wetnurse instead of a dairy and never learned of cowpox. But I was afraid to bring a wet-nurse into the house, and so I met Paul Skleros and his family."

"Everyone in Constantinople thinks he's a theologian," Riario grumbled. "Pure foolishness, if you ask me."

"I didn't," the magistrianos said shortly. He could not bear to think Helen and Sergios had died in vain, for no purpose at all.

But then he begged Riario's pardon. He would not have noticed the relationship between cowpox and smallpox without the doctor, either. In years to come, physicians would not have to grow so hard-shelled, so cynical, for they would have a true weapon against one deadly scourge of mankind. It might even keep some of them from despair-ing of God and going to hell.

Argyros did not mention that thought to Riario. He knew what the doctor would say about it.

With a grunt of displeasure, Pavlo sat down at his desk to draft his monthly report. The tourmarch of the border fortress of Pertuis inked his pen, sent it scraping over the parchment: "Events of the month of May, 1315—"

He looked at the year he had carelessly written, swore, and scratched it out. Bad enough he had to compose in Latin. Both men who would read his report—his immediate superior Kosmas the kleisouriarch of the Pyrenees, and Arkadios the strategos of Ispania—came from Constantinople. Greek-speakers themselves, they would sneer at his lack of culture. Despite still being one of the two official tongues of the Roman Empire, Latin had far less prestige than Greek.

Using the northern style of dating on an official document, though, might get him marked down as subversive, even if it was also popular in Ispania—and Italia too, come to that. He substituted the imperial year, reckoned from the creation of the world rather than the Incarnation: "—May, 6823, the thirteenth indiction."

He settled down to writing. Most of the report was routine: soldiers and horses out sick, deaths (only two—a good month), new recruits, supplies expended, traders traveling down through the pass of Pertuis into the Empire, tolls collected, traders going up into the Franco-Saxon kingdoms, and on and on.

The description of the garrison's drills was also something to get past in a hurry, except for one part. There he checked his own records, which he kept meticulously: "Liquid fire expended in exercises, two and five-sevenths tuns. Stock remaining on hand"—he flicked beads on his countingboard—"ninety-four and two-sevenths tuns. Seals of wholly expended tuns enclosed herewith."

He did not know what went into what the barbarians called "Greek fire"; nor did he want to. It was shipped straight from the imperial arsenal at Constantinople.

He did know that he had best start looking for a good place to hide if he could not account for every drop he used. What happened to officials who let the northerners get their hands on the stuff did not bear thinking about.

His pen ran dry. He inked it again and wrote, "One siphon was damaged during fire exercises. Our smith feels he can repair it." Pavlo hoped so; Kosmas would take weeks to send him another of the long bronze tubes through which the liquid fire was discharged.

The tourmarch scratched his head. What else needed reporting? "The Franco-Saxons have lately shown a good deal of interest in the woods just north of the fortress. The forest being on their side of the frontier, I have only been able to send a rider to make inquiry. They say they are after a nest of robbers; their count declined the help I offered."

Pavlo wondered if he should say more, then decided not to. Even if the barbarians had sent a lot of men into the woods, they were still comfortably out of arrow range. And they were such bunglers that they might need a couple of companies for a one-platoon job.

The tourmarch folded the parchment into an envelope, lit a red beeswax candle at the lamp he always kept burning to have a fire handy, and let several drops splatter onto the report. When he had enough, he pushed his signet ring into the soft, hot wax.

Shouting for a courier, he came from the gloomy keep into the bright sunshine of the courtyard.

Something hissed through the air and landed with a surprisingly gentle thud twenty paces in front of him: a wicker-wrapped earthenware pot, a little bigger than his head. A wisp of smoke floated up from the top. At the same time as the sentry on the watchtower cried "Catapult!" another one thunked down in the courtyard.

"To the walls! They're coming!" the sentry screamed. Troopers snatched up bows, spears, and helmets and dashed for the stairs to the rampart.

Pavlo cursed in good earnest and tore his report in half. He should have been more alert—the Franco-Saxons had been brewing mischief after all, though what they hoped to accomplish with a bombardment of crockery was beyond him.

Suddenly the very air seemed torn apart. Pavlo thought a thunderbolt had struck the fort—but the sky was clear and blue. Something hot and jagged whined past his face. A cloud of thick gray smoke shot upward.

The tourmarch looked around dazedly. Two men were down, shrieking; a third, who had been closest to the pot, was hardly more than a crimson smear on the ground. The cataclysmic noise had frozen the rest of the soldiers in their tracks.

Outside, Pavlo heard the drumroll of hoofbeats, the whoops and war cries of the barbarians, horse and foot. His stunned wits started working again. "Go on! Move!" he roared to his men. Discipline told. They began to obey.

Then another blast came, and a few seconds later another. Almost deafening, Pavlo could barely hear the wails and moans of the wounded. Smoke filled the courtyard; its acrid brimstone reek made the tourmarch cough and choke.

"The northerners have called devils from hell!" someone yelled.

The sentry's voice went high and shrill. "Heaven protect us, you're right! I can see them capering there, just at the edge of the forest, all in red, with horns and tails!"

"Shut up!" Pavlo bellowed furiously, to no avail. Half the garrison was screaming in terror now. Against devils, no discipline could hold.

And devils or no, those cursed catapults kept firing from the woods. A wrapped crock landed almost at the tourmarch's feet. Too late, his mind made an intuitive leap. "It's not demons!" he cried to whoever would listen. "It's whatever's in these—"

The explosion flung him against the wall of the keep like a broken doll. A few minutes later, a bigger one smashed the gates of Pertuis. The Franco-Saxons stormed in.

THE BEAMY MERCHANTMAN sailed slowly toward the Ispanic coast. "Won't be long now, sir," the captain promised.

"The Virgin be praised," exclaimed his passenger, a tall, thin, dark man with a neatly trimmed beard, bladelike nose, and oddly mournful eyes. "I've spent more than a month at sea, traveling from Constantinople."

"So you said, so you said." It meant nothing to the captain; he spent most of his life on the water. He went on, "Aye, now we've weathered that little island back there (Scombraria they call it—name means 'mackerel fishery,' y'know), we're home free. Island's not just for fishing, either—shields the New Carthage harbor from storms."

"Of course," the traveler said politely, though he had trouble following the man's guttural African dialect in Latin. He went back to the deckhouse to reclaim his duffel bag and wait for the vessel to anchor.

He had been aboard ship so long that the plain beneath his feet seemed to roll and pitch as he made the short walk to New Carthage, which sat on a hill. A bored guard asked his name and business. The fellow's lisping Ispanic accent did not trouble him; it was not much different from the flavor his own Greek gave the Empire's other tongue.

He answered, "I'm Basil Argyros, a trader in garum out of the city."

"You've come a long way for fermented fish sauce," the guard said, chuckling.

Argyros shrugged. "New Carthage's garum is famous around the Inner Sea. Would you be so kind as to tell me the way to the residence of the strategos? I'll need to discuss quantities, prices, and shipping arrangements with him."

The guardsman looked at his comrades, said nothing. Sighing, Argyros dug a handful of copper forty-follis pieces from his pouch and distributed them. After pocketing his share of the money, the soldier gave directions, adding,

"You know, Arkadios isn't there. He's up north someplace, campaigning against the barbarians."

"Not doing too bloody well, either," one of the other guardsmen muttered.

Argyros pretended not to hear that, but filed the information away. He sauntered into New Carthage. The city was large and well laid out, but of rather somber appearance because of the gray local stone from which it was built.

The gate guard's directions proved easy to follow. The strategos's headquarters was just up the main street from New Carthage's most splendid building, a church dedicated to the town's patron saint, who had been its bishop during the reign of the first Herakleios, seven centuries before.

"St. Mouamet, watch over me," Argyros murmured, crossing himself as he walked by the shrine, which was a smaller copy of the great church of Holy Wisdom in Constantinople. He found Mouamet one of the most inspiring saints on the calendar. "There is no God but the Lord, and Christ is His Son," Argyros chanted softly.

It took a bribe of half a gold nomisma and an hour's wait to get Argyros admitted to the presence of Isaac Kabasilas, Arkadios's chief deputy. Kabasilas, a large, comfortable man with a large, comfortable belly, said, "Well, what can I do for you, fellow? Something about fish sauce, my secretary said. He's really quite able to handle that sort of thing himself, you know."

"I would hope so. However"—Argyros glanced around—"as we are alone, I can tell you that I don't care whether all the garum in New Carthage turns to honey tomorrow." He produced a letter and handed it to Kabasilas.

The official broke the gold seal. His jaw dropped as he read. "You're one of the Emperor's magistrianoi!" The condescension was gone from his voice, and the comfort from his manner.

"Only you know that, and I'd sooner keep it so."

"Of course," Kabasilas said nervously. In theory, he outranked his visitor, but he knew what theory was worth. Wetting his lips, he asked, "What do you need from me?"

"If you tell me how the Franco-Saxons have taken eight fortresses and three cities in the last year, I'll take the next ship out."

"Four cities," Kabasilas said unhappily. "Tarrago fell three weeks ago. In the field we match the northerners, but no walls can keep them out. The traders who escaped from Tarrago rave of sorcery ripping the gates open." He crossed himself.

So did Argyros, but he persisted, remarking, "Sorcery is something heard of more often than met."

"Not this time," Kabasilas said. "It's all of a piece with what's happened at other places we've lost. The Franco-Saxons must be in league with Satan. As if what they've done to us isn't enough, honest men have seen the devils they've summoned—great red fiends, from the stories."

The magistrianos frowned. Of course he believed in demons; after all, the Bible spoke of them. But he had never come across one in action, or expected to. Like most educated citizens of the Empire, he drew a firm distinction between the Outer Learning (most of it drawn from the pagan Greeks), which concerned this world, and the Inner Learning of Christian theology. It was disconcerting to find the line between them blurred.

"I think I'd better talk to these traders out of Tarrago myself," he said. "Where are they staying?"

IOAN'S INN was a cheerfully ramshackle place that catered to merchants. The wine was good, the prices low to one used to those of Constantinople. In his guise as a buyer of fish sauce, Argyros sat in the taproom, listening to the gossip and spicing it now and then with the latest scandal from the capital.

He did not have to prompt to bring the talk around to Tarrago. The merchants who had got out of the city spoke of little else. But they did not tell him as much as he wanted; Kabasilas's summary had been depressingly accurate. The attack had taken place at night, which only made things worse.

He learned the most from a tin merchant from Angle-land and his niece, who was an apothecary at a nunnery near Londin. Their lodgings in Tarrago had been close to the gate by the cathedral, through which the Franco-Saxons had en-tered. But even their account was vague; a roar, a cloud of vile smoke that seemed to cover half the city, and the crash of the locked gates going down to admit the enemy.

"We rode like madmen and got out by the northwest gate, the one next to the forum," said the merchant, a ruddy-cheeked fellow named Wighard, "and spent the night in the graveyard half a mile west. The Franco-Saxons were too busy looting the town to go poking through old bones."

"Oh, tell him the whole story, uncle," his niece Hilda said impatiently. She was a small, intense woman in her mid-twenties, with the startling gray eyes and fair coloring of the northern peoples; no wonder the Emperor Maurice had called the Franks, Lombards, and other Germans "the blond tribes" in his military manual.

She turned to Argyros. "A squad *did* come out to look the necropolis over, but when they got close, uncle Wig-hard rose up and shouted 'Boo!' They ran harder than we had."

Wighard said sheepishly, "What with their consorting with demons and all, I figured they'd be even more afraid of 'em than I am!"

The magistrianos laughed and ordered more wine for the three of them. In Constantinople he had met only a hand-ful of men from distant Angleland (he thought of it as Bri-tannia), and their steadiness and ready wit had fascinated him. These two seemed cut from the same cloth.

It was only right for Britannia to be reunited to the Em-pire one day, as over the centuries Italia, Ispania, and part of the southern coast of Gaul had been. Somehow, though, Argyros was glad it would not be any year soon.

Having found no real answers in New Carthage, Argyros bought a horse and rode north to see at first hand what the Franco-Saxons were up to.

Arkadios's forces still held the line of the Eberu, but the magistrianos had no trouble slipping across the river. He did not worry about being in enemy-held territory. The blond tribes were savage in battle, but careless about every other aspect of warfare, including patrols. They had been so even in Maurice's time, before the days of Herakleios.

But they had something going for them, he thought as he rode past captured Tarrago. "Or what am I doing here?" he asked his horse. Unlike Balaam's ass, it did not answer.

Argyros did not do any poking about at Tarrago; there were Franco-Saxons on the walls (none looking particularly demonic). He had expected troops there, the town having fallen so recently. But he was surprised and dismayed to find Barcilo also garrisoned, though it had been lost the autumn before. The barbarians looked to be coming to stay.

Empurias was another three days' ride up the Roman coastal highway—and proved full of soldiers too. Argyros frowned again, not sure whether to strike inland or stay on the road the first Caesar's legionaries had tramped. The highway promised to be quicker. He pressed ahead.

He rode past fields of fennel toward the Pyrenees, which loomed tall before him. Then the mountains were all around him as the road swung inland to take advantage of the pass of Pertuis. He met a band of Franco-Saxon armored horsemen clattering south into Ispania. Seeing only a lone traveler with nothing worth stealing, they let him by.

Not far from the fortress of Pertuis lay a victory monument set up by Pompey before the Incarnation. Seeing it stiffened Argyros's resolve. No less than the ancient general, he had the tradition of Rome to uphold.

The late afternoon sun threw long, mournful shadows. The Franco-Saxons had not repaired Pertuis after they took it; apparently they planned to fix the new border farther south. Argyros dismounted and led his horse through the yawning gateway into the courtyard. Better to spend the night there than in the open, he thought; the walls would hide his campsite from bandits.

The courtyard was full of rank grass. Argyros hobbled his horse and let it graze while he got a small fire going. He stretched till his joints creaked, then, taking bread, olive oil, and a skin of sour wine from his saddlebags, sat down by the fire for supper.

Something sharp dug into the seat of his pants (flowing robes were all very well in Constantinople, but not for serious travel). He raised up on one cheek and removed the offending object. He had expected a rock, but it was a potsherd, a triangle with the longest side about as long as his middle finger—a flat piece from the bottom of a pot.

He was about to throw it away when he noticed the potter's mark stamped into the clay: a cross flanked by the letters S and G. "St. Gall!" he said and looked at the shard with a new and lively interest.

For one thing, the monastery of St. Gall lay in the Alps, far to the northeast of Pertuis. It was no great pottery center; why was one of its products so far from home? For another, Franco-Saxon monasteries interested Argyros professionally. Such learning as the barbarians had was confined to their clerics. And St. Gall was their chief monastic center, from which abbeys had spread all through the Franco-Saxon kingdoms. The magistrianos tugged at his beard. St. Gall might well be involved in whatever mischief they had concocted.

His examination of the potsherd made him certain he was on to something, even if he was not sure what. One side of the shard was blackened, as if by fire. Yet that was the side that had been face-down; a pillbug was still clinging to it. It could not have been charred during the sack of Pertuis.

Argyros reproached himself for not making a thorough examination of the fortress when he rode up. Too dark now, he thought. The morning would have to do. He took out his bedroll, spread it on the ground, prayed, and slept.

He woke with the sun. After wolfing down more bread and oil, he walked around the overgrown courtyard, scuffing through the grass to see if he could find more bits of pottery. After a while, he did. They were all of the same yellow-brown clay as the first, and all scorched on one side.

He could still make out traces of a big scorch mark near the base of one wall of the keep. He scrabbled through the matted grass there and was rewarded with several more tiny shards. One, he thought, bore part of the S of St. Gall's mark. He grunted in satisfaction.

He also found a couple of fragments at the gateway, but learned less than he wanted there. The gates themselves were gone; the Franco-Saxons had burned their timbers.

He saw motion out of the corner of his eye: two horsemen approaching. He ducked back into the courtyard, clapped a helmet on his head, strung his bow, and slung a quiver of arrows over his shoulder. Having armed himself, he returned to the gateway and cautiously peered out.

One of the oncoming riders waved as he drew close enough to recognize Argyros. "You'll not find much garum here," Wighard called. After a few seconds, Argyros saw that the tin merchant's companion was Hilda. Her gilt hair was tucked up under a broad-brimmed hat, and she rode astride like a man, but tunic and trousers could not disguise her small size or womanly figure.

The magistrianos emerged from cover, but did not set down his bow. "You don't have many ingots with you, either," he said.

"Left 'em behind when we got out of Tarrago, if you must know," Wighard said.

He was smiling. Argyros studied him. "I don't believe you care."

"Believe what you like," the Anglelander said calmly. He glanced toward the ruined fortress of Pertuis. "Looks like a fair place to stop for lunch."

The sun was less than halfway up the sky. Argyros raised an eyebrow, but kept silent.

Hilda stirred in the saddle. She remarked, "Back in Constantinople, his imperial majesty Nikephoros must be displeased at the way the Franco-Saxons have violated his borders."

"I daresay he is," the magistrianos agreed politely. In fact, he knew the Emperor was furious. The Master of Offices had made that quite clear.

"Well, so is our good king Oswy," Wighard said, seeming to come to a decision. "And well he might be, for they've used their foul sorcery on us as well as against you Romans."

"Have they?" Argyros said, pricking up his ears.

"Indeed they have. Their cursed pirates have sunk or taken more than a score of good Anglelander ships in the Sleeve this past year." That was the name the Anglelanders gave to the strait between Britannia and the Franco-Saxon lands. Wighard continued angrily, "No king will brook such an outrage for long, nor should he, even if the devil is behind it."

"You sound very sure of that," the magistrianos said.

"Of course I am. We always sailed rings round the lousy lubbers before. What else but black magic could give 'em the edge now? King Oswy, God bless him, is certain of it, I can tell you."

"And so," Argyros said, making the connection, "you plan on inspecting the stronghold here to see if you can find out how it's being done."

Wighard reddened. Hilda, though, looked the magistrianos in the eye. "Just as you've been doing," she challenged. "We're well met, I think."

She was, Argyros thought, altogether too astute. He shrugged and nodded. "We do seem to have a common interest, at any rate."

"So you are one of the Emperor's thegns, then?" Wighard said. Guessing at the strange Germanic word, the magistrianos nodded again. Wighard was also nodding, half to himself. "I thought it might be so, when I saw you here. Are we allies, then, in tracking down the Franco-Saxons' wizardry?"

Argyros hesitated. If he could solve the puzzle, he was not at all sure he wanted to share the answer with another nation of barbarians. On the other hand, the Anglelanders and Franco-Saxons were enemies of one another... and Wighard and Hilda might come up with a solution where he could not. That would be very bad. "We have a common interest," he repeated.

"If we do," Hilda said, lightly stressing the first word, "suppose you tell us what you've found here."

A hardheaded young woman, despite her exotic good looks, Argyros thought. In her position, he would have asked the same thing. Saying, "Fair enough," he took the two Anglelanders around the fortress.

Wighard sucked in his breath sharply when the magistrianos pointed out the scorched wall of the keep. "The sign of the hellfire, you say?" he grunted, touching a silver chain around his neck. Argyros guessed he wore a crucifix or some relic under his tunic.

"Perhaps so, but I'd be more inclined to believe it came from St. Gall," the magistrianos said. He dug the broken piece of pottery from his belt pouch and explained how he had found it and what he thought it meant.

He thought that would knock the Anglelanders' maunderings about demons over the head, but it did not. To Wighard, in fact, the connection even made sense. "Who better to call up demons than monks?" he asked. "If anybody could control the fiends, they would be the ones."

Argyros blinked; that had not occurred to him. He felt his picture of the world losing a little solidity. Who knew what evil the monks of St. Gall might work? They were heretics, after all, and capable of anything. "Suppose it is deviltry," he said at last. "What will you do then?"

"Me? I expect I'll be frightened enough to piss my pants," Wighard said, shivering. "All I'm for is getting Hilda to wherever the answers lie and keeping her safe afterward. Once she learns the summoning spells, Angleland will be able to use them too."

The magistrianos had to admit that had a certain logic to it. Dealing as they did with drugs and potions, apothecaries like Hilda were the next thing to magicians. And who would suspect a slip of a girl of being a spy? He hadn't himself.

Covering his stab of jealousy, he said, "To St. Gall, then?" The Anglelanders nodded. He went off to saddle his horse, resigning himself to weeks and probably months in the company of barbarians.

The journey was as wearing as he had expected: up the ancient Via Domitia across Franco-Saxon territory to Araus, the northwesternmost town in the reclaimed Roman province of Narbonese Gaul; then by boat north on the Rhodan to Vienne, and east along another one-time legionary highway to Agosta; from there by a lesser road, good only in summer, through the Pennine Alps; and then northeast to Turic and, after it, to St. Gall itself.

Long as the trip was, though, his companions made it fascinating in a way he had not expected. He sometimes found them so strange as almost to be from another world. The northerners he had known in Constantinople had been touched by Roman customs, and most did their best to ape them. Hilda and Wighard had none of that veneer.

They had not even come to Araus, for instance, when black, roiling, anvil-topped clouds blew toward them, whipped by a harsh wind from the Inner Sea. "Storm coming," Argyros said.

"Aye," Wighard said, hauling a rain cape out of his kit, "those're Thor's whiskers, right enough. I reckon the Thunderer'll be busy tonight."

The magistrianos had only gaped at him, too startled for speech. In the Empire, peasants in the countryside still clung to the vestiges of their old pagan cults, in spite of priests' fuming. But Wighard was one of King Oswy's personal retainers, a man of higher rank in his country than Argyros held in Constantinople. Yet he plainly took Thor as seriously as he did Christ and the saints.

But then, to the Anglelanders there were no sharp dividing lines between everyday reality, rank superstition, and faith. Still uncomfortable with the notion of demons loose in the world, Argyros had scoffed at the idea while the travelers sat around a fire one evening, waiting for a couple of hares to finish roasting.

Wighard's counterargument was of the "well, everyone knows" sort. Hilda, however, had what was by Anglelander standards a good education, and undertook a more reasoned reply. When she cited the Gadarene swine, Argyros conceded the point, but asked, "Is that truly meaningful today? I don't expect another flood to wash us away in the fashion of Noah's, or the sun to stand still in the sky as it did for Joshua.''

''Maybe not,'' she said, ''but evil spirits are known much later than in scriptural times. What of the nun who forgot to cross herself in the monastery garden and so swallowed a demon along with her lettuce?''

''That's a new one on me,'' the magistrianos said, hiding a smile. ''Where did you learn it?''

''It's in the writings of Pope Gregory the Great,'' Hilda answered proudly.

''Oh.'' Argyros thought of the jest about Pompey: great as compared to what? Gregory had been pope some time after the reign of Justinian, and the heretical northerners still made much of his thunderings about the ecclesiastical privileges that were rightfully the see of Rome's. In imperial eyes he was chiefly remarkable for having spent some years in Constantinople without bothering to learn Greek, and for fawning on the repulsive tyrant Phokas after he overthrew the emperor Maurice and murdered him and his five sons.

Yet despite the Anglelanders' rudeness of manner, the magistrianos came to value their company. Wighard might not have known his letters, but he had no trouble reading tracks. The snares he rigged from vines and branches rarely went empty, and he always knew what fish were likely to be in a stream.

And Hilda, for all her credulity about demons, was skilled at her chosen craft. When Argyros's back tightened up after long days in the saddle, she concocted a lotion from oil and various plants she searched out near their campsite: wild cucumber, centaury, fleawort, a couple of kinds of mint, and licorice root. Well rubbed in, it eased him remarkably.

The lotion's success and the praises he showered on her for it broke the slight wall of reserve that had existed between them. He began to treat her as he would a well-born imperial lady of similar attractiveness, casually flirting, quoting the poets, and praising her with the fulsomeness of a practiced courtier.

Wighard found it all very funny, chuckling at each new sally. And Argyros took Hilda's blushes and lowered eyes to mean what they would have from a woman of Constantinople: an invitation to continue.

He had stayed celibate for nearly two years after Helen's death and even thought of retreating into a monastery, but, as sorrow eased over time, the demands of his body showed that was not the proper course for him. He was inalterably of the world, and had to make the best of it.

One morning while Wighard was out checking his traps, Hilda came back to camp from a nearby stream where she had just bathed. Her clothes molded themselves magnificently to her still-damp body. Catching his breath, the magistrianos murmured the famous tag from the *Iliad*. It meant nothing to Hilda, who knew no Greek. Argyros translated: "'Small blame to the Trojans and strong-greaved Achaeans for suffering for a long time over such a woman.' Homer was speaking of Helen, of course, but then he was not lucky enough to have met you."

She flushed and stopped in confusion. Argyros had been on the road long enough to cloud his usually keen judgment. He strode forward and started to draw her into his arms.

She kicked him in the shin, or tried to, for he slid his leg aside with the unconscious ease of a veteran warrior. She sprang away, fumbling for the small knife at her belt. Her eyes blazed as she spat out, "Did you take me for one of your loose Roman baggages, who lies down with a man at whim?"

Since the answer to that was at least "maybe" if not "yes," the magistrianos prudently evaded a direct reply. Instead he apologized with as smooth a tongue as he had formerly used to compliment Hilda. All the while he was thinking that the strict morality that Tacitus had mentioned in the early Germans was still depressingly alive among their descendants.

Tacitus had also spoken of German women as sharing armed combat with their men. Seeing Hilda standing at the ready with her dagger, Argyros decided he believed that too.

His ardor quite cooled, he went about the business of breaking camp in thoughtful silence.

That afternoon, when Hilda had gone off into the bushes by the side of the road for a few minutes, Wighard leaned toward Argyros and said quietly, "As well for you that you stopped when you did." He touched his bow.

"I daresay," Argyros agreed with a raised eyebrow: evidently the famed Germanic chastity had more backing it up than mere moral force. "Still," the magistrianos added a moment later, "we could do worse than resting in a town tonight."

Wighard nodded, clapped him on the shoulder. "Aye, why not? Go off and get yourself a lively wench. You'll be better for it, and we'll all have less to worry about."

A practical people, these Anglelanders, Argyros thought.

EN ROUTE to St. Gall were several daughter monasteries patterned after the original foundation. The travelers lodged at more than one, both because they offered safe, comfortable shelter and to get to know them: they were all as like as so many peas in a pod. And why not? The pattern was a splendid success. A space only 480 by 640 feet formed a self-contained community for 270 men. Argyros did not agree with the doctrines espoused within St. Gall and the other western abbeys, but he could only admire the genius of the architects who had laid them out.

He passed himself off as a trader of amber with the pagan Lithuanians, calling himself Petro of Narbomart. The port on the Inner Sea was in the hands of the Franco-Saxons; he did not want to be known for an imperial. Yet Narbomart's Latin dialect was close to that of Ispania, and easy for him to mimic. He could never have pretended to hail from northern Gallia. He could hardly follow that braying, nasal dialect, let alone hope to imitate it.

One Sunday he attended Mass at a monastery church with Wighard and Hilda, but succeeded only in making her angry at him once more. The issue, naturally, was theological. During the liturgy, Argyros stood mute whenever the word *filioque* came up: the doctrine from the imperial church was that the Holy Spirit proceeded from God the Father alone, not from the Father *and the Son*.

Most citizens of the Empire did the same when traveling in those lands outside the control of Constantinople. It salved their consciences and, ninety-nine times out of a hundred, passed unnoticed by their fellow celebrants.

Not here, though. As they were riding away, Hilda said bitterly, "I might have known you would go flaunting your heresy."

"*My* heresy?" the magistrianos shot back. "The fourth Council of Constantinople condemned the doctrine of the dual procession of the Holy Spirit as heterodox four hundred years ago."

"I don't recognize that council as ecumenical," she replied. None of the northern Christians did. When Herakleios's grandson Constans II reconquered Italia from the Lombards, he had installed his own bishop of Rome. The incumbent, of whose doctrines Constans disapproved, fled to the Franks, and the Franco-Saxon kingdoms and Britannia still followed that shadowy line of popes (so, clandestinely, did some folk in Ispania, Italia, and even Illyricum).

Hilda lifted her chin in challenge. "Convince me by reasoning, if at all."

"Since you reject orthodoxy, suppose you convince *me*," Argyros said.

Wighard rolled his eyes and took out a wineskin. He had no concerns other than those of this world. Intricate religious argument, though, was meat and drink to the magistrianos.

And to Hilda, it proved. "Very well, then," she said: "The Holy Spirit, being the Trinity, is the Spirit of both the Father and the Son. Since They both possess the Spirit, He must proceed from Them both. The Father has the Son; the Son, the Father; and, since the Father is the principle of the Godhead—one might even say, the essence of the Godhead—the Holy Spirit *must* proceed from the Father and the Son, completely from each Person."

"Whew!" Argyros looked at her in startled admiration. She argued as acutely as an archbishop.

Wighard chuckled, a little blearily. He might not have cared about the dispute, but he was beaming with pride for his niece. "What do you say to that? Bright girl, eh?"

"Very." Argyros turned back to Hilda, giving her all his attention now, as if she were an underestimated swordsman who had almost run him through.

He remained intellectually unpunctured, however, and counterattacked, "You're clever, but your doctrine destroys the unity of the Godhead."

"Nonsense!"

"Oh, but it does. If proceeding from the Son is the same as proceeding from the Father, it has no point. But if the two processions are different, the fact that procession from the Son is necessary implies that procession from the Father alone is insufficient—and thus that the Father is imperfect, surely a blasphemy. Also, ascribing procession to the Son as well as to the Father implies that the Father and Son share this attribute. If the Holy Spirit lacks it, then Son and Holy Spirit cannot be consubstantial, as the Persons of the Trinity must. But if the Spirit does not lack it, then what do we have? Why, the Spirit proceeding from the Spirit, which is absurd."

It was Hilda's turn to regard Argyros with caution. "That's not the definition of faith your precious Council gave."

"The Council was ecumenical, and tried to satisfy everyone," he answered, "even if it did fail with you. I accept its dogma, but as far as my reasons go, I have to please only myself."

"For someone not in holy orders, you're a keen theologian."

"After the hippodrome, theology has always been Constantinople's favorite sport," the magistrianos said. "Nine hundred years ago, St. Gregory of Nyssa complained that if you asked someone how much bread cost, he told you that the Father was greater than the Son, and the Son subordinate to Him; and if you asked if your bath was ready, the answer came that the Son was created from nothing. Of course there are no more Arians to uphold those views any longer, but—"

"—the principle still holds," Hilda finished for him. "So I see. Still, how do you get around the fact that—"

Argyros went back to the argument, but with only half his attention. The rest was still chewing on Hilda's left-handed praise for his skill at dogmatics. In the Empire, knowledge belonged to those with the ability to understand, both the Outer and the Inner Learning. Whether one was layman or cleric did not matter.

The northerners, he thought, lost a great deal by keeping learning so limited. Here was Wighard, a fine man and far from stupid, but half heathen and quivering at the notion of facing a demon. And even Hilda, though educated in religious matters, had none of the history, law, mathematics, or philosophy that gave perspective and produced a truly rounded individual.

He sighed. The Anglelanders were all he had to work with. Despite their weaknesses, they would have to do.

It was just past high summer, but the air of the pass through the Pennine Alps had a chill to it and was so thin that a man or a horse started panting after the least exertion. As they started the last leg of the journey to St. Gall, the three travelers hammered out their plans.

Every mile closer to the monastery made Wighard less and less eager actually to set foot inside it. He kept making dark mutters about the forces of evil lurking there and what they would likely do to anyone coming to sniff them out. When Argyros, exasperated, suggested that he stay outside and help when the time came for escape, he eagerly agreed and at once grew more cheerful; it was as if a great weight was off his shoulders.

Secure in her own faith, Hilda had no qualms about entering St. Gall. Her task would stay what it had been before she fell in with Argyros: to search through the monastery's library, ostensibly to look for new medicines to bring back to Londin, in fact after clues to the Franco-Saxons' tame hellfire.

That worried the magistrianos—suppose she found the secret and kept it to herself? All he could think of to keep that from happening was to make himself such an obviously valuable ally that the idea would never occur to her.

He had every intention of going into the monastery himself. He could not hope to compete with Hilda when it came to pawing through old manuscripts. He could not even read some of the western book hands. But as a magistrianos he had other talents, interrogation among them. The Franco-Saxons liked to boast; no telling what some unobtrusive probing might bring out.

And then all their plans unraveled in Turic, a lakeside town a couple of days' ride west of St. Gall. It was raining when they came in, a downpour that turned the dung-filled streets to a muddy stinking quagmire. Argyros thought longingly of Constantinople's flagstones and cobbles—and of its sewers. Hilda and Wighard seemed to notice nothing amiss.

All three of them were looking for an inn when Hilda's horse slipped on a patch of slime and fell heavily. She had no chance to kick free. The beast came down on her. Argyros heard the dull snap of cracking bone, followed an instant later by her stifled shriek.

When the horse, which was unhurt, tried to scramble to its feet again, Hilda's next cry was anything but stifled. Argyros and Wighard leaped down into the mud together. Wighard grabbed the horse's head and held it while the magistrianos freed Hilda's right leg—the one that was on top—from the stirrup. He shifted position, then nodded to Wighard. "All right—let him up, but slowly, mind."

"Aye." As the horse rose, Argyros cut the left stirrup-leather with his knife. Hilda sat up, clutching at her leg. Beneath splattered muck, her face was gray. She had bitten her lip in pain; there was a smear of blood at the corner of her mouth.

"Stay as still as you can," Argyros ordered, using his dagger to slit her trouserleg. He saw with relief that no bone was poking through the flesh; in this filth such a wound would surely have rotted. But her calf was swelling as he watched, and he had heard the break himself.

"Bad?" Wighard asked. Argyros told him in a few words. The Anglelander nodded. "Let's get her under a roof, then. I've set a few bones in my time." To Hilda he said, "I'm sorry, chick; we're going to have to move you. It'll hurt."

"It hurts already," she got out.

"I know, lass, I know." Wighard turned to Argyros. "We've nothing for a proper splint. I'll tie her legs together, and we'll carry her. Lucky she's short; we can keep her feet from dragging on the ground."

"Nothing better to do," the magistrianos agreed. Hilda gasped as they lifted her. Argyros could see her clamping her mouth shut against a scream. "Brave girl," he said; she was taking it like a soldier.

She managed the ghost of a smile. "See, I have my arm around you after all, though maybe not the way you wanted."

Leading their horses, they started slowly down the street. By good fortune, there was a hostel close by. Its proprietress was a plump widow named Gerda. She clucked at their draggled state, but Argyros's good Roman gold softened her remarkably. A nomisma went much further among the Franco-Saxons than in the Empire.

They eased Hilda down onto a table. Wighard produced a small leather bag full of sand and sapped her behind the ear. She sagged into unconsciousness. As he had said, her uncle knew how to treat injuries like hers. He skillfully aligned the fracture and splinted her leg between boards padded with rags. "She'll heal straight, I think," he said at last. "Maybe not even a limp."

"Good," Argyros said, and meant it. He honestly liked Hilda, even if she would not give him her body. But there was also still the mission to consider. He looked Wighard in the face. "We need to talk, you and I."

In the end all three of them hashed it out in one of the pair of upstairs rooms they rented. Hilda lay on a straw pallet; Wighard and Argyros drew rickety stools up next to her.

"Do not think ill of me, I beg you," the magistrianos said, "but I plan to push on to St. Gall. If I wait for you to mend, Hilda, snow will close off the southern passes and lock me away from the Empire till spring."

"Quite right," she said. Her voice was blurry; she had drunk two winejars down to dull the fire in her leg. But her wits still worked clearly. "Uncle, you must go with him."

"And leave you here alone? Are you daft, girl?"

"This Gerda likes money," Hilda shrugged. "She'll care for me if we pay her well, I think, and I can make myself useful to her, doing accounts and such. No sense your staying here because of me."

"And what will I tell your father when he asked how I watched over you?"

"What will you tell King Oswy when he asks why Angleland has lost another dozen ships, or two, or three?" she retorted. "Winter will not wait for you any more than for Basil. I can be getting better while you and he go on; maybe when you get back I'll be able to travel again. And it's more likely you'll succeed working together than separately."

The Angelander made a sour face. "Let me nose around town tomorrow," he said grudgingly. "If this innkeeper wench has a decent name for herself, then maybe . . ."

ON INVESTIGATION, Gerda proved acceptable as caretaker for an invalid; her nickname in Turic was "Mother." "Yes, she likes her silver up front, does the Mother," said a miller who sold her flour, "but she'd not harm a flea."

"That I know," Argyros said, scratching. But no hostel in which he'd ever stayed, in the Empire or out, had been free of bugs.

Despite testimonials, Wighard was still fretting when he and the magistrianos rode east past the cathedral honoring Turic's three famous martyrs, Felix, Regula, and their servant Exuperantius. But he rode; Hilda's invocation of King Oswy's name might have been a spell in and of itself.

"Necessity is the master of us all," Argyros consoled his companion as they clattered over the old Roman fortified bridge to the left bank of the Lindimat. "What would you be doing for her had you stayed, past fetching porridge and helping her use the chamberpot?''

''Nothing, I suppose, but I mislike it all the same.'' Wighard's eyes went to the foothills ahead, their flanks dusky green with thick forests of fir and pine. Bare gray granite, some peaks snow-tipped even now, loomed in the distance. The Anglelander shivered. ''I'd not like passing a winter here, though.''

''Nor I,'' Argyros said. Unspoken went the other thing that bound the two of them together: their common desire for the Franco-Saxons' secret. Without Hilda, Wighard would be hard-pressed to ferret it out for himself, so he depended heavily on Argyros. For his part, the magistrianos knew that if he could solve the mystery and get out of St. Gall with it, the Anglelander's less intellectual talents would make escape more likely.

Late the next afternoon, Wighard pulled off the road into a patch of woods less than a mile short of the monastery. ''Here I stay,'' he declared. ''If you're bold enough to stick your head in the bear's mouth, why, go on and good luck to you. As for me, I give you ten days. After that I go back to Turic and see to Hilda.''

Argyros clasped his hand. ''You'll not be caught, or starve?''

''An old poacher like me? Never. I'd twenty times sooner brave the forest than chase after demons the way you are.'' He paused and eyed the magistrianos anxiously. ''We still share, not so? Should you find the spell and I help you get away with it, we share?''

''If there's a spell to find, you'll have it from me,'' Argyros declared, though his tongue was more certain than his heart.

He clucked his horse forward. Behind him, Wighard muttered, ''I'd better,'' and followed that half-threat with low-voiced prayers—or were they heathen charms?

A BROWN-ROBED MONK standing sentry on the wall hailed the magistrianos. That robe and the man's tonsure and shaven face reminded Argyros he was in a foreign land. The monks he knew wore black and kept their beards and hair.

He shouted back, once more calling himself Petro the amber trader. "You're faring all the way to Lithuania?" the monk said. "A long journey, that. May it be profitable for you."

"My thanks," Argyros replied, and asked if he might rest a few days at St. Gall. Receiving permission, he dismounted and led his horse into the monastery.

A large guesthouse for nobles and other prominent guests stood to the left of the entrance road; to the right were a smaller house for their servants and a building that lodged the monastery's shepherd and sheep. All were of timber, in the northern style, with steeply pitched roofs to shed snow during the fierce mountain winters.

The entranceway led to the western porch of the monastery church, where, Argyros knew, all visitors were received. The porch lay between two watchtowers, one dedicated to St. Michael, the other to St. Gabriel. The church itself was a basilica, long and rectangular. Most churches in the Empire were built to the more modern cruciform pattern, but the timber-roofed stone building had an archaic grandeur; Argyros felt transported back to the early days of Christianity.

A monk emerged from the semicircular atrium of the church. He greeted the magistrianos with the sign of the cross, which Argyros returned. "Christ's blessing upon you," the monk said. "I am Villem, the porter. Tell me your name and station, so I may know where to lodge you."

Argyros repeated the story he had given the sentry. Villem rubbed his chin. "What shall we do with you?" he said with a thin chuckle. "You are neither noble nor pilgrim nor pauper. Would you mind the pilgrims' hospice?" He waved southeast. "It's just on the other side of the passageway to St. Gabriel's tower."

"Whatever you suggest. I'm grateful for the charity."

Villem bowed. "As best I can follow you, you're well spoken." Latin was plainly not his birth-speech; he had a harsh Saxon accent. He shouted back into the atrium, "Get out here, Michel, you lazy good-for-nothing! See to the gentleman's horse."

"Coming, Brother Villem!" Michel was a freckle-faced novice with curly red hair and a look of barely suppressed mischief. Under Villem's glowering supervision, though, he greeted Argyros politely and took the horse's reins from the magistrianos.

"This way, sir, if you please." He led Argyros south, past the tower of St. Gabriel and kitchen and brewery for the hospice on his left and the lodgings for sheep and shepherds and goats and goatherds on his right.

Several monks were busy overturning the dungheaps in both animal pens and going through the compacted dung at the bottom of each heap. Trying not to breathe, Argyros looked a question at Michel. The novice guffawed. "They're after the breath of the Holy Spirit," he said. Seeing Argyros did not understand, he explained: "Saltpeter."

"'The breath of the Holy Spirit,' eh?" the magistrianos said. He also smiled. Monks were men too, and saltpeter was said to quench lust. "A breeze that keeps the brothers cooled?"

"Huh?" Michel stared, then laughed again. "That too, of course." He shouted the joke to one of the monks working at the midden. The monk gave back a rude gesture.

The stableman and his assistant were obviously capable, so Argyros left them his horse and let Michel take him back around the corner of the stable to the hospice. "They'll feed you after vespers, when they light the hearth," he said. The magistrianos nodded agreeably. Michel gave a half-shy bob of his head and hurried away.

An eight-bed dormitory lay on either side of the hospice's main hall. The interior walls were only waist-high, to let heat from the hearth reach the sleeping-rooms. Argyros tossed his saddlebags on an empty bed, then thought better of it and put them on the floor. He stretched out on the bed himself.

Several men were already in the hospice, some on their way to religious shrines and the rest beggars. About half spoke one Latin dialect or another. Argyros made idle con-

versation with them. Fortunately, none was from Narbomart to give him away: he did not know his pretended
hometown well.

As dusk descended, he listened to the monks chanting the
vespers service in the basilica. A few minutes later, as Michel
had said, two came in to light the central fireplace. One bore
a torch, the other a bucket of rags soaked in pitch. That
perplexed the magistrianos until he noticed the hearth was
full of charcoal, not wood; charcoal fires were always hard
to start. But then he was puzzled all over again. None of the
monasteries modeled after St. Gall had used charcoal,
though they tolerated few discrepancies from one to the
next.

The fire finally took light. The monks looked at each
other, pleased with themselves. "Coals from the fire of the
Father," intoned the one who had carried the rags—not in
prayer, Argyros judged, but as a comment he was used to
making. Nodding, the other monk went around the hall
lighting tapers. A charcoal fire burned hotter than wood,
but gave off no more light than glowing embers.

Novices brought in a tray of large loaves, one for each
man in the hospice, and several crocks of beer. The bread
was coarse and dark. It was half wheat flour and half rye,
the latter a grain Argyros had not known before this journey and one he did not much care for. He did not think
highly of beer, either. A lifetime of drinking wine made it
seem weak and bitter by comparison.

As he ate, the magistrianos paid desultory attention to the
chatter around him. Had it not been for his theological arguments with Hilda, he might not have noticed, but these
monks of St. Gall had a curious way of relating homely
things to the Persons of the Trinity. His eyes narrowed in
thought. Eastern or western, monks had a taste for allegory—and if St. Gall was what he suspected, what better
subject for allegory than its fearsome secret?

Emptying his mug, he turned to the man beside him on
the long bench, a tall thin fellow with the pinched cheeks
and racking cough of a consumptive. He glanced around.
No clerics were anywhere close. "So," he said casually, "if

charcoal's the Father and saltpeter the Holy Spirit, what's the Son?''

He had all he could do to keep from shouting when the fellow promptly answered, ''Must be that yellow stuff—what do you call it?—sulfur, that's it. The healer burned some t'other day to try and clear my lungs. Didn't help much, far as I could see—just made a stink. But old Karloman called it the Son's own kindling.'' The beggar let out a bubbling laugh; a fleck of spittle at the corner of his mouth was tinged with pink. He said, ''Father, Son, and Holy Spirit, eh? Funny I never thought of that myself.''

''Crazy sort of Trinity,'' Argyros agreed. Wits racing, he did not hear when the man said something else to him. Maurice was right, he reflected; these blond barbarians still knew nothing of security. Why, the Empire had kept the makeup of its liquid fire a mystery for centuries, but St. Gall's secret was out after hardly more than a year. Charcoal, sulfur, saltpeter—there could be no other ingredients, or the monks would not have drawn the analogy with the three Persons of the Godhead.

No demons, either, the magistrianos thought with relief.

It also occurred to him that here was a trinity where the spirit might indeed proceed from both the other two elements, for he was certain that charcoal and sulfur by themselves were harmless. In a sense, then, Hilda had been right—not, of course, that the products of this world were truly relevant to theology and its perfection.

He was on the point of springing from his seat and running for his horse when he realized he had not yet won the whole battle. He still needed to know what proportion of the constituents went into the mix. One part of wine in five of water was safe for two-year-olds, but five of wine to one of water would put a grown man under the table in short order. He dared not assume it was different here. He would have to stay a while longer.

Pilgrims, so long as they left with reasonable quickness, did not have to work for their meals; paupers did. Argyros worked before he was asked to. He spent a dreary half-day cleaning the monastery henhouse and goosepen before the fowlkeeper found out he was good with horses and sent him to the stables.

He walked west, the monastery granary on his left hand and on his right a square wooden building whose ripe aroma proclaimed it to be the monks' privy. Just beyond it was a similar but slightly smaller structure. A couple of monks crossed his path, carrying wicker baskets full of robes, tunics and bed linens.

They went into the building next to the privy: the laundry, Argyros realized. His head snapped around to follow them—what would red cloth be doing in a monastery's washing? He was sure he had spied some, nearly buried though it was under drabber shades. He remembered the tales of scarlet devils who touched off the Franco-Saxon hellfire and grinned to himself. A perfect disguise, he thought, and one that ought to settle Wighard for good.

The monks came out, their baskets empty. Argyros ambled lazily toward the laundry, wanting to get a better look at the devil-suits, if that was what they were.

"Here, you, who are you and where do you think you're going?" someone barked at him.

He turned slowly, found himself facing a stocky, craggy-faced monk of about fifty, with hard, cold eyes. "Your Brother Marco told me to go help look after the horses," he answered, as innocently as he could. He could tell at once that this was no fellow to trifle with.

"Hmm! A likely tale," the other said. "You come along with me."

He marched Argyros back to the fowlkeeper, and scowled when Brother Marco confirmed the magistrianos's story, quavering, "It's just as he said, Karloman." He seemed more than a little intimidated by Argyros's captor.

With poor grace, Karloman apologized to the magistrianos. "Get on with you, then, and no snooping about." Feeling the monk's eyes burning into his back, Argyros hurried past the laundry without so much as a sideways glance.

The stablemaster was a mine of gossip; Argyros learned every small scandal that had amused St. Gall in the past

year. He did not, however, find out any of what he was after, and ended the day annoyed and frustrated, a condition
that persisted for most of the next week. When his break
came at last, it was, oddly enough, Karloman who gave it to
him.

The magistrianos had been dreaming of roast goat and
onions soused with garum, of smooth white wine from Palestine and the famous red of Cyprus, said to come from
vines planted by Odysseus before he sailed for Troy. Waking up to rye bread and beer was disheartening.

Then any thoughts of breakfast, however mixed, vanished from his head, for one of his companions lay groaning in bed, staring fearfully at the fast-rising boil near his
armpit. Men crowded away from him and each other. The
terror of plague was never far away. Someone went pelting
off for the healer.

Argyros soon heard two men approaching the hospice at
a run. He recognized Karloman's gruff voice at once.
"Which one is he?" the monk demanded; his tonsure was
gleaming with sweat. Before the man who had fetched him
could answer, he went on, "No need to tell me—that one
grizzling over there, am I right?"

"Yes, sir."

The healer strode up to the terrified man. "Let's see it,
Ewald," he said with rough joviality, but his patient was too
frightened to raise his arm and have his fears confirmed.

"Grab him, you, you, and you," Karloman ordered,
pointing. Argyros was the second "you." Along with a
newly arrived pilgrim and the cadaverous man who had
known about sulfur, he seized Ewald so the fellow could not
wriggle. Karloman jerked the man's arm up.

The healer studied the eruption for a moment, then gave
a shout of relieved laughter. "It's nothing but a common
carbuncle, Ewald, you fool. I expect you'll die in the stocks
yet, just as you deserve."

"It hurts," Ewald whined.

Karloman snorted. "Of course it hurts. Stay there; I'll
bring you an ointment to smear on it." He stomped out of
the hospice, returning a few minutes later with a steaming

bowl full of what looked like honey but had a very different odor.

Ewald sniffed suspiciously. "What stinks?"

"You mean, besides you?" Karloman grunted. "This is half sulfur and half borax, mixed in hot olive oil. It'll draw the matter out of your boil. Ai! Grab him again, you all!" Ewald tried to bolt, but the men the healer had drafted were too strong for him. Karloman dipped a rag in the bowl, slathered his medicine on the pilgrim's carbuncle.

Ewald let out a pitiful wail. "It burns. I can feel it eating the skin off me!" He squirmed like a worm on a hook.

"Oh, twaddle," Karloman said. As Argyros had already seen, he did not have much kindness in him, despite being a healer. He laughed again, this time unpleasantly. "Now if you'd run across another, ah, potion, I dreamed up a while ago, one sulfur to four saltpeter and a charcoal, why that might have just taken the whole arm."

Ewald, horrified, nearly writhed out of Argyros's grasp. Karloman wheeled furiously. "What's the matter with you, merchant? Hold him tight, God curse you."

"Sorry."

Karloman was only making a rough joke to frighten the man a little. He could not have expected anyone there to take its full meaning, not even Argyros—his suspicion of the magistrianos had been based on general principles. But he had given the game away, and Argyros forgot what he was supposed to be doing and almost let Ewald get loose.

After Ewald was finally medicated to Karloman's satisfaction, Argyros waited until the crowd had dispersed, then gathered his gear and slipped away for the stables. He had just finished saddling his horse when the stablemaster stuck his head in the door. "I thought I heard someone here," he said in a shocked voice. "You must not ride out now, not before Sunday prayers."

Argyros blinked. In the excitement over Ewald, he had forgotten it was Sunday. He walked to the church with the monk. After what God had granted him this morning, He deserved thanks.

No lesser shrine could impress a man who had prayed in Hagia Sophia, but the church of St. Gall was not to be sneered at. Its proportions were noble, the colonnades that separated the two aisles from the nave fairly good work. Altars stood by every second column, all the way up to the transept.

The monks had the nave to themselves; laymen worshiped in the aisles, with wooden screens separating them from the clerics. Karloman and Villem the porter stood just on the other side of the screen from Argyros. Villem nodded pleasantly. "God with you, Petro," he whispered.

"And with you," the magistrianos replied.

The healer did not waste time on small talk.

The Mass began. Argyros had been in the west long enough to follow the Latin version with ease and to make the proper responses. But he was so full of excitement over his discovery that he did not notice he was automatically omitting the *filioque* clause whenever it came up in the liturgy.

He also did not see Karloman's eyes widen when the monk caught his first omission, or narrow as he left out the offending word time after time. "A heretic!" Karloman cried in outrage, pointing at Argyros. The magistrianos's blood ran cold. "He rejects the *filioque*!"

And then the healer must have remembered Argyros's unwonted curiosity about the monastery laundry and his own inadvertent revelation that morning. He clapped a hand to his forehead. "A spy!" he shouted.

The choir went on for a few ragged notes, then fell silent. There was a confused, half-angry murmur from clerics and laymen alike. Karloman's bellow cut through it: "Seize him!"

But Argyros had already whirled and was twisting past gaping pilgrims and beggars. He cursed himself for the carelessness that had thrown him into danger at the moment of his success.

The consumptive pauper grabbed at his wrist as he dashed by. He struck the man a blow that stretched him out groaning on the floor.

Two monks stood in the doorway that led out of the church's western porch. They were staring at each other, not sure what was going on. "I'll get help!" Argyros shouted, which held one of them in place.

The other had quicker wits. He sprang out to bar the way. He was slight, though, and in his late middle years. He went down like the beggar when Argyros lowered a shoulder and bowled him over.

The magistrianos ran out into the sunlight. He sprinted south past the tower of St. Gabriel for the stables. Having lodged in other monasteries modeled after St. Gall served him in good stead: he was more familiar with the layout of the place than he could have become in the few days since his arrival.

The sounds of pursuit rose behind him. Fortunately, nearly the entire monastic community had been in church. There was no one to answer shouts for help. Long legs flying, Argyros was some yards ahead of everyone as he reached the stable building.

Gasping thanks to the Mother of God for letting him get his horse saddled, he sprang onto the animal. By the time he spurred out the stable door, he had his sword unshipped.

His pursuers were very close, but fell back in dismay at the sight of the gleaming blade. Almost all: Karloman, brave as well as clever, leaped forward to lay hold of the horse's reins. Argyros slashed, felt the sword bite flesh. Karloman fell. Argyros roweled his horse into a gallop, rode down another overly intrepid monk, and dashed for the monastery gate.

Karloman was not dead; Argyros heard him shouting, "Never mind me, you fools. After him!" At the healer's bawled orders, monks ran to get weapons, saddle horses, turn loose the monastery hounds.

That command alarmed the magistrianos, but it was the last one he heard. Urging his mount ahead for all it was worth, he thundered through the open gates and down the road.

His horse's muscles surged against his thighs; the wind of its headlong gallop tore tears from his eyes. St. Gall's fields of wheat, rye and barley blurred by on either side. Someone in one of the watchtowers sounded a horn. Argyros had no trouble guessing what the call meant.

To escape the all-seeing eye up there, he made for the woods, where he hoped Wighard was still waiting. A glance over his shoulder showed there was still no mounted pursuit. He let his panting horse slow from its sprint to a fast trot. If it broke down, he was done for.

He slowed again at the edge of the woods to give his eyes a chance to adjust to the gloom. Silent as a shadow, Wighard stepped into the roadway. "Fine ruction you stirred up back there," the Anglelander observed. "D'you have the spell, man?"

"The answer, yes."

"Then we'd best not wait around, eh?" Wighard said, mounting and digging his heels into his horse's flanks. The magistrianos followed.

As soon as the road made a sharp bend, the Anglelander rigged a trip-rope. He grinned at Argyros. "They'll be coming hell for leather after you. With luck, this'll take out two or three and make the rest thoughtful."

"Splendid," Argyros said. He took a packet of finely ground pepper from his saddlebag and scattered it behind them. "The dogs will need distracting, too."

"Aye, so they will," Wighard agreed. "Best take no chances with 'em." After he and Argyros had ridden on for a few paces, he dug out an old rag and tossed it into a clump of brambles by the side of the road. Seeing Argyros's quizzical look, he explained, "Soaked in the piss of a bitch in heat."

The magistrianos burst out laughing. He heard the horn again, faint now in the distance. Thin as the buzz of summer insects came the monks' cries: "Hurry there!" "Don't let him get away!"

Too late, Argyros thought—I've already done it. He and Wighard rode in companionable silence until they came to an icy stream—a young river, in fact—that eventually ran north into Lake Constant. They splashed along in the shallows against the current for a couple of miles to finish confusing the hounds (they had heard yapping far behind them a while ago, first agonized, then suddenly frantic).

When they were sure they were safe, they doubled back across country for Turic. Argyros was already thinking of the trip back to the Empire. It would be easy, save perhaps for the Pennine pass; the idea of a September blizzard made the magistrianos shiver all over. The hostels in the pass bred big dogs to rescue stranded travelers, but they did not save them all.

The magistrianos thought for a moment that the chill against his throat was only a reflection of his reverie. Then he realized it was the edge of Wighard's dagger. "The spell, man," the Angelander said hoarsely. "How do you summon up the demons?"

"There are no demons," Argyros said.

The dagger dug in. "You lying kern! I could fair watch you plotting to go your merry way without keeping your promise, but you'll not get away with that, not alive. Tell me how to raise the devils or I'll slit your weasand on the spot."

Getting away with the secret all to himself had always been in the back of Argyros's mind, but the kiss of steel put an end to that scheme. His voice quivered: "Very well, then, here it is, just as I learned it...."

THE SEASONS SPIN around like wheels. By the Inner Sea, though, the turning is more gentle. Mellow autumn lay on Constantinople a month after snow had come to the Alps.

A toy fortress, its walls as high as a man's knee and three digits thick, stood in the center of a secluded grassy courtyard between two buildings in the palace compound. Argyros and an older, stouter man walked across the lawn to the miniature fortress. The magistrianos carried a small, tightly stoppered winejug in his left hand; a bit of oily rag protruded from a hole drilled through the center of a cork. In his other hand Argyros held a lighted torch. He was careful to keep it well away from the jug.

"I think we are finally ready to demonstrate this for you, your illustriousness," he said. "The craftsmen at the arsenal say the key to a reliable product is grinding all the ingredients to a fine powder before mixing.''

''Very well, my new Kallinikos, you've done splendidly thus far; by all means show me,'' George Lakhanodrakon said amiably. The magnitude of the compliment from the Master of Offices made Argyros flush; Kallinikos had invented the Empire's liquid fire.

The magistrianos set the winejug at a corner inside the model fort's walls. He stooped to touch the torch to the rag. Watching with interest, Lakhanodrakon asked, ''Now what?''

The flame caught. ''Now, sir, we retire in haste.'' Argyros dropped the torch and loped away. The Master of Offices followed more sedately. Not only was he heavier than the magistrianos; despite descriptions, he had no real sense of what was about to happen.

Argyros turned his head to warn him to make better speed. Too late—at that moment, the flame worked down the rag into the winejug. The explosion made his ears ring. The half-bricks from which the little keep had been built flew apart as if kicked. A tiny fragment of jug or brick stung Argyros's neck. He yelped and rubbed at the spot.

And George Lakhanodrakon shot by, running as though the blast had hurled him forward. When no further thunderclaps came, the Master of Offices warily turned back to see the results of the experiment. His strong, fleshy Armenian face had gone rather pale.

The corner of the model where Argyros had nestled the winejug was utterly thrown down; the walls that had met there leaned drunkenly. The breeze was thinning the cloud of gray smoke, letting the great shouldering bulk of Hagia Sophia dominate the northern skyline once more.

Lakhanodrakon licked dry lips. ''It's like your first woman,'' he whispered. ''All the telling in the world doesn't matter a damn.''

Argyros had put the echoing silence within the halls to either side down to the blast having stunned his ears, but it was real, brought on by startled people stopping dead. After a few seconds there were screams and exclamations:

"What was that?" "Help me, St. Andreas!"—Constantinople's patron. "Earthquake!" "Mother of God, help me!" Faces appeared in a score of windows.

A squad of excubitores came dashing around the corner, gaudy in their clinging white leggings, silk surcoats, and golden torcs and belts. Each soldier's brightly painted shield was blazoned with the sacred labarum: ☧. Brandishing their spears, they looked wildly in all directions until they recognized Lakhanodrakon. They crowded round him, pelting him with questions.

Argyros admired the way the Master of Offices pulled himself together and calmed the imperial bodyguards without revealing anything of importance. They were scratching their heads as they went back to their post, but they went. One by one, the staring servants and officials in the palace buildings also decided the excitement was over and returned to work.

Eyeing the wrecked model, Lakhanodrakon waited until everyone was out of earshot. Then he said, "You really mean to tell me there's no witchcraft in that, Basil?"

"None whatsoever," Argyros said firmly.

"Astonishing to think of such destruction springing from such ordinary stuffs as charcoal, sulfur, and—" Lakhanodrakon snapped his fingers in annoyance. "I always forget the third."

"Saltpeter," Argyros supplied, adding, "The monks of St. Gall remember them by associating each with a Person of the Triune Godhead."

The Master of Offices frowned. "Barbarous heretics. Why would they do that?"

"It does make a certain amount of sense, sir," Argyros said. "From what the men at the arsenals have told me, the saltpeter gives the explosion its blasting force: thus the monks term it the Holy Spirit's breath. The charcoal touches off the blast, and so they link it with the Father, the source of all things, while the sulfur catches fire from the kindling of the charcoal and ignites the saltpeter, just as the Son is the Father's Word through Whom He works."

"A blasphemous, unholy trinity if ever I heard one," Lakhanodrakon exclaimed.

"I agree."

After a few seconds, the Master of Offices said worriedly, "Even knowing how the hellpowder is made may serve us less well than I hoped when I sent you out, for how are we to defend against it? Why, even the walls of the city here, which have never been breached, might fall if enough of this villainous compound were set off beside them."

"I suppose so," Argyros said, but he did not believe it. Theodosios II's magnificent works had survived nearly nine hundred years and looked good for as many more. The magistrianos pointed out, "Now that we have the secret, with catapults on the walls we can give as good as we get, and the ditch in front of the city will keep enemies from coming up to the wall, and thwart undermining as well."

"That's so," the Master of Offices said, somewhat reassured. He fixed his sharp dark glance on Argyros. "Undermining, you say? I like that. One fine day we may give the Persians a surprise at Nisibis." The border between the Roman Empire and the successive dynasties ruling Persia had swung through Syria and Mesopotamia since the days of Pompey. Neither side could win the lasting victory both dreamed of.

Argyros said, "The arsenal artificers say that placing the explosive below the works to be attacked may prove even more effective than putting it alongside. They're thinking of mounting catapults aboard ships, too, as the Franco-Saxons are doing against the Anglelanders, to attack enemies at longer range than we can with fire and siphon."

"Ah, yes, the Anglelanders," Lakhanodrakon said. "True, they don't impinge on us directly, but I confess to misgivings over your cooperation with them. Do you honestly feel such a, er, young folk should be trusted with this potent secret you learned?"

"My lord, I puzzled over that from the Ispanic border all the way to St. Gall. One minute I would reckon them only ignorant barbarians; the next they would startle me with their courage or their native lore or even their wits, untrained but keen. I tell you frankly, I was of two minds."

"How did you decide, then?" the Master of Offices asked.

"When Wighard put a knife to my neck without warning and started growling of demons and spells, I knew they were savages after all. And since he wanted a spell, why, I gave him one. My barber swears it will grow hair; if the Anglelanders can make any military use of that, they're welcome to it. Wighard believed me; he judged me too frightened to lie. And in any case, how could he know the difference?"

Lakhanodrakon stared, then pounded the magistrianos on the back. "Well done, Basil, and quick thinking, too! That's one less worry for me."

He paused, running a hand across his own bald pate. "You must give me your barber's name."

"Why, of course, sir," Argyros said, carefully not smiling. "It would be a pleasure."

4 *ETOS KOSMOU 6825*

The knock on the door was tentative, the sort any secretary learns to make when he is not sure his superior wishes to be disturbed. But to Basil Argyros the interruption came as a relief. "Come in," he called, shoving papyrus scrolls and sheets of parchment to one side of his desk.

The magistrianos had been daydreaming anyhow, looking out from his office in the Praitorion toward the great brown stucco mass of the church of Hagia Sophia and, beyond it, softened by haze, the Asian coast across the Propontis from Constantinople.

The case he had been trying to ignore was an Egyptian land dispute, which meant it would not be settled in his lifetime no matter what he did, or probably for fifty years after that, either. The insane litigiousness of the Egyptians had angered the Emperor Julian almost a thousand years before. They had only grown worse since, Argyros thought. As a good Christian, he condemned Julian the Apostate to hell; as an official of the Roman Empire, he was convinced that dealing with Egyptians gave a foretaste of it.

And so he greeted his secretary with an effusiveness alien to his usually self-contained nature: "Good day, Anthimos! What can I do for you on this fine spring morning?"

Anthimos, a lean, stooped man whose fingers were always black with ink, eyed the magistrianos suspiciously; he wanted people to be as orderly and predictable as the numbers in his ledgers. At last he shrugged and said, "The Master of Offices is here to see you, sir."

"What?" Argyros's thick black eyebrows shot up in surprise. "Show him in, of course."

The solid portliness of George Lakhanodrakon seemed all the more imposing next to Anthimos, who fluttered about nervously until Argyros dismissed him. The magistrianos bowed low to Lakhanodrakon, waved him to a chair, offered wine. "Always a pleasure to see you, your illustriousness. What brings you here today? Not this wretched mess, I hope."

Lakhanodrakon rose, walked over to pick up one of the documents Argyros so described. He held it at arm's length; he was about fifty, a dozen or so years older than the magistrianos, and his sight was beginning to lengthen. He read for a moment. His strong, rather heavy features showed his distaste. "*Pcheris vs. Sarapion*, is it? I didn't know you were stuck with such drivel. No, it's nothing to do with that, I promise."

"Then you're doubly welcome, sir," Argyros said sincerely. "I've been praying to St. Mouamet for a new assignment."

"The patron of changes, eh?" Lakhanodrakon chuckled. The amusement fell from the Master of Offices' face. "Your prayers are about to be granted. Tell me what you make of this." He fumbled in the silk pouch that hung from his gold belt of rank, produced a rolled-up parchment, and handed it to Argyros.

The magistrianos slid off the ribbon that bound the parchment, skimmed through it. "It's bad Greek," he remarked.

"Keep going."

"Of course, sir." When he was done, Argyros said, "I take it this came from one of the cities in the east, from Mesopotamia or perhaps Syria?"

"Mesopotamia—from Daras, to be exact."

The magistrianos nodded. "Yes, it has all the marks of a Persian piece: a polemic against the orthodox faith and an invitation to the Nestorians and hard-core Monophysites and other heretics to abandon their allegiance to the Empire and go over to the King of Kings. Preferably, I suppose, bringing the fortress of Daras with them.''

''No doubt,'' Lakhanodrakon agreed dryly.

''Forgive me, sir,'' Argyros said, ''but I've seen a great many sheets of this sort. Why bring this particular one to my attention?''

Instead of answering directly, the Master of Offices took another parchment from his beltpouch. ''When you have examined this sheet, I trust you will understand—as well as I do, at any rate, which is not a great deal.''

The magistrianos looked at Lakhanodrakon in puzzlement after reading the first few lines. ''But this is just the same as the other—'' His voice trailed away, and his eyes snapped back to the parchment. He picked up the other sheet Lakhanodrakon had given him, held one in each hand. His jaw fell.

''You see it, then,'' the Master of Offices said. ''Good. You are as quick as I thought you were.''

''Thank you,'' Argyros said abstractedly. He was still staring at the two pieces of parchment. They both said the same thing—exactly the same. It was not as if a scribe had copied out a message twice. Each line on both sheets had exactly the same words on it, written exactly the same size. The same word was misspelled in the third line of each sheet. A couple of lines later, the same incorrect verb form appeared in each, then an identical dative after the preposition where a genitive belonged. Near the end, the letter pi at the beginning of a word was half effaced on both handbills. They even shared the identical small smear of ink between two words.

The magistrianos put one sheet over the other, walked to the window. He held the parchments up to the sun and worked them until the left edges of the two messages were precisely aligned. Any differences would have been instantly apparent. There were none.

''Mother of God, help me!'' Argyros exclaimed.

''May She protect the entire Empire,'' George Lakhanodrakon said soberly. ''Not just these two, but hundreds of such sheets, have appeared in Daras, nailed to every wall big enough to hold one, it seems. They may well provoke the uprisings they seek—you know how touchy the east always is.''

Argyros knew. Despite having been a part of the Roman Empire since before Christ's Incarnation, Syria and Mesopotamia were very different from its other regions. Latin was all but unknown there, and even Greek, the Empire's dominant tongue, was spoken only by a minority in the towns. Most people used Syriac or Arabic, as their ancestors had before them. Heresy flourished there as nowhere else.

And farther east lay Persia, the Empire's eternal rival. The two great powers had been struggling for 1,400 years, each dreaming of vanquishing the other for good. The Persians always fostered unrest in the eastern provinces of the Empire. Worshipers of the sun and fire themselves, they gave Nestorians refuge and stirred up religious strife to occupy the Romans with internal troubles. But never on such a scale as this—

"How are they doing it?" Argyros said, as much to himself as to the Master of Offices.

"That is what I charge you with: to find out," Lakhanodrakon said. "Your success in ferreting out the secret of the Franco-Saxons' hellpowder last year made me think of you the moment those"—he jerked a thumb at the parchments Argyros was still holding—"came to my attention."

"You flatter me, your illustriousness."

"No, I need you," the Master of Offices said. Harsh lines of worry ran from his jutting nose to the corners of his mouth. "I tell you, I fear this worse than the hellpowder. That was only a threat against our borders; we have dealt with such before, a hundred times. But this could be a blow in the heart."

Argyros frowned. "Surely you exaggerate, sir."

"Do I? I've lain awake at night imagining the chaos these sheets could create. Suppose one said one thing, one another? They could fan faction against faction, heretic against orthodox—"

His wave encompassed all of Constantinople. "Suppose a Persian agent smuggled even a donkeyload of these accursed things into the city! Men from every corner of the world live here—Jews, Egyptians, Armenians, Sklavenoi from the lands by the Ister, Franco-Saxons. Set them at each other's throats, and it could be the Nika riots come again!"

"You've seen further than I have," Argyros admitted, shivering. It had been eight hundred years since Constantinople's mob, shouting *Nika*—Triumph!—had almost toppled Justinian the Great from the Roman throne, but that was the standard against which all later urban uprisings were measured.

"Perhaps further than the Persians, too, or they would not waste their time at the frontier," Lakhanodrakon said. "But they will not stay blind long, I fear. Beware of them, Basil. They are no rude barbarians to be fooled like the Franco-Saxons; they are as old in deceit as we."

"I shall remember," the magistrianos promised. He picked up the parchments Lakhanodrakon had given him and tucked them away. "The rest of this pile of trash I shall cheerfully consign to Anthimos. I'll leave for Daras in a day or two. As you know, I'm a widower; I have no great arrangements to make. But I would like to light a candle at a church dedicated to St. Nicholas before I go."

"A good choice," the Master of Offices said.

"Yes—who better than the patron saint of thieves?"

"I'VE TRIED EVERYTHING I can think of," the garrison commandant of Daras said, slamming a fist down on his desk in frustration. "Every incoming traveler has his baggage searched, and I keep patrols on the streets day and night. Yet the damned handbills keep showing up."

"I can't fault what you've done, Leontios," Argyros said, and the soldier leaned back in his chair with a sigh of relief. He was a big, burly man, almost as tall as Argyros and thicker through the shoulders, but there was no question who dominated the conversation. Magistrianoi could make or break even the leader of an outpost as important as Daras.

"More wine?" Leontios extended a pitcher.

"Er—no thanks," Argyros said, he hoped politely. The wine, like much of what was drunk in Mesopotamia, was made from dates. He found it sickeningly sweet. But he would have to work with Leontios and did not want to hurt his feelings, so he held out his hand, remarking, "That's a handsome jug you have there. May I see it?"

"Oh, d'you like it? Seems ordinary enough to me."

"Hardly that. I'm not used to seeing reliefwork on pottery, and the depiction of our Lord driving the moneychangers from the Temple is well done, I think."

"If it pleases you so, take it and welcome," Leontios said at once, afraid to antagonize the magistrianos in even a small way. "I'm sure you've seen much better, though, coming from the city."

"There's nothing to match it in Constantinople. The potters there decorate with glazes and drawings, not reliefs."

"Fancy that, us ahead of the capital!" Leontios said. He saw that Argyros did not want the winejug, and put it down. "The style's been all the rage in these parts—both sides of the border, come to that—the last five or ten years. I got this piece from old Abraham last summer. He's a damned Nestorian, but he does good work. His shop is only a block or so away, if you think you might find something you'd fancy."

"Perhaps I'll look him up." Argyros stood, fanned himself with his broad-brimmed hat of woven straw. It did not help much. "Is the heat always so bad?"

The garrison commandant rolled his eyes. "My dear sir, this is only June—not even summer yet. If you're still in Daras in six weeks, you'll find out what heat is."

"Do you know that in the Franco-Saxon mountain country it sometimes snows in September? Last year that seemed the most hideous thing I could imagine. Now it strikes me as delightful."

Leontios ran a hairy, sweaty forearm across his face. "It strikes me as impossible. I wish you luck on this madness, more than I've had myself. If I can help in any way, you have only to ask."

"My thanks," Argyros said and left. The commandant's office had been very warm, shielded though it was by thick walls from the worst Daras could do. The noonday heat outside was unbelievable, stupefying. The sun blazed down mercilessly from the blue enamel bowl of the sky.

The magistrianos squinted against the glare. He wished he could strip off his boots, trousers, and tunic (even if that was gauzy linen) and go naked under his hat. Some of the locals did, walking about in a loincloth and sandals. More, though, covered their heads with white cotton cloths and swaddled themselves in great flowing robes, as if they were so many ambulatory tents.

The strange clothes only accented Argyros's feeling of being in an alien land. The houses and other buildings, save for the most splendid, were of whitewashed mud brick, not stone or timber. And the signs that advertised dyeshops or jewelers, taverns and baths, were apt to be in three languages: angular Greek, the tight curlicues of Syriac, and the wild, snakelike script Arabic used. If any was missing, it was usually the Greek.

A couple of men talking in the street moved on when they saw the magistrianos approaching. They might not know him for an agent, but even without his speaking, his outfit and his face—tanned but not very swarthy—branded him as one loyal to Constantinople and not to be trusted. He scowled. Such recognition was only going to make his job harder.

The shop across the street had to be the one Leontios had mentioned. There were dishes and jugs and cups in the window, and the Greek line of the signboard above them read FINE POTTERY BY ABRAAM: Greek, of course, could not show the sound of rough breathing in the middle of a word.

Abraam or Abraham stood in the doorway, crying his wares in guttural Syriac. Argyros watched as a smith came over from the foundry next door to bring him a flat, square iron plate. The two men eyed the magistrianos with the same

distrust the street idlers had shown. He was getting used to
that suspicious stare in Daras. He returned it imperturbably.

The smith, an enormous fellow baked brown as his
leather apron by the sun, spat in the dirt roadway and ambled toward his own place of business, still glowering Argyros's way. Abraham the potter turned his back on the
magistrianos with deliberate rudeness and went back into
the darkness of his shop. Argyros saw him put the iron plate
under a counter and talk briefly with a woman back there;
whether wife, customer, or what he did not know.

Operating out of Leontios's barracks would have made
him altogether too conspicuous, so he went looking for an
inn. He did not notice when the woman emerged from the
pottery and hurried after him.

The first taverner he tried spoke only Arabic and catered
to nomads out of the desert. As Argyros had but a few
phrases of Arabic himself, he decided to try somewhere else.

Two men were waiting for him when he came outside to
retrieve his horse. Something in their stance told him their
breed at once: street toughs. He walked past them without
a sideways glance, hoping his size would make them choose
another victim.

But one grabbed at his arm. "Where you go to, you
damned swaggering Melkite?" he grinned, showing bad
teeth. He used the eastern heretics' insulting name for one
loyal to the dogmas of Constantinople: it meant "king's
man."

"None of your concern," Argyros snapped, shaking off
the man's hand and springing back. With a curse, the ruffian leaped at him, followed by his companion. The magistrianos kicked the first one where it did the most good.
Two against one left no time for chivalry. The fellow went
down with a wail, clutching at himself and spewing his guts
out in the dust.

The other tough had a short bludgeon. Argyros threw up
his left arm just in time to keep his head from being broken. He bared his teeth as pain shot through him from el-

bow to fingertips. His right hand darted to the knife at his belt. "Come on," he panted. "Even odds now."

The local was no coward. He waded in, swung again. Argyros ducked and slashed, coming up from below. The point of his dagger ripped through his enemy's sleeve. He felt the blade slice into flesh. The tough hissed. He was not through, though; he was ready for more fight.

Then a woman behind Argyros screamed something in Arabic. The magistrianos did not understand, but his opponent did. He whirled and fled. Argyros chased him, but he knew Daras's twisting alleyways as an outsider could not, and escaped.

Breathing hard and rubbing his arm, the magistrianos walked back to his horse. He saw what the woman's shout must have meant, for a squad of Leontios's soldiers had gathered round the good-for-naught he had leveled. They were prodding the wretch up, none too gently, with the butts of their spears.

Someone who had watched the brawl pointed at Argyros, which drew the squad-leader's attention. "You ruin this fellow here," he demanded.

"Frankly, yes. I was set on for no reason and without warning. He had it coming." Anger made him careless with his words.

The squad-leader set his hands on his hips. "Talk like you're the Emperor, don't you? Anyone else see this little scramble?" He glanced at the swelling crowd.

Argyros's heart sank. He did not want to go back to Leontios and waste time on explanations, but he was sure the witnesses would side with a man of Daras rather than an obvious stranger. Unexpectedly, though, a woman spoke up for him: "It's as the tall man says. They attacked him first."

The squad-leader was as taken aback as the magistrianos. Seizing the initiative, Argyros took him aside and pressed a gold nomisma into his palm, along with some silver to keep his men happy. The trooper pocketed the bribe in a businesslike fashion. "Haul that scum out of here," he commanded, and his squad dragged the captive off; two men still had to support him. Onlookers began to drift away.

Argyros looked around to see if he could spot the woman who had come to his aid. She had been well back in the crowd, and he had not got a glimpse of her face. But he had no doubts, for she waited in the shadow of a building across the street instead of leaving with the rest of the spectators. Above a short veil filmy enough to be no more than token concealment, she looked saucily toward him.

"My thanks," the magistrianos said, walking over to her. Something beside mere gratitude put warmth in his voice. From tightly curled black hair to gilded sandals beneath henna-soled feet, she was a strikingly attractive woman. Her dark eyes were bright and lively, her mouth, half seen, full-lipped and inviting. The fitted ankle-length robe she wore displayed her figure to the best advantage; even in the shadow in which she stood, the red, gold, and green sequins at her bodice sparkled with each breath she took.

She said, "It would be wrong for so brave—and so mighty—a man to find himself in trouble he does not deserve." Her Greek had a slight throaty accent. That and her costume told Argyros she was of Persian origin. The border between the two empires went back and forth so often that such things were common on both sides.

"Thanks again," Argyros said; and then, not wanting the conversation to end as abruptly as that, he asked, "Would you happen to know of a decent inn?"

She burst out laughing. "It just so happens that I dance at the hostel of Shahin Bahram's son. It's clean enough, and the food is good, if you don't mind eating Persian fare." When Argyros shook his head, she said, "Come on, then; I'll take you there. Bringing you in will make me money, too. I'm Mirrane, by the way."

The magistrianos gave his own name, but said that he had come from Constantinople as inspector of Daras's water-works. The famous system of cisterns and drains and the dam across the nearby Cordes River added greatly to the strength of the town's fortifications.

"An important man," she murmured, moving closer to him. "Do you think your horse can carry two?"

"For a little way, certainly." He helped her mount in front of him; her waist was supple under his hands. When the horse started forward, she leaned back against him and did not try to pull away. It made for an enjoyable ride.

Shahin's tavern was in the western part of Daras, not far from the church of the Apostle Bartholomew that Justinian had built when he renovated the town's works. Shahin folded Argyros into a bearhug and called him his lord, his master, his owner—none of which prevented a sharp haggle when it came to the price of a room.

At last Mirrane spoke in Persian: "Don't drive him away." Argyros had a hard time holding his face straight: no use letting the girl know he was fluent in her language, though he did not think there was anything more to this than her not wanting to lose her finder's fee. Shahin became more reasonable.

As was his custom when starting an investigation, the magistrianos wandered into the taproom to drink a little wine and soak up the local gossip. Shahin's place was good for that; it featured a mixed clientele, and talk came fast and furious in the three tongues of the imperial east and Persian as well. There was more chatter about doings in Ctesiphon, the Persian capital, than over what was happening in Constantinople.

Naturally enough, the handbills were also a prominent subject, but not in a way that helped Argyros. The townsfolk seemed much less upset about them than George Lakhanodrakon or Leontios had been. One man, well in his cups, said with a shrug, "They're looking to break our nerve. I'll fret when I see a Persian outside the walls, and not until."

The magistrianos tried to prompt him: "Don't you think the Nestorians might invite—" Several people shushed him, and he had to subside, for four musicians emerged from a back room to take their seats on low stools by the fireplace. One carried two vase-shaped drums and had a tambourine strapped to his calf, another brought a pair of flutes, the third a long trumpet, and the last a short-necked lute played with a bow, something Argyros had not seen in Constantinople.

At a nod from the lutanist, they began to play. The drummer's beat was more intricate than Argyros was used to, the tune lively but at the same time somehow languorous. Again he was conscious of traditions older than the Roman Empire that lived on in the east.

Then Mirrane glided into the taproom, and the magistrianos worried about traditions no more. She wore only her veil and a few jeweled ornaments that sparkled in the torchlight; her smooth skin gleamed with oil. When she moved among the tables, it was as if she sought out a particular man to slay with lust. Sinuous as a serpent, she slid away from every arm that reached out to take hold of her.

"With a dance like that," Argyros whispered to the man at the table next to his, "why does she bother with the veil?"

The fellow was shocked enough to tear his burning gaze away from Mirrane. "It were a gross indecency for a woman to show her face in public!"

"Oh."

Mirrane's eyes flashed as she recognized the magistrianos, and he knew she had chosen him for her victim. Laughing, she waved to the musicians; the tune grew faster and more urgent. It would have taken a man of stone, which Argyros assuredly was not, to remain unstirred as she whirled in front of him. The oil on her skin was scented with musk; under it he caught the perfume of herself.

The music rose to a fiery crescendo. With a shout, Mirrane flung herself down on the seat by Argyros, cast her arms around his neck. With her warm length pressed against him, he hardly heard the storm of applause that filled the inn.

And later, when she went upstairs with him, he ignored with equal aplomb the jealous catcalls that followed them. Knowing what was important at any given moment, he told himself, was a virtue.

HE WOKE the next morning feeling considerably rumpled but otherwise as well as he ever had in his life. The soft straw pallet was narrow for two; Mirrane's leg sprawled over his calf. He moved slowly and carefully, but woke her anyway as he got out of bed. "Sorry."

She smiled lazily up at him. "You have nothing to be sorry for."

"I'm glad of that." He politely turned his back to use the chamberpot, then splashed water on his face and rinsed his mouth from a ewer that stood next to the bed. He ran his fingers through his hair and beard, shook his head in mock dismay at the snarls he found. "You'd think the dogs dragged me in, the way I must look."

"Do you always worry so much?" she asked, rising and stretching luxuriously.

"As a matter of fact, yes." He went over to his saddle-bags, which he had not yet unpacked, in search of a comb. Several jingling trinkets and her veil were draped over the leather sacks. She took them back from him while he rummaged.

He lifted out three or four small, tightly stoppered pots with bits of rag protruding from holes drilled through their corks. "What on earth are those?" Mirrane asked; they were not the sort of thing travelers usually carried.

Argyros thought fast. "They're filled with clay," he said. "I filter water from the cisterns through them; from the amount and type of sediment left behind, I can judge how pure the water is."

"Ah," she nodded, not revealing much interest in anything so mundane as the tools of his alleged trade.

All the same, he was relieved when he finally found his bone comb and stowed the pots away. They were filled, not with clay, but with the Franco-Saxon compound of charcoal, sulfur, and saltpeter the armorers of Constantinople had dubbed hellpowder. Argyros had no intention of advertising its existence without dire need.

He combed out his tangled whiskers. "That's—ouch— better." When he was done dressing, he said, "I know what I do seems dull, but Daras may need all the water I can find to hold out against a Persian attack if these parchments I've heard about stir up the rebellion they're after."

Mirrane's costume made a simple shrug worth looking at. "I've heard of them too, but there haven't been many here about Shahin's place." She hesitated. "Are you thinking we may be disloyal because we're of Persian blood? Shahin's grandfather converted to Christianity—orthodox, not Nestorian—and he worships every week at Bartholomew's church."

He believed her. There was no point in lying about something of that sort; it was too easy to check. "I wasn't thinking any such thing," he said. "I'd rather not get stuck in a siege, though, especially in a city that may run dry. And," he added a moment later, "it would be sinful to risk you."

Since he had used the story he did, he thought it wise to actually examine some of Daras's waterworks. One major cistern stood close to the church of the Apostle Bartholomew. He poked at the brickwork as if to check its soundness, then climbed the stairs to the top of the great tank and peered in to see what the water level was.

One of the faces he noticed while he was puttering about seemed familiar. After a while he realized that the hawk-faced fellow lounging against a wall and munching a pomegranate was the flute player at Shahin's tavern. The man was gone by the time he got down from the cistern, which left Argyros uncertain whether his presence was coincidental or the magistrianos's cover had satisfied him.

Leontios greeted him cordially when, having had enough playacting, he went over to the garrison commander's headquarters. "Any progress?"

"Not really," Argyros said. "I have more new questions than answers. First, are you sure your men have Daras sealed off from getting these handbills from outside?"

"I told you so yesterday. Oh, I'll not deny they'd take the gold to let some things through, but not that poison. We've lived through too many religious riots to want more."

"Fair enough. Next question: where can I find the best map of the city?"

Leontios tugged at his beard as he thought. "That would be in the eparch's office, not here. He collects the headtax and the hearthtax, so he has to keep track of every property in the city. My own charts are years out of date—the main streets don't change much, and they're mainly what I'm concerned with as a military man."

"No blame on you," Argyros assured him. "Now—third one pays for all. Do you keep note of where in Daras your troopers have pulled down the parchments?"

He waited tensely. Many soldiers would not have bothered with such trivia. But the Roman bureaucratic tradition was strong, even in the army, and there was a chance— Leontios's relieved grin told him he had won the gamble. "I have them," the garrison commander said. "I warn you, though, not all are in Greek. Do you read Arabic?"

"Not a word of it. But surely some bright young clerk in the eparch's chancery will. I shall go there now; when you gather your troopers' reports, please be so good as to send them after me."

"With pleasure." Leontios cocked an eyebrow at the magistrianos. "If I dared say no, I suppose you'd set upon me, as you did on those two hoodlums yesterday."

"Oh, that." Argyros had almost forgotten the incident. Doubting he would hear anything worthwhile, he asked, "What did you learn from the one your men took?"

"Ravings, I'm certain—what's the point of torturing a man who's just been kicked in the crotch? He keeps babbling of a woman who paid him and his partner to assault you. He's been drinking poppy juice, if you ask me. Anyone out to hire killers would pick a better pair than those sorry sods, don't you think?"

"I hope so," Argyros said, but the news disturbed him. The woman, he felt sure, was Mirrane, but he could not see the game she was playing. Had the attack been a setup to make him grateful to her? If so, why was the hired tough still around to speak of it? "Perhaps I'll have a word with the fellow myself, after I'm done at the eparch's."

"Feel free. Meanwhile, I'll hunt up those notes and get them over there for you."

The chief map in the eparch's office was several feet square, an updated papyrus facsimile of the master map of Daras inscribed on a bronze tablet in the imperial chancery at Constantinople. At Argyros's request, the eparch—a plump, fussy little man named Mammianos—provided him with a small copy on a single sheet of parchment.

As the magistrianos had predicted, several of Mammianos's secretaries were fluent in Arabic. "One has to have them here, sir," the eparch said, "if one is to transact the business necessary to the fisc." He assigned Argyros a clerk named Harun, which the magistrianos guessed to be a corruption of the perfectly good Biblical name Aaron.

After that there was nothing to do but wait for Leontios's messenger, who arrived an hour or so later with an armload of papyri, parchments, and ostraca. He dumped them in front of Argyros and departed.

The magistrianos sorted out the notes in Greek, which he could handle himself. "'In front of the shop of Peter son of Damian, on the Street of the Tailors,'" he read. "Where's that, Harun?" The clerk pointed with a stylus. Argyros made a mark on his map.

It was nearly sunset when the last dot went into its proper place. "Many thanks," Argyros said. He gave a nomisma to the secretary, who had proven a model of patience and competence, and waved off his stammered protests. "Go on, take it—you've earned it. I couldn't have done any of this without you. Mammianos is well served."

Leontios was on the point of going home when the magistrianos came back to his headquarters. "I'd about given up on you. What did you find? That the handbills are thickest in the parts of town where the most Nestorians live?"

"That's just what I expected," Argyros said, admiring the officer's quick wits. "But it isn't so. Here; see for yourself. Each dot shows where a parchment was found."

"The damn things are everywhere!" Leontios grunted after a quick look at the map.

"Not quite." Argyros bent over the parchment and pointed. "See, here's a patch where there aren't any."

"Isn't that big square building the barracks here? No wonder the filthy rabble-rousers stayed away. They're bastards, but they're not fools, worse luck."

"So it is. Odd, though, wouldn't you say, that your strongpoint is on the edge of the empty area instead of at the center? And what of this other blank stretch?"

"Over in the west? Ah, but look, there's the church of St. Bartholomew in it. The priests would be as likely to raise the alarm as my soldiers. Likelier, maybe; not all my men are orthodox."

"But again," Argyros pointed out, "the church is at the edge of the clear space, not in the middle. And look, here is the Great Church, in the very center of town, with a handbill nailed to one of its gates. The agitators aren't afraid of priests, it seems."

"So it does," Leontios said reluctantly. "What then?"

"I wish I knew. What puzzles me most, though, is this third empty area, close to the northern wall. From what Mammianos's clerk said, it's a solidly Nestorian district, and yet there are no parchments up in it."

"Where is that? Let me see. Aye, the fellow's right; that's the worst part of town, probably because of the stink. Dyers and butchers and gluemakers and tanners and such work there. To say nothing of thieves, that is—the one who went for you hailed from that section."

"Oh yes, him. He almost slipped my mind again. As I said, I'd like to ask him a few questions of my own."

Leontios looked embarrassed. "There's a harsher judge than you questioning him now, I'm afraid. He died a couple of hours ago."

"Died? How?" Argyros exclaimed.

"From what the gaoler says, pain in the belly, and I don't mean on account of your foot. If I had to guess, I'd think the fish sauce went over; you know how hard it is to keep in this climate."

"I suppose so," the magistrianos said, but the ruffian's death struck him as altogether too pat. He stared down at the map on Leontios's desk, trying by sheer force of will to extract meaning from the cryptic pattern there. It refused to yield. Grumbling in annoyance, he rolled up the map and walked back to Shahin's tavern. A copper twenty-follis piece bought the services of a torchboy to light his way through the black maze of nighttime Daras.

The taproom was jammed when he got to the inn, and for good reason: Mirrane was already dancing. Her eyes lit up when she saw him standing against the back wall drinking a mug of wine (real grape wine, and correspondingly expensive) and chewing on unleavened pocketbread stuffed with lentils, mutton, and onions.

Later that night she said petulantly, "If your things were not still in your room, I would have thought you'd gone away and left me. Are your precious cisterns so much more interesting than I am?"

"Hardly," he said, caressing her. She purred and snuggled closer. "I find you fascinating." That was true, but he hoped she did not realize in how many senses of the word he meant it.

THE MAGISTRIANOS visited the northern part of the city on the following day. He noted that his shadow was back. He doubted the fellow was enjoying himself much, or learning much either. All of Argyros's actions were perfectly consistent with what he would have done had he been a genuine cistern inspector.

The second of Daras's two major water storage areas was easy to examine, for Justinian's engineer Chryses had diverted the Cordes River to flow between the town's outworks and its main wall, thereby also serving as a moat and offering extra protection against attack. To check the level of the water, all Argyros had to do was climb to the top of the wall and look down over the battlements.

Not much of Daras's masonry still dated from Justinian's time. The city had fallen to the Persians in the reign of his successor, and again less than half a century later when the madman Phokas almost brought the Empire to ruin, and two or three more times in the years since. Once or twice it had had to stand Roman siege while in Persian hands. Just the same, the ancient fortifications had been designed well, and all later military architects used them as their model.

The wall, then, was of stone, about forty feet high and ten thick. Arrow-slits and a runway halfway up gave defenders a second level from which to fire at foes outside. The slits, though, were not wide enough for Argyros to stick his head through, and in any case he wanted the view from the top of the wall, so he climbed the whole long stairway. The man following him loitered at the base and bought some hot chickpeas.

The magistrianos was a little jealous; in Daras's heat, the trudge had made his heart pound. In another way, though, Argyros had the better of it, for he was above the smell. As Leontios had said, northern Daras stank. It reeked of terrified animals and their excrement from the butchers' shops; of stale, sour urine from the dyers'; of that same vile odor and the sharper tang of tanbark from the tanneries; and of a nameless but unpleasant stench from cauldrons that bubbled behind every gluemaker's establishment. Added to the usual city stink of overcrowded, unwashed humanity, it made for a savage assault on the nose. The faint breeze that blew off the Cordes carried the scent of manure from the fields outside of town, but was ambrosial by comparison.

Argyros walked along the track atop the wall, peering down into Daras. It was the broadest view he could gain of the northern district. Searching there street by street would have been fruitless, especially since he was not sure what he was looking for.

With such gloomy reflections as that, he paced back and forth for a couple of hours. The sentries at the battlements came to ignore him; down below, the musician from Shahin's inn grew bored and fell asleep sitting against the wall, his headcloth pulled low to shield his face from the sun.

The magistrianos could not have said what drew his attention to the donkey making its slow way down an alley, its driver beside it. Perhaps it was that the beast carried a couple of pots of glue along with several larger, roughly square packages, and he found it odd for an animal to be bearing burdens for two different shops. He certainly could not think of anything a gluemaker turned out that would go in those neatly wrapped bundles. They were about the size of—

His boots thumping on stone, he dashed down the steps and past his dozing shadow. Then, careless of the hard looks and angry shouts that he drew, he hurled himself into traffic, shoving past evil-tempered camels that bared their teeth at him and pushing merchants out of the way. As he trotted along, he panted out prayers that he could remember where he had seen that donkey and that he could find the spot now that he was at ground level.

It was somewhere near the three-story whitewashed building with the narrow windows, of that much he was sure. Just where, though, was another question. And of course the donkey, though it was only ambling, would have gone some distance by the time he got to where he had seen it. Staring wildly down one lanelet after another, Argyros thought of Zeno's paradox about Achilles and the tortoise and wondered if he would ever catch up.

There the beast was, about to turn onto Daras's main north-south avenue, called the Middle Street after Constantinople's Mese. Imitating Leontios's gesture of a few days before, Argyros wiped sweat from his forehead with his sleeve, and took a minute or two to let his breathing slow. He needed to seem natural.

A brisk walk let him come up behind the donkey's driver. "Excuse me," he said. "Do you speak Greek?"

The man spread his hands. "Little bit."

"Ah, good." As casually as he could, Argyros asked, "Tell me, are those parchments your donkey is carrying?"

He was tense as a strung bow. If the answer to that was yes, he half expected to be attacked on the spot. But the driver only nodded. "So they are. What about it?"

"Er—" For a moment, the magistrianos's usually facile tongue stumbled. Then he rallied: "May I buy one? I, uh, forgot to write out a receipt for several tenants of mine, and seeing you passing by with your bundles here reminded me of it."

How much of the explanation the local understood was not clear, but he knew what the word buy meant. After some brisk bargaining, they settled on half a silver miliaresion as a fair price. The donkey driver undid one of his packages. Again Argyros got ready for action, thinking that the man did not know what he was carrying and that the subversive handbills would now be revealed.

But the parchment the driver handed him was blank. "Is all right?"

"Hmm? Oh, yes, fine, thank you," he said, distracted. As if he were an expect testing the quality of the goods, he riffled the corners of the stacked sheets—maybe the first few were blank to conceal the rest. But none had anything on it. He gave up. "You have a very fine stock here. Whatever scribe it's going to will enjoy writing on it."

"Thank you, sir." The donkey-driver pocketed his coin and tied up the package again. "Is not to any scribe going, though."

"Really?" the magistrianos said, not very interested. "To whom, then?"

The driver grinned, as if about to tell a funny story he did not think his listener would believe. "To Abraham the potter, of all peoples. He the glue wants, too."

"Really?" Argyros's tone of voice was entirely different this time. "What on earth does he need with a thousand sheets of parchment and enough glue to stick half of Daras down?"

"For all I know, he crazy," the man shrugged. "My master Yesuyab, he work on this order the last month. And when he get it ready to go, Musa the gluemaker next door, he tell me he gots for Abraham too, so would I take along? Why not, I say. My donkey strong."

"Yes, of course. Well, thank you again." Argyros let the fellow go, then stood staring after him until a man leading three packhorses yelled at him to get out of the way. He stepped aside, still scratching his head.

Something else occurred to him. He went back to the chancery. With Harun's capable help, he soon added two marks to his map of Daras, then a third and, as an afterthought, a fourth. He studied the pattern they made. "Well, well," he said. "How interesting."

Mesopotamian night fell with dramatic suddenness. No sooner was the sun gone from the sky, it seemed, than full darkness came. Last night that had been a nuisance; now Argyros intended to take advantage of it. He had returned to Shahin's inn during the late afternoon, grumbling of having to go right back to the chancery, probably for hours. He had to stop himself from nodding at his crestfallen shadow, who looked up from a mug of beer in surprise and relief when he arrived.

The wretch trailed him again, of course, but he really did revisit Mammianos's headquarters. The scribes and secretaries eyed him curiously as he waited around doing nothing until his tracker grew bored and mooched off, convinced he was there for the evening as he had feared. The staff departed just before sunset, leaving the place to Argyros.

The magistrianos prowled through the back streets of Daras like a burglar, without any light to give away his presence. He slunk into a doorway when a squad of Leontios's troopers came tramping by. Soon he might need to call on the garrison commander for aid, but not yet.

The smithy next to Abraham's pottery shop made it easy to find, for which Argyros was grateful. As he had thought, the windows were shuttered and the place barred and locked, both front and back. Nothing surprising there—anyone in his right mind would have done the same.

He considered the lock that held the back door closed: a standard type. A hole had been drilled from top to bottom near one end of the door bar. There was a similar hole bored part of the way into the bottom board of the frame into which the bar slid. Before Abraham had gone home, he had dropped a cylindrical metal pin down through the barhole so that half of it was in the frame and the rest above it, holding the bar in place.

The top of the metal cylinder was still lower than the level of the upper surface of the bar, so no passerby could hope to pull it out. Abraham, no doubt, had a key with hooks or catches fitted to those of the boltpin to let him draw it out again.

There were, however, other ways. Argyros reached into his belt pouch and took out a pair of long-snouted pincers, rather like the ones physicians used to clamp bleeding vessels. His set, though, instead of having flat inner surfaces, was curved within.

He slipped them into the bolthole. After some jiggling, he felt them slide down past the top of the pin. When he tightened them, it was easy to lift the bolt out of its socket.

The magistrianos left the door ajar to let a little light into the shop and give him the chance to find a lamp. He worked flint and steel until he got the wick going, then closed the door after him. The shuttered windows would keep the lamp's pale illumination from showing on the street out front.

He prowled about the inside of the cramped little shop. At first everything seemed quite ordinary. Here were two kilns, their fires out for the evening but still warm to the touch. A foot-powered wheel stood between them. There lay great lumps of refined clay and jugs of water next to them to soften them. Abraham had molds in the shape of a hand, a fish, a bunch of grapes, and other things, as well as a set of what looked like sculptors' tools to create the reliefwork popular in Daras. Pots that were ready to sell filled shelves in the front of the store.

After a snarl of frustration, Argyros began to use his head. If anything here was not as it should be, it would be connected with the parchments Yesuyab had sent Abraham. Where were they? The magistrianos held the lamp high. He made a disgusted noise deep in his throat. He had walked right past them—they were stacked by a table just to the left of the back door.

Excitement flared in the magistrianos as he saw the gluepots sitting on top of the table. Beside them were a couple of smaller vessels that proved full of ink, along with the square iron plate the smith had given to Abraham. A low iron frame had been put in place around it. The only other thing on the table was a large paintbrush.

The frustration returned. Here were parchment and ink, right enough, but Argyros could not see how the rest of the strange array contributed to making handbills. It would take a score of scribes to turn out as many as Abraham had parchments, and in that case they would be far from identical with one another.

There were four shelves over the table, each with a dozen small clay jars on it (except the topmost, which had thirteen). Only because they were close to the parchments and glue, Argyros lifted down one of them. He turned it around in his hand and almost dropped it—on the side turned to the wall was written a large majuscule delta: Δ. He tore the stopper off, held the lamp over it, and peered in.

At first he saw nothing that looked like a delta. The jar held a number of small rectangular blocks of clay, each about as long as the last joint of his middle finger but not nearly so thick. He picked one up. Sure enough, there was a raised letter at one end. It was still black with ink. He lifted out another clay pot. It also had a delta on it. So did the next and the next.

No wonder Abraham was involved in the plot, Argyros thought. The potter was used to creating reliefwork of all kinds; letters would come as no challenge to him. And Leontios had said he was a Nestorian. He had reason to be hostile to Constantinople, which forced religious unity to go with the political unity it brought.

Whistling tunelessly, the magistrianos put the jar back and chose another one from a couple of shelves higher up. This one was identified by a minuscule beta: β. Like the first, it was filled with those little blocks of fired clay. Argyros took one out, confidently expected to find a beta on one end of it. And so, in a way, he did, but reversed: $\mathrm{\beta}$.

He thought a few uncharitable thoughts about the wits of anyone incompetent enough to make his letters backward. Certain it was a mistake, he removed several more clay blocks from the jar. They were all the same and all reversed.

He frowned. That was going to a lot of effort to perpetuate an error. He poured all but one of the little clay lumps back into their jar, turned the last one over and over as he thought. He held it so close to his face that he had to look at it cross-eyed. It was still backward.

He squeezed it between his thumb and index finger, as if trying to wring the answer from it by brute force. Naturally, and annoyingly, such treatment harmed the clay block not at all. It was harder on him. There was a square indentation in the meaty pad of his thumb from the base of the block. And on his forefinger—

He stared at the perfect, unreversed beta pressed into his flesh. "Of course!" he exclaimed, startled into speaking aloud. "It's like a signet ring, where everything has to be done backward to show up the right way in the wax." The delta, he thought, had misled him because it was symmetrical.

He dipped the backward beta into an inkpot, stamped it down on the tablepot, and grinned to see the letter appear right-side-to. He stamped it again and again. Each impression, inevitably, was just like all the rest. "This is how it's done, all right," he breathed.

He discovered that the jars on the top two shelves contained minuscule letters (they were arranged in alphabetical order, to make finding each one easy), while their counterparts on the lower shelves all held majuscules. The extra jar on the highest board proved to have slightly smaller blocks of clay without any characters on them. They puzzled Argyros until he realized they had to be used to mark the spaces between words—because they were lower than their fellows, the ink that got on them would not appear on the parchment.

Like a child with a new toy, he decided to spell out his own name. One by one, he selected the letters that went into it and set them on the iron plate, leaning them against the edge of the iron frame for security. Even so, they kept falling over. And that, he decided, was probably what the glue was for: spread over the surface of the plate, it would hold the blocks in place.

He inked the brush, painted the tops of the letters, then pressed a sheet of parchment over them. The result made him burst into startled laughter. There on the parchment, rather raggedly aligned, were the nonsense words soɹʎƃɹA lizaᙠ.

He thumped his forehead with the heel of his hand, muttering "Idiot!" under his breath. He quickly rearranged the clay blocks; naturally, if the letters themselves were backward, their order had to be that way too, in order to appear correctly on the sheet. He felt like cheering when the second try rewarded him with a smeary *Basil Argyros*.

He wondered what to compose next. Almost without conscious thought, the first words of the Gospel according to John came into his mind: "In the beginning was the Word, and the Word was with God, and the Word was God."

A letter at a time, the evangelist's famous sentence took shape. Argyros suddenly stopped, halfway through, as the magnitude of what he was doing began to sink in. The Persians, with their petty subversion in Daras, were only pikers, and George Lakhanodrakon's fear of the same at Constantinople seemed just as trivial.

Of course John had been speaking of the divine Logos, Christ Himself, but his words rang with eerie aptness. These simple little blocks of clay could spell *anything* and make as many copies of it as one wanted. What power was more godlike than that?

The magistrianos was so struck with awe that he did not pay any attention to the approaching footfalls in the alley behind Abraham's shop. But the soft cry of alarm one of the newcomers raised on seeing the bar down from the door tore Argyros from his reverie. He cursed himself for his stupidity—the only reason all this dangerous paraphernalia was so openly displayed had to be that the Persians were going to reproduce another handbill tonight.

There were three stout iron hooks-and-eyes screwed into the inside of the door panels and the doorframe. Abraham, evidently, was the sort of man who tied double knots in his sandal straps—and in his sandals, Argyros would have done the same. The potter's caution was the only thing that saved him. He had just hooked the last closure when someone large heaved an ungentle shoulder against the door. It groaned but held.

Familiar, throaty laughter came from the alleyway. "Is that you, dear Basil?" Mirrane called mockingly. "Where will you run now?"

It was an excellent question. The pottery's front door was barred on the outside, just as the back had been. So were the stout wooden shutters, which—damn Abraham—had locks on both inside and out.

Mirrane let Argyros stew just long enough, then said, "Well, it seems we shan't raise Daras yet. A pity—but then, bagging one of the Emperor's precious magistrianoi (oh yes, I know who you are!) is not the smallest prize either."

"*You're* behind this!" he blurted. He had thought she was merely a pleasant distraction thrown his way by the real plotter—Shahin maybe, or Abraham, or Yesuyab, whom he had never seen.

She might have been reading his thoughts. Bitterness edged her voice as she answered, "Aye, by the Good God Ormazd, I am! Did you think I lacked the wit or will because I am a woman? You'll not be the first to pay for that mistake, nor the last." She shifted from Greek to Persian and spoke to one of her henchmen: "I'll waste no more time on this Roman. Burn the place down!"

Someone let out a harsh protest in Arabic.

"Don't be a donkey, Abraham," Mirrane snapped. "The noise of breaking in the door might bring the watch—we're too close to the barracks to risk it. The King of Kings will pay you more than you would earn from this miserable hovel in the next fifty years. Come on, Bahram, set the torch. The bigger the blaze, the more likely it is to destroy everything we need out of the way, Argyros included.

"...Isn't that right, Basil?" she added through the door.

The magistrianos did not answer, but could not argue with her tactics. A very accomplished young woman indeed, he thought ruefully—and in such unexpected ways. He had no doubt several armed men would be waiting when smoke and flames drove him to try bursting out through the door. He could see Bahram's torch flame flickering, hot and yellow, under the doorjamb.

But Mirrane, for all her ruthless efficiency, did not know everything. Along with his burglar's pincers, Argyros had fetched a couple of the tightly corked clay pots he had passed off to her as sediment testers. Stooping, he set them at the base of the back door.

His lamp was beginning to gutter, but it still held enough oil for his need. He touched the flame to the rags that ran through the stoppers. Those were soaked in fat themselves, and caught at once.

As soon as the magistrianos saw they were burning, he put down the lamp and dove behind Abraham's counter. He clapped his hands over his ears.

It was not a moment too soon. The hellpowder bombs went off, the explosion of the first touching off the second. The blast was like the end of the world. Shattered bits of pottery flew round the shop, deadly as slingers' bullets. The double charge of the charcoal, sulfur, and saltpeter mix the Franco-Saxons had discovered flung the door off its hinges, hurling it outward at Mirrane and her companions.

Dagger in hand, Argyros scrambled to his feet. His head was ringing, but at least he knew where the thunderbolt had come from. To Mirrane and her friends in the alleyway, it was a complete and hideous surprise.

The magistrianos charged through the cloud of thick, brimstone-smelling smoke that hung in the shattered doorway. He discovered one of Mirrane's henchmen at once, by almost tripping over him. The fellow was down and writhing, his hands clutched around a long splinter of wood driven into his groin. He was no danger and would not last long.

Several other men went pelting down the alley as fast as they could run. Through half-deafened ears, Argyros heard their shouts of terror: "Devils!" "Demons!" "Mother of God, protect me from Satan!" "It's Ahriman, come to earth!" That last had to come from a Persian: Ahriman was Ormazd's wicked foe in their dualist faith.

One of the nearby shadows moved. Argyros whirled. "A trick I did not know about, it seems," Mirrane said quietly. Her self-possession was absolute; she might have been talking of the weather. She went on, "The game is yours this time, after all."

"And you with it!" he cried, springing toward her.

"Sorry, no." As she spoke, she opened the door behind her, stepped through, and slammed it in Argyros's face. The bar locked it just as he crashed into it. He rebounded, dazed at the impact. Mirrane said, "We'll meet again, you and I." He heard her beat a rapid retreat.

Only then did he think of anything beyond the predicament from which he had just escaped. As Mirrane had said, Abraham's pottery was only a block from the main barracks of Daras. Already Argyros could hear cries of alarm and then the disciplined pound of a squadron running his way.

"Here!" he shouted.

The squad-leader came puffing up, torch held high. He gaped at the wrecked doorway to Abraham's shop. "What's all this about?"

"No time to explain," the magistrianos snapped. He gave the underofficer his rank; the man stiffened to attention. "Have some of your troopers break down that door," Argyros ordered, pointing to the one through which Mirrane had escaped. He quickly described her, then sent the rest of the squad around the corner to where the front entrance of the house or store or whatever it was let out.

They returned empty-handed. At Argyros's urging, Leontios sealed the gates of Daras within the hour, and for the next two days the garrison forces searched the town from top to bottom. They caught Abraham hiding with Yesuyab the tailor, but of Mirrane no sign whatever turned up.

Argyros was disappointed, but somehow not surprised.

"VERY CLEVER, Basil, your use of the map to ferret out the nest of spies," George Lakhanodrakon said.

"Thank you, sir." Argyros's office chair creaked as he leaned back in it. "I'm only annoyed it took me as long as it did. I should have seen that the Persians deliberately avoided putting their parchments in certain parts of Daras so as to give Leontios no reason to search in them. But it wasn't until I found out that Yesuyab's tanning-works (and the gluemaker's next to it), Abraham's pottery, and Shahin's tavern were all in the exact centers of the empty areas that things began to make sense."

"A pretty piece of reasoning, no matter how you reached it." The Master of Offices hesitated, clearing his throat, and went on, "All the same, I'm not entirely sure the situation you left behind satisfies me."

"I'm not certain what else I could have done, your illustriousness," the magistrianos said politely. "No more inflammatory handbills are appearing in Daras, the town was calm when I left it, and I discovered the means by which the Persians were producing so many copies of the same text." Excitement put warmth in his voice. "A means, I might add, which could be used to—"

"Yes, yes," the Master of Offices interrupted. "I don't intend to slight you, my boy, not at all. As I said, you did splendidly. But all the same, there is no final resolution of the problem underlying this particular spot of trouble. It could crop up again anywhere in the east, in Kirkesion or Amida or Martyropolis, the more so as the tricksy Persian baggage in charge of the scheme slipped through your net."

"There you speak truly, sir," Argyros said. Mirrane's getaway still rankled. Also, it piqued him that the enjoyment she showed in his arms had probably been assumed to lull him. It had seemed very real at the time, more, he thought, than with any woman he had known since Helen. He hoped her parting warning would come true; one way or another, he wanted to test himself against her again.

He went on, "In any case, a second outbreak is not likely to be as serious as the first was. Now that we know how the thing is done, the local officials should be able to search out clandestine letterers on their own. And if the government issues them sets of clay archetypes on their own, they can easily counter any lies the Persians try spreading."

"Issue them archetypes of their own?" Lakhanodrakon spread his hands in something approaching horror. "Don't you think this is a secret as dangerous as hellpowder? It should be restricted in the same way, and the production of documents written with it limited to the imperial chancery here in the city."

"I'd like to believe I could convince you that this new way of lettering has more applications than simply the political."

The Master of Offices' scowl was like a stormcloud. "My concern is for the safety of the state. You'd need a powerful demonstration to alter my opinion here."

"I suppose so," Argyros said with a sigh. He seemed to change the subject: "Will you still be giving another reading next week, sir?"

Lakhanodrakon's frown vanished. He was composing an epic on Constans II's triumph over the Lombards in Italia, in iambic trimeters modeled after those George of Pisidia had used in his poems celebrating Herakleios's victories. "Yes, from the third book," he said. "I hope you'll be here?"

"I'm looking forward to it. I only wonder how many of your guests will be familiar with what you've already written."

"To some degree, a fair number, I suppose. Many will have been at the earlier readings last year and this past winter, and of course the manuscript will have circulated somewhat. I intend to summarize what's gone before, anyhow."

"No need for that." Argyros opened a desk drawer and handed a pile of thin papyrus codices to Lakhanodrakon.

"What on earth are these?"

"Books one and two of your *Italiad*, sir," Argyros said innocently. "I've given you thirty-five copies, which I believe will be enough for you to pass one on to everyone who is coming. If not, I still have the letters in their frames. I would be happy to make as many more as you need."

A couple of days ago Argyros would have sung a different tune. He did not fret about the cost of seven hundred sheets of papyrus. The stuff was cheap in Constantinople, because the government used so much of it. And finding a potter from Mesopotamia who could be made to understand how to make the clay archetypes had not been difficult for one who knew the city as the magistrianos did.

But Argyros was still squinting from the unaccustome
effort of putting twenty pages of poetry into frames a lette
at a time—backward. Anthimos had helped, some, but h
never did get the hang of it, and the magistrianos spent al
most as much time fixing his secretary's mistakes as he di
making progress of his own. After a while, he had excuse
the hapless scribe. And then, halfway through page eigh
teen, he had run out of *omegas* and had to rush back to th
potter to get more.

It was all worth it now, though, watching the astonish
ment on the Master of Offices' face turn to delight. "Thirty
five copies?" Lakhanodrakon whispered in wonder. "Why
saving the Bible and Homer, I don't know of thirty-fiv
copies of any work here in the capital. Perhaps Thucydide
or Plato or St. John Chrysostom—and me. I feel ashame
to join the company you've put me in, Basil."

"It's a very good poem, sir," the magistrianos sai
loyally. "Don't you see now? With this new lettering, we ca
make so many copies of all our authors that they'll neve
again risk being lost because mice ate the last remaining on
three days before it was due to be redone. Not just litera
ture, either—how much better would our armies fare i
every officer carried his own copy of Maurice's *Strate
gikon*? And lawyers and churchmen could be sure their text
matched one another, for all would come from the sam
original. Ship captains would be able to take charts an
sailing guides from port to port—"

At last the Master of Offices was beginning to catch som
of the younger man's enthusiasm. "The Virgin protect me
you may be right after all! I can see how this invention coul
prove a great boon for government. Imperial rescripts woul
become much easier to produce. And—oh, think of it! W
could make endless copies of the same standard forms an
send them throughout the Empire. And it might not even b
too much labor to have other forms, on which we could kee
track of whether the first ones had been properly dis
patched. I can fairly see the scheme now, can't you?"

Argyros could, only too well. He wondered if he would b
able to change his boss's mind back again.

Had he not decided to pray at the church of St. Mouamet, Basil Argyros would never have got caught in the riot.

The church was in a poor part of Constantinople, not far from the Theodosian harbor on the Sea of Marmara. It held only about twenty people. As a magistrianos, Argyros could have chosen a more splendid holy place. He had prayed in Hagia Sophia often enough.

But St. Mouamet was one of Argyros's favorites. He had a fine church in distant New Carthage much grander than the little shrine dedicated to him here in the capital. Argyros had seen it a couple of years ago, when he was in Ispania to ferret out the secret of the Franco-Saxons' hellpowder. Come to think of it, he had also prayed to St. Mouamet before he set out for Syria last year to see what mischief the Persians were stirring up in the border fortress of Daras. He wondered idly if this visit to Mouamet's church portended another voyage.

He picked his way through the winding alleys of the harbor district toward the Mese. Once or twice toughs eyed him speculatively, but decided it wiser to leave him alone. He might wear a gold ring on one finger, but he also slung a smallsword on his belt. Moreover, he was a tall, solidly built man, still strong though close to forty.

Unlike the back alleys, the Mese was paved with blocks of stone; Argyros scraped mud from his sandals. Colonnades on either side of the street supported roofs that gave shelter from sun and rain. When it had been showery the night before, as was true now, they also dripped. Argyros walked in the middle of the street, dodging mules, small carts, and heavily laden porters.

The Mese widened out into the Forum of Arkadios. The other squares in the city were named for great Emperors: Augustus, Constantine, Theodosios. Theodosios's halfwit son, Argyros thought, hardly belonged in such exalted company.

A crowd had gathered at the base of the tall column in the center of the square. Once a statue of Arkadios had topped the pillar, but an earthquake had sent it crashing down about a hundred years after Mouamet's time. Only a colossal hand and forearm survived, set up next to the column. Standing balanced on two man-sized fingertips, a monk was haranguing the crowd.

The fellow was scrawny, swarthy, and not very clean. He wore a ragged black robe and let his hair grow long, so that it fell in a tangled mat past his shoulders. A fanatical light burned in his eyes as he shouted out his message, whatever it was.

His Greek, Argyros noticed as he approached, had a strong Egyptian accent. That sent the first trickle of alarm through the magistrianos. Egyptians were volatile and still reckoned themselves a folk apart despite having been part of the Roman Empire since before the Incarnation. As if to emphasize their separateness, many still clung to the Monophysite heresy; even those nominally orthodox had strange notions about the relationship between Christ's human and divine natures.

The monk came to his peroration just as Argyros reached the back edge of the crowd. "And so," he cried, "you can see how these icons are a desecration and an abomination, a snare of Satan to deceive us into circumscribing the uncircumscribable." He drew an image of Christ from within his robe, held it over his head so his audience could see what it was, then dashed it with all his strength against the column beside him.

Cheers rang out; so did shouts of "Blasphemy!" Someone flung a large melon at the monk. He ducked, only to be caught in the side of the head by a stone. He toppled to the ground. The stone-thrower's triumphant bellow turned to a howl of pain and fury when someone punched him in the face.

Crying, "Down with the icons!" several young men dashed for the first church they could find, hot to match action to word. An old woman hit one of them over the head with her basket of figs, then kicked him as he sprawled on the cobbles.

The Egyptian monk was on his feet again, laying about him with a stick. Argyros heard it thud into someone's ribs. Then his interest in the broil abruptly went from professional to personal. Without bothering to find out which side he was on, a fat man ran up and kicked him in the shin.

His yelp was reflexive. So was his counterpunch. The fat man reeled away, a hand clapped to his bleeding nose. But he had friends. One of them seized Argyros's arms from behind. Another hit him in the stomach. Before they could do him worse damage, a ferret-faced man neatly bludgeoned the rioter who had hit the magistrianos. He fell with a groan.

Argyros stomped on the foot of the man behind him. As his sandals had hobnails, the fellow shrieked and let go. By the time the magistrianos whirled around, his smallsword drawn, the rioter was retreating at a limping run.

"Thanks," Argyros said to the chap who was so handy with a cudgel.

That worthy was on his knees next to the man he had felled, busily rifling his beltpouch. He looked up for a moment, grinning. "Don't mention it. Down with the icons!"

Like most educated Constantinopolitans, Argyros fancied himself a theologian, but it had never occurred to him to wonder if religious images were wrong. They were simply there: the iconostasis in front of the altar, the mosaics and paintings on the walls and ceilings of churches. At the moment, however, he lacked the leisure to meditate on their propriety.

As riots have a way of doing, this one was rapidly outgrowing the incident that had spawned it. Already several merchants' stalls had been overturned and looted, and another went over with a crash as Argyros watched. A woman ran past him with her arms full of cheap seashell jewelry. A man struggled to drag away a chair and was set upon and robbed in his turn before he had got it thirty feet. The magistrianos sniffed fearfully for smoke; a maniac with a torch or the burning oil from a broken lamp could set half the city ablaze.

Through the shouts and screams that filled the square, through the sound of splintering boards, Argyros heard a deep, rhythmic tramping coming down the Mese from the east, getting closer fast. Nor was he the only one. "The excubitores!" The warning cry came from three throats at once.

A company of the imperial bodyguards burst into the square. A barrage of rocks, vegetables, and crockery greeted them. They ducked behind their brightly painted shields, each of which was inscribed with the labarum— ☧ —Christ's monogram. One excubitor went down. The rest surged forward, swinging long hardwood clubs.

The rioters stood no chance against their grimly disciplined efficiency. Here and there a man, or even two and three together, would stand and fight. They got broken heads for their trouble. The excubitores rolled across the Forum of Arkadios like a wave traveling up a beach.

Argyros fled with most of the rest of the people in the square. Approaching an excubitor and explaining that he too was an imperial official struck him as an exercise in futility—and a good way to get hurt.

As it happened, he got hurt anyway. The alley down which he and several other people ran proved blocked by a mulecart that did not have room to turn around. A squad of excubitores came pounding after. The magistrianos's cry of protest and fear was drowned by everyone else's, and by the triumphant shouts of the guardsmen. He felt a burst of pain. His vision flared white, then plunged into darkness.

It was nearly sunset when he groaned and rolled over. His fingers went to the knot of anguish at the back of his head. They came away sticky with blood. He groaned again, managed to sit up, and, on the second try, staggered to his feet.

As he shakily walked back toward the Forum of Arkadios, he discovered someone had stolen his smallsword and slit his purse. Maybe, he thought, pleased with his deductive powers, it was the same ruffian who had sapped the man in the plaza and then robbed him. And maybe it wasn't. Trying to decide which only made his headache worse.

The Forum of Arkadios, usually crowded, was empty now except for a couple of dozen excubitores. "On your way, you," one of them growled at Argyros. He did his best to hurry.

There were excubitores on the Mese down toward the Forum of the Ox, and more in that square. Constantinople was buttoned up tight, trying to keep trouble from breaking free again. Another soldier approached the magistrianos. "Move along, fellow. Where are you supposed to be?"

"Mother of God!" Argyros exclaimed. "I'm supposed to dine with the Master of Offices tonight!" The engagement had been beaten out of his memory.

Seeing his bedraggled state, the excubitor set hands on hips and laughed. "Sure you are, pal, and I'm playing dice with the Emperor tomorrow."

Waving vaguely to the trooper, Argyros hurried down the Mese toward George Lakhanodrakon's residence. The Master of Offices lived in a fashionable quarter in the eastern part of the city, not far from the great church of Hagia Sophia and the imperial palaces.

The magistrianos hurried through the Forum of Theodosios and that of Constantine, with its tall porphyry column and its waterclock. He passed the Praitorion, the government building where he worked when he was in Constantinople. Darkness was falling as he lurched into the Augusteion, the main square of the city, which was flanked by Hagia Sophia, the palace district, and the hippodrome. Dinner was set for sunset. He was going to be late.

George Lakhanodrakon's doorman, a Syrian named
Zacharias, knew Argyros well. He exclaimed in polite horror as the magistrianos came up. "By the Thrice-Holy One,
sir! What happened?"

"Why? What's wrong?" Argyros said indignantly. "I
know I'm not quite on time, and I'm sorry, but—"

The doorman was gaping at him. "On time? Sir, your
face, your clothes—"

"Huh?" His wits muddled by the blow he had taken, the
magistrianos had been so intent on getting to Lakhanodrakon's house that he had not even thought about his appearance. Now he looked down at himself. His tunic was
torn, filthy, and bloodstained. A swipe of his hand across
his face brought away more dirt and dried blood.

"Sir, you'd better come with me." Calling for other servants to help him, Zacharias took Argyros's arm and half
led, half carried him through the doorway. Like the houses
of most wealthy men, Lakhanodrakon's was built in a
square pattern around a court, with blank, marble-faced
walls fronting the street. On a fine, mild evening like this
one, the dinner party would be held in the court, amid the
fountains and trees.

Argyros did not get that far. Lakhanodrakon's servants
took him to a guestroom and laid him on a couch. One ran
for a physician while others washed his face and the ugly
wound on the back of his head. They fetched him wine,
stripped him of his tunic, and dressed him in one belonging
to the Master of Offices.

He was beginning to feel human, in a sorrowful way,
when Lakhanodrakon himself hurried into the room, concern on his strong, fleshy features. "St. Andreas preserve
us!" he burst out, swearing by Constantinople's patron.
"Don't tell me the ruffians waylaid you this afternoon,
Basil!"

"Well, actually, no, your illustriousness," Argyros said
ruefully. "As a matter of fact, it was an excubitor." He
added, "I think he hit me with Arkadios's column." Despite the wine, his head was still splitting.

"You stay here until the doctor has had a look at you," Lakhanodrakon commanded. "Then if you'd sooner go home, I'll have Zacharias send for a linkbearer for you. Or if you're well enough to join us outside, of course we'll be delighted to have you."

"Thank you, sir; you're very kind."

The physician arrived a few minutes later; anyone summoned to the Master of Offices' residence hurried. The man shaved the back of Argyros's scalp, applied an ointment that smelled of pitch and stung ferociously, and bandaged his head with a long strip of linen. Then he held a lamp to the magistrianos's face and peered into each of his eyes in turn.

"I don't believe there is a concussion," he said at last. "Your pupils are both the same size." He gave Argyros a small jar. "This will reduce the pain; it has poppy juice in it. Drink half now, the rest in the morning." Businesslike to the end, he waved aside Argyros's thanks and departed as quickly as he had come.

The magistrianos would have recognized the odd scent and flavor of the poppy without the doctor's explanation. They brought back grim memories of the time when his infant son died of smallpox. As he forced himself to, he shoved the memories aside.

Though he still felt slow and stupid, he went out to the courtyard. Having come this far, he was not about to miss the dinner party, no matter what Lakhanodrakon said.

The Master of Offices' other guests, naturally, swarmed around him and made much of him, when he would rather have taken his quiet place on a couch and drunk more wine. Not everyone knew what had touched off the riot. There was a thoughtful silence after Argyros told them. Then the imperial grandees began arguing the propriety of images among themselves.

Normally, the magistrianos would have played a vigorous part in the debate. Now, though, he was content merely to seize the opportunity to recline. Servants offered him fried squid, tuna cooked with leeks, roast kid in a sauce of fermented fish. He turned everything down. The smell of food made him queasy.

He slapped at a mosquito; the torches and lanterns that made Lakhanodrakon's courtyard bright as day drew swarms of them. He wondered why the Master of Offices had so many lights set out. Half the number, he thought, would have been plenty.

Then a servant passed among the guests, handing each one a papyrus folio. Argyros caught Lakhanodrakon's eye. "You didn't tell me you would be reading your poetry tonight," he called.

"I was not sure I would finish the fourth book of my *Italiad* in time for this evening," the Master of Offices said. "I'm distributing book three here, to bring everyone up to date in the story. Thanks to you," he went on, bowing politely, "the company is already familiar with books one and two." If this was a printed version of book three—and Argyros saw it was—it seemed Lakhanodrakon had tried lines on him, and he had even contributed a suggestion or two himself, so he knew the poem fairly well.

"Now that you've been refreshed as to the background, my friends, I shall commence," the Master of Offices declared. To read, he held his manuscript at arm's length; he was growing more farsighted year by year.

Some of the verses were quite good, and Lakhanodrakon read well. His faint Armenian accent suited the martial tale he was telling. The magistrianos wished he could pay closer attention. The poppy juice and the lingering effects of the blow combined to make him feel detached, almost floating above his couch...

A polite patter of applause woke him. He guiltily joined in, hoping no one had seen him doze off. The dinner party began to break up. When he went over to the Master of Offices to say his good-byes, Lakhanodrakon would not listen to them. "You spend the night here, Basil. You're in no shape to go home alone."

"Thank you, sir," the magistrianos said, though he wished Lakhanodrakon had not been so insistent. It only made him certain his boss had noticed him asleep.

ARGYROS'S SECRETARY unceremoniously dumped a handful of rolled-up papyri on his desk. "Thank you, Anthimos," the magistrianos said.

Anthimos grunted. He always reminded Argyros of a
mournful crane. Capable but without enthusiasm or real
talent, he would never be anything more than a secretary,
and knew it. When he returned to his own work, Argyros
forgot about him the moment his back was turned.

The magistrianos read rapidly over the interrogation reports taken from the men and women the excubitores had
captured during the riot. They showed him little he had not
learned from his own brief encounter. The rabble-rousing
monk's name, he found out, was Sasopis, which confirmed
the fellow's Egyptian origin. Accounts of just what he had
preached varied, depending on how each witness felt about
icons.

Sasopis himself had escaped. As would any Constantinopolitan official, Argyros thought that a shame. Ever since
the Nika uprising, its specter haunted the city. Anyone who
thought to bring back such chaos deserved what he got.

For the next couple of weeks, the city stayed calm. The
magistrianos accepted that with gratitude but no great trust,
as he might have welcomed one of the last fine days before
the autumn storms began. He used the respite to try to track
down Sasopis, but to no avail. The miserable monk might
have vanished off the face of the earth, though that, Argyros thought sourly, was too much to hope for.

When the trouble broke out again, Sasopis had nothing
to do with it. Yet still it sprang from Egypt: as the plague
had in Justinian's day, strife came now via grain ship from
Alexandria. Sailors went off to wench and drink and roister, and took with them the exciting tales of the turmoil they
had left behind. Up and down the Nile, it seemed, men were
at each other's throats over the question of the icons.

Argyros could imagine what happened next, in some
dockside tavern or brothel lounge. Someone would have said
scornfully, "What foolishness! My grandfather venerated
images, and that's enough for me." And someone else
would have answered, "Because your grandfather burns in

hell, do you want to join him?'' That would have been
plenty to bring out the knives.

The second round of rioting was not confined to the
Forum of Arkadios, and took the excubitores, the scholae,
and the other palace regiments four days to put down. Several churches had their icons defaced with whitewash or
scraped from the walls, while one was put to the torch.
Luckily, it stood alone in a little park, and the fire did not
spread.

The day after peace—more a peace of exhaustion than
anything else—returned to the city, word came of disorders
in Antioch, the third city of the Empire.

George Lakhanodrakon summoned Argyros that afternoon. The magistrianos was shocked to see how worn he
looked; although Master of Offices was not a military post,
Lakhanodrakon was a member of the Emperor's Consistory and had had to attend privy council meetings day and
night. He also oversaw the civil servants who prepared orders and recorded testimony, all of whom had been over-
worked in the emergency.

"You should rest, sir," Argyros said.

"So I should," Lakhanodrakon agreed. "I should also
exercise until I lose this belly of mine, should learn better
Latin to go with my Greek, and should do a great many
other things I have no time for."

No doubt one of the things he had no time for was well-
meaning but useless suggestions. The magistrianos flushed,
expecting a dressing-down.

But his superior surprised him, asking, out of the blue it
seemed, "Basil, where do you stand on this fight over the
images?"

"For them, I suppose," Argyros said after a moment's
hesitation. "I'm no Jew, to say an icon is a graven image.
And since it was a breaker of images (is 'iconoclast' a
word?) who started the troubles here, I can't look kindly on
their case—all the more so because I had my head split in the
brawl."

"I happen to agree with you," Lakhanodrakon said. "I
respect the tradition of the church, and icons have been a

part of it for many, many years. Still, you'll find honest men who think we're wrong. In Consistory the other day, the Count of the excubitores called icons a pagan holdover and said that was reason enough to suppress them.''

"It must have made quelling the riot interesting, if you couldn't decide which faction to put down,'' Argyros said dryly.

The Master of Offices rolled his eyes. ''Joke all you like, but it's nothing to laugh at. Both sides can't be right: either it's proper to give reverence to icons, or it's not. The Emperor and the patriarch have to lay down the proper doctrine for the people to follow. We can't have icons destroyed here and hallowed there. One Empire, one faith.''

"Of course," Argyros nodded. "Since there can be only one true creed, everyone should follow it.'' In theory, as Lakhanodrakon had said, the whole Empire worshiped as Constantinople decreed. In fact, heresy persisted in Egypt, in Syria, in the western provinces reconquered from their German kings—Italia, Ispania, Africa, Narbonese Gallia. Only fitting to root it out wherever it sprang up.

"You have a good knowledge of the inner learning, Basil,'' Lakhanodrakon said. ''If you were going to justify the use of images in worship, how would you go about it?''

The magistrianos considered. As George Lakhanodrakon had said, he knew his theology; only in the barbarous lands of northwest Europe was such wisdom reserved for priests. He said, ''Of course the argument that an icon is a graven image falls to the ground as soon as it is made. The Pauline dispensation frees us from the rigor of the Jewish law. I would say the chief value of images is to remind us of the holy ones they represent—Christ, the Virgin, or a saint. When we look at an icon, we contemplate the figure behind the portrait. Also, icons teach the truths of the faith to those who cannot read Scripture.''

The Master of Offices had been jotting down notes. "That last is a good point; I don't recall it coming up in any of the council meetings I've attended. I'll pass it on to the patriarch. Have no fear, I'll mention whose suggestion it was.''

"You're very kind, your illustriousness," Argyros said, and meant it. Most imperial officers would have appropriated both the idea and the credit that went with it. Then the import of what Lakhanodrakon had said hit him. "The patriarch is collecting arguments in favor of icons?"

"Sharp as usual, aren't you?" The Master of Offices was smiling. "Yes, so he is, to be ready in case of need. One of the options raised for putting an end to this quarrel over images is for the Emperor to convene an ecumenical council."

Argyros whistled, soft and low. "They're taking it as seriously as that, then?" Ecumenical councils were watersheds in the history of the church; in the thousand years since Constantine the Great, only nine had been called. Groups that refused to accept their decrees passed into heresy: notably the Nestorians of Syria, with their undue emphasis on Christ's humanity; and the Monophysites, strong in Egypt and all through the Roman east, when the council of Chalcedon would not accept the way they overstressed His divinity.

"I think the Emperor was going to wait and see if things blew over," Lakhanodrakon said, "until last night. That was when the grand logothete called the city prefect a filthy pagan-minded heretic and broke a crystal decanter over his head."

"Oh, my," the magistrianos said, blinking.

"Yes. Officially, of course, the prefect fell down a flight of stairs, and don't forget it—the saints have mercy on you if you go around telling the other tale. But it was about then that Nikephoros decided a council might not be out of place."

"When will the order summoning the bishops go out?" Argyros asked.

"Soon, I think. It's late July now—or has August started yet? In any case, fall will be starting by the time prelates in places like Carthage and Rome and Ispania receive the call. By then it will be too late for them to travel—no ships will be sailing till spring. I imagine the synod will be held then."

"Good. We'll have some time to prepare a solid theological case."

"Among other preparations," the Master of Offices said with a grin. Ecumenical councils were as much exercises in practical politics as they were religious disputes. Most of the time, they ran as the Emperors who called them wanted them to. Nikephoros III was a thorough ruler; he would have no intention of letting this one go wrong.

Lakhanodrakon went on, "Write me a statement giving your views on the icons; let me have it some time in the next couple of weeks. I'll convey it to the patriarch, as I said. Don't expect any immediate acknowledgment, though—it won't be the only document he's getting, I'm sure."

"I daresay." Everyone in the city who fancied himself a theologian—which meant, for all practical purposes, everyone in the city who could write—would be sending impassioned missives to the patriarchal residence attached to Hagia Sophia. Most of them, as was the way of such things, would end up in braziers or have their ink scraped off so they could be reused.

Lakhanodrakon made a gesture of dismissal, saying, "I'll look forward to seeing that commentary of yours." Argyros bowed his way out, then hotfooted it over to the library in Hagia Sophia: best to start taking notes before half the tomes he needed disappeared.

THE MAGISTRIANOS submitted his long memorandum on the icons to George Lakhanodrakon. He was proud of the document, which he had thickly studded with quotations from such venerable authorities as St. John Chrysostom, St. Ambrose of Milan, St. Sophronios of Jerusalem, St. Athanasios of Alexandria, and the church historian Eusebios, who had been at the very first ecumenical council, the one Constantine had convened at Nikaia.

While he worked and afterward, reports of strife over the images kept coming into Constantinople. A riot convulsed Ephesos, with half the town burnt. Several monasteries were sacked outside of Tarsos when the monks refused to yield up their icons. The Jewish quarter of Neaplis in Italia was plundered because the Neaplitans blamed the Jews, who rejected images for their own reasons, for stirring up iconoclasm in the first place.

It was almost a relief when the stormy season set in and news grew harder to acquire. One of the last grain ships from Alexandria brought word that Arsakios, the patriarch of that city, had convened a local synod there to try to settle the issue for his ecclesiastical province. No one on the big merchantman knew how the synod had come out; it had still been going on when they sailed.

Argyros wondered how much the gathering could accomplish. The patriarchate of Alexandria leaned over backward to avoid antagonizing the Monophysites, who were probably a majority in Egypt, and the Monophysites had always opposed images. As their name implied, they felt Christ had but one nature, the divine, after the Incarnation, with His humanity entirely subsumed. And since God by definition was uncircumscribable, the Monophysites rejected all attempts to portray Christ.

Come to think of it, the magistrianos remembered, that was the line the Egyptian monk Sasopis had taken. Despite Argyros's best efforts, the magistrianos thought gloomily, he was halfway across the Empire by now, spreading trouble as he wandered from town to town.

As winter wore on, Argyros forgot about Sasopis. The Master of Offices shared responsibility with the patriarch for lodging the bishops during the upcoming council, for one of his duties was seeing to embassies that came to Constantinople. George Lakhanodrakon passed the job on to Argyros, who went through the city checking on available cells in monasteries and on grander quarters for the more important or more luxury-minded prelates.

"After all this running about, the council itself will be a relief," he told the Master of Offices one cold February day.

"That's as it should be," Lakhanodrakon replied calmly. "Let the country bumpkins from Sicily or Rome see the proper way to do things. If everything is planned well in advance, it will go properly when the crucial moment comes and there's no more time for planning."

"You're not the one getting blisters," Argyros muttered, too low for his boss to hear. But that was unfair, and he knew it. Lakhanodrakon was doing enough work for two men, each half his age.

The first bishops began arriving in mid-April, a bit earlier than the Master of Offices had expected. Thanks to his elaborate preparations, though, they were housed without difficulty.

There were representatives from all five patriarchates: that of Constantinople, of course, and Antioch, Jerusalem, Rome, and Alexandria. The Alexandrian contingent, led by Arsakios himself, was the last sizable one to reach the imperial capital. The Egyptians virtually took over the monastery of Stoudios, in the southwestern part of the city. They behaved as if it were a citadel under siege, not a place of worship and contemplation. Muscular monks armed with very stout walkingsticks constantly patrolled the grounds, glowering at passersby.

"Egyptians!" Lakhanodrakon snorted when that was reported to him. "They always act as though they think it would pollute them to have anything to do with anyone else."

"Yes, sir," Argyros said, but inside he wondered. He had watched Arsakios disembarking from his ship. The patriarch of Alexandria had been friendly enough then, distributing blessings and coppers among the longshoremen and other dock laborers at the Theodosian harbor. The grin on his foxily handsome face, in fact, had been enough to rouse the magistrianos's ever-ready suspicions.

But diligent checking had turned up nothing more incriminating than the fact that Arsakios had brought a woman with him. If only the priests who held to their vows of celibacy were allowed to take part in the ecumenical council, Argyros thought, Nikephoros could hold it in St. Mouamet's little church, not Hagia Sophia. Nevertheless, he filed the information away. No telling when a hint of scandal might come in handy.

The Emperor and his courtiers gathered in the Augusteion to greet the assembled prelates before they went into the great church and called the council to order. Argyros stood in the first rank of the magistrianoi, behind George Lakhanodrakon, whose position of honor was at the left hand of Nikephoros III's seat.

Nikephoros III, Autocrat and Emperor of the Romans, rose from his portable throne and bowed to the hundreds of clerics in the square. They in their turn performed the proskynesis before him, going down to their knees and then their bellies as they prostrated themselves. Sunlight flashed from cloth-of-gold and pearls, shimmered off watered silks, was drunk by plain black wool.

After the bishops, priests, and monks had acknowledged the Emperor's sovereignty as vicegerent of God on earth, most of Nikephoros's courtiers went back to their duties. Several magistrianoi, however, Argyros among them, accompanied Lakhanodrakon as they followed Nikephoros into Hagia Sophia. The churchmen came after them.

The atrium of the great church was magnificent enough, with its forest of marble columns, their acanthus capitals bound with gilded brass. Then the clerics passed through the exonarthex into the nave, and Argyros heard gasps. He smiled to himself. Throughout the Empire, churches were modeled after Hagia Sophia. The models and their prototype, however, were not identical.

For one thing, Hagia Sophia was huge. Counting the side aisles, the open space under the dome was about eighty yards square; that dome itself reached sixty yards above the floor. With forty-two windows all around the base admitting bright beams of light, the golden mosaic and cross in the dome seemed to float above the rest of the church, as if, as Prokopios had written, it were suspended on a chain from the sky.

Justinian had lavished the wealth of the entire Empire on the church. Rare marble and other stone faced the columns and walls: white-veined black from the Bosporos, two shades of green from Hellas, porphyry out of Egypt, yellow marble from Libya, red and white marble from Isauria, multicolored stone from Phrygia. All the lamps were silver.

Before the altar, itself of solid gold, stood the iconstasis with its images of Christ, the Virgin, and the Apostles. Another portrait of Christ ornamented the crimson altar curtain; He was flanked by Paul and Mary. It hurt Argyros to think of destroying such beauty, but he heard some of the bishops hiss when they saw the icons and other divine images.

The Emperor ascended the pulpit. His courtiers stayed inconspicuously in one of the side aisles, while the churchmen gathered in the central worship area.

Nikephoros III waited for silence. He was the one man recognizable to everyone in the empire, for his features appeared on every coin, gold, silver, or copper. He was between Argyros and Lakhanodrakon in age and, like the Master of Offices, had the heavy features and strong nose associated with Armenian blood.

"Dissension, friends, is the worst enemy our holy church knows," Nikephoros declared. His words echoed in the church; he was a soldier-Emperor, used to pitching his voice to carry on the field. He went on, "When this controversy over images came to our notice, we ached in our soul; it is unbecoming for religious men to be in discord, as you are properly men of peace. Thus we have summoned you together for this council. Examine the reasons behind your turmoil, and with the help of the Holy Spirit seek an end to it, and to the evil designs of Satan, who through envy creates the disturbances among you. Hear now the words of Constantinople's holy patriarch Eutropios, who shall convey to you the thoughts that have occurred to us concerning the propriety of icons."

Eutropios began his statement, which Nikephoros and his officials intended as the point of departure for the council. Argyros was pleased to hear two or three phrases from his own little treatise in the patriarch's oration.

The clerics gave Eutropios varying amounts of attention. Many of those from the lands close to Constantinople—from the Balkans or western Asia Minor—were already familiar with his arguments. The western bishops, those under the jurisdiction of the bishop of Rome, could be

expected to follow along. Ever since Constans II had installed his own candidate on the Roman patriarchal throne
to replace the pope who fled over the Alps to the Franks,
Rome remained subservient to Constantinople.

The clerics about whom Argyros worried came from the
three eastern patriarchates. Even aside from the heretical
tendencies in their sees, the prelates of Alexandria, Antioch, and Jerusalem still looked on Constantinople as an
upstart town a thousand years after its founding.

The magistrianos stiffened. "Look there," he hissed to
George Lakhanodrakon, pointing into the delegation of
Arsakios of Alexandria. "That's Sasopis! The skinny fel-
low there, next to the bishop in the green robe."

"Do the best you can to keep an eye on him," the Master
of Offices said. "It wouldn't do to drag him out of the
opening session of the council in chains."

"No," Argyros admitted reluctantly. "But what's he
doing with Arsakios? Alexandria's already had its synod on
icons." He stopped. "What did that synod decide?"

"I don't recall hearing," Lakhanodrakon said. He ran his
hands over his bald pate, adding in a worried tone, "We're
about to find out, I think."

Indeed, Eutropios was running down: "Just as Christ's
two natures are linked by a single will, may everyone be
joined in concord at the close of our discussions here."

The amen resounded through the great church. Before its
echoes had died away, Arsakios stepped forward, his hand
upraised. "May I add a few words to your brilliant discus-
sion of the issues, your holiness?"

"Er, yes, go ahead," Eutropios said nervously. Like
everyone else, he knew the patriarch of Alexandria was a
better theologian than he. Emperors tended to pick the prelates with whom they worked most closely for pliability
rather than brains.

"Thank you." Arsakios bowed with exquisite politeness.
Despite a vanishing trace of Egyptian accent in his Greek,
his smooth tenor was an instrument he played masterfully.
"Your address covered many of the points I wished to make,

thus enabling me to achieve the virtue of brevity." Stifled cheers rose here and there; Arsakios ignored them.

He went on, "I am not quite certain, for example, your holiness, of your conception of the relationship between this present dispute over images and previous disagreements over how Christ's humanity and divinity coexist."

"I do not see that there is a relationship," Eutropios said cautiously. Argyros frowned; he did not see it either.

But Arsakios raised an eyebrow in feigned disbelief. "But is not an icon of our Lord a statement of christology in and of itself?"

"The man's mad," Lakhanodrakon whispered to Argyros at the same time as Eutropios demanded, "In what way?" of Arsakios.

And the patriarch of Alexandria, smiling, sank the barb: "Let me state it in the form of questions: What does an image of Christ portray? If it depicts His human nature alone, is this not separating His humanity from His divinity, as the heretic Nestorians do? But if it portrays His divinity, does it not attempt both to circumscribe what may not be circumscribed and to subordinate His humanity altogether, in a Monophysite fashion? In either case, then, the validity of the use of images comes into question, does it not? So, at least, decided the synod held in my city this past fall." With another elegant bow, he gave the floor back to his brother of Constantinople.

Eutropios gaped at him in dismay. Nikephoros III scowled from his high seat, but he could do little, autocrat though he was. The Egyptian's attack on the icons had been perfectly respectful and raised an important question Eutropios's opening statement had left untouched.

The prelates from the three eastern patriarchates also realized that. They crowded round Arsakios, showering him with congratulations. Eutropios was no great theologian, but he did have some political sense. "I declare this first session of the council adjourned!" he cried.

His own supporters left quickly and quietly. The Emperor stalked off toward the private passageway that led back to the palaces. No sooner had he disappeared than the clerics still crowding the floor of Hagia Sophia raised an exultant shout: "We've won! We've won!"

"Arrogant devils, aren't they?" Lakhanodrakon said indignantly.

"Hmm?" A glimpse of motion behind the screen of the second-story women's gallery had distracted Argyros. For a moment he saw a pair of dark, avid eyes peering down through the filigreework at the churchmen below. He wondered to whom they belonged. The Emperor's wife and mistress were both blue-eyed blondes; Nikephoros had a weakness for fair women. In any case, neither Martina nor Zoe was devout. The magistrianos scratched his head. He had the nagging feeling that barely seen face was familiar.

Shrugging, he gave it up and accompanied the Master of Offices out of the great church. The Augusteion was crowded with people wondering how the first day of the council had gone. Some of Arsakios's monks harangued the Constantinopolitans: "Anathema to the worship of lifeless wood and paint! Destruction to idolatry!"

When an iconophile took violent exception to the anathemas hurled at him, a monk ducked under his wild swing and hit him in the pit of the stomach with his staff. The evasion and counter showed soldierly skill. Truly Arsakios had come ready for anything.

"His imperial majesty is not going to be pleased at the prospect of a council out of control," the Master of Offices said.

"No," Argyros agreed, "but what if the Alexandrians are right?" His head was still spinning from the subtlety of their argument: to justify the use of images now, somehow the Emperor's theologians would have to steer between the Scylla of Monophysitism and the Charybdis of the Nestorian heresy.

Lakhanodrakon looked at him reproachfully. "Not you, too?"

"The Holy Spirit will guide the assembled fathers to the truth," the magistrianos said confidently. Being a veteran of years of bureaucratic infighting, he added, "Of course, we may have to help things along a bit."

THE SUMMONS to return to Hagia Sophia, or rather to the residence of the patriarch, which was attached to it, woke Argyros in the middle of the night. "What is it?" he asked, yawning in the face of the messenger.

"A gathering of scholars seeking to refute Arsakios," the man replied. He was one of Lakhanodrakon's servants. "I am to tell you that your earlier exposition was clever enough to make Eutropios hope you can help find a way out of our present difficulty."

Eutropios was an amiable nonentity who barely knew Argyros existed. Like the fellow standing in front of the magistrianos, the order came from the Master of Offices. That made it no less flattering. Rubbing his eyes once more, Argyros dressed quickly and followed the messenger, who had a linkbearer waiting outside.

"Careful here," the magistrianos warned, steering them around a pothole in the street in front of the house of his neighbor Theognostos, who was a senior member of the bakers' guild.

"That should be filled in," Lakhanodrakon's servant said. "I almost fell into it a few minutes ago."

On the way to the great church, they passed the hostel where the archbishop of Thessalonike was staying. The archbishop supported the use of icons. A couple of dozen of Arsakios's monks stood in the street, ringing cowbells and chanting, "Bugger the images! Bugger the images!" A few more, their throats tired from such work, sat around a bonfire, passing a jar of wine from one to the next.

"They'll make no friends that way," Lakhanodrakon's man observed.

"No, but they may wear down their foes," Argyros said.

The monk's chant broke off as someone hurled a chamber-pot at them from a second-story window. The ones befouled shouted curses that made their previous vulgar chant sound genteel by comparison.

"Go on ahead," Argyros told his companions. "I'll catch up soon." They stared at him as if he were a madman, but went after a little argument, the linkbearer gladly, the servant with misgivings. He yielded only when Argyros pulled rank.

Whistling, the magistrianos strode up to the men by the bonfire and said cheerily, "Down with the icons! How about a swallow of wine for a thirsty man?"

One of the monks rose, none too steadily, and handed him the jug. "Down with the filthy icons it is," he said. Showing decayed teeth, he opened his mouth in a tremendous yawn.

"Wearing work, going to the council of the day and harassing the damned iconodule in there by night," Argyros said.

The monk yawned again. "Ah, well, we're just little fellows out here. Arsakios and his bishops are sleeping sound, but we're caterwauling for all the head picture-lovers tonight, and we'll serenade 'em again tomorrow, and the next day, and as long as it takes to bring home the truth."

"A clever man, Arsakios, to come up with such a scheme," the magistrianos said.

"Here, give me a slug of that," the monk said. His throat worked. He wiped his mouth with the sleeve of his black robe, then chuckled. "Aye, Arsakios'll sleep sound tonight, with that doxy of his to warm his bedding."

"Doxy?" Argyros prodded.

The monk made curving motions with his hands. "Can't fault his holiness's taste, that's certain. If you're going to sin, it may as well be sweet, says I. I don't think she's an Egyptian wench, from her accent, though he's had her since last summer, the lucky dog."

That was mildly interesting. "What's her name?" the magistrianos asked.

"I forget," the monk said. "She's no interest in the likes of me, I can tell you that, not that she doesn't have Arsakios wrapped around her finger." *Finger* was not quite what he said. Pausing to hiccup, he went on, "She's no fool herself, though; I give her that. In fact, someone told me this night's vigil was her plan."

"You don't say." A formidable female indeed, Argyros thought. He rose from his squat, stretched, and said, "I must be off. Keep this stinking image-worshiper wide-eyed till dawn, and thanks for the wine.''

"Always happy to help an honest pious man." The monk smacked himself in the forehead with the heel of his hand. More to himself than to Argyros, he exclaimed, "Mirrane, that's what the hussy calls herself.''

It took all the magistrianos's training to hold his face and walk steady. Mirrane had come unpleasantly close to killing him in Daras; despite her sex, she was a top agent of Persia. And Argyros could also well understand how she had gained Arsakios's favor.

Argyros's fists clenched as he hurried toward Hagia Sophia. The Persians loved to stir up religious dissension in the Roman Empire: if the Romans battled among themselves, it could only profit their rival. And Mirrane had been playing that very game in Daras, rousing the local heretics against the orthodox faith.

Now, though, she was embarking on a far more dangerous course. This quarrel over images threatened to tear all the eastern provinces away and to set faction against faction through the rest of the Empire.

The magistrianos cursed. Exposing the furor over iconoclasm as a Persian plot would not help. Arsakios, whether inspired by Satan or more likely by Mirrane, had raised a real, thorny theological point, and no doubt had more in his arsenal. The only way to bring back religious peace would be to show he was in error. That made the conclave in the patriarchal residence all the more vital.

There were no shouting monks in the square of the Augusteion. Their din had disturbed not only the patriarch but also the Emperor, and the imperial guards had driven them off. Things inside the patriarch's apartments were quite hectic enough without them. The distinguished theologians and scholars there were going at one another like a kettle of crabs.

"You idiot!" an archbishop with a long white beard shouted at an abbot. "St. Basil clearly states that—''

"Don't tell me, show me!" the abbot interrupted. "I wouldn't take your word the sun was shining without looking outside. Show me the text!"

"Someone's filched the codex!" the archbishop howled in frustration. The abbot laughed and snapped his fingers in the other man's face. Just then, someone pulled someone else's hair, and abbot and archbishop alike rushed to separate the two combatants, both of whom were close to seventy. Eutropios, who was supposed to be presiding over the gathering, looked as though he wanted to hide.

Argyros unobtrusively made his way to an empty chair and spent the next several minutes listening, as if he were trying to pick up gossip at a waterfront tavern. As sometimes unfortunately happens with brilliant men, the meeting had got sidetracked. Here someone was declaring that the writings of the church fathers obviously sanctioned images; there somebody else announced that images were not consubstantial with their prototypes. It was all fascinating, and probably true, and none of it, sadly, the least bit relevant.

Intellectually the magistrianos did not belong in such company, and knew it. But he did have a feel for what was important. To the man next to him, he said, "God became man in the person of Jesus Christ."

"Amen," the man said. He wore the pearl-ornamented robes of an archbishop. "And God made the world in seven days. What of it?" The nightlong wrangling had left him cranky.

The magistrianos felt himself flush. He was groping after a concept and could not pin it down. Maybe talk would help, even if it did make the archbishop take him for a simpleton. He went on, "In the Incarnation, the Word—the divine Logos—took flesh."

"And the immaterial became material," the archbishop echoed. "There, you see, whoever you are, I can spout platitudes too."

Argyros refused to let himself be baited. Without meaning to, the archbishop had helped him clarify his thoughts. He said, "Before the Incarnation, God was only immaterial; it would have been blasphemous to try to depict Him. That, no doubt, is why the Old Testament forbade graven images."

"Yes, and the foolish Jews still keep to that law, waiting for the Messiah and not knowing He has already come," the archbishop said. He did not sound so scornful now, only contemptuous of the ignorant, stubborn Hebrews.

"But for us Christians—" Argyros began.

Excitement flamed on the archbishop's face. He broke in, "Yes, by all the saints! For us Christians, since God has appeared among us and become a part of history, we can portray His human form!"

"To say otherwise would be to deny the validity of the Incarnation."

"It would! It would!" The archbishop shot from his chair as if he had sat on a pin. His shout filled the room: "I have it!" Almost word for word, he bellowed out the chain of thought Argyros had developed.

There was silence for half a minute when he was through. Then the prelates and savants crowded round the archbishop, slapping his back and showering him with congratulations. Eutropios kissed him on both cheeks. The patriarch was fairly babbling in his relief; he had been quivering at the prospect of having to report failure to Nikephoros.

"Wine!" he shouted to a servant. "Wine for everyone!" Under his breath, Argyros heard him mutter, "Saved from Kherson!" The monastery at Kherson, on the peninsula that jutted into the Black Sea from the north, was the bleakest place of exile in the Empire. Argyros had been to the god-forsaken town in his younger days. No wonder poor Eutropios was nervous, he thought.

The magistrianos slipped out of the patriarchal residence while the celebration was just getting started. He did his best to fight down his anger at the archbishop's stealing his ideas. No way to claim them back now. Even if he did stand well with the Master of Offices, that meant little to the ecclesiastics he had left.

Perhaps it was just as well, he thought. Arsakios and the other iconoclasts would be more likely to take seriously a proposal put forward by a churchman than one that came from an official of the imperial government.

The racket under the archbishop of Thessalonike's window was still going on. The miserable archbishop undoubtedly wished he was back conducting services at the church of St. Demetrios in his hometown. Argyros went a couple of blocks out of his way, not wanting anything further to do with the vociferous Egyptian monks.

The magistrianos heard a low whistle from the direction of the hostel. A woman's voice, low and throaty, said, "There he is." Her Greek had a Persian flavor.

"Mirrane?" he called.

"Indeed, Basil. Did I not say, back in Daras, we would meet again?" Then, to her companions, she issued a sharp command: "Get him!"

The slap of their bare feet said they were Arsakios's monks. They came dashing down the narrow street toward Argyros. Some held torches to light their way, while others brandished clubs. "Heretic!" they shouted. "Worshiper of lifeless wood and pigments!"

Argyros turned and fled. A Franco-Saxon might have taken pride in a glorious fight against overwhelming odds; he was a sensible Roman, and saw no point in enduring a beating he did not have to. A proverb survived from pagan days: "Even Herakles can't fight two."

As he ran, he wondered how Mirrane had known he was coming. She must have stopped to see how her chanters were doing and talked with the one of whom he had been asking questions. If he had come back the same way he had gone, he would have fallen into her hands. As it was, she had a gift for putting him in difficult spots.

It had been worse in Daras, though. Now he was on the streets of his own city. He knew them; his pursuers did not. If they were going to catch him, they would have to work at it.

He darted through an alleyway that stank of rotten fish, turned sharply left and then right. He paused to catch his breath. Behind him he heard the monks arguing in Greek and hissing Coptic. "Split up! We'll find him!" one of them shouted.

Moving more quietly now, the magistrianos came to the mouth of a blind alley. He picked up half a brick and flung it at the wall that blocked the way, perhaps twenty paces down. It hit with a resounding crash. "Mother of God, what was that?" a woman cried from a second-story bedroom. Several dogs yapped frantically.

"There he is!" The shout came from three directions at once, but none of the monks sounded close. Argyros hurried down a lane that ended about three minutes' walk from his home.

At the first cross street, he almost bumped into a monk. It was hard to say which was the more surprised. But the monk had only Mirrane's description of him. That led to a fatal second of doubt. Argyros hit him in the face, then stamped on his unshod foot. As the monk started to crumple, the magistrianos kicked him in the pit of the stomach, which not only put him out of the fight but also kept him too busy trying to breathe to be able to cry out. The whole encounter lasted only a few heartbeats.

Argyros turned onto his own street. He walked along jauntily, pleased at having escaped Mirrane's trap. She had been someone to fear in Daras, he thought, but here at the heart of the Empire all the advantage was on his side.

Thus filled with himself, he did not see the dark-cloaked figure come out of a shadowed doorway and glide after him. Nor, thinking back on it, did he really hear anything, but at the last moment he sensed the rush of air from behind. He threw himself to one side, far enough to keep the knife that should have slipped between his ribs from doing more than taking a small, hot bite out of his left arm.

He stumbled away, groping for his dagger. His foe pursued. Starlight glittered coldly off the assassin's blade. Argyros's own knife came free. He dropped into a crouch, his arms outspread, and began slowly circling to his right.

Seeing he knew what he was about, his attacker went into a like posture. They moved warily, each seeking an opening. The assassin leaped forward, stabbing up from below, underarm style. The magistrianos knocked his knife hand aside with his own left forearm, stepped in close, and thrust himself. His blow was similarly parried. Both men sprang back, resumed their circling dance.

Argyros's eyes flicked to one side. He was in front of his neighbor Theognostos's house. He took a few cautious steps backward, dragging his heel to feel at the hard-packed ground under his feet. Then he staggered and, with a groan, went to one knee.

Laughing—the first sound he had made in the whole encounter—the assassin rushed toward him, knife upraised for the easy kill. His right foot came down in the same hole the magistrianos had walked around earlier in the evening. His arms flailed as he strove for balance. Argyros lunged forward under his faltering stroke and buried his dagger into his foe's belly.

The iron scent of blood and the death-stench of suddenly loosed bowels filled the street. "Sneaky—bastard," the assassin wheezed. His eyes rolled up in his head as he fell.

Argyros approached him with caution, wondering if he was hoarding his last strength for a try at vengeance. But his assailant was truly dead, as the magistrianos found by feeling for a pulse at his ankle. He turned the man onto his back. This was no monk from Alexandria, but a Constantinopolitan street tough. Argyros knew the breed, with their half-shaven heads and puff-sleeved tunics pulled tight at the wrists by drawstrings.

Something had jingled as the man bonelessly went over. There was a well-filled purse at his belt. The magistrianos tucked it into his own beltpouch and, sighing, went to look for a guardsman.

What with explanations, formal statements, and such, Argyros did not see his bed until dawn was beginning to lighten the eastern horizon. The sun streaming through the window woke him much sooner than he wanted. He splashed cool water on his face, but that did nothing to relieve the gritty feeling in his eyes, the tiredness that made him fumble as he laced up his sandals.

He also had trouble remembering why his pouch was heavier than it should have been. Digging, he found the little leather sack he had taken from his assailant. The nomismata that rolled into his hand were smaller and thicker than the goldpieces minted in Constantinople. Instead of the familiar CONOB mintmark, they bore the legend ΑΛΕΞ, for Alexandria.

The magistrianos nodded, unsurprised. He should have figured Mirrane would have more than one string for her bow. Woman or not, she knew her business. It was unfortunate, he thought, that part of that business was getting rid of him.

THE EMPEROR attended the second session of the ecumenical council, as he had the first. This time his retinue included fewer courtiers and more imperial guardsmen. Their gilded armor and scarlet capes were hardly less splendid than the costumes of the great prelates whom they faced, impassive, over their painted shields.

The hint of force, however, did nothing to deter Arsakios. He returned to the same respectful attack he had launched against the images of the previous day. He even allowed a sardonic grin to flicker on his lips as he reiterated his theological paradox.

But his amusement slipped when Eutropios was quick to reply. The patriarch of Constantinople surreptitiously glanced down at his notes from time to time, but his presentation of the ideas hammered out only the night before was clear and lucid. George Lakhanodrakon paid him the highest compliment: "I didn't think the old fraud had it in him."

"Amazing what fear will do," Argyros agreed.

Yet anyone who had expected the patriarch of Alexandria and his followers to yield tamely to Eutropios's defense of images and their veneration was wrong. No sooner had Eutropios finished than half a dozen eastern bishops were shouting at each other for the privilege of replying.

"Why should I hear you?" Eutropios thundered from the pulpit as Nikephoros III watched. "By denying the reality

of the Incarnation, you deny Christ's perfect humanity and
brand yourself Monophysites!''

"Liar!" "Fool!" "Impious idiot!" "How can base
matter depict divine holiness?" Turmoil reigned for several
minutes as iconoclasts and iconophiles hurled abuse at one
another. The two sides went from there to shaking fists and
croziers, and seemed about to repeat on a larger scale the
squabbling that had gone on in Eutropios's apartments.

The Emperor Nikephoros uttered a low-voiced command. His bodyguards advanced two paces, their ironshod
boots clattering on the stone floor. Sudden silence fell. The
Emperor spoke: "The truth should be sought through contemplation and reason, not in this childish brawling." He
nodded to Eutropios. "Let them all speak, that errors may
be demonstrated and those who wander be returned to the
proper path."

The patriarch bowed in obedience to his master. The debate began in more orderly fashion. Argyros listened for a
while and was impressed to find that many of the points the
opponents of images raised had been anticipated the night
before. When an iconoclast bishop from Palestine, for example, claimed that icons were of the same substance as
their prototypes, the skinny little man who had thought of
that problem used elegant Aristotelean logic to deny their
consubstantiality.

Biblical quotations and texts taken from the church fathers flew like rain. After a while, Argyros regretfully tore
himself away from the argumentation and left for the Praitorion to try to catch up on the work he had neglected for
the sake of the council.

Arsakios's monks were very much in evidence on his short
walk down the Mese. During the day, they scattered through
the city to preach the dogmas of iconoclasm to whoever
would listen. The magistrianos passed no fewer than three,
each with a good-sized crowd around him.

"Do you want to be Monophysites?" the first monk
shouted to his audience.

"No!" "Of course not!" "Never!" "Dig up the Monophysites' bones!"

"Do you want to be Nestorians?"

The same cries of rejection came from the crowd.

"Then cast aside the pernicious, lying images you wrongly reverence!"

Some of his listeners gave back catcalls and hisses, but most looked thoughtful. A couple of hundred yards down the street, another Egyptian was preaching the same message in almost identical words. It was Argyros's turn for thought, mostly about the organization that implied. He suspected Mirrane's hand there; she had been extremely efficient in her placard campaign at Daras. The clergy of Constantinople far outnumbered Arsakios's determined band, but they were not prepared for such disciplined assault on their beliefs. By the time they realized the danger, it might be too late.

Full of such gloomy musings, the magistrianos climbed the stairs to his office. To his surprise, his dour secretary greeted him with enthusiasm. "How now, Anthimos?" he asked, bemused.

"If you're really back at it, maybe I'll be able to catch up on my own work for a change," his secretary said.

"Ah." That, sadly, was a reason altogether in accord with Anthimos's nature. Still, the warmth of the secretary's first response left Argyros more effusive than he usually would have been. He gossiped on about the proceedings of the ecumenical council; Anthimos, a typical Constantinopolitan, listened avidly.

His long, narrow face froze in disapproving lines as the magistrianos described the battalion of monks harassing their opponents by night and advancing their own cause by day. "They'll pay for their impudence in the next world," he predicted with grim relish.

"That's as may be," Argyros said, "but they're a damnable nuisance in this one. What happens if the council ends up deciding the icons are proper and the city mob tears Hagia Sophia down around its ears because they've decided the images are traps of Satan to drag them down to hell?"

Anthimos clucked distressfully. "Our own priests and monks should settle these upstart Egyptians."

"So they should, but will they? Most especially, will they in time, before the city gets convinced iconoclasm is right?" Argyros explained his pessimistic reasoning as he had walked from the great church.

"But there are many more clerics native to Constantinople than the Alexandrian has brought," Anthimos protested. "They should be able to vanquish them in debate by sheer weight of numbers, if in no other way."

"But too many keep silent." Argyros paused. "Sheer weight of numbers," he echoed. His voice was dreamy, his eyes far away.

"Sir?" Anthimos said nervously, after the magistrianos had stayed absolutely still for three solid minutes. If Argyros heard, he gave no sign.

Another little while went by before he stirred. When at last he did, it was into a blur of activity that made his secretary jump in alarm. "What are you loafing there for?" Argyros snapped unfairly. "Get me ten thousand sheets of papyrus—get it out of storage, beg it, or borrow it from anyone who has it, but get it. No—go to Lakhanodrakon first; get a letter of authorization from him. That way you won't have arguments. When you've brought the papyrus back, round up fifty men. Try to get them from all parts of the city. Tell them to come here tomorrow morning; tell them it's three miliaresia for every man. The prospect of silverpieces should get their attention. Do you have all that?"

"No," Anthimos said; he found the magistrianos worse as King Stork than King Log. "But it's to do with those damned clay lumps of yours, isn't it?"

"With the archetypes, yes," Argyros said impatiently. "By the Virgin, we'll see who shouts down whom! Now, here's what I told you—" Only slightly slower than in his outburst of a moment before, he repeated his orders to Anthimos, ticking off points one by one on his fingers. This time, his secretary scrawled shorthand notes, his pen racing to keep up with Argyros's thought.

"Better make it a hundred men," the magistrianos said. "Some won't show up. And on your way to the Master of Offices, stop at the shop of Stavrakios the potter and send him to me."

"I'll do whatever you say, as long as you don't set me to spelling words backward and upside down," Anthimos declared.

"I won't, I promise," the magistrianos said. He was still burning with urgency. "Go on! Go on!"

Anthimos had hardly slammed the door behind him before Argyros was setting a square metal frame on an iron pan and painting the surface of the pan with glue. On shelves beside his desk he kept jars of clay archetypes.

Images again, he thought. If the Egyptian monks had abhorred them before, they would really hate them soon.

He was still composing the text of his message when someone tapped on the door. "Come in," he called, and Stavrakios did. He was surprised the potter had got there so fast; Anthimos must have headed for his shop on the dead run.

"What can I do for you today, sir?" Stavrakios asked. He was a stocky man of about Argyros's age, with open, intelligent features and the hands of an artist: large, long-fingered, delicate. Those hands, and the native wit guiding them, made him the perfect man to produce the molds that in turn shaped the archetypes in clay.

"I want a set of archetypes five times the usual size of our letters," the magistrianos said, hastily adding, "I don't mean I want the blocks five times as tall. I want them the same height as the rest. I just want the letters five times as big, so people can read them at a distance."

"I understand," Stavrakios said at once. He tugged his beard in thought. "You won't be able to get much of a message on your sheet with letters that size."

"I realize that," Argyros said, nodding in respect for the potter's quick thinking. "I just need one line, to draw people's attention. The rest of the page will be made from regular archetypes."

"Ah. That's all right, then." Stavrakios considered. "If you'll tell me the one line, I can make it as a single unit. That will be faster than doing the mold for each new archetype by itself. From what your secretary said, or what I understood of it through his panting, you'll want this as fast as I can make it."

Argyros nodded and told Stavrakios what he needed. The potter, a pious man, crossed himself. "Well, of course He did. Is there anything more? No? Then I'm off. I'll bring you the line directly it's done."

"That's splendid, Stavrakios," the magistrianos said gratefully. The potter left. Argyros went back to composing, setting letters in the frame one by one. Every so often he would spot an error or come up with a better idea and have to pull a few archetypes—once, a whole line—out of the glue, which was starting to get tacky.

A commotion on the stairs gave him an excuse to stop. He stepped out of his office and was almost run down by a stream of workmen carrying boxes. "Where do you want these, pal?" the one in front asked.

"In there," he said weakly, pointing. He had worked with papyrus in lots of a few hundred sheets at a time. He had never thought about how much room ten thousand sheets would require. They ended up taking over his office. When Anthimos got back, Argyros congratulated him on a job well done and sent him out again for more ink.

Then it was just a matter of waiting for Stavrakios. It was late afternoon when the potter came in, carrying a bundle wrapped in several thicknesses of cloth. "Fresh from the kiln and still hot," he said, walking crab-fashion between the mountains of boxes to hand his prize to the magistrianos.

"Let me undo the swaddling clothes here," Argyros said. Thanks to the potter's warning, he left cloth between the new-fired clay and his fingers. "Oh yes, very fine. People should be able to read that a block away. I'd say you've earned yourself a nomisma, Stavrakios."

"For this little thing? You're crazy," the potter said, but he made the coin disappear.

The magistrianos set the big line of text in the space he had reserved for it at the top of the frame. He took a flat board and laid it over his composition to force all the letters down to exactly the same level. When he was satisfied, he inked a paintbrush and ran it over the letters, gently pressed a sheet of papyrus down on them. After reading the result, he used a tweezer to pluck out a couple of improper letters and insert replacements. Then he lit a brazier. Once it was hot, he put the frame and tray on a rack above it to dry the glue and lock the letters in their places.

He used the cloths Stavrakios had brought to remove the tray and frame from the brazier and to protect his desktop from the hot metal. As soon as they were cool, he inked the letters, imprinted a piece of parchment, set it to one side, plied the inky brush again.

Ink, press, set aside; ink, press, set aside. His world narrowed to the brush, the tray and frame full of letters, the box of papyrus from which he was pulling sheets. When he emptied a box, he would fill it with imprinted papyri and go on to the next one. That was the only break in the routine consuming him.

After some eternal time, he realized it was too dark to see the letters in front of him. He also realized he was cramped and hungry. He went out and bought a chunk of bread, some goat's-milk cheese, and a cup of wine from a little eatery near the Praitorion. Then, sighing, he went back to his office, lit a lamp, and got back to work.

A half-moon rose in the southeast over Hagia Sophia, so it had to be close to midnight. The magistrianos was a bit more than halfway done. He labored on, steady as a waterwheel, only pausing to yawn. He had not had much sleep the night before, and it did not look as though he would get much tonight.

Darkness still ruled the city when he finally finished, but by the stars he could see through the window it would not last long. He filled the last box with papyri and set it to one side. Then he sat down to rest, just for a moment.

Anthimos's voice woke him: "Sir?"

He roused with a start, crying, "Nails! St. Andreas preserve us, I forgot nails!"

His secretary held up a jingling leather sack. "I have them. There are more downstairs, along with the men I hired, or as many of them as showed up. They can use stones or bricks for hammers."

"Excellent, excellent." When Argyros rose, his abused shoulders gave twin creaks of protest. He followed his secretary out to the Mese, where a crowd of men waited. Most of them were raggedly dressed. "First things first," the magistrianos said, fighting back a yawn. "Let's have some of you come up with me and haul some boxes down here."

A dozen men went upstairs with him. "First time I been in *this* part o' the building," one said. Several more chuckled: along with its offices, the Praitorion also served as a prison.

Once the papyri were downstairs, the magistrianos distributed them among the men Anthimos had assembled, then gave his instructions: "Post these in prominent spots—at street corners, on tavern doors if you like. But don't go in the taverns—not till you're done."

That got a laugh, as he had expected. He went on, "I'll give you one miliaresion now, and two more when you're done. And don't think you can chuck your share of the work down the nearest privy and get paid for doing nothing, either. Someone will have an eye on you all the time, sure as I'm a magistrianos." He was lying through his teeth, but the men looked fearful, and one or two of them disappointed. As secret agents, magistrianoi had a reputation for owning all sorts of unpleasant—possibly unnatural—abilities.

His gang of men trooped off; before long, he heard the first sounds of pounding. This time he could not hold back his yawn. He said, "Anthimos, pay them as they come back. I can't stay awake any longer. I'm going back to my office to sleep; I don't think I'd make it home. Wake me in the early afternoon, would you?"

"Whatever you say," Anthimos agreed dolefully.

Argyros thought he could have slept in the fiery furnace prepared for Shadrach, Meshach, and Abednego. By the time Anthimos shook him awake, his office was a fair approximation of it, with Constantinople's summer mugginess only making things worse. The magistrianos wiped sweat from his face with his sleeve.

"Like Satan," he told Anthimos, "I am going up and down in the city, to see how my work has turned out."

He had walked only twenty paces when he saw his first poster. Only the headline was visible above the crowd of people in front of it. Argyros was pleased at how far away he could read that message: CHRIST DIED FOR YOU.

The rest of the sheet was a boiled-down version of the argument that came from the gathering at the patriarchal residence: that once God became man too, His humanity was portrayable, and that to say otherwise was to deny the truth of the Incarnation. The broadside concluded: "Impious men have come to Constantinople to reject the images and to try to force their will on the ecumenical council the Emperor has convened. Don't let them succeed."

There was a continual low mutter around the poster. Not everyone in Constantinople, of course, could read, but close to half the men and a good fraction of the women did know how. Those who were literate passed the text on to their letterless friends and spouses.

"I don't know," a man said, scratching himself. "I don't want to be one of those accursed Nestorians the Egyptian monks go on about."

"Do you want to go to hell?" someone else demanded. "Without Christ, what are we but Satan's meat?" The people close by him nodded agreement.

"I don't know," the first man said again. "I have Christ in my heart. Why do I need an icon, if having one makes me a heretic?"

"You're a heretic now, for talking that way!" a woman screeched and threw an apple at him. That seemed to be the signal for several people to advance on the would-be-iconoclast. He fled.

Argyros smiled to himself and kept walking down the Mese. He heard one of Arsakios's monks preaching to a crowd, but now the cleric had to shout against hecklers and continually backtrack to try to defend what he was saying.

People were trickling into the Augusteion, gathering in front of the atrium of Hagia Sophia. The palace guards outside the great church looked at the growing crowd with suspicion. Here and there a guardsman hefted a spear or loosened a sword in a scabbard, readying himself for trouble.

Men and women began shouting down the Egyptian monks in the Augusteion, then raised a chant of their own: "Dig up the iconoclasts' bones! Dig up the iconoclasts' bones!" At that old Constantinopolitan riot call, all the guardsmen looked to their weapons. But the swelling crowd showed no inclination to attack. Instead, they stood and shouted, the noise rising like the tide. Argyros wondered how Arsakios, inside Hagia Sophia, enjoyed this new din.

He saw one of the monks who had accompanied the patriarch of Alexandria tear a sheet from the front of a building, hurl it to the ground, and step on it in execration. A moment later the monk was on the ground himself, taking a drubbing from several Constantinopolitans. They were shouting, "Blasphemer! Atheist!" as they pummeled him.

That night it was Arsakios who got no sleep. A throng of people ringed the monastery of Stoudios, where the Alexandrian delegation was staying. Their racket kept half the city up. It bothered Argyros not at all. He reveled in his first full night of sleep since the ecumenical council had begun.

In the morning, the Augusteion was packed even tighter than it had been the day before. The magistrianos was glad he had dressed in his most resplendent robe; the fancy outfit made people press back to let him by as he made his way toward Hagia Sophia . . . except for one young woman who clasped his hand, saying, "Bless me, your reverence!"

"First time I've ever been mistaken for an archbishop," he remarked to George Lakhanodrakon once he was inside the great church.

"I daresay," the Master of Offices chuckled. "You've been a busy lad with the archetypes, haven't you? You used so much papyrus, you'll make half the government grind to a halt."

Privately, the magistrianos could think of worse things. All he said, though, was, "I thought the situation demanded it."

"I suppose so." Lakhanodrakon shook his head in wonder. "What a curious thing: little sheets of papyrus rallying a people to a cause."

"*Lots* of little sheets of papyrus," the magistrianos pointed out. "Daras showed how words could stir a town close to rebellion. I thought they might work as well for the Empire's unity as against it, and on a larger scale than anything the Persians tried. With a new idea as powerful as the archetypes, discovering all the things they can do is as important as finding out about them in the first place."

"That's true." Lakhanodrakon was not sure he liked the notion. Then, remembering an ancient procedure, he brightened. "Caesar did something of this sort, did he not, posting a daily bulletin of events in the Forum of Rome for the people to read?"

"Yes, I—" Argyros broke off when an altarboy came trotting up and asked which of the gentlemen was Basil Argyros. "I am," the magistrianos said.

"Here, then, sir," the altarboy said, handing him a note. "The lady told me to give this to you."

Lakhanodrakon raised an eyebrow. "The lady?"

Argyros was reading. "It's not signed," he said, but he had no trouble figuring out who the lady was. The note read: "If you care to, meet me this afternoon in front of the shop of Joshua Samuel's son in the coppersmiths' quarter. Come alone. Be sure that if you are not alone, you will not see me. By the supreme god of light Ormazd I swear I shall also be alone; may I be damned to Ahriman's hell if I lie."

"An old acquaintance," he told the Master of Offices while he thought it over. He was certain he would not be able to ambush Mirrane; if she said she could escape a trap, she could. He knew her skill from Daras. What he did not know was how much trust to put in her oath. There was no stronger one a follower of Zoroaster—as most Persians were—could swear. But many so-called Christians would cheerfully invoke Father, Son, and Holy Spirit whenever it was to their advantage.

"I need to get away this afternoon," he said, making his decision. Lakhanodrakon nodded, smirking; no doubt he thought Argyros had made an assignation. Recalling Mirrane's other talents, the magistrianos half-wished it were so.

The district of the coppersmiths lay not far from the Augusteion, but it might have been a world away. Here, as nowhere else in the city, Argyros's handbills earned only a passing glance. Most of the metalworkers were Jews; Christian doctrinal disputes concerned them only if likely to lead to persecution.

Questions led Argyros to the shop Mirrane had named. Passersby eyed his fine robes with curiosity. A crone limped past, her gray hair ragged, a wine-colored birthmark disfiguring one cheek. The magistrianos waited impatiently, wondering if Mirrane had lured him here so she could work some mischief elsewhere unimpeded.

"Have I changed so much then, Basil?"

He whirled at the unexpected sound of that smooth, familiar contralto. The crone was leaning against a wall, saucily grinning his way. The sparkling brown eyes might have belonged to the woman he had known, but—

She laughed, seeing his stricken expression. Three of her teeth were black. She tapped one of them with a grimy forefinger. "It all washes off, even this. I've not aged thirty years overnight, I assure you, for which the god of light be praised."

"A good disguise," he said, giving credit where it was due and hoping his relief did not show. Beauty was too rare in the world to be wasted. That, he thought, was why he had instinctively rejected iconoclasm, all theological considerations aside. But Mirrane was too dangerous to let even remembered beauty lull him. "What sort of murderous scheme do you have planned for today, since your last two went awry?"

"None, now, I'm sorry to say," she smiled. "What would be the point? The council is already going the wrong way. Arsakios will squirm and fuss and fight through both the Old and New Testaments of your Bible, but he will lose the fight, whether or not he knows it; the Emperor and most of the church are against him. The only real hope was to raise the city mob against the icons, and that seems to have failed. ...Was it your idea, spreading those handbills far and wide?"

"Yes."

Mirrane sighed. "I thought as much. Such a pity you escaped my monks and the knifeman. I thought you might have lost your wariness, once the first attack failed."

"The second one almost did catch me napping," he admitted. He explained how he had beaten the hired killer; Mirrane grimaced in chagrin. He said, "I'm sure you would have got free of any trap I set in Ctesiphon or Ecbatana; operating on home ground is always an advantage."

It was odd, talking so with a professional from the other side. Argyros had worked many times against agents of the Persian Empire, and Mirrane against the Romans, but despite their masters' agelong rivalry, their posts gave them more in common than either had with fellow citizens.

Mirrane must have been thinking along the same lines. She said, "A shame we could not act together once, instead of against each other."

He nodded, but said, "Not likely, I fear."

"One never knows. The nomads on the northern plains are stirring, and they threaten the Roman Empire as much as Persia. Against them, we could share a common goal."

"Maybe," Argyros said for politeness's sake, though he did not believe it. He changed the subject. "What will you do now that you no longer need your liaison with Arsakios?"

"Him I'll not be sorry to leave," she said with a curl of her lip. "You were much more enjoyable, those couple of times in Daras." She chuckled as the flush mounted under his swarthy skin. She returned to his question: "I suppose I'll travel back to Persia, to see where the Grand Wazir will send me next: maybe into the Caucasus, to turn a client-king toward Ormazd and away from Christ."

"I think not," Argyros said, and leaped at her. The two of them were alone, he was certain. He was bigger, stronger, and quicker than Mirrane, and she was too great a threat to the Empire to let her leave Constantinople.

She made no move to flee. For an instant, in fact, she pressed herself against him as he seized her, and he felt the ripe body her old dirty clothes concealed. Her lips brushed his cheek; he heard her laugh softly in his ear.

Then she was fighting like a wildcat and crying, "Help! Help! This Christian seeks to ravish me!"

Men came boiling out of shops all along the street. They converged on the struggling couple, some brandishing makeshift bludgeons, others armed only with their fists. They tore Argyros away from Mirrane, shouting, "Leave her alone!" "You gentile dog, you think because you have money you can take any woman who pleases you?" "See how you like this!"

"Let go of me!" Argyros yelled, struggling against the angry coppersmiths. "I am a—" Somebody hit him in the pit of the stomach, leaving him unable to speak. Fighting on instinct alone, he grabbed a man and pulled the fellow down on top of him to protect him from the Jews' punches and kicks.

At last he managed to suck in a long, delicious lungful of air. "Stop, you fools!" he shouted from beneath his unwilling shield. "I am a magistrianos of the Emperor, making an arrest!"

The mention of his rank was enough to freeze his attackers for a moment. "It was no rape," he went on into the sudden silence. "The woman is an agent of Persia, and not even a Jew. Bring her here, and I will prove it to you. And if you help me find her, I will forget your assault on me—you were deceived."

With a grunt, Argyros got to his feet and helped up the smith who had covered him. The man was holding his ribs and groaning; he had taken a worse beating than the magistrianos. The rest of the coppersmiths scattered, some dashing this way, some that.

By then, though, Mirrane had disappeared.

THE SHAFTS OF SUNLIGHT streaming through the windows that pierced the base of Hagia Sophia's great dome were paler than they had been when the ecumenical council convened two months before. High summer was past and fall approaching; if the assembled clerics were to return to their churches this year, they would have to sail soon, before the stormy season set in.

With the rest of the court, Basil Argyros stood in the aisle, listening to the patriarch Eutropios read out the acts of the council. "Anyone who declares henceforth that an icon is a graven image, let him be anathema," the patriarch intoned.

"Let him be anathema," the ecclesiastics echoed.

"Anyone who declares henceforth that to paint an image or give reverence to an image is either Nestorian or Monophysite, let him be anathema," Eutropios said.

"Let him be anathema," the clerics agreed. Argyros glanced toward Arsakios of Alexandria, who joined in the anathema with poor grace. Only that "henceforth" preserved his orthodoxy. If it had not been conceded, however, he might have led his men into schism and more strife.

"Anyone who declares henceforth that our incarnate Lord Jesus Christ may not be depicted, let him be anathema."

"Let him be anathema."

"Anyone who declares henceforth that—" The anathemas rolled on and on. When they were finally through, Eutropios bowed his head and went on, "With the aid and intercession of the Holy Spirit, we have determined and do proclaim these the true and correct doctrines of our holy orthodox church. Anathema to any man who dares contradict them."

"Amen," said everyone in the church, prelates and courtiers together. The Emperor Nikephoros rose from his high seat, bowed to the clerics, and left the church.

"This council is now ended," Eutropios said, and let out an inconspicuous sigh of relief. As he left the pulpit, ecclesiastics began hurrying away; sailors would not put to sea in stormy weather even for archbishops.

The courtiers followed more slowly. "Once again, error is driven from the church," George Lakhanodrakon said, rubbing his large, knobby-knuckled hands in satisfaction.

"Is it?" Argyros asked with some bitterness. The Master of Offices turned to look at him sharply. He went on, "How can we have the gall to claim the Holy Spirit descended to inspire the ecumenical council? It was a Persian scheme that threw fuel on the controversy in the first place, and pamphleteering that helped swing it back toward the way the Emperor wanted it to go. Not much room for divine intervention in any of that."

"Wasn't it you who said we'd have to help the Holy Spirit along?" Lakhanodrakon reminded him. "God works through men; that is why He created them, to unfold His scheme for the world." He patted the magistrianos on the shoulder. "You were also the one who pointed out that God had to become a man to save mankind."

Both men crossed themselves. "Yes, but that was a miracle," Argyros persisted.

"Must all your miracles be showy?" the Master of Offices asked. "St. Athanasios and St. Cyril of Alexandria, if you read their writings, show themselves to be arrogant men, hungry for power. Yet the doctrines they fought for we still hold today, though the one has been dead almost a thousand years and the other close to nine hundred. Is that not something of a miracle?"

"Put that way, I suppose it is. And yet—"

"I know," Lakhanodrakon sighed. "Examined closely, any human institution is sadly imperfect; with your job, you know that better than most. Should you be shocked it's also true of the church? If you still hanker for miracles, I'll give you one: in Egypt, Palestine, and Anatolia; in Thrace and the lands by the Danube; in Italia and Carthage and Ispania, churchmen will be going home from this council all bearing the same doctrines to pass them on in their sees, and all over the Empire townsmen who will never see Constantinople, farmers who could never even imagine Constantinople, will hear the same teachings and follow them, and so will their sons and grandsons after them. If that is not a miracle, what is it?''

"It might just be good organization," Argyros said. "Those same peasants and townsmen pay their taxes to the government every year, and so will their sons and grandsons."

Lakhanodrakon frowned at his obstinacy, then gave a snort of laughter. He said, "Too damned many of them don't. And the Holy Spirit doesn't inspire tax collectors, either; of that I'm woefully certain. They have to do the best they can, the same as you and I and poor Eutropios swimming out of his depth."

"The best they can," Argyros mused. He thought it over. "That's not so bad, I suppose." He and the Master of Offices walked down the Mese toward the Praitorion. He wondered what Anthimos would have waiting for him there.

The man next to Basil Argyros in Priskos's tavern near the church of St. Mary Hodegetria took a long pull at his cup, then doubled up in a terrible coughing fit, spraying a good part of his drink over the magistrianos. *"Kyrie eleison!"* the fellow gasped: "Lord, have mercy! My throat's on fire!" He kept choking and wheezing.

Argyros's eyebrows went up in alarm. "Innkeeper! You, Priskos!" he called. "Fetch me water and an emetic, and quickly! I think this man is poisoned." He pounded the fellow on the back.

"Sir, I doubt that very much," replied Priskos, a handsome young man with a red-streaked black beard. He hurried over nonetheless, responding to the sharp command in Argyros's voice, a vestige of his tenure as an officer in the imperial army before he came to Constantinople.

"Just look at him," Argyros said, dabbing without much luck at the wet spots on his tunic. But he sounded doubtful; the man's spasms were subsiding. Not only that; several of the men in the tavern, regulars by the look of them, wore broad grins, and one was laughing out loud.

"Sorry there, pal," the coughing man said to Argyros. "It's just I never had a drink like that in all my born days. Here, let me buy you one, so you can see for yourself." He tossed a silver coin to the taverner. Argyros's eyebrow rose again; that was a two-miliaresion piece, a twelfth of a gold nomisma, and a very stiff price for a drink.

"My thanks," the magistrianos said, and repeated himself when the drink was in front of him. He eyed it suspiciously. It looked like watered wine. He smelled it. It had a faint fruity smell, not nearly so strong as wine's. He picked up the cup. The regulars were grinning again. He drank.

Mindful of what had happened to the chap next to him, he took a small sip. The stuff tasted rather like wine, more like wine than anything else, he thought. When he swallowed, though, it was as the man had said—he thought he'd poured flames down his gullet. Tears filled his eyes. Careful as usual of his dignity, he kept his visible reaction to a couple of small coughs. Everyone else in the place looked disappointed.

"That's—quite something," he said at last; anyone who knew him well would have guessed from his restrained reaction how impressed he was. He took another drink. This time he was better prepared. His eyes watered again, but he swallowed without choking. He asked the innkeeper, "What do you call this drink? And where do you get it? I've never had anything like it."

"Just what I said," the fellow next to him declared. "Why, I—" He was off on a story Argyros did not want to listen to. Anything new and interesting Argyros wanted to hear about; his fellow drinker's tale was neither.

Luckily, Priskos was proud of his new stock in trade, and eager to talk about it. "I call it *yperoinos*, sir." *Superwine* was a good name for the stuff, Argyros thought. At his nod, the innkeeper went on, "We make it in the back room of the tavern here. You see I'm an honest man—I don't tell you it comes from India or Britain."

A good thing too, Argyros said, but only to himself: I'd know you were lying. No customs men were better at their job or kept more meticulous records than the ones at the imperial capital. If anything as remarkable as this dragon's brew had entered Constantinople, word would have spread fast. The magistrianos drank some more. Warmth spread from his middle.

He finished the cup and held it out for a refill. "And one for my friend here," he added a moment later, pointing to the man who had inadvertently introduced him to the potent new drink. He fumbled in his beltpouch for the right coins. They seemed to keep dodging his fingers.

By trial and error, he found out how big a draught of superwine he could swallow without choking. The tip of his nose began to turn numb. Usually that was a sign he was getting drunk, but that could hardly be possible, not when he was just finishing his second cup. He could drink all night in a tavern and still handle himself well. Indignant at himself and at his nose, he waved to the innkeeper again.

He had not gone far into the third cup when he realized how tight he was. By then it was too late. He prided himself on being a moderate man, but the superwine had snuck up on him. The more he drank, too, the easier the stuff was to drink. Feeling most expansive, he ordered a fresh round for everyone in the place, the taverner included. Cheers rang out. He had never, he thought, drunk with such a splendid lot of fellows.

He fell asleep with a finger's width of drink still in the bottom of his cup.

ANTHIMOS STUCK HIS HEAD into Argyros's office. "His illustriousness is here to see you," the secretary declared, and seemed to take mordant pleasure at his boss's groan. Mordant pleasure, Argyros sometimes thought, was the only kind Anthimos really enjoyed.

George Lakhanodrakon came in while the magistrianos was still pulling himself together. "A fine morning to you, Basil," the Master of Offices said cheerfully; only the slightest eastern accent flavored his Greek. Then he got a good look at Argyros and at once went from superior to concerned friend. "Good heavens, man! Are you well?"

"I feel exactly like death," Argyros replied. He spoke quietly, but his voice hurt his ears; his eyes were vein-tracked and found the sun oppressively bright. His mouth tasted as if the sewers had drained through it and, judging by the state of his digestion, maybe they had. He said, "I slept in a tavern last night."

Lakhanodrakon's jaw fell. "You did what?"

"I know what you're thinking." Argyros shook his head and wished he hadn't. "Aii! I haven't had a hangover like this since—" He paused, trying to recall the last time he'd hurt himself so badly. The memory brought sudden sharp pain, though it was a dozen years old now: not since he drank with Riario the Italian doctor after his wife and infant son died of smallpox. He forced his mind away from that. "Do you want to hear something truly absurd? I had only four cups."

Concern returned to the Master of Offices's face. "And you're in this state? You ought to see a physician."

"No, no," Argyros said impatiently. "The innkeeper told me it was something new and strong." His eyes went to the icon on the wall, an image of the patron saint of changes. "By St. Mouamet, he wasn't wrong, either." He dipped his head and crossed himself, showing respect for the image of the saint.

Lakhanodrakon was eyeing the image, too. He was a pious man, but one who also turned his piety to practical ends. "Just as they were in Mouamet's time, the Persians are stirring again."

That was plenty to alarm Argyros, decrepit though he felt. "Troops on the move?" he demanded. The Roman Empire and Persia, Christ and Ormazd, were ancient rivals, dueling every generation, it seemed, for mastery in the near east. Few wars were waged on the scale of the one that had forced Mouamet to Constantinople, but any attack would lay provinces waste.

"Nothing quite so bad, praise God," Lakhanodrakon answered, following Argyros's thought perfectly. "There's trouble in the Caucasus, though."

"When isn't there?" Argyros replied and drew a cynical chuckle from the Master of Offices. Precisely because all-out war between them could be so ruinous, Rome and Persia often dueled for advantage on the fringes of their empires, intriguing among the client kings of the mountains between the Black and Caspian seas and the tribal chieftains of the Arabian peninsula. "What have you heard now?" the magistrianos asked.

"It's Alania," Lakhanodrakon said; Argyros abruptly realized this was what the Master of Offices had come to see him about. He wished Lakhanodrakon had named a different principality. Alania really mattered to both Rome and Persia, because the most important passes from the Caucasus up into the steppe were there. A prince of Alania who went bad could let the nomads in and channel them toward one empire or the other.

The magistrianos asked, "Is Prince Goarios thinking of going over to sun-worship, then?"

"God may know what Goar is thinking, but I doubt if anyone else does, Goar himself included." Lakhanodrakon betrayed his eastern origin by leaving the Greek suffix off the prince's name. After a moment, the Master of Offices went on, "Truth to tell, I have very little information of any sort coming out of Alania, less than I should. I thought I would send you to find out how things are there."

"Alania, eh? I've never been in the Caucasus," Argyros murmured. He glanced at the image of St. Mouamet. His life, it seemed, was about to see one more change.

That thought led to another, as yet only half-formed. "I suppose I'll go in as a merchant."

"Whatever you like, of course, Basil." George Lakhanodrakon valued results more than methods, which made him a good man to work for.

Still thinking out aloud, Argyros mused, "I ought to have something new and interesting to sell too, to get me noticed at Goarios's court." The magistrianos rubbed his temples; it was hard to make his wits work, with his head pounding the way it was. He snapped his fingers. "I have it! What better than this popskull drink that has me cringing at my own shadow?"

"Is it really as vicious as that?" Lakhanodrakon waved the question aside. "Never mind. I think you have a good idea there, Basil. Nothing would make Goar happier than a new way to get drunk, unless you could figure out how to bottle a woman's cleft."

"If I knew that one, I'd be too rich to work here." But Argyros, headache or no, focused too quickly and thoroughly on the problem he had been set to leave much room for jokes. "Superwine ought to be a good way to pry answers out of people too; they're drunk before they know it—

I certainly was, anyhow. The more anyone wants to talk or sing or carry on, the more I'll learn."

"Yes, of course. I knew in my heart you were the proper man to whom to give this task, Basil. Now my head also sees why that's so." It was Lakhanodrakon's turn to glance again at the icon of St. Mouamet. "When something new comes up, you know what it's good for."

"Thank you, sir." Argyros knew the Master of Offices was thinking of such things as hellpowder and the archetypes. He did not believe Lakhanodrakon knew of his role in showing that a dose of cowpox could prevent smallpox. He claimed no credit there; losing his family was too high a price for glory.

As he had so often before, he shoved that thought down and returned to the business at hand. "I'm off to Priskos's wineshop, then."

"Excellent, excellent." Lakhanodrakon hesitated, added, "Bring back a bottle for me, will you?"

ARGYROS RODE EAST down the Mese from the Praitorion to the imperial palaces. There he picked up a squad of excubitores, reasoning that Priskos might need persuading to part with the secret of his new drink. Having a few large, muscular persuaders along seemed a good idea.

For their part, the imperial bodyguards had trouble believing the assignment that had fallen into their laps. "You're taking us to a tavern, sir? On duty?" one trooper said, scrambling to his feet as if afraid Argyros might change his mind. "I thought I'd get orders like that in heaven, but no place else."

The magistrianos led his little band north through the Augusteion. The morning sun turned the light-brown sandstone exterior of Hagia Sophia to gold. Still, that exterior was plain when compared to the glories within.

The church of St. Mary Hodegetria lay a few furlongs east and north of Hagia Sophia. It was close by the seawall; as he approached, Argyros heard the waves of the Sea of Marmara slap against stone. None of Constantinople was more than a couple of miles from the sea, so that sound pervaded the city, but here it was foreground rather than background.

Argyros had to use the church as a base from which to cast about a bit to find Priskos's tavern. It was not one of his usual pothouses; he'd stopped in more or less by accident while on his way back to the Praitorion from the sea-wall gate of St. Barbara. He got no help finding the place from the locals, who had a tendency to disappear as soon as they spotted the gilded shields and long spears the excubitores carried.

The magistrianos spotted an apothecary's shop and grunted in satisfaction—Priskos's was only a couple of doors down. Argyros turned to the excubitores. "Follow me in. I'll stand you all to a couple of drinks. Back me if you need to, but St. Andreas help you if you break the place apart for the sport of it."

The soldiers loudly promised good behavior. Knowing the breed, Argyros also knew how little promises meant. He hoped for the best and hoped Priskos would cooperate.

The taverner was sweeping the floor when Argyros came in. So early in the day, only a couple of customers were in the place, nodding over winecups. Looking up from his work, Priskos recognized the magistrianos. "Good morning to you, sir," he said, smiling. "How are you tod—" He stopped abruptly, the smile freezing on his face, as the excubitores tramped in and plunked themselves down at a pair of tables.

"Fetch my friends a jar of good Cypriot, if you'd be so kind," Argyros said. To remove any possible misunderstanding, he handed Priskos a tremissis, a thin gold coin worth a third of a nomisma. "I expect this will even pay for two jars, since they'll likely empty the first."

"I think it should," Priskos said dryly; for a man still in his twenties, he did not show much of what he was thinking. He brought the jar and eight cups on a large tray; while he was serving the excubitores, one of his other customers took the opportunity to sidle out the door.

Once the soldiers were attended to, Priskos turned back to Argyros. "And now, sir, what can I do for you?" His tone was wary, no longer professionally jolly.

Argyros gave his name and title. Priskos looked warier yet; no one, no matter how innocent, wanted a magistrianos prying into his affairs. Argyros said, "I'd be grateful if you showed me how you make your *yperoinos*."

"I knew it! I knew it!" Try as he would, the innkeeper could no longer keep frustrated rage from his voice. "Just when I begin to work my trade up to where I can feed my family and me with it, somebody with a fancy rank comes to steal it from me."

The excubitores started to get up from their seats. Argyros waved them down. "You misunderstand. What stock of yours I buy, I will pay for," he told Priskos. "If you use some process only you know (as I daresay you do, for I've had nothing like your superwine, and I've traveled from Ispania to Mesopotamia), the fisc will pay, and pay well, I promise. Can't you see, man, what a boon such a strong drink could be to those in my service?"

"Pay, you say? How much?" Priskos still sounded scornful, but calculation had returned to his eyes. "By St. Andreas, sir, I'd not sell my secret to another taverner for a copper *follis* less than two pounds of gold."

"A hundred forty-four nomismata, eh? You'd only get so much once or twice, I think; after that, people who wanted to learn would be able to pit those who knew against one another and lower the price. Still—" Argyros paused and asked, "Do you read and write?"

Priskos nodded.

"Good. Fetch me a pen and a scrap of parchment, aye, and a candle too, for wax." When Argyros had the implements, he scrawled a few lines, then held the candle over the bottom of the parchment until several drops of wax fell. He thrust the signet ring he wore on his right index finger into the little puddle. "Here. It's no imperial chrysobull with a golden seal, but the staff at the offices of the Count of the Sacred Largesses, in whose charge the mint is, should accept it. Ask especially for Philip Kantakouzenos; he will recognize my hand.''

The taverner's lips moved as he worked his way through the document. Argyros knew when he got to the key phrase, for he stopped reading. ''Four pounds of gold!'' he exclaimed. He studied the magistrianos with narrowed eyes. ''You swear this is no fraud to deceive me?''

''By the Father, the Son, and the Holy Spirit, by the Virgin, by St. Andreas who watches over the city, by St. Mouamet whom I have come to recognize as my own patron, I swear it. May they damn me to hell if I lie,'' Argyros said solemnly. He crossed himself. So did Priskos and a couple of the excubitores.

The innkeeper tugged at his beard for a moment, then tucked the document inside his tunic. ''I'm your man. You deal fairly with me, and I will with you.'' He held out his hand.

Argyros shook it. ''Good enough. Maybe you'll fetch these good fellows that second jar of Cypriot, then, and show me what there is to see.''

Priskos set the wine before the soldiers, then went to a door at the back of the taproom. It had, Argyros saw, a stouter lock than the one that let out to the street. Priskos took a key from his belt. The lock clicked open. ''Right this way, sir.''

Argyros felt his head start to swim as he stepped in. A small fire burned in a stone hearth sunk in the center of the floor. Above it hung a cauldron that, by the smell, was full of hot wine. The combination of heat and wine fumes was overpowering.

Over and around the cauldron was a copper contraption, a large cone of thin metal. The hearth's high walls shielded most of it from direct exposure to the fire. The bottom of the cone had a lip that curved inward and lay in a basin of water shaped to match it.

Priskos put out the fire. ''I would have had to do that soon anyway,'' he told Argyros. He stuck his finger in the basin and nodded to himself. ''The cooling bath is getting too warm.'' He undid a plug; water from the basin ran into a groove in the floor and out under a door that led, Argyros supposed, to the alley behind the tavern. The innkeeper put the plug back, lifted a bucket, and poured fresh and presumably cool water into the basin till it was full again. The water level was just below the edge of the inner lip.

"I hope you'll explain all this," Argyros said.

"Yes, yes, of course." Priskos splashed water on the copper cone till it was cool enough to touch. Then he picked it up. That inner lip also had a cork. He held a cup under it, pulled it out. An almost clear liquid flowed into the cup. "Taste," he invited.

Argyros did. The way the stuff heated the inside of his mouth told him it was superwine.

Priskos said, "I got the idea from my brother Theodore, who makes medicines."

"Is he the one with the apothecary's store a few doors down?"

"You saw it, eh? Yes, that's him. One of the things he does is to boil down honey to make it thicker and stronger." Priskos paused. Argyros nodded; he knew druggists did that sort of thing. The innkeeper went on, "I thought what worked with honey might do the same with wine."

The magistrianos waved at the curious equipment. "So why all this folderol?"

"Because it turned out I was wrong, sir, dead wrong. The more I boiled wine, the less kick whatever was left in the pot had. I was boiling out what makes wine strong, not—what word do I want?—concentrating it, you might say."

Argyros ran his hands through his neat, graying beard. He thought for a moment, then said slowly, "What you're doing here, then, is getting back what you were boiling away, is that right?"

The taverner eyed him with respect. "That's just it, sir, just it exactly. Have you ever seen how, when you blow your warm breath on a cold window, the glass will steam over?" Again he waited for Argyros to nod before resuming, "That's what I do here. The wine fumes steam on the cool copper, and I collect them as they run down."

"No wonder you charge so much," the magistrianos observed. "You have the fuel for the fire to think about, and the work of tending this thing, and I don't suppose one jug of wine yields anything like a jug's worth of *yperoinos*."

"Not even close," Priskos agreed. "It's more like ten to one. Besides the fumes that get away, if you boil the stuff too long, you see, then it starts weakening again. You have to be careful of that. One way to up your yield a little is to keep sprinkling cold water on the outside of the cone. But you have to keep doing that, though, or pay someone to. I don't pay anyone—he'd just sell the secret out from under me."

"You sound as though you have all the answers." Argyros rubbed his chin again. "How long have you been playing around with this scheme, if I may ask?"

"I guess it's about five years now, if you count a couple of years fooling about with things that turned out not to work," the taverner answered after a moment's thought. "Once I figured out what I had to do, though, I spent a lot of time building up my stock; I wanted to make *yperoinos* a regular part of my business, not just a passing thing I'd brew up now and again. I still have hundreds of jars down in the cellar."

"Well, God be praised!" Argyros exclaimed. He was normally a taciturn, even a dour man, but that was better news than he had dared hope for. "What do you charge for each jar?"

"Two nomismata," Priskos said. "You have to remember, it's not like Cypriot. Two jars would have your bully boys out there asleep under their tables, not just happy."

"I'm quite aware of that, I assure you." Remembering how he had felt the day before made the magistrianos shudder. But the strength of the stuff was the reason he wanted it. "I'll give you three a jar, on top of what I've already paid you, if I can buy out every jar you have."

"Yes, on two conditions," Priskos said at once.

Argyros liked the way the younger man made up his mind. "Name them."

"First, I have to get my gold from the Count of the Sacred Largesses. Second, let me keep half a dozen jars for myself and my friends. Out of so many, that won't matter to you."

"Yes to the first, of course. As for the second, keep three. You'll be able to afford to make more later."

"I will at that, won't I? All right, I'd say we have ourselves a bargain." Priskos stuck out his hand. Argyros clasped it.

THE CARAVAN WOUND through the mountains towards the town of Dariel, the capital, such as it was, of the kingdom of the Alans. Even in late summer, snow topped some of the high peaks of the Caucasus. The mountains were as grand as the Alps, which till this journey had been the most magnificent range Basil Argyros knew.

"Good to be in big city, eh?" said one of the caravan guards, a local man wearing a knee-length coat of thick leather reinforced with bone scales and carrying a small, round, rivet-studded shield. His Greek was vile; Argyros was sure he had never been more than a couple of valleys away from the farm or village where he had been born. No one who had traveled would have called Dariel a big city.

In many ways, the magistrianos thought as the caravan approached the walls of the town, the Caucasus was the rubbish-heap of history. Dariel was a case in point. The Romans had built the fortress centuries ago, to keep the nomads from coming down off the steppe. When the Empire was weak, the Georgians manned it themselves, at times supported by Persian gold. The Alans, the present rulers hereabouts, had been nomads themselves once. A crushing defeat on the steppe, though, sent them fleeing into the mountains. Though they played Rome and Persia off against each other, they were as interested as either in guarding the pass that lay so near Dariel.

They had been, at any rate, until Goarios. Neither the Emperor nor the King of Kings could count on what Goarios would do. Trouble was, the king of the Alans was as lucky as he was erratic. All that did was make him twice the nuisance he would have been otherwise.

The gate guards had been dealing with the merchants in the caravan one by one. When they reached Argyros and his string of packhorses, he had to abandon his musings. "What you sell?" an underofficer asked in bad Persian. Both imperial tongues, like money from both realms, passed current all through the Caucasus, more so than any of the dozens of difficult, obscure local languages.

For his part, Argyros spoke better Persian than the Alan trooper. "Wine, fine wine from Constantinople," he replied. He waved at the jugs strapped to the horses' back.

"Wine, is it?" White teeth peeked through the tangled forest of the underofficer's beard. "Give me taste, to see how fine it is."

The magistrianos spread his hands in sorrow. "Noble sir, I regret it may not be," he said, using the flowery phrases that come so readily to Persian. "I intend to offer this vintage to no less a person than your mighty king himself, and would not have his pleasure diminished." Seeing the guard scowl, he added, "Here is a silver drachm. May it take away your thirst."

The gate guard's grin reappeared as he stuffed the Persian coin into his pouch. He waved Argyros forward into Dariel.

One of the magistrianos's comrades, a gray-eyed man named Corippus, came up and murmured, "A good thing he didn't check the jars." He spoke the guttural north African dialect of Latin, which no one in the Caucasus would be likely to understand; even Argyros had trouble following it.

Since he could not use it himself, he contented himself with saying, "Yes." All the jars looked like winejars, but not all of them held wine, or even superwine. In the same way, the couple of dozen men who had accompanied the magistrianos from Constantinople looked like merchants, which did not mean they were.

The horses moved slowly through Dariel's narrow, winding streets. Small boys stared and pointed and called out, as small boys will anywhere. Some of them were touts for inns. After some haggling, Argyros went with one. From the way the lad described it, his master Supsa's place was what God had used as a pattern for making heaven.

The magistrianos carefully did not ask which god the boy meant. Dariel held both Christian churches with domes in the conical Caucasian style and fire-temples sacred to the good god Ormazd whom the Persian prophet Zoroaster praised. Churches and fire-temples alike were thick-walled, fortresslike structures; most had armed guards patrolling their grounds. Nowhere but in this region that both empires coveted did their faiths have such evenly balanced followings; nowhere else was there such strife between them. Goarios was a Christian (or at least had been, the last time Argyros heard), but it would not do to count on that too far.

Native Georgians and their Alan overlords were both on the streets, usually giving one another wide berths. Language and dress distinguished them. Not even Satan, Argyros thought, could learn Georgian, but the Alan tongue was a distant cousin of Persian. And while the natives mostly wore calf-length robes of wool or linen, some Alans still clung to the leather and furs their ancestors had worn on the steppe. They also let their hair grow long, in greasy locks.

Some real nomads, slant-eyed Kirghiz, were also in the market square. They stared about nervously, as if misliking to be so hemmed in. Their fine weapons and gold saddle-trappings marked them as important men in their tribe. Argyros almost wished he had not spotted them. They gave him one more thing to worry about, and he had plenty already.

Supsa's inn proved more than adequate. The stableman knew his business, and the cellar was big enough to store the winejars. Argyros, who from long experience discounted nine-tenths of what he heard from touts, was pleased enough. He did his best not to show it, dickering long and hard with Supsa. If he had more money than a run-of-the-mill merchant, that was his business and nobody else's.

The mound of pillows he found in his chamber made strange but surprisingly comfortable bed. The next morning, fruit candied in honey was not what the magistriano was used to eating for breakfast, but not bad, either. H licked his fingers as he walked toward Goarios's palace, bleak stone pile that seemed more citadel than seat of gov ernment.

One of Goarios's stewards greeted him with a supercil iousness the grand chamberlain of the Roman Empero would have envied. "His highness," the steward insisted "favors local wines, and so would have scant interest i sampling your stock."

Argyros recognized a bribery ploy when he heard one. H did not mind paying his way into Goarios's presence; he wa not, after all, operating with his own money. But he di want to take this fellow's toploftiness down a peg. He ha brought along a jar of *yperoinos*. "Perhaps you would car to see that its quality meets your master's standards," h suggested, patting the jar.

"Well, perhaps, as a favor for your politeness," th chamberlain said grudgingly. At his command, a lesser ser vant fetched him a cup. Argyros worked the cork free poured him a good tot, and watched, gravely silent, as hi eyes crossed and face turned red when he drank it down a a gulp. The steward came back gamely, though. "I may hav been in error," he said, extending the cup again. "Pray giv me another portion, to let me be sure."

Goarios's great hall was narrow, dark, and drafty. Peti tioners worked their way forward toward the king's hig seat. The magistrianos waited patiently, using the time i which he occasionally lurched ahead to examine the other in the hall who sought the king's favor.

He did not like what he saw. For one thing, the Kirghi nobles he had spied in the market were there. For another while one Christian priest, plainly a local, waited to make request of Goarios, a whole delegation of Ormazd's cleric in their flame-colored robes sat a few paces ahead of th magistrianos. He could hear them talking among them

elves. Their Persian was too pure to have been learned in
he Caucasus.

As he drew closer, Argyros also studied the king of the
Alans. Goarios was close to his own age, younger than he
had thought. His face was long, rather pale, with harsh lines
on either side of his mouth that disappeared into his thick
beard. His eyes were black and shiny; he had somehow the
air of a man who saw things no one else did. Whether those
things were actually there, Argyros was not sure.

Goarios spent some time with the Kirghiz, even more with
he Persian priests. The rumbles of Argyros's stomach were
reminding him it was time for the noon meal when at last the
steward presented him to the king. He stooped to one knee
and bowed his head; only before the Emperor of the Romans or the Persian King of Kings would he have performed a full prostration, going down on his belly.

The steward addressed Goarios in Georgian. The king
made brief answer in the same tongue, then spoke to Argyros in Persian: "You have, Tskhinvali here tells me, a remarkable new potation, one I might enjoy. Is this so?"

"Your majesty, it is," the magistrianos answered in the
same tongue. He handed the jar to the steward to pass on to
Goarios. "Please take this as my gift, to acquaint you with
he product."

Those opaque eyes surveyed Argyros. "I thank you. You
must have great confidence, to be so generous." Goarios still
used Persian. Argyros had heard he knew Greek, and suspected he was the victim of a subtle insult. He showed no
annoyance, but waited silently while the king, as his steward had before him, had a cup brought. Unlike Tskhinvali,
Goarios drank from silver.

The king drank. His eyes widened slightly, and he rumbled deep in his throat, but he tolerated his first draught
better than anyone else Argyros had seen. "By the sun!"
Goarios exclaimed, a strange oath if he still followed Christ.
He drank again, licked his lips. Suddenly he switched languages: he *did* speak Greek. "This is something new and
different. How many jars have you to sell, and at what
price?"

"I have several hundred jars, your majesty." Argyros also shifted to Greek. "They cannot, I fear, come cheap: not only is the preparation slow and difficult, but I have incurred no small expense in traveling to you. My master back in Constantinople would flay me for accepting less than twenty nomismata the jar."

He expected dickering to begin then, or Goarios to dismiss him to bargain with Tskhinvali or some other palace dignitary. He would have been satisfied to get half his first asking price. But the king of the Alans simply said, "Accepted."

Disciplined though he was, Argyros could not help blurting, "Your majesty?" The first confused thought in his mind was that his might be the only government-financed expedition in the history of the Empire to turn a profit. He had never heard of any others; he was certain of that.

Goarios took another pull. "Agreed, I said. Rarity and quality are worth paying for, in wine or women or—" He let his voice trail away, but his eyes lit, as if for an instant his inner vision grew sharp and clear. The moment passed; the king returned his attention to Argyros. "I have a banquet planned this evening—I am pleased to bid you join me. Perhaps to further the pleasure of all those present, you will consent to bring with you ten jars of your brew."

"Certainly, your majesty." Argyros had hoped the superwine would make him popular at court, but had not expected to succeed so soon. He regretted having to stay in character. Any failure, though, might be noticed, so he said, "Your majesty, ah—" He made what he hoped was a discreet pause.

"You will be paid on your arrival, I assure you," Goarios said dryly. He added, "If you have found a companion, you may bring her to the feast. We do not restrict our women to their own quarters, as the tiresome custom is in Constantinople."

"You are most generous, your majesty." Argyros bowed his way out. The audience had gone better than he dared wish. He wondered why he was still nervous.

For the banquet the magistrianos dug out the best robe he had brought. He had several finer ones back in Constantinople, including a really splendid one of thick sea-green samite heavily brocaded with silk thread. For a merchant of moderate means, though, that would have been too much. Plain maroon wool fit the part better.

The reputation of the *yperoinos* must have preceded it; eager hands helped Argyros remove the jars from the pack-horses. Too eager—"Come back, you!" he shouted at one servitor. "Your king bade me bring ten jars. If my head goes up on the wall for cheating him, I know whose will be there beside it." That was plenty to stop the fellow in his tracks, the magistrianos noted: Goarios's men feared their king, then.

Horns, flutes, and drums played in the banquet hall. The music was brisk, but in the wailing minor key the Persians and other easterners favored. Argyros had heard it many times but never acquired the taste for it.

The servants had not yet set out the tables for the feast. Guests and their ladies stood and chatted, holding wine-cups. When the chief usher announced Argyros's name and the other servants carried the jars of superwine into the hall, King Goarios clapped his hands above his head three times. Silence fell at once.

"Here we have the purveyor of a new and potent pleasure," the king declared, "than which what praise could be higher?" He spoke Persian. By now, Argyros had decided he meant no mockery by it; more courtiers used Persian than Greek here. Goarios beckoned the magistrianos toward him. "Come and receive your promised payment."

Argyros pushed his way through the crowded hall. He had no trouble keeping the king in sight; they were both taller than most of the people in the hall. Behind him, he heard the first exclamations of amazement as the guests began sampling the *yperoinos*.

"Two hundred nomismata," Goarios said when he drew near, and tossed him a leather purse over the heads of the last couple of men between them.

"I thank your majesty," Argyros said, bowing low when he and Goarios were at last face to face.

"A trifle," the king said with a languid wave.

A woman stood by his side. Argyros had not got a good look at her before, for the crown of her head was not far above Goarios's shoulders. Her hair fell in thick black waves to her shoulders. She had bold, swarthy features and flashing dark eyes that glittered with amusement as she smiled saucily at the magistrianos.

"Mirrane, this is Argyros, the wine merchant of whom I told you," Goarios said. Recognizing her, the magistrianos felt ice form round his heart. He waited woodenly for her to denounce him.

She turned her mocking gaze his way again. "I've heard of him," she said, speaking Greek with the throaty accent of her native tongue. "He is, ah, famous for his new products he purveys." Her attention returned to Goarios. "For what marvel did you reward him so highly?"

"A vintage squeezed, I think, from the thunderstorm," the king of the Alans replied. "You must try some, my dear." His hand slid around Mirrane's waist. She snuggled against him. Together they walked slowly toward the table where Goarios's servants had set out the *yperoinos*.

Argyros stared after them. He was too self-possessed to show his bafflement by scratching his head, but that was what he felt like doing. If Mirrane had become Goarios' concubine, she had to have influence over him. Of that the magistrianos had no doubt. Mirrane, Argyros was certain, could influence a marble statue, as long as it was a male one.

Why, then, was she letting him stay free? The only answer that occurred to Argyros was so she could ruin him at a time that better suited her purpose. Yet that made no sense either. Mirrane was skilled enough at intrigue to see that, the longer a foe stayed active, the more dangerous he became. She was not one to waste so perfect a chance to destroy him.

He shrugged imperceptibly. If she was making that kind of mistake, he would do his best to take advantage of it.

After a while, servants began fetching in tables and chairs. Goarios, Mirrane still beside him, took his seat at the head table. That was the signal for the king's guests to sit down too. Soon all were in their places but the group of Kirghiz, who would not move away from the superwine. One of them was already unconscious; two of his comrades had to hold him up. Stewards of ever higher rank came over to remonstrate with the nomads. At last, grudgingly, they went up to sit across the table from Goarios.

Back in the kitchens, Argyros thought, the cooks must have been tearing their hair, waiting for the dinner to start. They quickly made up for lost time. Grunting under the weight, servants hauled in platters on which rested roast kids, lambs and geese. Others brought tubs of peas and onions, while the sweet smell of the new-baked loaves that also made their appearance filled the hall.

What was left of the superwine seemed reserved for Goarios's table, but jars from the sweet Caucasian vintages in the Alan king's cellars kept those less privileged happy. Argyros drank sparingly. He kept his eyes on Mirrane, again wondering what game she was playing.

None of his tablemates—minor Alan nobles, most of them, along with a few townsmen rich enough for Goarios to find them worth cultivating—found his staring obtrusive. Desirable though she was, the magistrianos did not think they were watching Mirrane. The Kirghiz were busy making a spectacle of themselves.

Argyros knew the privation steppe nomads endured, and knew how, to make up for it, they could gorge themselves when they got the chance. Reading of the huge feasts Homer described, he sometimes thought the heroes of the Trojan War had the same talent. Maybe the Alans' ancestors did too, when they were a steppe people, but this generation had lost it. They gaped in astonished wonder as the Kirghiz ate and ate and ate.

The nomads drank too, swilling down *yperoinos* as if it were the fermented mare's milk of the plains. The one who had been wobbling before the banquet slid quietly out of his chair and under the table. Another soon followed him. The rest grew boisterous instead. They slammed fists down on the table to emphasize whatever points they thought they

were making, shouted louder and louder, and howled song
in their own language. Argyros understood a few words o
it; not many other people in the hall did. It sounded dread
ful.

Servants cleared away platters, except, after a snarle
warning, the ones in front of the Kirghiz. Goarios stood up
held his hands above his head. Silence descended. Eventu
ally the Kirghiz noticed they were roaring in a void. They too
subsided, and waited for the king to speak.

"Thank you, my friends, for sharing my bounty to
night," Goarios said in Persian. He paused for a moment to
let those who did not know the tongue have his words inter
preted, then resumed: "I know this would not seem like
much in the ways of riches to one used to the glories o
Constantinople or Ctesiphon, but in our own small way we
try."

This time, being safely inconspicuous, Argyros did
scratch his head. Modesty and self-depreciation were no
what he had come to expect from the king of the Alans.

Goarios continued, "Still and all, we have learned much
from the Romans and from the Persians. Of all the folk
under the sun"—here he glanced at Mirrane, who fondly
smiled back his way (if Goarios had embraced the creed o
Ormazd, Argyros was doubly sure now it was because he
had first embraced an eloquent advocate for it)—"they are
strongest, and also cleverest. That is no accident; the two
qualities go hand in hand."

The king paused. His courtiers applauded. The Kirghiz
nobles, those still conscious, looked monumentally bored
Argyros sympathized with them. If Goarios had a point, he
was doing his best to avoid it.

Or so the magistrianos thought, until the king suddenly
adopted the royal we and declared, "Though our realm is
small at present, we do not see ourself as less in wit than
either the Emperor or the King of Kings." Both those rulers,
Argyros thought tartly, had the sense not to go around
boasting how smart they were.

Nevertheless, Goarios's words did have a certain logic, if
a twisted one: "Being so astute ourself, it follows naturally

that power will accrue to us on account of our sagacity and on account of our ability to see the advantages of policies heretofore untried. As a result, one day soon, perhaps, the rich and famous in the capitals of the empires will have cause to envy us as we now envy them."

The courtiers applauded again. They seemed to know what their king was talking about—but then, Argyros thought, the poor devils had likely listened to this speech or something like it a good many times before. He had heard Goarios was a cruel man; now he was getting proof of it.

A couple of Kirghiz envoys also cheered the king of the Alans—or maybe the fact that he was done. The rest of the nomads had slumped into sodden slumber. Speaking of envy, Argyros envied them that.

Goarios was plainly convinced his address marked the high point of the evening, for no singers, dancers, or acrobats appeared afterward to entertain his guests. Instead, the king waved to the doorway, showing that the festivities were over.

The banquet did not break up at once. As in Constantinople, the custom was for departing guests to thank their host for his kindness. Argyros joined the procession, sighing inwardly. He wished he could somehow get into Goarios's good graces without having anything to do with the king.

Still, Goarios greeted him effusively. "We are in your debt. You and your *yperoinos* have helped make this evening unique."

He used Greek, so as not to leave the name of the new drink dangling alone and strange in an otherwise Persian sentence. One of the Kirghiz understood the Roman Empire's chief tongue and even spoke it after a fashion. Before Argyros could respond to the king, the nomad poked him in the ribs. "You this drink make, eh? Is good. Where you from?"

"Constantinople," the magistrianos replied. The Kirghiz's prodding finger distracted him from Goarios, whom etiquette demanded he should have answered.

"Ah, the city." The nomad was too drunk to care about etiquette, if he ever had. He poked Goarios in turn. "You, I, maybe one fine day we see Constantinople soon, eh?"

"Who would not wish such a thing?" Goarios's voice was smooth, but his eyes flickered.

Argyros bowed to the king. "To serve you is my privilege, your majesty." He turned to Mirrane. "And your lady as well." Maybe his directness could startle something out of her, though he knew what a forlorn hope that was.

Sure enough, her equanimity remained absolute. With dignity a queen might have envied, she extended a slim hand to the magistrianos. He resented being made to dance to her tune, yet saw no choice but to take it. She said, "My master speaks for me, of course."

The magistrianos murmured a polite phrase and bowed his way out of the king's presence. Outside the castle, he hired a torchboy to light his way back to the inn. The boy, a Georgian lad, could follow Persian if it was spoken slowly and eked out with gestures. "Stop a moment. Hold your torch up," Argyros told him as soon as buildings hid them from Goarios's castle.

The boy obeyed. Argyros unrolled the tiny scrap of parchment Mirrane had pressed into his palm. He had to hold it close to his face to make out her message in the dim, flickering light. "Meet me alone tomorrow by the vegetable market, or I will tell Goarios who you are," he read.

Nothing subtle or oblique there, he thought as he put the parchment in his beltpouch. That did not mean she would not get what she wanted. She generally did.

"You're going to meet with her?" Corippus, when he heard Argyros's news the next morning, was openly incredulous. "What will the rest of us do once she's dealt with you? You can't tell me she has your good health foremost in her mind."

"I doubt that," Argyros admitted. He tried to sound judicious, and not like a man merely stating the obvious. He did bolster his case by adding, "If she wanted to bring me down, she could have done it simply last night, instead of going through this rigmarole. By the look of things, she has Goarios wrapped around her finger."

Corippus grunted. "This is folly, I tell you."

"Being exposed to Goarios is worse folly. One thing I know of Mirrane: she does not threaten idly."

Corippus made a noise deep in his throat. He remained anything but convinced. Argyros, however, headed the team from Constantinople, so the north African could only grumble.

The magistrianos tried to tease him out of his gloom. He waved round the cellar of Supsa's inn, pointing at the three *yperoinos*-cookers Corippus and his team had going. "You worry too much, my friend. Even if something does happen to me, the lot of you can go into superwine for true, and likely end up rich men here."

Corippus fell back into his harsh native dialect. "In this God-forsaken lump of a town? Who'd want to?"

He had a point, Argyros thought. Nevertheless, the magistrianos turned a benign eye on Dariel as he made his way to the vegetable market. That was partly because, if he got through this confrontation with Mirrane, he would have a hold on her to counter the advantage she now held on him— he did not think, at any rate, that Goarios would be pleased to learn his paramour was arranging a secret rendezvous with another man. More important, though, was the prospect of matching wits with the best Persia had. Mirrane was that, as Argyros had found more than once to his discomfiture.

To one used to the bounty of Constantinople, Dariel's vegetable market was a small, mean place. The city prefect's inspectors would have condemned half the produce on display. Argyros bought a handful of raisins and waited for Mirrane to come into the little square.

He was not sure what to expect. When with Goarios, she had dressed as a great lady, with brocaded robe and with bracelets and necklace of gleaming gold. He had also seen her, though, in a dancer's filmy garb, and once when she was artfully disguised as an old woman. Just recognizing her would constitute a victory of sorts.

He was almost disappointed to spot her at once. She wore a plain white linen dress, something that suited a moderately prosperous tradesman's wife, but she wore it like a queen. Copper wire held her hair in place; apart from that, she was bare of jewelry. Seeing Argyros, she waved and walked toward him, as if greeting an old friend.

"You have another new toy, do you, Basil?" Her voice held a lilting, teasing tone, of the sort a cat would use to address a bird it held between its paws. "What better way to swing a man toward you than dealing with him drunk, the more so if he's had so little he doesn't know he is?"

If anyone would realize why he had brought the *yper-oinos*, it was she. He answered, "I'm not trying to turn a whole city on its ear, the way your handbills did in Daras."

"You turned the tables neatly enough on me in Constantinople." She shook her head in chagrin, put her hand on his arm.

He pulled free. "Enough empty compliments," he said harshly. "Unfold your scheme, whatever it is, and have done, so I can start working out where the traps lie."

"Be careful what you say to me," she warned, smiling still. "Ormazd the good god knows how backward Alania is, but Goarios's torturer, I think, would have no trouble earning his keep in Ctesiphon. In some things, he accepts only the finest."

"I daresay."

"Oh, think what you will," Mirrane said impatiently. "I serve the King of Kings no less than you your Avtokrator. If my body aids in that service, then it does, and there is no more to be said about it." She paused a moment. "No, I take that back. I will say, Basil, that Goarios is not one I would have bedded of my own free choice, and that that is not true of you."

Ever since those few nights in Daras, Argyros had wondered whether the passion she showed then was real or simply a ploy in an unending struggle between Persia and the Roman Empire. He wondered still; Mirrane might say anything to gain advantage. That mixture of suspicious curiosity and anger roughened his words: "Say whatever you like. Whether or not you care a follis for him, Goarios dances to your tune, in bed and out.''

Mirrane's laugh had an edge to it. ''Were that so, I'd not be here talking with you now—you would have been a dead man the instant Tskhinvali called your name. But I need you alive.''

For the first time, Argyros began to think she might be telling the truth, or some of it. She had no reason not to unmask him if she did fully control the king of the Alans. Trusting her, though, went against every instinct the magistrianos had, and against the evidence as well. ''If Goarios is his own man, as you say, why has he turned his back on God's only begotten Son Jesus Christ and embraced your false Ormazd? Whence comes that, if not from you?''

''I find my faith as true as you yours,'' Mirrane said tartly. ''As for Goarios, he is his own man, and his own god as well—the only thing he worships is himself. The words he mouths are whichever ones suit him for the time being. I saw that too late, and that is why I need your help.''

''Now we come down to it,'' Argyros said.

Mirrane nodded. ''Now indeed. What he intends, you see, is opening the Caspian Gates to the Kirghiz and as many other nomad clans as care to join them. His own army will join the nomads; he thinks he will end by ruling them all.'' Her sigh was full of unfeigned regret. ''And to think that that was what I labored so hard to accomplish, and here I find it worse than useless.''

Argyros found it appalling: it was George Lakhanodrakon's worst nightmare, come to life. The magistrianos said, ''Why should you not be glad to see the nomads ravage Roman provinces?''

''I told you once—if that were all, you would be dead. But Goarios and the men from the steppe have bigger plans. They want to invade Persia too. Goarios thinks to play Iskander.'' Argyros frowned for a couple of seconds before recognizing the Persian pronunciation of the name Alexander. Many had tried to rule both east and west in the sixteen hundred years since Alexander the Great; no one had succeeded.

Then again, no one had tried with the backing of the nomads. "You think he may do it, then," the magistrianos
said slowly.

"He might; he just might," Mirrane answered. "He is a
man who believes he can do anything, and those are the ones
who are sometimes right." She hesitated, then added, "He
frightens me."

That admission startled Argyros, who had never imagined hearing it from Mirrane. All the same, he said, "It's
hard to imagine a conquering army erupting out of the
Caucasus. The mountains here are a refuge of defeat, not
stepping-stones to triumph." He spelled out the chain of
thought he'd had coming into Dariel.

Mirrane's eyes lit. She followed him at once. He knew
how clever she was. Her wit rather than her beauty made her
truly formidable, though she was twice as dangerous because she had both.

She said, "This once, though, the Alans have raised up a
leader for themselves. He is . . . strange, but sometimes that
makes people follow a man more readily, for they see him
as being marked by—well, by whatever god they follow."
Her smile invited Argyros to notice the concession she had
made him.

He did not rise to it. Over the centuries, the agents who
served the Roman Empire had learned to gauge when di-
plomacy would serve and when war was required, when to
pay tribute, and when instead to incite a tribe's enemies to
distract it from the frontier. If a hero had appeared in
Alania, that long experience told Argyros what to do. "Kill
him," the magistrianos said. "The chaos from that should
be plenty to keep the Alans safely squabbling among themselves."

"I thought of that, of course," Mirrane said, "but, aside
from being fond of staying healthy and intact myself, it's too
late. The Kirghiz control the pass these days, not the Alans."

"Oh, damnation."

"Yes, the whole damn nation," Mirrane echoed, her
somber voice belying the lighthearted tone of the pun.
"Their khan Dayir, I would say, is using Goarios for his own

ends as much as Goarios is using him. And where Goarios
would be Iskander if he could, Dayir also has one after
whom he models his conduct.''

Argyros thought of the nomad chieftains who had
plagued the Roman Empire through the centuries. "Attila," he said, naming the first and worst of them.

Mirrane frowned. "Of him I never heard." The magistrianos was briefly startled, then realized she had no reason
to be familiar with all the old tales from what was to her the
distant west: Attila had never plundered Persia. But she
knew of one who had: "I was thinking of the king of the
Ephthalites, who long ago slew Peroz King of Kings by a
trick.''

Argyros nodded; Prokopios had preserved in Roman
memory the story of that disaster. "Enough of ancient history, though," he said with the same grim pragmatism that
had made him urge Mirrane to assassinate Goarios. "We
need now to decide how to deal with this Dayir." Only when
he noticed he had said "we" was the magistrianos sure he
believed Mirrane.

She accepted that tacit agreement as no less than her due.
"So we do. Unfortunately, I see no easy way. I doubt we'd
be able to pry him and Goarios apart. Until they've succeeded, their interests run in the same direction.''

"And afterward," Argyros said gloomily, "will be too
late to do us much good.''

Mirrane smiled at the understatement. "Ah, Basil, I knew
one day Constantinople would get around to sending someone to see what was going wrong in Alania: Goarios *will*
brag, instead of having the wit to let his plans grow in the
quiet dark until they are ripe. I'm glad the Master of Offices chose you. We think alike, you and I.''

A hot retort rose to the magistrianos's lips, but did not get
past. Despite the differences between them, there was much
truth in what Mirrane said; he was reminded of it every time
he spoke with her. Certainly he had more in common with
her than with some Constantinopolitan dyeshop owner
whose mental horizon reached no further than the next

day's races in the hippodrome. "We use different tongues,"
he observed, "but the same language."

"Well said!" She leaned forward, stood on tiptoe to plant
a kiss on his cheek. She giggled. "You keep your beard
neater than Goarios—there's more room on your face. I like
it." Laughing still, she kissed his other cheek, just missing
his mouth.

He knew she took care to calculate her effects. He reached
for her all the same. The touch of her lips reminded him
again of those few days back at Daras.

Sinuous as an eel, she slipped away. "What would be left
of you, if you were caught molesting the king's kept
woman?" She abruptly turned serious. "I must get back.
Leaving the palace is always a risk, but less so at noon, because Goarios sleeps then, the better to roister at night. But
he'll be rousing soon, and might call for me."

Argyros could say nothing to that, and knew it. He
watched Mirrane glide across the market square; she moved
with the grace of a dancer and had once used that role as a
cover in Daras. The magistrianos stood rubbing his chin in
thought for several minutes after she finally disappeared,
then made his own way back to Supsa's inn.

All the way there, his mind kept worrying at the problem
she posed, as the tongue will worry at a bit of food caught
between the teeth until one wishes he would go mad. Equally
stubborn in refusing to leave his thoughts was the feel of her
soft lips. That annoyed him, so he prodded at his feelings
with characteristic stubborn honesty until he began to make
sense of them.

In the years since his wife and son died, he'd never
thought seriously about taking another woman into his life.
That came partly from the longing he still felt for Helen.
More sprang from his unwillingness to inflict on any woman
the lonely life a magistrianos's wife would have to lead,
especially the wife of a magistrianos who drew difficult
cases. In the past five years he had been to Ispania and the
Franco-Saxon kingdoms, to Daras, and now he was here in
the Caucasus. Each of those missions was a matter of

months, the first close to a year. It was not fair to any woman to make her turn Penelope to his Odysseus.

With Mirrane, though, that objection fell to the ground. She was at least as able as he to care for herself in the field. And if—if!—she spoke the truth about how she reckoned their brief joining in Daras, he pleased her well enough, at least in that regard. There was, he remembered, far more to love than what went on in bed, but that had its place too.

He started laughing at himself. Mirrane was also a Persian—enemy by assumption, in almost Euclidean logic. She worshiped Ormazd. She was sleeping with Goarios and keeping his nights lively when the two of them were not asleep. The only reason she was in the Caucasus at all was to seduce the king of the Alans away from the Roman Empire, in the most literal sense of the word. Not only that; if—if!—she spoke the truth, both Constantinople and Ctesiphon faced deadly danger from Goarios's machinations.

When all those thoughts were done, the thought of her remained. That worried him more than anything.

CORIPPUS SCOWLED at the magistrianos. "That accursed potter has raised his price again. And so has the plague-taken apothecary."

"Pay them both," Argyros told him. "Yell and scream and fume as if you were being bankrupted or castrated or whatever suits your fancy. That's in keeping with our part here. But pay them. You know what we need."

"I know you've lost your wits mooning over that Persian doxy," Corippus retorted, a shot close enough to the mark that Argyros felt his face grow hot. He was glad they were in the dimly lit cellar, so his lieutenant could not see him flush. But Corippus, after grumbling a little more, went on, "However much it galls me, I have to say the wench is likely right. There'd not be so many stinking Kirghiz on the streets if they weren't in league with Goarios, and she'd've long since nailed us if she didn't think they meant to do Persia harm along with the Empire."

Argyros had reached exactly the same conclusions. He said so, adding, "I'll be hanged if I can tell how you'd know how many Kirghiz are in Dariel. You hardly ever come up out of here, even to breathe.''

Corippus chuckled dryly. "Something to that, but some-one has to keep the superwine cooking faster than Goarios and his cronies guzzle it down. Besides which, I don't need to go out much to know the nomads are thick as fleas. The stench gives 'em away.''

"Something to that," the magistrianos echoed. Strong smells came with cities, especially ones like Dariel, which had only a nodding acquaintance with Roman ideas of plumbing and sanitation. Still, the Kirghiz did add their own notes, primarily horse and rancid butter, to the symphony of stinks.

Corippus said, "Any which way, I'm happier to be down here than upstairs with you and Eustathios Rhangabe. Worst thing can happen to me here is getting burned alive. If Eustathios buggers something up, I'll be scattered over too much landscape too fast to have time to get mad at him.''

That was a truth Argyros did his best to ignore. He said, "The innkeeper thinks Rhangabe's some new sort of here-tic who isn't allowed to eat except with wooden tools. I don't know whether he wants to burn him or convert.''

"He'd better convert," Corippus snorted. He and Ar-gyros both laughed, briefly and self-consciously. They knew what would happen if Eustathios Rhangabe struck a spark at the wrong time.

The magistrianos went upstairs to the room the man from the arsenal at Constantinople was using. He knocked—gently, so as not to disturb Rhangabe. He heard a bowl being set on a table inside the room. Only then did Rhan-gabe come to the door and undo the latch.

As always, he reminded Argyros of a clerk, but a clerk with the work-battered hands of an artisan. "Hello, Ar-gyros," he said, "It goes well, though that thief of a drug-gist has raised his price for sulfur again.''

"So Corippus told me.''

Rhangabe grunted. He was not a man much given to conversation. He went back to the table where he had been busy. He had shoved it close to the room's single small window, to give himself the best possible light—no lamps, not here.

Along with the bowl (in which a wooden spoon was thrust), a stout rolling pin lay on the table. Judging its position, Rhangabe had been working on the middle of the three piles there, grinding it from lumps to fine powder. The pile to the left was black, that middle one (the biggest) a dirty gray-white, and the one on the right bright yellow.

Argyros was perfectly willing to admit that Eustathios Rhangabe knew much more about hellpowder than he did these days. Rhangabe had headed the man at the arsenal who concocted the deadly incendiary liquid called Greek fire (the magistrianos did not know, or want to know, what went into *that*). When something even more destructive came along, he was the natural one to look to to ferret out its secrets. That he had not blown himself up in the process testified to his skill.

He took the spoon out of the bowl, measured a little saltpeter from the middle pile into a balance, grunted again, and scooped part of the load back onto the table. Satisfied at last, he tipped the balance pan into the bowl, vigorously stirred the contents, squinted, wetted a finger to stick it in so he would taste the mixture, and at last nodded in reluctant approval.

He picked up a funnel (also of wood) and put it in the mouth of a pottery jug. He lifted the bowl, carefully poured the newly mixed hellpowder into the jug. When it was full, he plugged it with an unusual cork he took from a bag that lay next to his bed: the cork had been bored through, and a twist of oily rag forced through the little opening.

Only when Rhangabe was quite finished did he seem to remember Argyros was still in the room. He jerked a thumb at the jars that lined the wall. "That's forty-seven I've made for you since we got here, not counting the ones we fetched from the city. All in all, we have plenty to blow a hole in Goarios's palace you could throw an elephant through, if that's what you want."

A couple of weeks before, the magistrianos would have seized the chance. Hearing Mirrane had made him wonder, though, and made him watch the fortress to check what she said. He was certain now she had not misled him. Goarios might still rule Alania, but the Kirghiz ruled Goarios. The comings and goings of their leaders were one sign; another was the growing numbers of nomads on Dariel's streets.

By themselves, those might merely have bespoken alliance, but other indications said otherwise. The Kirghiz nobles treated Goarios's guards and courtiers with growing contempt, so much so that Tskhinvali, arrogant himself, complained out loud to Argyros of their presumptuousness. In the markets, the men from the steppe treated traders like servants.

That sort of thing could go on only so long. The Alans were themselves a proud people, while their Georgian subjects remembered every slight and carried on feuds among themselves that lasted for generations. Dariel did not have the feel of a place about to become a world-conqueror's capital. It seemed, Argyros thought, more like one of Eustathios Rhangabe's jugs of hellpowder a few seconds before someone lit the rag stuffed in the cork.

The magistrianos wished he could see Mirrane again. Partly because he wanted to get a better feel for what was happening in the palace, and partly just because he wanted to see her. He avoided thinking about which desire was more important to him. In any case, he could not casually make an appointment with the king's mistress. She had to arrange to come to him.

He thought from time to time about changing that, about letting Goarios get hold of her note to him. Each time he held off. Doing that was dangerous and, worse, irrevocable. Moreover, with endless chances she had not betrayed him. Yet he fretted every day at how little he really knew of what was going on.

As things turned out, he found out with no help from Mirrane. He had broken a bronze buckle on one of his sandals and was in the market dickering, mostly by signs, with a Georgian coppersmith for a replacement. Another local had set out several trays of knives in the adjoining stall.

Half a dozen Kirghiz rode by. One leaned down from the saddle with the effortless ease the nomads displayed on horseback, plucked a fine blade from a tray, and stuck it in his belt. His companions snickered.

The knifesmith shouted angrily and ran after the Kirghiz. The thief, amused at his fury, waited for him to catch up, then gave his beard a yank. The nomads laughed louder. Then the one who had taken the knife bellowed in pain—the knifesmith had bitten his hand, hard enough to draw blood.

The nomad lashed out with a booted foot. The knife-smith reeled away, clutching his belly and gasping for breath. All the Kirghiz rode on; now they were chuckling at their comrade.

Had the Georgian knifesmith been made of less stern stuff, the incident would have been over. But the local staggered back to his stall. "Kirghiz!" he shouted as he snatched up a blade. The nomads looked back. The Georgian had known exactly what weapon he was grabbing. He threw the knife. It went into the thief's chest. The nomad looked astonished, then slowly slid from the saddle.

The rest of the Kirghiz stared for a moment, first at their friend and then at the knifesmith. Quickly but quite deliberately, one of the nomads strung his bow, pulled out an arrow, and shot the Georgian in the face. The man gave a great bass shriek of anguish that made heads jerk round all over the market square. He ran a few steps, his hands clutching the shaft sunk in his cheek, then fell. His feet drummed in the dirt.

Argyros looked around to exchange a horrified glance with the coppersmith, but that worthy had disappeared. He was, the magistrianos decided, no fool. The locals in the square were surging toward the Kirghiz, as the sea will surge when driven by an angry wind. Argyros heard a harsh cry somewhere as a nomad on foot was mobbed. All the mounted ones near him had their bows out now.

He slipped away before any of the Kirghiz chanced to look in his direction. He had not got half a block out of the

square when the noise behind him doubled and doubled
again. He went from a walk to a trot. He had been caught
in a street riot once before, in Constantinople. Once was
plenty.

The tumult had not yet reached the inn where Argyros
and his men were staying. All the same, Corippus was
prowling around the courtyard, wary as a wolf that has
taken a scent it mislikes. "How bad?" he asked when the
magistrianos told him what had happened.

"With all the nomads in town? Bad," Argyros replied.
"The Georgians hate 'em, the Alans hate 'em, and they hate
everyone. I'd say we have to look to ourselves—Goarios's
men will be too busy guarding the king and his nobles to pay
attention to much else."

"Goarios's men will be hiding under their beds, more
likely," Corippus snorted. His cold eyes raked the wall that
surrounded the courtyard. He made a disgusted noise deep
in his throat. "Too low, too shabby. How are we supposed
to hold this place?" He shouted to a couple of stableboys,
cursed them when they began to protest. They helped him
close and bar the gates.

Supsa the innkeeper came rushing out at the noise of the
gate panels squealing on their hinges. "What you doing?"
he cried in bad Greek.

"He is trying to save you from being killed," Argyros
snapped; the officer's rasp he put in his voice straightened
Supsa up as if it had been a cup of icy water dashed in his
face. The magistrianos added, "There's rioting in the market square, and it's spreading."

Supsa needed only a moment to take that in. "I have
heavier bar in back," he said. "I show you where."

As soon as the stouter bar was in place, Argyros called all
of his crew except Eustathios Rhangabe out of the inn. Like
Corippus, the rest of the men were top combat troops. Some
were imperial guards, others, like their leader, ex-soldiers
who had joined the corps of magistrianoi. Every one was
deadly with bow, spear, and sword.

"Fetch benches," Corippus ordered Supsa, "so they can
see over the top of the wall to shoot." This time the tavern-

er and his staff obeyed without question. Other traders came rushing out, clutching whatever weapons they had. Corippus put them on the wall too. "Who knows how well they'll do?" he grunted to Argyros. "The more bodies the better, though."

That got put to the test in minutes. Even while everyone in the courtyard had been working to turn it into a fortress, the noise of strife outside came closer and closer. The white-faced stableboys were just dragging a last bench against the wall when the mob came baying round the corner.

Supsa clambered onto a bench, stood on tiptoe so the rioters could recognize him. He shouted something in his native Georgian, presumably to the effect that he was just another local and so they should leave him alone.

Stones, bricks, and clods of horsedung whizzed past him. One caught him in the shoulder and sent him spinning to the ground. Argyros, less optimistic, had already ducked behind the wall. He peered over it again a moment later. A dozen rioters had hold of a thick wooden beam; the others, after much yelling, cleared a path so they could charge for the gate.

"Shoot!" the magistrianos cried at the same time as Corippus, in his excitement forgetting where he was, bellowed the identical word in Latin. Even without a command, everyone knew what to do. Argyros's men pumped arrows into the mob with a speed and accuracy that left the genuine merchants gasping. Screams rose. The improvised ram never got within twenty feet of its intended target. The men who had carried it were down, moaning or motionless. The rest of the rioters suddenly discovered urgent business elsewhere.

"Mobs," Corippus said scornfully. "The bravest bastards in the world, till somebody fights back." Argyros was nodding grateful agreement when shouts of alarm came from the rear of the inn. Men leaped down from their benches and rushed to help the few beleaguered fellows there. "No, damn you, not everyone!" Corippus howled. "The same bloody thing'll happen here if we all go haring off like so many idiots!"

That plain good sense stopped several defenders in their tracks. By then, though, Argyros was already dashing round the inn toward the stables and other buildings. The rioters had found or stolen a ladder; more dropped down over the wall every minute.

Bowstrings thrummed. One of the invaders fell, screaming, while two more cursed. Others ran forward. They waved knives and clubs. But for all their ferocity, they were only townsmen, untrained in fighting. Even the merchants who ran with Argyros had better gear and knew more of what they were about. His own men went through their foes like a dose of salts.

Part of that, he suspected, was what helped some women get through childbirth so much better than others: knowing and understanding the process would hurt and carrying on regardless. He saw a rioter who took a minor knife wound in his forearm forget everything else to gawk at it. The fellow never saw the bludgeon that stretched him senseless in the dirt.

An instant later, the magistrianos got the chance to test his theory. A club thudded into his ribs. He gasped, but managed to spin away from the rioter's next wild swing. After that, drilled reflex took over. He stepped in, knocked away the club—it looked to be a table leg—with his left hand, thrust his dagger into the man's belly. The Georgian might never have heard of defense, and it was too late for him to learn it now.

By then, Argyros had come quite close to his real target, the ladder leaning against the rear wall. A man was climbing over the wall. The magistrianos displayed his bloodsmeared knife, grinned a ghastly grin. "Your turn next?" he asked. He had no idea whether the man knew Greek, but the message got through, one way or another. The fellow jumped down—on the far side of the wall. From the curses that followed, he landed on someone. Argyros knocked over the ladder.

The last few rioters inside Supsa's compound had been pushed back against the wall of the stable. Only traders still fought with them hand to hand. Argyros's men, professional survivors, shouted for their allies to get out of the way so they could finish the job with arrows.

"A lesson the townsfolk will remember," the magistrianos told Corippus. He rubbed at his rib cage, which still hurt. He knew he would have an enormous bruise come morning. But to his relief, he felt no stabbing pain when he breathed. He'd had broken ribs once before, and knew the difference.

"Bodies strewn here and there will make a mob think twice," Corippus agreed. "I'm just glad they didn't try to torch us."

Ice walked the magistrianos's spine. He'd forgotten about that. With jar after jar of hellpowder in Supsa's inn—He crossed himself in horror. *"Mè genoîto!"* he exclaimed; "Heaven forbid!"

"I don't think even a mob would be so stupid," Corippus said. "Fire'd mean the whole stinking town would go up. Of course," he added, "you can't be sure."

Argyros told his archers to shoot anyone they saw outside with a torch. For the moment, the inn seemed safe enough. Like any other scavengers, the mob preferred prey that did not fight back. Rioters went by—at a respectful distance—carrying their loot. At any other time, Argyros would have wanted to seize them and drag them off to gaol. Now, caught in chaos in a country not his own, all he did was scan the sky to make sure no plumes of smoke rose in it.

"Night before too long," Corippus observed. "That'll make things tougher."

"So it will." The magistrianos laughed self-consciously. In his concern for fire, he had not even noticed the deepening blue above. The din outside was still savage and getting worse. Of itself, his hand bunched into a fist. "What's Goarios doing to stop this mess?"

"Damn all I can see—probably under the bed with his soldiers." Contempt filled Corippus's voice. "I'd say our new Alexander can't even conquer his own people, let alone anybody else's."

Yet soldiers did appear. Darkness had just settled in when a heavily armed party approached the front gate of Supsa's inn. Argyros recognized its leader as an officer he had seen several times in the palace. He stayed wary even so—the fellow might be taking advantage of the riot, not trying to quell it. "What do you want?" he shouted in Persian.

The officer's answer startled him too much to be anything but the truth: "You're the wine merchant? His majesty has sent us to collect the next consignment of your *yperoinos*. Here's the gold for it." He held up a leather sack.

With a curious sense of unreality, Argyros let him come up the barred gate. The magistrianos counted the nomismata. The proper number were there. Shaking their heads as they went back and forth, Argyros's men fetched the jars of superwine and handed them to the officer's troopers over the top of the gate. When he had all of them, the officer saluted Argyros and led his section away.

All the magistrianos could think of was Nero, singing to his lyre of the fall of Troy while Rome burned around him. Dariel was not burning, but no thanks to Goarios.

The stout defense Argyros's band and the real traders had put up gave the rioters a bellyful. They mounted no fresh assaults. The magistrianos found the night almost as nervous as if they had. All around was a devil's chorus of screams, shouts, and crashes, sometimes close by, sometimes far away. They were more alarming because he could not see what caused them. He kept imagining he smelled more smoke than cooking fires could account for.

"Who's that?" one of his men called, peering at a shadow moving in the darkness. "Keep away, or I'll put an arrow through you."

A woman laughed. "I've been threatened with worse than that tonight, hero. Go wake Argyros for me."

"Who are you to give me orders, trull?" the Roman demanded. "I ought to—"

"It's all right, Constantine. I know her," the magistrianos said. He looked out, but saw little. "I'm here, Mirrane. What do you want?"

"Let me inside first. If Goarios learns I've come, we're all done for. We may be anyhow."

"Are you going to open the gate for her?" Despite Mirrane's alarming words, Corippus plainly did not like the idea. "No telling who's lurking there out past our torchlight."

Argyros nodded. Trusting Mirrane was harder than wanting her. He remembered, though, her supple dancer's muscles. "Can you climb a rope if we throw one out to you?" he called over the fence.

She laughed again, not in the least offended. "Of course I can." A moment later she proved good as her word, dropping into the courtyard as lightly and quietly as a veteran raider. She was dressed like one, too, in nondescript men's clothes, with her fine hair pulled up under a felt hat that looked like an inverted flowerpot. Few marauders, however, smelled of attar of roses.

Ignoring the curious glances the men in the courtyard were giving her, she baldly told Argyros, "Goarios knows you were in the marketplace where the riot started this afternoon. In fact, he thinks you're the person who got it started."

"Mother of God!" The magistrianos crossed himself. "Why does he think so?"

"You can't deny you were there—one of my, ah, little birds saw you." Mirrane sounded very pleased with herself. "As for why he thinks you threw that knife at the Kirghiz, well, I told the little bird to tell him that." She grinned as if she had done something clever and expected Argyros to see it too.

All he saw was disaster. Those of his men who heard shouted in outrage. "I should have let Constantine shoot you," he ground out, his voice as icy as Corippus's eyes.

"Ah, but then you'd never have known, would you, not till too late. Now you—we—still have the chance to get away."

"I suppose you expect my men to give you an armed escort back to Persia."

Mirrane paid no attention to the sarcasm. "Not at all, because I'm not planning to go south." She paused. "You do know, don't you?"

"Know what?" Argyros's patience was stretched to the breaking point, but he would sooner have gone under thumbscrews than reveal that to Mirrane.

"That the whole Kirghiz army is through the Caspian Gates and heading for Dariel."

"No," Argyros said woodenly. "I didn't know that." With the chaos inside the town, that at first seemed a less immediate trouble than many closer at hand. Then the magistrianos ran Mirrane's words through his head again. "You're going to the Kirghiz?"

"To stop them, if I can. And you and yours are coming with me."

Argyros automatically began to say no, but checked himself before the word was out of his mouth. The pieces of the puzzle were falling together in his mind. "That's why your man fed Goarios that lying fairy tale!"

"To make you work with me, you mean? Well, of course, dear Basil." She reached out to stroke his cheek, which warmed and infuriated him at the same time. He hoped that did not show on his face, but suspected it did; Mirrane's smile was too knowing. But she held mockery from her voice as she continued, "I told you once that the nomads endanger both our states. Besides, you have a weapon we may be able to turn against them."

"The superwine, you mean?"

"Of course. The more Kirghiz who are drunk, and the drunker they are, the better the chance my plan has."

Being caught in her web himself, the magistrianos had a certain amount of sympathy for the nomads. There were some thousands of them and only one of her, but he was not sure that evened the odds. "We'll load the wagons," he said resignedly. He did not mention the hellpowder. He had used a little at Daras, but only a little. Mirrane would have trouble imagining how powerful more than half a ton of the stuff could be.

As Argyros set his men to work, Supsa came rushing up. "You leaving?" the innkeeper wailed. "No leave!"

"I fear I have little choice," the magistrianos said. He glared at Mirrane. She smiled sweetly, hoping to annoy him further. He stamped away.

It was nearly midnight before the miniature caravan—wagons, packhorses, and all—rumbled out of the courtyard. The men on horseback looked less like traders than they had coming into Dariel. Some of them had worn mail shirts then too, but that was not where the difference lay. It was in their posture, their eyes, the hard set of their mouths. They were no longer pretending to be anything but soldiers. Even drunken rioters took one look and got out of their way.

"A good crew you have," Mirrane remarked. She was sitting by Argyros, who drove the lead wagon. It was full of *yperoinos*. In the last wagon of the four came Eustathios Rhangabe—as far as everyone else was concerned, he was welcome to baby the hellpowder along all by himself. If by some disaster that wagon went up, the magistrianos thought, it would take the flank guards and everything else with it, but sometimes the illusion of safety was as important as the thing itself.

Argyros's mouth twisted; that could also be said for the illusion of command. "They're dancing to your tune now," he growled. He would have lost his temper altogether had she come back with some clever comment, but she merely nodded. She was, he reminded himself, a professional too.

He had worried about whether the gate crew would let them pass (for that matter, he had wondered if there would be a gate crew, or if they had left their posts to join the looting). They were there and alert, but their officer waved Argyros through. "Getting out while the getting's good, are you?" he said. "Don't blame you a bit—in your shoes, I'd do the same."

"Not if you knew where we were going you wouldn't," the magistrianos said, once the fellow was out of earshot. Mirrane giggled.

Argyros called a halt a couple of miles outside Dariel. "This is far enough," he said. "None of the trouble from town will follow us here, and we need rest to be worth anything come morning. We also need to find out just what this scheme is that we're supposed to be following." He gave Mirrane a hard look.

So did Corippus. "Why?" he asked bluntly. "Now that she doesn't have Goarios protecting her, why not turn her into dogmeat and go about our business?" Several men grunted agreement.

Mirrane stared back, unafraid. She said, "I might point out that, were it not for me, Goarios's soldiers would have you now."

"Were it not for you," Corippus retorted, "Goarios's soldiers would never have been interested in us in the first place." Again many of his comrades paused in the business of setting up camp to nod.

"She could have given us to the Alan king any time she chose," Argyros said. "She didn't."

"Till it served her purpose," Corippus said stubbornly.

"True enough, but are you saying it fails to serve ours too? Do you really want the Kirghiz rampaging through Mesopotamia, or grazing their flocks in Kappadokia from now on? They endanger us as well as Persia. And if you're so eager to be rid of Mirrane, let us hear *your* plan for holding the nomads back." He hoped the north African would not have one.

When Corippus dropped his eyes, the magistrianos knew he had won that gamble. His subordinate, though, did not yield tamely. He said, "Maybe we could use the *yperoinos* to get the buggers drunk, and then—" He ran dry, as a water clock will when someone forgets to fill it.

"And then what?" Argyros prodded. "Sneak through their tents slitting throats? There are a few too many of them for that, I'm afraid. If you have no ideas of your own, getting rid of someone who does strikes me as wasteful."

Corippus saluted with sardonic precision, shook his head, and stalked off to help get a fire started.

Mirrane touched Argyros's arm. In the darkness, her eyes were enormous. "I thank you," she whispered. "In this trade of ours, one gets used to the notion of dying unexpectedly, but I'd not have cared for what likely would have happened before they finally knocked me over the head."

Having been a soldier, Argyros knew what she meant. He grunted, embarrassed for a moment at what men could do—and too often did—to women.

"Why did you choose to save me?" Mirrane still kept her voice low, but the newly kindled fire brought an ironic glint to her eye. "Surely not for the sake of the little while we were lovers?" She studied the magistrianos's face. "Are you blushing?" she asked in delighted disbelief.

"It's only the red light of the flames," Argyros said stiffly. "You've been saying you know how to stop the Kirghiz. That's more than anyone else has claimed. You're worth keeping for that, if nothing else."

"If nothing else," she echoed with an upraised eyebrow. "For that polite addition, at least, I am in your debt."

The magistrianos bit back an angry reply. Mirrane had a gift for making him feel out of his depth, even when, as now, power lay all on his side. No woman since his long-dead wife had drawn him so, but Mirrane's appeal was very different from Helen's. With Helen he had felt more at ease, at peace, than with anyone else he had ever known. The air of risk and danger that surrounded Mirrane had little to do with the settings in which he met her; it was part of her essence. Like his first cup of *yperoinos*, it carried a stronger jolt than he was used to.

To cover his unease, he returned to matters at hand. "So what is this precious plan of yours?" She stayed silent. He said, "For whatever you think its worth, I pledge I won't slit your throat after you've spoken, or harm you in any other way."

She watched him. "If your hard-eyed friend gave me that promise, I'd know what it was worth. You, though ... with that long, sad face, you remind me of the saints I've seen painted in Christian churches. Should I believe you on account of that? It seems a poor reason."

"Sad to say, I am no saint." As if to prove his words, memories of her lips, her skin against his surged in him. Angrily, he fought them down.

Her lazy smile said she was remembering too. But it faded, leaving her thoughtful and bleak. "If I tell you, I must trust you, and your land and mine are enemies. May you fall into the fire in the House of the Lie if you are leading me astray."

"I will swear by God and His Son, if you like."

"No, never mind. An oath is only the man behind it, and you suit me well enough without one." Still she said nothing. Finally Argyros made a questioning noise. She laughed shakily. "The real truth is, the plan is not very good."

"Let me hear it."

"All right. We spoke of it once, in fact, in Goarios's palace. You said you remembered how the White Huns lured Peroz King of Kings and his army to destruction—how they dug a trench with but a single small opening, then concealed it. They fled through the gap, then fell on his army when it was thrown into confusion by the first ranks charging into the ditch. I had hoped to do something like that to the Kirghiz. They have little discipline at any time, and if they were drunk on your superwine, drunker even than they knew—"

Argyros nodded. The scheme was daring, ruthless, and could have been practical—all characteristics he had come to associate with Mirrane. "You do see the flaw?" he said, as gently as he could.

"Actually, I saw two," she replied. "We don't have enough people to dig the ditch, and we don't have an army to use to fight even if it should get dug."

"That, ah, does sum it up," the magistrianos said.

"I know, I know, I know." Bitterness as well as firelight shadowed Mirrane's features. "At the end, I kept telling Goarios he was giving his country away by not keeping a tighter check on the nomads; I was hoping to use the Dariel garrison to do what I had in mind. But he still thinks he'll ride on the backs of the Kirghiz to glory—or he did, until the riots started. For all I know, he may believe it even now.

He's had less use for me outside the bedchamber since I stopped telling him things he wanted to hear.'' She cocked her head, peered at Argyros. "And so here I am, in your hands instead.''

He did not answer. His eyes were hooded, far away.

Mirrane said, "With most men, I would offer at once to go to their tents with them. With you, somehow I don't think that would help save me.''

It was as if he had not heard her. Then he came far enough out of his brown study to reply, "No, it would be the worst thing you could do.'' Her glare brought him fully back to himself. He explained hastily, "My crew would mutiny if they thought I was keeping you for my own pleasure.''

She glanced toward Corippus, shivered. "Very well. I don't doubt you're right. What then?''

"I'll tell you in the morning.'' The magistrianos's wave summoned a couple of his men. "Make sure she does not escape, but don't harass her either. Her scheme has more merit than I thought.'' They saluted and led Mirrane away.

Argyros called Corippus to him and spoke at some length. If defects lurked in the plan slowly taking shape in his mind, the dour north African would find them. Corippus did, too, or thought he did. Argyros had to wake up Eustathios Rhangabe to be sure. Through a yawn wide enough to frighten a lion, Rhangabe suggested changes, ones not so drastic as Corippus had thought necessary. The artisan fell asleep where he sat; Corippus and the magistrianos kept hammering away.

At last Corippus threw his hands in the air. "All right!'' he growled, almost loud enough to wake Rhangabe. "This is what we came for—we have to try it, I suppose. Who knows? We may even live through it.''

A small wagon train and a good many packhorses plodded north toward the Caspian Gates. The riders who flanked the packhorses seemed bored with what they were doing: a routine trip, their attitude seemed to say, that they had made many times before. *If I see Constantinople again,* Argyros thought half seriously, *I'll have to do some real acting, maybe the next time someone revives Euripides.*

A glance up from beneath lowered brows showed the
magistrianos Kirghiz scouts. He had been seeing them for
some time now, and they his band. He had enough horsemen with him to deter the scouts from approaching by ones
and twos. For his part, he wanted to keep pretending he did
not know they existed.

For as long as he could, he also kept ignoring the dust
cloud that lay ahead. When he saw men through it, though,
men who wore furs and leathers and rode little steppe
ponies, he reined in, drawing the wagon to a halt.

"We've just realized that's the whole bloody Kirghiz
army," he called to his comrades, reminding them of their
roles as any good director would. "Now we can be afraid."

"You're too late," someone said. The men from the Em
pire milled out in counterfeit—Argyros hoped it was coun
terfeit—panic and confusion. His own part was to leap
down from the wagon, cut a packhorse free of the string
then scramble onto the beast and boot it after the mounts his
men were riding desperately southward.

The Kirghiz scouts gave chase. A few arrows hissed past
Then one of the nomads toppled from the saddle; Corip
pus was as dangerous a horse-archer as any plainsman. Tha
helped deter pursuit, but Argyros did not think it would
have lasted long in any case. The Kirghiz scouts were only
human—they would want to steal their fair share of what
ever these crazy merchants had left behind.

Argyros looked back over his shoulder—cautiously, as he
was not used to riding without stirrups. One of the nomad
was bending to examine the broken jars the magistrianos'
horse had been carrying. Some of the contents must stil
have been cupped in a shard, for the Kirghiz suddenl
jumped up and began pointing excitedly at the packhorse
and wagons. Argyros did not need to hear him to know wha
he was shouting. Nomads converged on the abandoned
yperoinos like bees on roses.

The poor fools who had provided such a magnificen
windfall were quickly forgotten. Before long, they were able
to stop and look back with no fear of pursuit. Corippus gav
the short bark that passed for laughter with him. "After

haul like that, most of those buggers will have all the loot from civilization they ever dreamed of."

"Something to that," Argyros admitted. The thought made him sad.

One of his men put hand to forehead to shield his eyes from the sun as he peered toward the Kirghiz. He swore in frustration all the same and turned to Argyros. "Can you get a better view, sir?"

"Let's see." At his belt, along with such usual appurtenances as knife, sap, and pouch, Argyros carried a more curious device: a tube fitting tightly into another, with convex glass glittering at both ends. He undid it from the boss on which it hung, raised it to his eye, and pulled the smaller tube partway out of the larger one.

The image he saw was upside down and fringed with false colors, but the Kirghiz seemed to jump almost within arm's length. The artisans in Constantinople still had trouble making lenses good enough to use—most far-seers belonged to Roman generals, though the savants at the imperial university had seen some things in the heavens that puzzled them and even, it was whispered, shook their faith. Only because Argyros had learned of the far-seer in the first place was he entitled to carry one now.

He watched the Kirghiz nobles, some of whom had sampled superwine in Dariel, trying to keep their rank and file away from the wagons. They were too late. Too many ordinary nomads had already tasted the potent brew. The ones who'd had some wanted more; the ones who'd had none wanted some. Even under the best of circumstances, the nomads obeyed orders only when they felt like it. These circumstances were not the best. Argyros smiled in satisfaction.

"They all want their share," he reported.

"Good," Corippus said. The rest of the men nodded, but without great enthusiasm. If this part of the plan had failed it could not have gone forward. The more dangerous portions lay ahead.

The Romans rode back toward Dariel. Eustathios Rhanabe was bringing up the last wagon, the one so different

from the rest. A couple of outriders were with him; Mir
rane's horse was tethered to one of theirs. Argyros had told
them to shoot her if she tried to escape, and warned her o
his order. All the same, he was relieved to see her with hi
men. Orders were rarely a match for the likes of her.

"You have your spots chosen?" the magistrianos asked
Rhangabe.

The artisan nodded. "Six of them, three on either side.'

"Basil, what are these madmen playing at? They won'
talk to me," Mirrane said indignantly. "They aren't fol
lowing what we talked about at all. All they've done is dig
holes in the ground and put jars of your strong wine i
them. What good will that—" Mirrane stopped in the mid
dle of her sentence. Her sharp brown eyes flashed from Ar
gyros to the wagon and back again. "Or is the *yperoinos* i
them? Back in Daras, you had some trick of Ahriman—"

Argyros would have said "Satan's trick," but he under
stood her well enough. He might have known she would
make the connection. His respect for her wits, already high
rose another notch. He said, "Well, without that army be
hind us, we do have to modify things a bit."

"The good god Ormazd knows that's true." Suddenly
startlingly, she grinned at the magistrianos. "You won'
need to worry about my running off any longer, dear Basil
I wouldn't miss seeing this for worlds." So I can bring new
of it back to the King of Kings, Argyros added silently.

He said, "Let's hope there's something interesting for yo
to see." He knew she was clever enough to add her own un
spoken commentary: if not, nothing else matters, becaus
we'll be dead.

He told off the half-dozen men who had done the dig
ging, sent them back to the holes they had made. He de
tailed two more to keep Mirrane under guard. Regardless o
what she said, he took no chances where she was con
cerned. Eustathios Rhangabe, of course, stayed with hi
wagon.

That left—Argyros counted on his fingers—fifteen men
He wished for four times as many. Wishing failed to pro
duce them. "Double quivers," the magistrianos told th

men he did have. Each of them carried, then, eighty arrows. If every shaft killed, they could hardly slay one of five Kirghiz.

How long would the nomads take to get thoroughly drunk? Certainly not as long as any of them expected. Argyros gauged the sun in the sky. He could not afford to wait for nightfall. He did not think he would have to.

Corippus had spent even more time in the imperial army than Argyros. Their eyes met; they both judged the moment ripe. Argyros raised his right hand. His comrades clucked to their horses, trotted north once more behind him.

They rode in silence, alert for Kirghiz scouts. Argyros used the far-seer from horseback, though it made him vaguely seasick to do so. He saw no one. His confidence rose, a little. If the nomads were too busy soaking up their unexpected loot to bother with scouts, so much the better.

The horsemen topped a low rise. Corippus barked sudden harsh laughter. "Look at them!" he exclaimed, pointing. "They're like a swarm of bees round a honeypot."

The comparison was apt. The Kirghiz were milling in a great disorderly knot around the abandoned wagons and packhorses. Pulling out the far-seer again, Argyros saw jars going from hand to hand. He watched one nomad, wearing a foolish expression, slide off his horse. Another reached down to snatch away the jug the fellow was holding.

"They're as ripe as ever they will be," the magistrianos said. "Let's go kick the honeypot over—and hope we don't get stung."

Some of the Kirghiz must have seen Argyros and his followers approach, yet they took no alarm. Argyros could hardly blame their leaders for that. No sane attackers would approach a foe so grotesquely outnumbering them, any more than a mouse would blithely leap into the fox's jaws.

The magistrianos drew up his tiny battle line not far inside archery range. He raised his arm, then dropped it. Along with his men, he snatched up an arrow, drew his bow back to his ear and released it, grabbed for the next shaft.

They had all shot three or four times before the racket from the Kirghiz began to change timbre. Some of the no-

mads cried out in pain; others pointed and yelled at the su
icidal maniacs harassing them, just as a man will point and
shout at the mosquito that has just bitten his leg and buzzed
off.

A few nomads began to shoot back, those who happened
to be facing the right way, who were not too tightly pressed
by their fellows, and who were sober enough to remember
how to use their bows. Argyros and his comrades methodi
cally emptied their quivers into the tight-packed mass.
Those who knew fragments of the Kirghiz speech shouted
insults at the nomads. They were not out to strike and skulk
away; they wanted to be noticed.

When the outer ranks of nomads moved away from th
wagons, the magistrianos's little force retreated a corre
sponding distance, but kept plying the Kirghiz with arrows.
More and more nomads came after them.

Argyros yelled the most bloodcurdling curses he knew
then turned his horse and roweled it with his spurs. Thi
flight was not like the one when he had abandoned th
yperoinos wagons; the nomads were pursuing in earnes
now.

One of his men shrieked as an arrow sprouted from hi
shoulder. The magistrianos knew others would also perish
either because some arrows had to hit with so many in th
air or because some nomads had faster horses than some o
his men. With the thunder of thousands of hooves behin
him, he hoped some of his men had faster horses than th
Kirghiz. Were the chase longer than the mile and a half o
so that lay between Argyros's men and Eustathios Rhan
gabe's wagon, he knew none of his people would be likel
to survive.

He glanced ahead and to the right. Yes, there behind
bush was one of the men who had come from Constanti
nople. Unless one knew where to look for him, he was al
most invisible. Only the stragglers of the Kirghiz, who wer
pursuing with scant regard for order, would come near th
fellow.

Argyros had to keep his attention on more immediat
concerns. He did not see his countryman thrust a lighted

candle at an oil-soaked rag, and noticed only peripherally when the fellow leaped up and dashed for another hole not far away.

What happened moments after that was difficult to ignore, even for one as single-mindedly focused on flight as the magistrianos. The hellpowder in the buried jars ignited, and, with a roar louder and deeper than thunder, the ground heaved itself up. Earth, stones, and shrubs vomited from the newly dug crater.

Argyros's horse tried to rear. He roughly fought it down. He and the rest of the men from the Roman Empire had encountered hellpowder before and knew what the frightful noise was. Even as the thought raced through Argyros's mind, another charge of the stuff went off, far over on the Kirghiz left. It should have been simultaneous with the one on the right, and was in fact close enough for Argyros to let out a pleased grunt.

The nomads, taken by surprise as much as their mounts, naturally shied away from the blasts. That bunched them more closely together and made it harder for them to keep up their headlong pursuit. Still, they were bold men, not easily cowed by the unknown. They kept after their quarry.

Another pair of blasts crashed forth, almost at the same instant, as the Romans dashed past the second prepared set of charges. These were nearer each other and nearer the path than the first ones had been. Argyros felt the booming reports with his whole body, not merely through his ears. Again he had to force his mount to obey his will.

He swung around in the saddle to look back at the Kirghiz. They were packed more tightly now, wanted nothing to do with the eruptions to either side. He saw two horses collide. Both went down with their riders, and others, unable to stop, tumbled over them. Now the magistrianos's men were lengthening their lead over the nomads, except for the frontrunner out ahead of the pack. He grabbed an arrow, tried a Parthian shot at one of those. He missed, swore, and concentrated again on riding.

The Romans manning the third set of charges had their timing down to a science. They waited until their country-

men were past before touching off their stores of hellpowder. This last pair was so close to the path that dirt showered
down on Argyros. His mount bolted forward as if he had
spurred it. The nomads' ponies, on the other hand, balked
at the sudden cataclysmic noise in front of them.

The last wagon appeared ahead. Eustathios Rhangabe
dove out of it, then sprinted for the shelter of the rocky
outcrop where, Argyros presumed, the last two Romans
were holding Mirrane. The magistrianos hoped Rhangabe
had accurately gauged the length of candle he had left
burning atop one of the jars in the wagon. On second
thought, hope did not seem enough. Jolts from Argyros's
galloping horse made his prayer breathless, but it was no less
sincere for that.

Around the wagon, invitingly set out, were open jars of
yperoinos. None of the Romans paid any attention to them.
The Kirghiz whooped with delight when they spied the familiar jars. Most of them tugged on the reins to halt their
horses. Drinking was easier and more enjoyable work than
chasing crazy bandits who shot back.

Several Roman riders were already diving behind the
rocks where Rhangabe had found shelter; more dismounted and ran for them as Argyros drew up. He sprang
from his horse. An arrow buried itself in the ground, a
palm's breath from his foot. Not all the nomads, worse
luck, were pausing to refresh themselves.

The magistrianos peered over a boulder. He lofted a shot
over the last few Romans at the pursuing Kirghiz. His fingers told him only three shafts were left in his quiver. He
reached for one. If something had gone wrong with that
wagon, saving them would not matter.

"How much longer?" Mirrane shouted at him.

"Why ask me?" he yelled back, irrationally annoyed.
"Rhangabe lit the candle—why don't you ask—"

He was never sure afterward whether he said "him" or
not. He had thought the blasts from a couple of jars of
hellpowder loud and terrifying; this sound put him in mind
of the roar that would accompany the end of the world. The
earth shook beneath his feet. He threw himself face-down,

his eyes in the dust and his hands clapped to his ears. He felt no shame at that; the rest of the Romans were doing exactly the same thing.

He was, though, the leader of this crew. Pride quickly forced him to his feet—he did not want his men to see him groveling in the dirt. He brushed at his tunic as he started to scramble over the rocks to find out what the blast had done.

Two others, he noticed, were already up and looking. One was Eustathios Rhangabe. Argyros did not mind that; if anyone could take hellpowder in stride, it would be a man who had dealt with the stuff for years. The other, however, was Mirrane.

He had only an instant in which to feel irked. Then she threw herself into his arms and delivered a kiss that rocked him almost as much as the hellpowder had. Her lips touched his ear. That was not a caress; he could feel them moving in speech. He shook his head. For the moment, at least, he was deaf. He was sorry when Mirrane pulled her face away from his, but she did not draw back far, only enough to let him see her mouth as she spoke. "It worked!" she was yelling over and over. "It worked!"

That brought him back to himself. "Let me see," he said, mouthing the words in the same exaggerated style she had used: her hearing could be in no better shape than his.

He peered over the piled rocks behind which he had huddled. "Mother of God, have mercy!" he whispered. Of itself, his hand leapt from his forehead to his breast as it shaped the sign of the cross.

He had been a soldier; he knew only too well that war was not the clean-cut affair of drama and glory the epic poets made it out to be. All the same, he was not prepared for the spectacle the lifting veils of acrid smoke were presenting to him.

The titanic blast had not slain all the Kirghiz, or even come close. A large majority of the nomads were riding north. From the desperate haste with which they used spurs and whips on their ponies, Argyros did not think they would pause this side of the pass. Observing what they were fleeing from, the magistrianos could not blame them.

In adapting the plan the Ephthalites had used against the King of Kings, Argyros knew he needed to force the Kirghiz to group more tightly than usual: thus the hellpowder charges that funneled them toward the wagon. Now he saw how appallingly well he had succeeded.

Close by the crater where the wagon had stood, few fragments were recognizable as surely being from man or horse. Freakishly, however, one of the jars of superwine that helped lure the nomads to disaster remained unbroken, though it, like much of the landscape there, was splashed with red.

Argyros had anticipated that central blast zone and hoped it—and the noise that went with its creation—would be enough to intimidate the Kirghiz. He had not thought about what would lie beyond there, about what would happen when fragments of the wagon and fragments of the jars that had held the hellpowder were propelled violently outward after it ignited.

The results, especially when seen upside down in the surreal closeness the far-seer brought, reminded him of nothing so much as hell in a hot-tempered monk's sermon. Scythed-down men and horses, variously mutilated, writhed and bled and soundlessly screamed. That silence, somehow, was worst of all; it began to lift as the minutes went by and Argyros's hearing slowly returned.

Yet despite the horror, the magistrianos also understood Mirrane's delight at the scene before them. Never had a double handful of men not only vanquished but destroyed an enemy army; the stand of the Spartans at Thermopylai was as nothing beside this.

One by one, the rest of Argyros's crew nerved themselves to see what they had wrought. Most reacted with the same mixture of awe, horror, and pride the magistrianos felt. Others tried to emulate Eustathios Rhangabe's dispassionate stare; the artisan reacted to the grisly spectacle before him as if it were the final step in some complex and difficult geometric proof, a demonstration already grasped in the abstract.

For his part, Corippus looked as though he only regretted the carnage had not been greater. "Some of them will be
a long time dying," he shouted Argyros's way, sounding
delighted at the prospect. His eyes, for once, did not seem
cold. He was savage as any Kirghiz, Argyros thought; the
chief difference between him and them was in choice of
masters. He made a deadly dangerous foe; the magistrianos was glad they were on the same side.

That thought brought his mind back to the woman next
to him. Mirrane might have been able to see into his head.
She said, "And now that they are done with, what do you
plan to do about me?" She no longer sounded full of nothing but glee, and Argyros did not think that was solely concern for her own fate. She had been examining the results of
the blast for several minutes now, and a long look at those
was enough to sober anyone less grim of spirit than Corippus.

The magistrianos stayed silent so long that Mirrane
glanced over to see if he'd heard. Her mouth tightened when
she realized he had. She said, "If you intend to kill me, kill
me cleanly—don't give me to your men for their sport. Were
we reversed, captor and captive, I would do as much for
you." Somehow, she managed one syllable of a laugh. "I
hate to have to bellow to beg, but my ears ring so, I can't
help it."

"Yes, I believe you might give me a clean death," Argyros said musingly, though the ferocity of the King of
King's torturers was a bugbear that frightened children all
through the Empire. The magistrianos paused again; he had
been thinking about what to do with Mirrane since they left
Dariel, without coming up with any sure answer. Now, under her eyes, he had to. At last he said, as much to himself
as to her, "I think I am going to bring you back to Constantinople."

"As you will." Mirrane fought to hold her voice tone-
less, but beneath her swarthiness her face grew pale; the in-
genuity of the Emperor's tortures was a bugbear that
frightened children all through Persia.

"I think you misunderstand me." Like Mirrane, Argyros found it odd to be carrying on this conversation near the top of his lungs, but had little choice. Spreading his hands, he went on, "If you had your henchmen here instead of the other way around, would you let me go back to my capital?"

"No," Mirrane answered at once; she was a professional.

The magistrianos had looked for no other reply from her. "You see my problem, then." She nodded, again promptly—as he had once said, in many ways the two of them spoke the same language, though he used Greek and she Persian. That reflection was part of what prompted him to continue, "I hadn't planned to put you in the gaol in the bowels of the Praitorion, or to send you to the Kynegion"—the amphitheater in northeastern Constantinople where the imperial headsmen plied their trade. "I meant that you should come back to the city with me."

"Did you?" Mirrane lifted an eyebrow in the elegant Persian irony that could make even a sophisticated Roman less than self-assured. "Of course you know I will say yes to that: if I slept with you for the sake of duty in Daras, I suppose I can again, if need be. But why do you think you can make me stay in Constantinople? I escaped you there once, remember, on the spur of the moment. Do you imagine I could not do it again, given time to prepare?"

Argyros frowned; here, perhaps, was more professionalism than he wanted to find. He said, "Come or not, sleep with me or not, as you care to, not for any duty. As for leaving Constantinople, I daresay you are right—there are always ways and means. I can hope, though, you will not want to use them."

Mirrane looked at him in amusement. "If that is a confession of wild, passionate, undying love, I must own I've heard them better done."

"No doubt," Argyros said steadily. "The Master of Offices writes poetry; I fear I haven't the gift."

"Battle epics." Mirrane gave a scornful sniff.

The magistrianos supposed he should not have been surprised she knew what sort of poetry George Lakhanodrakon composed; the Romans kept such dossiers on high Persian officials. But he admired the way she brought it out pat.

He shook his head. This was no time to be bedeviled with side issues. He said, "I doubt you could pry a confession of wild, passionate, undying love from me with barbed whips or hot irons. To mean them fully, I fear one has to be half my age and innocent enough to think the world is always a sunny place. I'm sorry I can't oblige. I will say, though, I've found no woman but you since my wife died with whom I care to spend time out of bed as well as in. Will that do?"

It was Mirrane's turn to hesitate. When she did speak, she sounded as if she were thinking out loud, a habit Argyros also had: "You must mean this. You have the power behind you to do as you like with me here; you gain nothing from stringing me along." She still kept that inward look as she said, "I told you once in Constantinople we were two of a kind—do you remember?"

"Yes. Maybe I've finally decided to believe you."

"Have you?" Mirrane's voice remained reflective, but something subtle changed in it: "I suppose Constantinople has its share of fire-temples."

She was, the magistrianos thought, a master of the oblique thrust, murmuring in one breath how alike they were and then hammering home a fundamental difference. He said stiffly, "I would never give up hope that you might come to see that the truth lies in Christ." Seeing her nostrils flare, he made haste to add, "Those who follow the teachings of Zoroaster may worship in the city and the Empire, however, in return for the King of Kings not persecuting the Christians under his control...as I am sure you know perfectly well."

That last little jab won a smile from her. "Fair enough," she said, "though how you Christians can fail to see that evil is a live force of its own rather than a mere absence of good has always been beyond me." Her smile grew wider, more teasing. "I expect we will have time to argue it out."

He took a moment to find her meaning. When at last he did, his breath caught as he asked, "You'll come with me, then?"

"Well, why not? Didn't the two of us—not forgetting your men, of course—just put paid to a threat to both our countries? What better sets the stage for a more, ah, personal alliance?" Now she was wearing an impish grin.

Argyros felt a similar expression stretch his face in unfamiliar ways. He looked again at the blast that had ruined the hopes of the Kirghiz and of Goarios. His eye lit on the miraculously unbroken bottle of *yperoinos*. Suddenly it seemed a very good omen. He pointed it out to Mirrane. "Shall we pledge ourselves with it?"

"Well, why not?" she said.